FORTRESS OF ICE

C. J. CHERRYH

FORTRESS OF ICE

An Imprint of HarperCollinsPublishers

FORTRESS OF ICE. Copyright © 2006 by C. J. Cherryh. All rights reserved. Printed in the United States of America. No part of this book may be used or reproduced in any manner whatsoever without written permission except in the case of brief quotations embodied in critical articles and reviews. For information address HarperCollins Publishers, 10 East 53rd Street, New York, NY 10022.

EOS is a federally registred trademark of HarperCollins Publishers.

Designed by Sunil Manchikanti

ISBN-13: 978-0-380-97904-2

The Events of

FORTRESS IN THE EYE OF TIME, FORTRESS OF OWLS,

FORTRESS OF EAGLES, FORTRESS OF DRAGONS

A VERY LONG TIME AGO, LONG BEFORE THE TIME OF MEN, GALASIEN RULED. ITS world was wide with trade and commerce, and sustained by wizardry.

But besides wizardry, there was native magic in the world. Far to the north, in the frozen wastes, the Sihhë existed. They might have been first of all. The Galasieni seemed to believe so.

The Sihhë were immortal. So the Galasieni believed.

And the Galasieni pursued those secrets of long life. One wizard, Mauryl Gestaurien, was very close. But his apprentice, Hasufin Heltain, wanted that secret, and seized power, a wizard-war that drove Mauryl to the Sihhë-lords themselves, asking help.

In the struggle that followed, all of Galasien went down in ruins. One tower survived, Ynefel, where Mauryl defeated Hasufin and drove him into the Shadows.

When the dust settled, the faces of Galasien's greatest wizards looked out from the walls of that ravaged tower, imprisoned in the stone, still living. Mauryl alone survived.

The five Sihhë-lords had come down, and ruled the land, as Men began to move into the west, and Sihhë blood mixed with that of Men.

For a number of centuries thereafter the land saw the rule of the innately magical Sihhë-lords, of whom there were five, and not all of whom were good, or kind.

Some Men thrived; some learned wizardry. Others rebelled, and plotted to seize power—hopeless as long as the five lords remained. But in the passage of time the Sihhë-lords either perished, or retreated from the world. They left a thinner and thinner bloodline, half Sihhë, half Man.

Now Hasufin made his bid for life, stealing his way into a stillborn infant.

It was Selwyn Marhanen, a warlord under the High King Elfwyn Sihhë, who betrayed his lord and murdered him and all his house—while the court wizard, Emuin, killed Hasufin for the second time.

Selwyn Marhanen proclaimed himself king, in the kingdom that he called Ylesuin. He put down the old religion and all veneration of the Sihhë-lords, and established the Quinalt, the Five Gods. He built the Quinaltine in Guelemara, and perished, obsessed with nightmares and fear of damnation.

His son, Inárreddrin, succeeded him, in a reign distinguished by wars and internal disputes.

Inárreddrin had two sons, Cefwyn, the firstborn and heir, and Efanor, the son of Inárreddrin's heart. Inárreddrin set his eldest son to oversee restive Amefel, the old Sihhë district, where assassins abounded, in fondest hope of having him die and Efanor inherit.

Magic was moving again, subtly, but old Mauryl saw it coming. Locked away at Ynefel among his books, he nevertheless watched over the world, and he became more and more aware that his old enemy Hasufin, dead and not dead, had found his way back from his second death.

Feeling mortality on him, Mauryl created a Summoning, a defender, a power to oppose Hasufin, but his weakness—or in the nature of magic—things went awry. What he obtained was Tristen, bereft of memory.

Hasufin indeed brought Mauryl down, but missed Tristen, who wandered into the world and found himself in Amefel, a guest of Cefwyn Marhanen.

Hasufin's power moved against Cefwyn, against the Marhanen, attempting to stir up trouble in Amefel—but the seeds of discontent in Amefel were the old loyalties to the Sihhë-blood kings—a bloodline which thinly survived in Amefel, in the house of Heryn Aswydd.

There was, ironically, one other in whom it ran very strongly: it was Tristen, who had become Prince Cefwyn's friend.

King Inárreddrin died in an ambush Heryn Aswydd arranged. That meant Cefwyn became king, and he hanged Heryn Aswydd—but he spared the lives of Heryn's twin sisters, Orien and Tarien, both of whom had been Cefwyn's lovers—and one of whom, which he did not know, was with child. He married the Lady Regent of Elwynor, an independent kingdom which still honored the traditions of the lost Galasieni, and she produced a legitimate son.

Tristen, gathering more and more of his lost memories, stood by Cefwyn, to the resentment of Cefwyn's own people—even when Cefwyn's victory in a great battle at Lewen Field, in Amefel, drove Hasufin from the world in a third defeat.

By now Tristen was known for much more than a wizard: people in the west openly called him Tristen Sihhë, and all of Elwynor and Amefel would have been glad to proclaim Tristen High King and depose Cefwyn. Emuin, Cefwyn's old tutor, advised Cefwyn to be careful of that young man and never to become his enemy—and Cefwyn heeded the old wizard's advice. He bestowed arms on Tristen, the Sihhë Star, long banned, and would have made him Duke of Amefel.

Hasufin, however, was not done: he used the Aswydd sisters—one of them the mother of Cefwyn's bastard son. In the end, Tarien, her baby taken from her, was imprisoned in a high tower, spared her sister's fate by Tristen's intercession.

And in years that ensued, Cefwyn regarded Tristen as a brother, and leaned on his advice and Emuin's.

But Emuin left the world, and Tristen himself lived in the world only as long as Cefwyn truly needed him: his presence roused too much resentment from Cefwyn's people, the eastern folk of the divided kingdom. He set things in order in Amefel, saw a good duke in power over that land, and retreated increasingly into Mauryl's haunted tower.

Cefwyn's queen now had a son, an heir for Ylesuin, and then produced a daughter, who would inherit her own Regency of Elwynor. In these two children of loving parents, east and west were united, and peace settled on the land for the first time since Sihhë rule.

The bastard son lived happily enough in rural Amefel, foster brother to old Emuin's former servant. The world went back to its old habits, and forgot, for a few years, that its peace was fragile.

PROLOGUE

SNOW CAME DOWN, LARGE PUFFS DRIFTING ON A GENTLE WIND, WAFTING ABOVE the stone walls of the courtyard. Snow fell on dead summer flowers, on the stones of the broken walls, a fat, lazy snow for a quiet winter's afternoon.

Tristen watched it from the front doors of the ancient keep, walked out and let it fall onto his hands, let it settle in his hair and all about his little kingdom. The clouds above were silken gray, so far as the great tower of Ynefel afforded him a view above the walls, and the leaves, clinging to dry flower stems, regained a moment of beauty, a white moment, remembering the summer sun.

He kept a peaceful household in the grim old fortress of Ynefel, with Uwen and his wife—Cook, as she had been when Uwen married her, and Cook she still liked to be—though her real name was Mirien. They fared extremely well, never mind the haunts and the strangeness in the old keep, which Cook and Uwen had somewhat, though haphazardly, restored to comfort.

The snows had come generously this winter, good for next year's crops, of which Ynefel had none but Cook's herbs and vegetables, and for good pasturage, of which it had very little, cleared from the surrounding forest. This snow brought a quiet cold with it, no howling wind, only a deep, deep chill that advised that the nights would be bitter for days. The Lenúalim would continue to flow along under the ancient bridge, collecting a frozen edge of ice up against the keep walls, possibly freezing over, but that was rare. Though it would be well, Tristen thought, to take care of the rain barrel today, bring the meltwater they had gathered into the scullery and move the barrel in, before nightfall.

A lord, a king, could do that damp task for himself quite handily, but Cook would likely send her nephew to do the chore, in her notion of propriety. Uwen would be in the thick of the weather by now, doing his work up on the hill pasturage, bringing hay up to the horses and the four goats—a little spring flowed there, assuring that the animals had water in almost all weather. Cook would be fussing about down in the cottage, stuffing cracks, being sure she had enough wood inside the little house that flanked the keep: easiest to have that resource inside, if the snow became more than a flurry, and there was, Tristen thought, certainly the smell of such a snow in the air.

So, well, what had a lord to do, who had only three subjects?

He could let the snow carry his thoughts to his neighbors across the river, beyond Marna Wood. He could stand here, missing old friends today, with his face turned toward the gates that so rarely opened to visitors. He knew a few things that passed in the land, but not many. He knew that Cefwyn queried him; he answered as best he knew, but he thought less and less about the world outside the walls, beyond the forest. He wondered sometimes, and if he wondered, he could know, but he rarely followed more than the thread of Cefwyn's occasional conversation with him, a warm, friendly voice. He was reluctant, otherwise, to cast far about, having no wish to trouble old and settled things in the land. Occasionally, in summers, he entertained visitors, but lately only two, Sovrag and Cevulirn, who came as they pleased, usually toward the fading of the season. Emuin—Emuin, he greatly missed. Emuin had used to visit, but Emuin had ceased to come, and drew a curtain over himself. Whether his old mentor was alive or dead remained somewhat uncertain to Tristen—though he was never sure that death meant the same thing to Emuin as to other Men.

Uwen traveled as far as Henas'amef from time to time, with Cook's boy. Uwen reported that Lord Crissand fared quite well in his lands, and from Crissand Uwen gathered news from the capital of Guelemara, where Cefwyn ruled. The queen had had a daughter this fall, so Uwen reported, and that family was happy. It was good to hear.

He longed to see the baby. He so greatly longed to see Cefwyn . . . to be in hall when the ale flowed and the lords gathered in fine clothes, to celebrate the return of spring—he might go if he chose.

But it was not wise. It was not, in these days, wise. He had fought the king's war. He had settled the peace.

He had been a dragon.

He could not forget that, and in that memory, he stayed to his ancient keep, hoped for the years to settle what had been unsettled in those years, and let his friends live in peace.

SNOW FELL THICKLY ON GUELEMARA, GRAY CLOUDS SHEETING ALL THE HEAVENS and snow already lay ankle deep in the yard, but the threatening weather had not brought quiet to the courtyard. His Royal Highness Efanor, Prince but no longer heir of Ylesuin, tried manfully to concentrate on his letters, while young lords laid on with thump and clangor below the windows, shouting challenges at one another and laughing. Efanor penned delicate and restrained adjurations to two jealous and small-minded priests of the Quinaltine, while sword rang against sword—fit accompaniment to such a letter, in Efanor's opinion.

The clergy was in another stew, a matter of a chapel's income and costs, a niggling charge of error in dogma on the one hand and finance on the other hand—when, among priests, was it not?—and ambition in another man: the latter was, in His Royal Highness's opinion, the real crux of the matter.

Bang and clang. Pigeons flew up from off the roof in a wild flurry of wings past the window, and Efanor calmly sanded the ink on his second letter, tipped wax onto the paper, and sealed it.

Pigeons settled, fluttering and arranging their feathers. Efanor rose from his chair and walked toward that diamond-paned window—another storm of wings, wheeling away toward the Quinaltine roof, not so far across the processional way.

He had a view of the courtyard from here. And it was not just any two lords' sons battering at each other below. It was Cefwyn's sons, his nephews, neither beyond sixteen years. It was a game. It was high spirits. Metal flashed in gray light, and the snow that had already fallen was trampled in a wide circle, the pale stone walls of the Guelesfort echoing with mock battle.

So he and Cefwyn had used to do, in the days when their father Ináreddrin was king.

He still had his skill with the sword. He opted now for a gray goose quill, in battles more constant and with less-defined outcomes.

His brother the king had invited his other son, his illegitimate son, to Guelemara, to spend the holidays. It was not what he would have advised the king to do. But his brother had planned it, planned it for too many years to think now whether this was the right year. The boy was growing up. It was this year, perhaps, or forever too late. Were not the court's controversies full of brothers who found things to divide them?

Too much had divided these two. Yet they found a way to be friends.

Gods protect them, Efanor thought.

SNOW CAME DOWN, AS KING CEFWYN STOOD ON THE BALCONY OF HIS BEDchamber, watching two boys at arms practice in the yard, boys on the verge of becoming men.

Elfwyn was the elder, nicknamed various things, but his caretaker, in the distant countryside of Amefel, had called him Otter, that being a safer name than the one his mother had given him. So Otter he had been for all his life, and the name well fitted him: a dark, quick boy, wary and wild, as free and merry as an otter in a brook: Cefwyn had seen all that before the boy had ever crossed the river or taken up residence under his roof—much as he had restrained himself from loving this boy, his firstborn son. The eyes alone should be a caution—gray as the distant sea, and quick, and denying everyone a direct stare. It was too early to know what he would do in the world or what paths these two young men would take in their lives.

But today, in the snow, in the blurring of distant lines and the changing of the landscape below this window—Cefwyn found himself moved to hope that bringing the boy to Guelemara was a good idea, that Otter's was a wild heart, but a good one, overall.

His son, now, his legitimate son and heir—Aewyn, a few months the younger—was very much the Marhanen prince: sturdy, blond, and blue-eyed as Guelenfolk ought to be—and where his queen had found such a head of hair in her dark northern ancestry was a wonder: it curled, it bounced, it refused confinement, much like its owner.

Who would have thought it so apt a brotherhood, the slim dark, wily brother, and the sunny, headlong one? Aewyn could overpower his elder brother by sheer strength—but first he had to lay hands on him.

Brothers they had been, partners in mischief from their first meeting. The boys had found each other, in fact, with no one quite ready for it to happen. Ceremonial occasions, the annual visits to the duchy of Amefel, had regularly brought Cefwyn past a certain tiny farm on the roadside, just at the outskirts of Amefel's capital of Henas'amef. He had paused there, every year that he took this trip, for a dipper of water from the well. Every year he talked to the old woman who held that farm, just to be sure things were still as peaceful as he had left them.

Came the year Aewyn had gotten on his pony and ridden with him, his first long ride out from Guelessar to Amefel, to show himself to the people he would someday rule.

And on the very first visit on which Aewyn had gone with him, Aewyn being barely six—he had spied the dark-haired lad by the shed, the lad by the shed had spied him, and Aewyn, no one quite noticing, had slid down from his pony and escaped through the fence to make his own visit. Otter had been shy and retreating, Aewyn quite bent on his acquaintance.

Every year after that, whenever the royal procession had stopped at Gran's little farm, Otter had been quick to appear, and Aewyn had been just as quick to get down and renew acquaintances—so eager for that, that the festivities of the Amefin court, the presents and the sweets, proved far less allure to Aewyn than the annual meeting with the boy on the farm. The annual stop at Gran's place therefore extended itself into half an hour, and an hour—became long enough for the guard to dismount, water their horses, and take a cup of cider; became long enough for a king and a hedge-witch to share a mug of country ale and discuss affairs of curious range, since he had found that the old woman could give him more sense of local events in half an hour than a meeting of the town ealdormen in half a day. The boys had played together at tag, gathered eggs, milked goats—certainly things the Crown Prince never would have done under ordinary circumstances. In earliest days Aewyn had sulked at being set back on his pony, and Otter, in Cefwyn's keenest memory, had stood silent, grave, and equally unhappy in Gran's rustic goat yard, watching their departure. Otter had darted one keen glance at him, that first year, a dark, wing-browed glance that had haunted him for miles, it was so like his mother's.

Last fall, leaving the goats and geese, both boys had vanished for far too long—to be discovered far down by the brook, by Gran's craft and her boy Paisi's knowledge of Otter's habits.

Aewyn, unrepentant at the guardsmen's discomfiture, unabashed to have had the king of Ylesuin wading the brook to retrieve him, had declared he had just invited his brother to come to Guelessar and live with them.

Had the king of Ylesuin quite planned it that way? No. But from the beginning, from Otter's birth, Cefwyn had had advisement not to make this bastard son Aewyn's natural enemy—or his own. And he had intended to have Aewyn come down to rustic Amefel to pass a summer, perhaps before he was old enough to get into a man's kind of mischief in the town.

Perhaps, he had mused on the way home, friendship between the boys had been very good advice, far wiser than trying to conceal one from the other or keep them apart. He already knew power was at issue, not just Gran's hedge-witchery, but the craft of the woman he had been fool enough to get a son on—the woman kept prisoner all these years in Henas'amef, because there was nowhere else safe to put Tarien Aswydd, and because the old woman at the farm and the lord of Amefel himself and the lord of Ynefel, who was not too far removed, beyond Marna Wood, all were in a position to watch her continually and prevent her from mischief.

Wizardry had always been at issue, in the boy's getting and in his life. And where wizard-work or worse was at issue, items found ways to reposition themselves, to walk on two feet to where they needed to be, to someone's fortune or misfortune.

Best know where this one was, at all times. Very wise advice had told him that at the same time he had locked the mother away.

Even the queen his wife, Ninévrisë, had told him the same, when he had told her what Aewyn had promised. At summer's end she had just given him another child—one Aewyn had so hoped would be a brother, and predicted would be, against all Ninévrisë's advisement to the contrary. Aewyn had, just after his ride south this summer, gained a little sister, Aemaryen. The birth was a great relief to the people of Ylesuin, who had wanted an heir to be Regent of Elwynor after Ninévrisë—treaty had sworn that the next child of their union would rule that adjacent kingdom, which Ninévrisë now ruled. And if it had been a disappointment to the Elwynim to have a girl born, it had also been a quiet disappointment to a fifteen-year-old prince, who had so earnestly counted on a brother.

The consequence had been foreseeable: Aewyn, a loving, loyal brother to his little sister, had nevertheless fallen off his food, pushed items about on his plate, and sighed a great deal, staring out the windows to the west and south, never once mentioning Otter.

If the baby had been another boy, a prince, Cefwyn thought, he might have had second thoughts about bringing Otter here. But it had been a princess, and he had been entrapped. Aewyn had written him a formal letter, in his own untidy hand, requesting formal audience, and had come into that audience with a written list of reasons why Otter would be no trouble at all in the household, where Otter might live, in an unused apartment down the hall, and how if he had a brother, he would apply himself to his lessons again and forever after.

Well, what could a father say? He had not forced Aewyn to reach the desperate bottom of his list.

And clearly his son suffered from want of companionship. Aewyn had not gotten on as well as he might with certain nobles' sons—their backbiting of one another and their politicking were not engaging traits, and Cefwyn did not force that society. Otter perhaps had enjoyed a certain gloss in Aewyn's memory because he was distant, and forbidden. But a father could well understand the situation of a prince—gods, indeed, he knew the taste of solitude and endless lessons and long court sessions. He knew the other side of such matters, too: his father had praised Efanor's accomplishments extravagantly and driven his elder son to low company and bad behavior with those same bickering lordlings. Without those bad habits he himself had gained, being determined to spite his own father, there would have been no royal bastard to worry this generation, that was the plain truth of matters. So he knew well how a boy's misery could turn to bad behavior and very foolish actions.

He had already been quite understanding in the matter of tutors; he had given Aewyn every gift, every understanding; he had excused him from lengthy sessions; he had taken him hither and yon about the countryside, and let him milk goats and gather eggs, because he saw value in it. He was already far too open-handed, his father would have told him, far too ready to give the Prince what he wanted.

But the desperation in Aewyn was clear. The promise had been made to the other boy, even if he had intended otherwise. The solution was one he had already leaned toward and dithered over—which was clearly why Aewyn had taken the notion he was leaning toward it. So he had found himself saying, "Perhaps this winter," and receiving a wild hug that sealed the bargain and became agreement before he had quite thought the realities of the matter to conclusion . . . a bastard son living down the hall from his proper son, subject to all the jealous stares and gossip the lordlings his son so despised could muster.

Otter, at least, was well aware of his unfortunate connections and his difficulties. He was not baseborn; oh, not in the least—his mother, Lady Tarien Aswydd, imprisoned for life by her remote cousin, Lord Crissand—was alive, like Otter, because those had been Tristen's orders, before the army had come back to Henas'amef. Let her live, Tristen had said, when others said differently. But Tristen had also said, by no means give her the child.

Tristen's advice had been law in Amefel. It was also advice Cefwyn took, above all other.

And although Cefwyn had had no stomach for hanging a woman who'd been his mistress, and none at all for doing away with the helpless infant, circumstances had given him no choice but to have that child brought up almost within sight of Tarien's prison. Again at Tristen's word, he had had him brought up by a hedge-witch who would spot sorcery if it reared its head in the boy and who might educate him in needful ways.

The boy had the Aswydd look. The gray eyes very certainly couldn't have come from the Marhanen side of the bed: eyes gray as old ice, in a face dark of complexion, dark-browed and dark-lashed. He was a handsome boy, but not one whose stare Guelenfolk much liked . . . now that they had finally seen him up close.

Now . . . gods knew the rumor of his origins was out, now that he was walking the corridors in the Guelesfort. No good to call him Otter any longer. Everyone knew what name his mother bestowed on him: Elfwyn. Elfwyn, after the last Sihhë king of the old kingdom, the enemy of the Marhanen. The name alone had counseled the boy's demise, all those years ago. The name his mother had given him was a direct challenge to the king of Ylesuin: kill your own son. Do it, and kill me, and see how your life turns.

Mercy was its own revenge. Tarien Aswydd lived. And sixteen years on, her naming had lost much of its sting. The people knew the name. That the boys were friends and the queen accepted him had been delicious gossip for the late fall season, then faded into simple fact—it evoked a little shiver, the Sihhë being a recent memory; but that was a matter no one dared broach with Cefwyn—by the gods, they would not, and knew it. Best now if a boy bearing that name could publicly befriend a Marhanen prince, become his good right hand, and let people see the name sat, not on a wizard, but a sober, studious boy—let them see that dark, somber face break into smiles and laughter as it had, this late fall in Guelemara; as it did now, while the boys caught their breath. And Cefwyn had made his decision: he could have sent the boy home, as seasons turned. But he had not. Festival approached, and the new year. He could send him home. But he purposed not to.

Aewyn was by a finger or two the taller of the two boys, certainly the stronger—he broke things: he had a reputation for it, to as much mortification as a prince was allowed to suffer. On the brighter side of that coin, the people of the city compared him to his fair-haired great-grandfather, a true Marhanen, a throwback to the blond, bluff Marhanens, and never, in any of his tutors' imagination, destined for scholarship. But a father knew. A father knew that Aewyn did think, that the boy who had been his riding companion out and about the country wanted to know things—and was no fool. Otter had found that side of Aewyn. Otter was priest-taught: Cefwyn had seen to that, in his visits to Amefel, and now Aewyn, who had rejected tutor after tutor, had taken a sudden deep interest in scholarship, taking books of natural history from the library, of all things, he and Otter together, and seeking out the room of royal curiosities, which the library had under lock and key: the hide of a two-headed calf, the egg of an unknown bird, and various strange bones. The librarian had reported their visits in some distress, fearing damage or mischief particularly with the precious books, which only scholars ordinarily had license to take from the room.

But the Prince had his way, and when they were not bashing each other with blunt swords in the courtyard, the boys had read, explored, and looked up maps, Aewyn's one scholarly passion. Maps of the realm. Maps from beyond the borders. Old maps, new ones—they had visited the chart room, where only lords and officers were supposed to be . . . and pored over military maps. Aewyn had begun this interest as a child: he had been lured into literacy only because the colorful maps had words on them he wanted to read, and, oh, count on it, to this hour he knew his maps and directions down to the most obscure hamlet in Osenan, with any detail of who lived there and how—

A perfect young tax collector, Cefwyn had used to say to his queen, perfect, if he were not the heir to the throne. Now he had drawn Otter into his passion, and of all things, the boys *read* to each other, would anyone believe it? They had gone out and about the halls mapping the passages, and down into the cellars looking for hidden halls and unknown rooms—there were none, but it did turn up a hidden cache of wine.

And who knew? There might be more to Aewyn yet than people suspected. Aewyn had hated the sessions with the Quinalt priest who taught him and attempted to sneak catechism into the reading; Aewyn had sabotaged those lessons with numerous pranks, and the priest, being discharged, had predicted that such an irreverent prince was never going to be a scholar of any sort. The next tutor had come in saying that the best they could do was instill doctrine in him and keep him on the straight and narrow, while his armsmasters turned him into a warrior. That tutor had been discharged in a week, and in that dismissal, of a man the Holy Father had provided, Aewyn had not even had to make the request.

The priestly tutors were wrong. A loving father had concluded that beforehand purely on faith, but with, of all things, Otter's coming to Guelemara, he was finally vindicated. His legitimate son would have the size, yes, to bully his way through situations: that was what all the tutors wanted to foster in their prince and future king.

But Aewyn's petition for his brother's coming to Guelessar had shown certain traces of scholarship, had it not?

Aewyn's fidgeting, a fond father could suspect, was not after all the restlessness of a simple mind but that of a boy who, contrary to his bluff appearance, had long since understood the point at issue, was bored beyond endurance, particularly by catechisms—had not he been similarly bored? If Aewyn had not had Otter, Aewyn might not have imagined there were better teachers . . . as Otter, who could dive and dart with native skill, had never learned the value of keeping an enemy a sword's distance away from his skin. Each learned from the other.

As now. Bang and clang, all measured, interspersed with prankish feints and laughter. A month and more of those two together, more than two fortnights without so much as a quarrel between them or a cross word for the staff from Aewyn . . . and that, too, was a marvel. Too great a silence and compliance from Aewyn had never boded well for the household's tranquillity, until now.

But everything was changed, with this boy's coming. Had he ever seen Aewyn as happy as he was?

Bang, and down went the shield, the royal prince thrown onto his rump, but not defeated. Aewyn scrambled and threw a handful of snow. Snow came back, as Otter shook a sapling branch down on him in a cloud of white. With a shout that rang off the walls, Aewyn surged to his knee, sword be damned, and gathered a mighty snowball behind his shield, but not in time. A well-thrown snowball hit him, but on the fast-moving shield.

Oh, then the fight started, snowballs and shieldwork, as fast as two rascals could form and throw.

Aewyn had the Marhanen knack for offense: his snowballs were accurate, and he flung them with all the strength in his arm, stubborn and strong—but with his namesake's quickness, Otter dived behind the hedge and worked up the row, to throw from ambush.

Now that, Cefwyn thought, was a boy brought up by a witch and a thief, not an armsmaster. Then Aewyn, baffled at first, took to the hedges that rimmed the little practice-yard, a warfare on which Cefwyn held grand vantage, neither boy paying the least attention upward.

An otter's cunning was no small gift to bring to the royal line. For all the years these two lads had lived, the realm had been at peace, the two boys born within months on either side of the great battle—but the skills of attack and defense had to come down to them, no matter. Aewyn had the classic training—rode well, stood well, swung well, while Otter had never sat a horse before he rode to Guelessar.

Aewyn, on the other hand, had never had to hunt an otter in the bushes, but he was gaining the knack after being ambushed. An impartial father simply watched from on high, offering no advice.

Snowballs from either side. Neither hit a thing but winter hedge. And both boys ducked. Aewyn had abandoned his shield. So had Otter. A fast scramble ensued, each seeking new positions. New snowballs formed.

A gust of wind came down off the Guelesfort roof, a white cloud enveloping balcony and garden alike. Cefwyn found snow on his sleeves, on the balcony rail—a second gust and a third, and the boys below, hit by avalanche, shoveled snow at each other with their hands.

But the wind that had come over the roof brought new snow with old, a gray veil rapidly drawn between the yard and the spires and spiked roof ridge of the Quinaltine, across the wall. The noble houses round about grew dimmer still. New snow and old mixed together in sudden violence.

A prudent man knew when to step back into the sheltering room. A father wondered when his sons would have the same good sense. A blast came down from the dark cloud that had crept up behind the Guelesfort. Now the afternoon light darkened, and the wind began to whip the snow off all the eaves.

"The weather's turning." He said it conversationally, as to an old friend, closing his hand on the amulet he wore beneath the leather and velvet—he conversed, one-sided, at times when his world grew strange or his nobles grew fractious. He rarely had any sense from the locket whether Tristen heard him or not. Faith was a certain part of his wearing it, faith and remembrance, and the warm confidence of friendship, which rode there, close as his own heartbeat—it was not an amulet he wore too openly, nor ever showed the Quinaltine fathers, whose business it was not. Now he did imagine a presence, poised between winter and warmth, and he lingered there, gazing outward into gray.

"My dear friend," he murmured. "Do you hear? The wind's rising. The fickle warmth before, and now the snows come hard. A late winter, and an edge in the wind. Is it snowing where you are?"

Perhaps the sensation was false, wishful thinking. The cold seemed fresh and keen, and a venture to the balcony rail showed the boys heading for shelter, sensibly taking their gear with them, then vying to get through the door at the same time, like sheep.

"I wish you were here this season, my friend. I wish you could see how the boys have grown. I was doubtful. But they teach each other. They teach themselves."

They made it through the door, which shut. The king had memories of winter practice with his own brother, of scampering through that hall to the stairs, and down to the kitchens, where the ovens maintained the warmest spot in all the Guelesfort.

A memory of berry jam and butter, on fresh-baked bread, while one's fingers were still numb. Efanor with berry stain on his cheek, chiding him for stain on his nose.

"There's happiness here, this winter, old friend, there is, never mind Efanor's dire predictions. There are good qualities in them both."

Taste of berries that he could have at any time, being king. But jam baked into a twist of dough and hauled out just when brown and hot, that was sweetest, the best thing on a winter day. One had to get such things straight from the oven, not ported up through a chain of ceremony.

"The holidays are on us—well, none so cheery, our Guelen holidays, as those we kept in Amefel. I shall keep the boy with us. And I wish you could see them. You know you would come welcome, if you would come east this winter—after Festival." He spoke, but more faintly, the wind skirling about him. "I make the offer, at least." And doubt welled up, cold as the wind. "Do you still hear me, my friend? Are you well? It's been so long since you wrote. You know me: magic has to thunder to get my attention."

Nothing from the amulet. The wind whipped up and drove him to retreat into his chambers. He pulled the doors shut as the draperies whipped about and tried to flee outside, like escaping ghosts.

The latch thumped down and secured the door, imprisoning the curtains and the warmth. The fire in the hearth ceased whipping about.

Outside the diamond panes of the windows, the whole world had gone white.

Mist on the glass, it was, clouding the world outside.

A pattern streaked across that moist surface, the appearance of writing on the inside glass.

Be careful, the writing said.

BOOK ONE

CHAPTER ONE

i

THEY HAD A PANFUL OF JAM-FILLED TREATS, AND TEA FROM THE KETTLE, THE baker's boy being so obliging as to run a heavy tray straight upstairs, and if they spoiled their supper, they were satisfied. The royal table hosted the duke of Osenan tonight, and Aewyn was ever glad enough to forage and not to have to sit still at his father's table, at some long-winded state dinner. The fireside in his own room was ever so much nicer, himself and his brother lying on the rug by a well-fed fire, having dessert first. There were two kinds of sausage for later, three kinds of cheese, and a crusty loaf, besides their treats, and the tea, which they drank down by the cupful.

They were warm again, after their battle. The wind howled about the tall windows, sleet rattling against the diamond panes, and they had drawn the drapes against the cold. The fire before them made towers and battlements of coals, glowing red walls that tumbled and sent up sparks into the dark of the flue, which they imagined as the dark of night above the world.

It was Aewyn's own room, his private realm—at fifteen going on sixteen he had gained this privacy from his father: his own quarters, near if not next to the king's and the queen's chambers, but with his own door and a separate foyer room for his guard and a second small sleeping room for his two constant domestic servants—they were his father's guard and his father's staff, in all truth, but they were the same men who had been attending him since he was first out and about the halls and the courtyards on his own recognizance, so they were as good as his.

Most of all he had his own sitting room and his own bedchamber, and this meant Nurse had finally retired to her own numerous children down in Dary, beyond the city walls.

And that meant he no longer had anyone to make him sit in a chair, at a table, like a proper boy, and be served by servants. Otter preferred the fireside, and the warm stones, and the prince of Ylesuin found the close warmth of the fire a thorough delight, the best place in the room. They had their tray of food beside them, and a pitcher of watered wine—very watered, it was—and their book, which Otter read to them both—a record, really, of the properties and the building of the royal lodge at Maedishill. The account had all its local legendry, and it had maps, the most wonderful colored and whimsically detailed maps of a place Aewyn had known from earliest childhood.

"Here," Aewyn said, tracing a line with his finger, "here is the spring and its outflow. And just down from here, it joins this larger brook." In his mind was a wonderful place, on an autumn day when he was about five. He had sailed leaf-barges down the current from the spring, to see them wreck in the great rapids of the great brook—he could stride across it now—where the water flowed over rounded rocks. He would never, now, admit to having sailed leaf-boats, but he cherished the memory of them. He snatched a bite of sweet and pointed with the stick of crust to the place where the rapids ended and the brook ran by the lodge. "A falls there, with an old log. See, even the log is on the map. Brother Siene drew it. I remember him. He had a white beard down to his belt. He was caretaker there until I was seven."

"Why do you have a map of the lodge?"

"Well, because Brother Siene loved to do maps, and he lived there alone most of the time, so he just did. But now anyone who ever wants to know about Maedishill can look in this book and see the lodge and know all its properties, and how far they go, and where the next holding starts. It makes it a legal record, because Brother Siene wrote a date on it, and the library has a date when the book came here. That proves, for instance, that it's my father's brook. It starts here, where it comes out of the rocks, so he has title over it until it reaches the boundary with the farmers, and if it had any fish in it—it doesn't, no matter that Brother Siene drew them in—they would be his only until they reach the boundary."

"The fish wouldn't know that," Otter remarked, so soberly Aewyn had to laugh.

"Fish don't know anything."

"I don't know if they do. Maybe they do." Otter touched the painted fish with his fingers, ever so carefully. "I like his laughing fish."

"So do I," Aewyn said, remembering sun on water, sparkling rays through thick green leaves. "My mother and I used to go there for a month before Papa could get time to come, and when he did, everything would change. Messengers, messengers at all hours, and lords coming in for visits with dozens of servants, all full of arguments, with papers to read, and if two came, there wasn't room for the second one, and there was dust all over everything if there wasn't mud, just from the horses. They'd trample the grass down and spoil the meadow, they'd get drunk in the great room, and their sons would be out chasing the rabbits and trying to shoot them. Mother had the duke of Marisyn's sons and his servants rounded up by her guard, and Papa—my father—said if he had his choice, he was going to run away to Far Sassury and not tell anybody where he was going. But the next year, the grass would be green again and the brook would have its moss back, and it would be just us, until Papa came."

"No!" a feminine squeal came from the guards' room, and several men laughed. "The scriptures is against immodesty," the girl said, "an' ye keep your nasty hands t' yourself."

There were remarks below hearing, and then the girl began citing scripture: "Cursed is the flesh and the desires of it, cursed is the lustful man and the issue of his . . ."

Aewyn surged up to his feet, outraged. "Hush, now, hush," his guards were saying, wishing to keep the peace in the hall, but the undercook's daughter was a righteous girl: so she said at every chance. Madelys was her name, she had probably come up looking for used dishes, and she was too holy for a nunnery, was what everyone said—which was why Cook thought she was proper enough to be waiting on a young lord in his own premises—and spying, meanwhile, on his household.

It was a very furious and upset Madelys, as Aewyn faced the hall—Madelys with her serving tray and used dishes snatched under her arm and a fury on her thin face. She scarcely bobbed a curtsy as she stood there confronting him and glaring at his bodyguards.

"Out!" Aewyn said.

"It ain't me!" Madelys said, with not a *Your Highness* nor any other grace. "It ain't me at any fault. They was pullin' my skirt!"

"No one ha' touched the lass, Your Highness." This from his oldest guard, Selmyn, and if he had any discernment in him, or cared at the moment, this was the source of truth, far more than this surly girl.

"Out," Aewyn said the second time, and not loudly at all. If he were his father, Cook's daughter would already have been running; but he was not, and she stood there glaring at him like a badger in its den. He said, more harshly: "Get out!"

She hunched her tray closer, turned, and stalked out the door, which one of his guards opened for her, without a second curtsy or a mollifying word.

He was truly not supposed to swear. His father and his mother would hear about it if he did, though not, perhaps, from these men. He turned a carefully serene face toward them, then walked with a certain embarrassed dignity back to the fireside, where Otter stood utterly dismayed.

"Madelys," Aewyn said, his face burning, "is the only maid Mother will let come through my doors, and she has to come because the menservants aren't to touch the dishes."

"Do you have to mind what she says?" Otter asked him. "Are we in trouble?"

"No." He plumped down whence he had risen, signaling Otter to do the same. "Oh, I could be rid of her like that if I took my nurse back. I know Nurse would send her away. But I'm too old for Nurse telling me what to eat and when to eat and always scolding me about my clothes." He missed Nurse. Sometimes he missed her keenly. But when she visited, as she did, she always hugged him like a baby, straightened his hair, and more particularly, would never let him sit on the floor with his half brother. The notion of pretending they were in Gran's little house in Amefel just would never occur to Nurse, who had one notion of the way things should be and never left it. "Madelys is just a fool, is all. She really does want to be a nun, but you have to have a dowry for that, and being undercook's third daughter, she has two sisters to marry first." He gave a laugh. "If she doesn't mend her ways, I'll save up my market pennies for a year and give her one."

Otter didn't seem to understand. He shot a troubled look toward the short hallway and the door.

"It's a joke, goose."

Otter showed a shy smile, then. His country brother was sometimes slow to laugh at angry people, although he had a very quick wit in private. Aewyn fell onto his belly and shut the little book, which was done up in goatskin with a painted picture of the lodge in a little medallion. "It's a silly little book. It was a present, really. Brother Siene used to be a copyist in the monastery—he was Bryalt—and he could read, besides. He made it for my father to give to my mother on her birthday: he can't give her the lodge, which he would like to have done, because she's Elwynim and he can't give away Guelen land, but he could give it to me. He says he will, when I'm nineteen. And my mother gave me the book because I was always borrowing it."

"Will you live there when you can?"

"As often as I can. I'll put fish in the brook. I'm tired of waiting to see one."

That, Otter clearly thought was worth laughing at. Aewyn laughed, himself, and rolled onto his back on the bearskin rug, looking up at the laquear ceiling. The beams were dark polished wood, with boars' heads set where they met the walls. The center of the squares had sheaves of barley in some, and deer in others, with the crest of Guelessar in the centermost, in gold. He had never really seen these things for what they were, until Otter came: like the book, they were the accounting of the wealth of the kingdom, which was his to enjoy and spread about in charity, dispensing justice and making sure the wealth went where it ought, to men of peace. Otter had grown up otherwise, in a little farmhouse, over in Amefel, with his gran, who was a wisewoman, but a witch, really, as the Quinalt saw it, and who was not really Otter's own grandmother. Otter had never ridden a horse, only practiced with a wooden sword, with Paisi, who was Gran's real grandson. Paisi was peasant-born, and in Guelessar, Paisi, being a farmer, would not have known about swords, but he had learned a little. It was all very different where Otter had lived. There had been wars in Amefel. And even the farmers had learned to fight.

The wind blew at the windows and fluttered the fire in the fireplace.

"When the storm blows itself out," Aewyn said, "we could go riding." He had a second, glum thought. "If it weren't holiday coming. If the weather clears by tomorrow, we could do it, but it doesn't sound like it out there, does it?"

"No."

A deep sigh. "Besides, it's a great fuss, getting the horses up from pasture, then only having to send them down again. But we shall go after. There'll still be snow all about. And by then the merchants will wear down the snow. And then—" He had brought out the book and shown Otter this special prize of his, and now he had a keen notion what would be a great treat. "Then, after Festival, we shall go to the lodge. It's not that far. The brook may be frozen, but you can see it all the same. We can spend a night or two there."

"If your father will let us," Otter said.

"I'll tell you what's not in the book," Aewyn said, rolling back onto his stomach and his elbows, looking straight into Otter's pale gray eyes. He dropped his voice to a whisper. "The lodge has its own ghost."

"A haunt?" Otter asked, duly impressed.

"It's supposed to be a grave from before the lodge was built, and nobody knew it was there, nor ever has found it. But late at night pans fall in the scullery, and footsteps go up and down the stairs."

Otter's eyes were wide as could be. "Is it a man or a woman?"

"Her. It's a lady. Well, a woman. She could be a farmer or a herder. Nobody knows. But cakes go missing out of the kitchen, and everyone says it's the ghost."

Now Otter looked doubtful and grinned. "I can think of another way cakes disappear."

Aewyn laughed, too. "We'll stay up late and see if cakes disappear," he said. "We just have to endure Festival to get there."

"Day after tomorrow," Otter said.

"Three days earlier than yours, in Amefel, isn't it? And no dancing." He understood that Otter was Bryalt, like his mother. "I like your holidays much better. But I daren't say that, being the Prince. I have to be good. Have you tried your clothes?"

"Clothes?" Otter asked, confused, so he hoped he had not spoiled their father's surprise.

"Papa sent some. For the whole Festival. Mother said so. I thought they'd have come this morning. They were supposed to."

"I haven't seen them."

"Oh, well, they'll be there. Probably the servants are brushing them. They had better be there."

"Where am I supposed to wear them?"

"To services every day."

Otter wore a look of slight dismay. Perhaps he shouldn't have said that.

"Papa says you should sit with us in sanctuary," Aewyn said.

"What does the queen think about that?"

"Mother wants you there, too."

Otter didn't say anything to that, only looked unhappy.

"Papa says it will be a good thing if you come. People will know you're my brother. You'll be welcome. You will. You're to walk in with us and sit with us, and the people will see who you are."

A small silence. "I don't know why."

"Because you *are* my brother."

"I'm not, quite. It's pretending."

"It's not," Aewyn said fiercely. "You are my brother. You will be, in public, so everyone knows who you are, and that my father and my mother agree. I heard them talking about it, and my mother says it's a good idea."

"If His Majesty says so," Otter said faintly. "I've never been to Quinalt services. What am I to do?"

"Oh, all you have to do is sit when we sit and stand when we stand and stay next to me and do just as I do. The choir sings and the Holy Father gives a sermon every day. We listen, and we get up and go home. The first day is Fast Day. That's the worst. You have to dress in the dark every day. But we go without eating from dawn to dark on Fast Day, and it's always breakfast before the sun comes up, because we have to be there at sunrise. But it's just five days." It was what his mother used to say to him to cheer him up. "And then the Bryalt holiday starts, midway through. My mother puts up decorations in her chambers when that starts. You could put them up, in yours, well, after Fast Day. You shouldn't put them in the sitting room, though. We can't do that."

"The Quinalt doesn't allow it?"

"No." Aewyn lowered his voice, and confessed: "I like my mother's holiday ever so much better, with the evergreen and candles. Especially the cakes. Do they make the sweet cakes in Amefel, the brown ones with the nuts?"

"Oh, nut cakes, yes. And braided bread with apples in it." Otter's eyes brightened. "Do you have that for holiday?"

"Well," Aewyn admitted, "no one downstairs knows how. But Mother's maid knows how to bake the cakes herself, and she goes down to the kitchen, and tosses Cook out, and we have them for days." He saw how Otter's eyes brightened at that news. "They pass the cakes out among all my mother's staff, all through the Bryalt holiday, and she puts the evergreen up and lights bayberry candles in her private chambers at night, and they go to the Bryalt shrine on the last night, or at least Mother does, and her maids. My father can't, and I can't, not even when I was a babe in arms." That was always a sore spot with him and with his mother. "She misses the dances. But they sing songs in her rooms. What else do they do in Amefel?"

"They give out the little cakes, free, in the shrine, except if you have coin in your purse you have to make an offering to keep all your other coins lucky. And there's a penny baked into some of the cakes. The aetheling—the duke—throws pennies all up and down the street when he rides to the front gate to open it for the year. I've picked up three, all told. They're supposed to be lucky." He pulled out the plain braided cord he wore about his neck, and showed three dull brown pennies, pierced through. Aewyn had seen it before, and wondered then if it was a charm.

"Is it magical?" he asked warily.

"Oh, it's Gran's; it could be. She made it for me, from the lucky pennies. Holiday pennies. It's bad luck to spend them."

"The Quinalt takes the money we give," Aewyn said. "It doesn't give it out. Everybody has to give something. The priests do give out food to the poor on the last day and set up long tables in the square. First day is the day I hate."

"Fast Day?"

"That's the hardest. Fasting daylight to dark. And praying at sunrise in the Quinaltine. We have to go there while it's still dark, it's always cold, because the sanctuary hasn't heated up yet, and it's long, long praying. You get tired, you mustn't fidget, and you can't eat or drink anything, not even water, on the day, from the first the sun rises. Even the horses and the cattle can't eat or drink until the sun goes down."

"But they don't know what day it is!"

"Oh, truth is, they'll feed themselves off browse. That's why we put most of the horses we can down in pasture."

"But it's thick snow down there now. Will they put out hay?"

"They're not supposed to, really. If the wind's blowing, you'll hear the cattle bawling clear up on the hill. Lamenting the sins of the world, the fathers say. And the horses that have to stay in stable, the courier horses and such, they're pent in, and there's no hay."

Otter had been on his belly, leaning on his elbows before the fire. Now he had sat up. "That's outright cruel, not to feed them."

"Well"—Aewyn looked to see where his guards were, and lowered his voice—"the fact is, the grooms up on the hill always spill a lot of grain in empty stalls before the day, and leave buckets full of water, then let the horses across to the empty stalls where the grain is, that afternoon, for all the horses that have to be up on the hill. It is sort of a sin, if the priests had to rule on it, but nobody mentions it happens, so nobody ever complains. And I don't know for sure, but I'd wager with all this snow that the stableboys leave a gate open so the livestock down in pasture can get into a section where there's a haystack. The priests say one thing, but the grooms always get around it because nobody wants the horses tearing up the fences."

"That's lying, isn't it?"

Aewyn gave a second look toward the guards' hallway. And back. "It's not really lying. It's just pretending. Pretending isn't a sin."

"It's still lying. And starving the horses is a sin."

"Well, you can't say that to the priests. Nor even where the guards can hear you."

"I can say it to you, though. Don't *you* think it's wrong?"

Sometimes Otter's questions were worrisome. "I don't know I ever thought about it. We're not supposed to lie. Or be cruel. But my father says sometimes people have to, anyway, for good reasons. The horses not knocking the boards down would be a good, practical reason for sneaking the grain in, wouldn't it? And we're lying so we don't have to be cruel. So I suppose that one cancels the other."

"Well, what if we went down to the stable tomorrow and dropped a whole sack of apples?"

Sometimes Otter's schemes were as troubling as his questions. But he also came up with intrigues Aewyn never would have thought of. "Us high folk daren't get caught doing it. The priests would be very put out. But if we paid the grooms to go get a batch of nice big apples and carrots and such and strew it all through the stalls, nobody would care."

It was a plot hatching, a plot that required all sorts of delicious connivance. Otter's ways had never gotten them caught, particularly when he had Paisi's advice. For a country lad, Otter was very good at figuring out the byways and back ways of the palace—besides their careful mapping. But this was something that, besides theft, required diplomacy, and arrangements, and picking the right people to carry it out, those who would keep a secret.

He knew just the ones.

And, he thought, if they were very clever, there was the big kitchen apple barrel, there were always old flour sacks in the kitchen, and if they sneaked quite skillfully, they needn't spend a penny of his market money, or have to trust the stable lads to do the buying.

ii

A LITTLE PLAN, WITH AEWYN, ALWAYS ENDED UP FAR BIGGER THAN IT STARTED. Otter was not thoroughly happy: he would rather have put his hand in fire than have to attend Quinalt services, though he had to respect the king's faith, and he could see that there were advantages to his mother's son not sitting in his rooms while Guelenfolk were praying and fasting and being pious. But that inconvenience palled in the face of the adventure Aewyn proposed: he was very glad to think they would be feeding the horses—his own among them—and that Aewyn agreed with him. His own stomach was full of good food. He trusted his half brother Aewyn, who, despite his grand notions, never had led them wrong. And his father—in private, he dared think of the king as his father—had made provision for his going to the Quinalt Festival in public with the family. That was at once scary and exciting. He had not been in public with his brother before.

He walked back to his room, a track that led down the hall, across the landing of the great stairs, and farther down the hall four doors, just as the servants were putting out the east wing candles—all but the single candle in each hall sconce, which would burn for safety and for convenience of anyone whose night candle had gone out. The west wing, where Aewyn's room lay next the king's and the queen's chambers, still burned bright with multiple candles, and the sounds of revelry still came up the stairs from the corridor below, where a veritable forest of candles burned bright and numerous. By comparison, with the dimming of the candles in the east wing, the way to his own door began to feel like deepest night, and the sleet rattling at the high windows of the grand stairway at the landing predicted the revelers below might wade knee deep to their lordly houses before morning.

It was a lonely hour, and he had no bodyguard to walk with him: his father had appointed him none, though the captain of his father's guard had given him the name of the sergeant of the upper hall night guard and orders to go to him if he ever felt uneasy. Aewyn's bodyguard, likewise, would have walked him home on such late visits, but he never availed himself of what Aewyn had ceased to offer—he could not imagine Guelen guardsmen, the Prince's Guard more to the point, armored and carrying weapons, walking him down the hall to his room. He had no enemies that he knew, nor any great notoriety, so far as he knew; there were no bogles on the short way, only disconcerting echoes and a fluttering activity of shadows in the dim light, all of which were due to drafts—there was a well-reported and much-deplored draft in the upper hall when certain doors downstairs were open, but he had no idea which ones those were. He was reasonably sure the shadows were the wind fluttering the last candles, and nothing due to haunts—the Guelesfort had nothing of the reputation of the Zeide, down in Amefel.

He was a guest in his father's house and had no desire to disturb the household, or make demands, or take his welcome for granted. He was Otter, was all, on a visit that would last only as long as he amused his brother, and he would go back to Amefel, probably before too much longer—as soon as he had assured his father he was a quiet soul and without great expectations. He had used to dream of being swept up by his royal father on one of his visits and made a prince, well, at least a landed lord—had not his father provided him an education, and put him under the personal care of Lord Crissand?—but a surer knowledge of the world beyond Gran's farm had begun to tell him that was not at all likely, and that the reason he was under Lord Crissand's care had more to do with Lord Crissand's having his mother in prison.

Going to Festival with the family, now: that was a surprise to him. He had not been sure he would be this long in Guelemara.

He found his own door and whisked inside as if ghosts were on his heels—always, these snug, painted doors chased a little breeze inside, and the doors, easy on their polished hinges, felt snappish and scarily sharp in their closing, fierce things that would love a taste of peasant skin.

"M'lord?" Paisi was waiting up for him—Paisi, Gran's true grandson, as happened, Gran's proper heir, a grown man—while he himself was Gran's ward, a guest even under the roof he called home. Paisi had never settled easily into what he called "lordly doin's," and avoided locals—so it was a lonely watch Paisi had assumed, and not uncommon for Otter to find Paisi sitting exactly this way at the fireside, having had his supper alone. It was not to his will that Paisi regularly stayed behind in quarters when he was with Aewyn, but that was what Paisi chose. Paisi oversaw the servants who made free of every door in the Guelesfort—"so's to see what fancy servants do," was Paisi's way of putting it, in his choice to stay much about their rooms. But Paisi, who had been a thief when he was a boy, had his own suspicions of anyone opening drawers—even with the best of excuses and bearing clean linens when they did it.

Paisi was a small wiry man with dark hair and dark eyes, like most Amefin-born—clean-shaven, like most from the west and north. His hands were callused and his face was tanned dark from work in the sun. The habit of good humor was etched around his eyes, lines which the fire smoothed to a look of youth. Country-bred might be an insult in this grand house; but that was Paisi, through and through; and wherever Paisi was, was safe and comfortable, in Otter's thinking, a little bit of Gran's house that stayed constantly near him in this strange place.

Paisi rose as Otter unfastened his cloak, and Paisi took it from him, snatching it deftly away, though Otter perfectly well knew for himself where the peg was. Paisi hung his cloak up by the guards' room, just off the little entry hall, and Otter, ignoring both hearthside chairs, sank down on the warm, smooth, polished stones: nothing escaped the relentless polishing in the Guelesfort.

Paisi sat down by him, cross-legged, picked up the poker, and began to settle the fire down for the night.

"Did you have supper?" Otter asked him, to be sure the servants had come and done their jobs. He was prepared to go down and raid the kitchen with Paisi, well fed as he was: Aewyn's supper invitation had been unexpected. "I didn't think I'd be so long."

"Oh, when 'Is 'Ighness called ye in to supper, I went straight down to kitchen on me own, bein' a canny fellow."

A frown. "You're entitled to call the servants to bring it, you know."

"Oh, but 'Is Majesty's banquet's all spread out down below, and staff gettin' all the dishes that come back, ain't they? So the pickin's is better if I go down meself—I ain't lived in a great house for nothin'. I'd ha' brought some tarts up when I come back, but didn't seem likely there was short commons in 'Is 'Ighness's rooms, neither, was there?"

"I couldn't eat another bite," Otter said, which was the truth—though he and Aewyn had, regrettably, seen no tarts at all: he was a little envious, for the tarts. "We laid plots to feed the horses."

"For Fast Day, was ye meanin'?"

"Aewyn told me about it. Paisi, we intend to steal a sack of apples from the kitchen."

"Now, ye ain't pilferin' any apples, lad. If you're bent on annoyin' the priests, leave pilferage to one who knows how to slip about."

"I think His Highness insists to do it himself."

"An' the kitchen barrel is in the storeroom, an' there's a lock on all. You got to get down there after supper, is what, if you're going to get in. And then you got to know when the baker'll be in, and 'e'll be in and out of that room in the night, to start the dough for mornin' bakin'. I know when."

"You could get in trouble."

"I might if I was caught. Which I won't be." Paisi wriggled his fingers, a ripple in the firelight. "An' who's sayin' this is a good idea, now?"

"His Highness says they always do it. Well, the grooms always do it, spread grain here and there so the horses don't go hungry. We just thought apples would be good for holiday."

"So how many sacks is this to be? There's twenty-some horses up 'ere."

"I don't know. At least a good big one. His Highness says there are always flour sacks in the kitchens."

"Oh, so this is a proper plan, is it, wi' sacks an' all. An' ye'll be tellin' the stableboy what, when ye come in with these 'ere sacks?"

"See, you should have come with me."

"Well, I didn't know ye'd be plottin' theft and knavery with 'Is 'Ighness. Filch ye a couple coin, that I can do, an' we got a few o' Gran's, which is far easier, then I go down an' get your sack of apples in town, none the wiser, wi'out stirrin' up the whole hill an' gettin' the Prince in trouble. You just let me tend to it."

"No! Coin's not apples. You can get in so much trouble . . ."

"Apples an' coin is the same to the law, an' coin o' th' realm's a sight lighter an' easier to hide. If you're goin' to thieve, lad, ye got to be light. Besides, if ye bribe the stableboy, 'e won't remember a thing when they find the flour sack."

"Well, you'd have to get the whole sack of apples up past the Guelesfort gate. That's where you'd get caught."

"Wi' what? A sack of apples I paid for wi' good coin? I'm bringin' it up-stairs t' m'lord."

"For Fast Day?"

"Ah, that is a point."

"And neither you nor I has money. We shouldn't spend Gran's."

"An' Gran'll skin us both for fools for good an' all for even thinkin' it, an' me for lettin' ye risk your neck! Whoever come up wi' this wild notion in the first place?"

"Maybe I did," Otter admitted. "I don't know."

"Well, how can ye not know?"

"It was mostly both of us. Prince Aewyn said they don't feed the horses on Fast Day, or well, they do, but they don't, and he said they scatter grain around and let them into the stalls where it is. But it just seemed right to give them a real treat. We already have coin. Or Prince Aewyn does. He gets pennies for market day. We could just tell the grooms to go buy apples because they're the ones to do it."

Paisi made a rude face, not letting him get further. "An' who knows if the grooms takes 'alf your coin an' spends it in the tavern, neither? I don't trust them lads, especially not that shifty fellow who's the stablemaster's get. Ye give 'im a bribe, so's he knows it's his, an' 'e don't have to get all stirred up and sweaty to pilfer it, so's he can lie wi' a pure, clear face when authority comes askin'."

He was sure that, where it regarded thievery, Paisi was the one to ask. He and Paisi had shared little mischiefs at home in Amefel, minor misdeeds, like filching windfall apples during harvest from an unwatched orchard, and Paisi had taught him how to lie low and cover his tracks. But here, Paisi was right, it was priests, and law, and very skilled guards stalking up and down the halls; and whether it was because they were in the strange and Guelen west, or because it was priests lying about being cruel and calling it good deeds, he had no idea of the ground he stood on in Guelenish lands. He had come to the Guelesfort, it had turned out, because Prince Aewyn wanted him to come and not because, as he had always hoped would happen, his father had had the idea. So he was not the king's guest. He was here on Aewyn's whim, and they liked each other, but it was a question how far Aewyn would stand up for him if something went wrong. Here in the Guelesfort the penalty wasn't just paying extra chores to Gran and delivering simples to the offended orchard owner. It was the priests, the law, and the Guelen Guard, and Paisi, who wasn't the king's son, and had no protection, wanted to get between him and the law.

"I just felt badly about my horse," he said, the only moral sense he could come up with. "He loves his grain. Gran wouldn't hold with these priests, would she?"

"Nor would she hold wi' you stealin'," Paisi said. "Gran'd box my ears for lettin' you find your way into mischief, here in the king's own house, an' the Prince with ye, good gods! Ye're here to find your fortune wi' your father, is what."

"I'm not, really. It wasn't my father who wanted me here."

"Well, same as. An' finding your fortune ain't likely if the guards catch you an' the Prince filchin' apples."

"So what's right? The Prince won't like it if I back off now. And Aewyn wouldn't get into trouble if he was caught. I know it's right what you say about the kitchen, and the locks, and all, but he won't get caught. They won't dare catch him, the same as they pretend to starve the horses, won't they?"

"Let me tell you about priests an' morality, little brother. They're apt to be more upset if them apples is in the Prince's hands after sunrise, because he's the prince, havin' food when he ain't supposed to, never mind it's horsefeed. Stealin', that's not the matter. The *food* is. That's priests for you."

"But—"

"You hear me, you hear me on this, lad. There was a time the pious priests—they was Bryalt ones, in this case—was preaching in the square about charity, an' the holiday penny, and feedin' the poor, an' all. An' we was starvin', Gran and me, an' it sounded like a miracle. We was desperate. I was, oh, about nine. An' hearin' that about charity, an' believin' what I heard, I went to the shrine to get the 'oliday gift they promised. And do you know, them rascal priests wouldn't give me the penny for a loaf o' bread, because I wasn't goin' to swear again' wizards, when the whole reason we was starvin' was that Gran couldn't sell her cures on account of the town marshal put out some damned edict about wizards an' charms? That was when Heryn was duke in Amefel, and there was laws again' most things, from wall to wall o' the town, an' a tax on ever'thing that moved, an' there was two thieves 'angin' at the gate that very day. Well, I was mad. An' it didn't fright me none. That was the first time I stole, right from the offerin' plate. Weren't the last, neither. I were a damn good thief before all was done. An' I went on bein' a good thief. I got back at the cheats as deserved it, and got paid for havin' a sharp eye by the same guards as would ha' hanged me if they'd caught me at thievin'. Oh, I was clever. Well, till I met Lord Tristen, I was."

"Tell that time," Otter said, snugging down against his arms, down on the warm hearthstones, full as he was and close to bedtime. They were far from the matter of Aewyn and the apples now, and a tale, one he'd heard a hundred times, was much better at settling the day's worry than thinking about Festival and apple theft, which he hoped would just work itself out without involving Paisi at all. "Tell it, about how you met Lord Tristen."

"Well," Paisi said, gathering his knees into his arms, as they'd sat many a cold night on the rough masonwork of Gran's fireside. One could all but see the flash of Gran's spindle spinning beside them. "Well, it was like this. I was on the street, me a little younger 'n you, now—" That one detail had changed slowly over the years he had heard the tale. "And I see this young man walkin' along, looking lost, 'im wi' the look of a noble, but all dirty an' lookin' as if 'e'd slept rough. Now here's a young lord a little drunk an' lookin' for 'is next tavern, says I to meself, an' maybe havin' money left on 'is person, an' maybe I can find that purse. So I goes up to him, and 'e asks me if 'e can stay the night in my room, bein' kind of odd-spoke when he does it. Well, now, I hadn't any room, bein' as Gran an' I was livin' in sheds and such as we could find 'em, up an' down the town. I says, well, a gentleman like you c'n stay up to the Zeide, can't ye? An' he wants to know where that is. Well, now, any fool, even a drunk fool, knows the way to the Zeide hill, which is plainly uphill all over town, from the walls up, an' at first I'd the notion to laugh at 'im, but 'e just looked at me in that way he had. So, says I, I'd guide him, says I, figurin' there'd be coin somewheres—'e 'ad no purse about 'im, such as I'd been able to see first off, but some hides it, an' the gate-guards up there, they'd pay 'andsome, if so happen this was some lord's son in trouble, an' more 'n that if so happen this odd young man were some out-land spy—the Elwynim was keen on doin' in your da in those days, an' now an' again they tried. It wasn't just thieves they had hangin' at the town gate when your da was there. So I showed me visitor up to the gate, an' the guards took 'im in an' give me a penny for 't. But it were that look 'e had, them gray, gray eyes as could look right through you, gentle as could be—I didn't like what I'd done, an' I thought an' thought about it. But if ye ever get involved with 'is kind, ye never can untangle the threads, can ye? An' 'e fell in with your da. So came the day I'd got meself in trouble, an' 'e remembered, and 'e asked me to be 'is servant, which I was. And 'e give me ever'thing I needed, and enough for Gran a room, too, never a question, never asked what I did wi' the last coin. 'Is hands could heal, they could, and 'e cured Gran, too, didn't he, just easy as thinkin'?"

Gran always nodded at this point in the story, so in Gran's absence, he did, which went unnoticed. Paisi's eyes were shut, remembering.

"And I was a servant to Master Emuin, after, which was the same, almost, as to him. And sometimes I slipped in me manners, but Lord Tristen, 'e forgive me, an' 'e spoke for me. And after 'e forgive me, I felt different, at least about stealing from honest craftsfolk. Not about stealing from the priests, who was always talkin' charity and who always ate well enough and had a roof over their own heads—them I never got on with; but I didn't steal again, so's when Lord Tristen left the town, and after Master Emuin left, I went to the Bryaltines an' gave three good Amefin pennies at the shrine, to have it all paid, every penny I could ever remember stealing from the priests in the lean years. Lord Crissand set me and Gran up in the country—with you. With an Otter to bring up."

Here Paisi always came alive and gave a playful dig at Otter's ribs. He did it now, and Otter tumbled over and laughed as he always had, so that for a moment a fine lordly fireside in the Guelesfort had the feel of a little Amefin farmhouse with its rough stone fireplace, and winter fire after winter fire, before this one.

"Which the Bryalt seems all right with," Paisi added, aside from his story, resuming his place on the hearthstones as Otter rolled back onto his elbows. "I ain't never feared curses from the Bryaltine since I paid them coins. I'd come in there while you was studyin' letters an' never feared no curse. And now you got them lucky pennies round your own neck, the same number as I gave back. It's spooky, is what it is."

Paisi hadn't always added that bit. But it was true, and he knew it. Otter touched the coins, which dangled free about his neck, and thought of Gran, and wondered what spell she had put on them.

"I'm going to miss the Bryalt festival, being here this long," Otter said quietly. "They don't dance." And then he added, remembering: "They want me to attend services here, with the Prince. Were there clothes sent for me?"

"Oh, damn," Paisi muttered, and leapt up.

"What?" Otter asked, bewildered by this change of countenance.

"I was to tell ye. 'Is Majesty's man was 'ere hours ago, and servants, and they left all sorts of things, which ye—ye must see, m'lord."

"I'm not 'm'lord,' here," Otter murmured, which he had protested a hundred times by now, but he gathered himself to his feet as Paisi asked. The king had bestowed all manner of gifts on him, as was: he could by no means think what Paisi could so disapprove, but he rose, following a suddenly worried Paisi to the clothespress.

"Here 't is," Paisi declared, opening the door and drawing out a bright red cloak of fine cloth.

And besides the fine cloak, there was a quilted red coat, with the gold Dragon quartered in a black shield, the beast worked in close stitches, with a marvelous bright eye picked out in real gold—an eye that pierced right through him and made him ask whether this could possibly be a tailor's mistake. It was not all the Marhanen device, quartered like that; but it was an appearance of that royal emblem, every bit a prince's coat in the quality of it: quartered like that, it meant kinship with the Marhanen, at very least, but the black—he had no right to Crissand's blue and gold, certainly. The black and a darker red were the provincial colors of Amefel. But he certainly had no right to those, either: Duke Crissand had heirs, and the king would not disinherit *them*.

Paisi, sober of countenance and surely knowing as well as he did that this gift of device and colors marked some turn in their fortunes, mutely showed him the hose and boots that went with it.

"Which I got to think 'Is Majesty surely knows what's what and where's where," Paisi said, still with a worried look, "as 'Is Majesty's man give me the livery to match, an' I said somebody made some mistake, an' 'e said no, it were no mistake." Paisi showed it, too, bright red, a plainer, twill-woven cloth, but very fine, with never a slub to be seen, and new black boots. Paisi's holiday coat had the same Dragon in a shield worked smaller, in leather cut-work, with stitches for the eye, and sewn on.

"Summat like the Guard, the shield, summat like, but this ain't the same, is it? The servants said 't was for the Fast Day," Paisi rattled on, "an' it was the king's man who said it, an' 'e 'ad to know it's proper, didn't 'e? It's as if 'e's goin' to give ye a title. Feel the boots, there, that 'e give ye. Ain't they splendid?"

They were, indeed, the finest leather imaginable, soft and sturdy at once, not the sort of thing ever to scuff up in the practice-yard or wear on the road, beyond any question—not the sort of thing either of Gran's lads had ever worn, not even in the palace of Guelemara.

"Marhanen colors, m'lord! It is, which ever'body is going to remark, seein' it."

The colors of the king, with a passing acknowledgment of Amefel, no acknowledgment at all of his bastardy or the banned Aswydds—the cloth whispered past his fingers with a darker thought, that the only colors he was actually entitled to were those of another dragon, green and gold: his mother's colors. And those were death to wear: all perquisites, including the duchy and the colors, had been stripped from the Aswydds by the king's decree. The priests had told him, most particularly, those perquisites and grants Lord Crissand held, and those to which a bastard, even a Marhanen bastard, would not even appear to aspire, in any degree. He must never, for specific instance, wear any species of red, not dark like the Amefin or bright like the Marhanen, nor any appearance of the Aswydds' personal green and gold, or Lord Crissand's blue. And here he held the Marhanen device in his hands, no matter what his mother might think of his wearing it—and there was no one at this hour to ask what it meant.

"Tomorrow," he said to Paisi. "Tomorrow, before we get into any other sort of trouble, I have to run down the hall and ask Aewyn what His Majesty intends."

"I was afraid to ask twice, me," Paisi said in a low voice. "I thought I should, an' then when I didn't get a proper answer, I thought I shouldn't, the king's men bein' so sure an' so quick, an' it coming straight from the king. I ain't sure, m'lord, I ain't at all sure. But 'Is Majesty clearly means what 'e gives. Ye're to go to Festival in the king's company, the king's man says. And what else is there? 'E certainly can't fit ye out in the Aswydd colors, what ye own by right. Can 'e?"

"No," he said. "Don't ever say it, Paisi. And we should never count on this. It's very likely a mistake."

"I'm sure your royal father knows what 'e's about."

"I'm not sure his tailor does."

"But I'm sure 'Is Majesty's man does, m'lord."

"And livery!" He was unhappy with that assumption. "You're not my servant, Paisi. You're my brother. My uncle, if anything."

"Well, servant is right enough, by me, and what 'm I ever to wear in me life as fine as this?" Paisi held up the twill coat, admiring it before he hung it back in the clothespress. "What the man said, the king's man, was that these here is for the first day, Fast Day, and then there'll be others come, day by day, but the tailor's workin' daylight an' candlelight to be done, as is, on short notice. You'll have a wardrobe t' be proud as a prince."

"And as like the tailor's made a mistake. A terrible mistake." He surrendered the fine coat to the clothespress, which Paisi hung for him, with the cloak, and set the boots down in the bottom of it.

"No, now, don't ye fret about it," Paisi said. "Ye'll have tomorrow to ask. An' if there's aught wrong, it's the tailor's fault, ye've easy access to the Prince, an' he'll get his father's ear. None'll blame ye. Ye just be proper. Proper as ye can. Ye do ever'thing right, ye walk by the king, an' all, an' ye just do the rituals, never mind ye don't have to agree in 'em."

"Quinalt." He was afraid of the Quinaltine, which loomed so large beside the Guelesfort. That priesthood had sent out decrees to trouble the lives of Amefin folk and Bryaltines and most of all wizard-kind, which was Gran, and him, as well as his wicked mother, all his life.

"Well, ye got to do some things different than 'oliday at home. These Quinaltines, mark ye, tomorrow they'll just stuff themselves wi' breakfast before the sun comes up, and again after the sun goes down, same as the grooms goin' about to feed the horses. They don't ever starve. It's all show. It's a lot of prayin', an' fine talk. An' bluster."

"It's lies!"

Paisi's face shadowed the second time with a look Otter could read as plain as words. "Don't ye say that! Don't ye ever say that except to me."

"I'm no fool, Paisi."

"Well, but ye're honest, which can be right dangerous, 'specially if ye're come at by surprise. Which I got to tell ye."

"About what?"

"That there's words in the Quinalt service that ye may have to hear an' keep quiet, an' ye're not to look up when they say 'em or ask about 'em after."

"How, words?"

"They curse the Bryalts. Now, mind, they may not do it nowadays. They used to do it in Amefel, till m'lord Crissand said otherwise, an' then they don't do it no more there, as I've heard. But this bein' Guelessar, and the Quinaltine itself, I ain't sayin' they don't, still, especially at Festival. It's in the singin'. They used to say over an' over, Death to them as is under the Star—which means the Sihhë; an', Death to them as drinks the cup—which is the cup the Bryalts drink at 'oliday sunset. It's about the old wars, an' the king. An' it's just words."

"Gran says nothing is just words if you have any sense. Why do they do that?"

"Well, the Quinalt 'olds it's different gods we drink the cup to, and in their heads it's witchcraft. An' the Bryaltine in Henas'amef has a shrine they don't talk about, which they don't like. An' ye know the Quinalt don't 'old with wizards. Even the Bryalts is a little put off by 't, except old Master Emuin used to come an' go there, bein' Teranthine, which is no different than bein' a wizard."

Gran was a witch, and Bryalt, and the Bryalt priests never had complained about his manners in services in town, except to show him how to make a proper blessing sign and not to do it Gran's way.

"The Bryalt priests don't mind a charm or two," Paisi said. "But the Quinalts, you know they're strong again' the Sihhë." Paisi had closed the clothes-press. Now he settled on the end of the bed. "And sure enough, the first Festival after Lord Tristen went west, the Quinaltines started doin' the old hymns again, all upset, puttin' things back in what they hadn't done all the years. So 'e's gone, an' here they are, an' the Bryalts bein' foremost in Henas'amef—still, the Quinalt there got ambitious an' was goin' to put the words back, so the Bryalts said. So I went to the Quinalt service meself, an' heard it plain as plain. The Star is *his* banner, ye recall."

Lord Tristen's banner, that was, the old Sihhë banner.

"So they were cursing him."

"No question at all that was what they was about. I 'eard it plain, just the way the fathers said it would happen, an' I was upset. And old Father Haidur—you don't remember him: he died when you was scarcely up to me elbow—but 'e was Lord Abbot in the Bryalt shrine, then, and he went right to Market Square an' raised a famous fuss in town, tellin' ever'body what the Quinalts was sayin'. After that, a couple of Quinalt priests got soaked in ale an' tossed in a manure pile. So the Quinalt Patriarch went to Lord Crissand all hot and steamin' about the disrespect, and Lord Crissand had hot words back with the Patriarch about them doin' the hymn about Lord Tristen again, and the upshot was they stopped singin' that hymn the next services, an' ever' year after. Far as I know, they still don't do it. But here's the Quinaltine, an' ye just got to expect 'em to be Quinalt."

Be on your guard, that was to say, in a place where the walls echoed to listening servants, and even the report of a dour look raced off to places there was no accounting. There's spies, Paisi had said before they ever rode inside the walls of Guelemara, or up its cobbled streets. There's spies in every hall up there. Look 'appy no matter what, an' don't fight. Don't ye never let anybody provoke ye, boy.

"Well, well," Paisi said in the stillness, "the king is lookin' out for you, he's goin' to bring ye out in front o' ever'body, an' granted them colors is what ye're to wear, he ain't goin' half measures. But there's those here that don't like the Amefin, and sometimes they say so, and act so, an' puttin' on a red coat is only goin' to turn them heads your way—not too many of that mind, maybe, but ye don't want to do nothin' to make folk uneasy. Ye don't get to laughin' wi' the Prince an' ever forget it's a solemn place, or let yourself frown when ye shouldn't, so's somebody can be whisperin' about it after an' sayin' ye was talkin' again' the Quinalt or that ye wasn't grateful t' be there. Otters is slippery, but they shouldn't ever, never get too confident."

Otter nodded solemnly, with a colder and colder feeling coiling inside, after the first blush of pride at being invited with the family, then the unsettling matter of the red coat. Priests always made him anxious, even Bryalt ones, and he never had had dealings at all with the Quinalt sort before— Quinaltines were few in number in Henas'amef, sullen and aloof from most of the poorer sort of townsman and holding their services in a mostly empty sanctuary, for a handful of clerks, mostly travelers from Guelessar. In Guelemara, in the capital, the Quinaltines were foremost, and ruled everything, while it was the Bryaltines who kept one solitary shrine: it stood near the great Quinaltine, so far as he knew, while everyone important would go to Quinalt services. Even the queen, who was Bryalt herself, went to Quinalt services, even if she went to the Bryalt shrine later.

And by what her son had just hinted was the case, even the queen of Ylesuin daren't put up holiday lights outside her own rooms, or hold holiday dancing or pass out festive cakes outside her own chambers, for fear of what Quinalt priests would say. There were bloody wars in the history of the Bryaltines and Quinaltines. There were riots, and murders. His father was king, but apparently even the queen didn't dare do what she wanted, or speak her mind; nor could Aewyn, so that should warn him.

It appeared a grim sort of holiday, already. And the clothes by no means comforted him. The supper he'd had with Aewyn, so blithe and happy with naive plans an hour ago, sat uneasily on his stomach. But he was well sure that Paisi, who had spent his time in Lord Crissand's halls, and in Lord Tristen's service, was a clever man and generally good at finding out things, and very quick to warn him about things that could go wrong. The matter of the king's gift had Paisi baffled, that much was clear: Paisi was warning him to walk carefully, and Paisi had found no way to ask deeper into the matter without, as Paisi might put it, starting every hare in the hedge.

He had to do the next asking, was what. Aewyn would likely sleep until noon—it was not at all uncommon. But Aewyn, when he did wake tomorrow, was the best person to ask—Paisi was right: he could get to Aewyn, easy as that, and if Aewyn himself said wear the clothes and ask no questions, well, then that was the Prince's order, wasn't it, and as high as he could reasonably reach.

So that was the wisest thing to do. He made up his mind to it. And he looked sidelong at Paisi, putting complete confidence into his voice. "I have no great worry about it. Aewyn will solve it when he gets up. And if it's wrong—I can trust him to smooth things over."

"He brung ye here. Ye ain't fallen out, ha' ye? He's agreein' t' ye bein' wi' the family."

"Oh, he's happy about it. He says—he says we only have to get through Festival, then we'll take the horses afield and ride out to a hunting lodge he may have someday. He showed me the maps. And while we're there, it'll be the Bryalt festival, well, at least the last of it, and he says we can put up evergreen and candles. It's five days. Just five days, and we can go."

Paisi gave a deep sigh, as if that settled matters. "Well, if we ain't neck deep in snow by then, which it's lookin' like out there, tonight."

"We'll go, all the same. We'll camp in the lodge and cook for ourselves and not worry about whoever might be listening, because it won't be anybody but you and Aewyn's guard."

"Oh, now, you be careful wi' that notion there, lad. If there's anybody reports to 'Is Majesty, it's that lot."

"Well, but we won't do anything to deserve reporting, will we? We'll just eat sausages and holiday cakes—I think I can make them, myself, fair enough, if we have the makings—and we'll have a good time and wear plain clothes, and you won't have to call me m'lord there, either, because there won't be servants. I'll just be Otter again."

Paisi grinned. "Ain't no difference where we sit, I'm bound to be your man, m'lord, until we're back under Gran's roof, an' who knows? We're still here, an' things is goin' right well for ye. If ye please your father an' win them colors proper, maybe I'll be your man after."

"Never after, Paisi."

"Now ye mind your words, there. You was born a king's son, m'lord, ye was, no question, an' if justice is done, an' if 'e's truly bent on sayin' so in public, then, so—ye ain't just Otter, ever again."

"I'm not sure I want that, Paisi."

"Of course you do. An' how 'm I t' stay with any king's son except I'm a rare good servant? Which I was! I was Master Emuin's helper, and Lord Tristen's man, an' it was Lord Tristen himself set me to watch you, wasn't it? So I ain't goin' against *his* word, no, I ain't. I'm stayin' what I was told to be, 'cause I ain't facin' *him* to say no, no sir, I give up."

It was a glum and sobering thought, never to be Otter again. But he was verging on a man's estate, his voice already changed, and his upper lip needed just a touch of Paisi's razor now and again—there was no hope yet of more.

"Watered wine," Paisi said, sliding down off the bed. "There's the proper cure for a troublin' night and a howlin' cold wind. Maybe wi' just a little less water 'n usual, it bein' late. What d' ye say?"

"I'd drink it," he said. And Paisi poured it, with only a little water, and they went back to the warmth of the hearthside and drank it, while Paisi heated coals in a bedwarmer, and took the pan to warm the sheets—there never was such a fine thing in Gran's house, but then, Gran's house was all one room, and the fireside never far, so their bed there never took such a chill as this one could, in its separate room. Paisi had a second cup, he added wine himself—which was very much hedging Gran's strict instructions to keep the measure of water in the cup at two of water and one of wine—and they took themselves to bed.

To the same bed, there being ample room for both. It was the way they were accustomed to sleep at home in winter—all their lives were in that one room, the comfortable kitchen nook, their bed and Gran's. No sleeping in the guards' post for Paisi, though they mussed the bed there daily to make the servants think they had town manners, and laughed about it.

Tomorrow's troubles for tomorrow, Gran would say, and Paisi very soon snored. Otter found the exact center of the warmed spot for his cold feet, in sheets otherwise smooth and fine as ice itself, and listened to the wind prying about the fine windows. No one stood guard over them, as bodyguards stood guard over the king and Prince Aewyn and every lord and lady under the Guelesfort roof. They themselves had no enemies except the general sort who fiercely deplored Amefin folk and Bryaltines, and none of those, Otter was sure, would care to risk the guards who stood watch over the Guelesfort. Or even raise their voices too much when he appeared with Aewyn.

So they slept, innocent, under the king's roof.

iii

LATE TO BED, AND FAR TOO MUCH WINE, CEFWYN DECIDED, WHEN HE AND HIS queen, Ninévrisë, reached the sitting room. She had been more prudent at supper—but too long speech-making from the duke of Osenan and a tendency to moralize on the part of the Patriarch, on this eve of the holidays, had driven him to his old bad habits. He hoped no one had noticed.

And being far too heated from the desire to cut the Holy Father off short, he had smiled, and had a second dessert, which he regretted more than the wine.

"Tedious old man, the Holy Father," he said to his queen, with a kiss on the cheek and a long embrace, which somehow alleviated the weariness. "I wish we were both in Elwynor. Or he was."

"Oh, never afflict my kingdom with your priest," Ninévrisë said, her hands slipping to his arms. Those wonderful eyes stared straight into his. "You tolerate him."

"He's an old, old man. There's no mending him at this point. And the Crown needs no contests. Not now."

"With this son of yours visiting, no, by no means."

"Are you at ease with this? Are you truly at ease with him going to services?"

Those great eyes blinked, once, twice. And never wavered. "I held him when he was born. He had no choice in mothers. Of pity for her, however—I have little."

"I have none at all. Nor would ever, ever offend you in bringing him to Festival. He could have gone home. He still might. Be sure. Be sure, now. Later—would be very hard."

"I held him, I say. He looked like any baby."

"The gods know what he is. He's quick. He's clever."

"He's Otter. And he could go on being Otter, if you sent him back . . . but that would be hard, now. What you do—what you do, be ever so sure of. For my own part—"

"What, for your part?" He had yearned for Ninévrisë's true opinion on the matter of this son of his—and never felt he had it.

"He's respectful, and modest. A good Bryalt lad."

"If only he were *only* that."

"Whatever he is, he makes our son laugh."

"I have greatest reliance on the old woman. I believe her. But what I risk by believing this much in her—"

"It's Tristen you believe in," Ninévrisë said. "Isn't it, after all? And Tristen said you should spare that woman, and he said you should take care of this boy. Me, he never advised in that regard . . . so I think my part is simply to watch you both and be on my guard. And I find he has a good face."

"His mother's eyes."

"Oh, no such thing. They're gray. Sihhë gray."

"That didn't come from my house."

"That may be. But he has none of her wicked ways. Not a lie, not a prank—"

"Except our own son instigated them."

Ninévrisë laughed the laugh that could cure his darkest mood and laid her head against his shoulder. "Daily," she said, and looked up. "Wit and grace, both. Have you noticed? Aewyn has taken to books, under his influence."

"More than his tutors ever managed. The last, I hear, went into cloister."

"A good place for him." Ninévrisë cast herself down in the chair by the fire, looking up at him. "He was dull and far too full of catechism. And the one before that was ambitious."

"Ambitious, do you say?"

"Trust my word. Ambitious. I never liked him. Now he eels his way into the Patriarch's service. He may be a good clerk, but what he writes I would never trust."

"Efanor is too clever for him."

"So was Aewyn."

"That I have always maintained." Cefwyn sank into the other chair, with the warmth of the fire instant on his outstretched feet as he folded his hands across his middle. "Otter. Elfwyn, as he is and will be—what would you think, Nevris, were I to send him to Elwynor to study?"

Brows lifted. "Take him from the old woman *and* our son?"

"A difficulty. An admitted difficulty. But he's at that age. He has to find his way in the world. And he could rise in scholarly ranks, he well could. He has the wit, he has the skill, and he has the discretion to be very valuable to our son someday. Or to our daughter."

Ninévrisë frowned, thinking on it—before a distant baby's cry rose above the crackling of the fire. Aemaryen had waked. The nurse was with the baby, in the next room. But Ninévrisë rose from her chair to open the door and bade the nurse bring in the little princess—a red-faced and angry little bundle, who wanted her mother and generally got her way in the world.

Ninévrisë took the baby, and Cefwyn got up to touch the little face, which frowned at the light and squinted up at him—not half a year old, and already with her own notions of royal prerogatives. She was Elwynor's longed-for heir. He would lose her entirely to Elwynor when she gained her majority, and she would spend more and more time in that land as she grew. Already he mourned that future, but it was for the peace, and for the future of both his children . . . all his children.

The tiny princess collected a kiss from her father and screwed up her face in protest, wanting less light and her mother's attention.

"He might certainly go to Elwynor," Ninévrisë said, finishing their former conversation. "With my blessing." She offered a bent finger to the baby's furious grasp. Pink, tiny fingers turned white, holding tight. "Hush, hush, Maryen. There's a dear."

Aemaryen shrieked.

"The Marhanen temper," her father said ruefully.

"And Syrillas stubbornness in one," Ninévrisë said, hugging the baby against her shoulder, which produced no diminution of the cries. "La, Saleyn, open the door."

Conversation was over. Ninévrisë carried the Princess away, diminishing into quiet, and Saleyn shut the door, restoring peace, at least in the king's chambers.

He missed the quiet evenings. He looked forward to the time, however brief, when the little princess would be up and about, eyes shining, finding wonder in everything new—he had had fifteen, now sixteen years between children, and Aemaryen their second and likely last, born when Aewyn was about to be a man. Everything they had learned with Aewyn they attempted with Aemaryen, and nothing quite applied. Aewyn had been so deceptively placid, well, until his young feet hit the ground, and this one—this one had come into the world demanding her way.

Perhaps she would become sweet-tempered once she could walk and do things with her own hands. Perhaps she would be the model of her mother, and that anger would be only at what she could not yet do.

Did it ever apply? he wondered. Were ever two infants quite the same?

This one would never, he feared, be a complacent child—this babe destined to be Regent in Elwynor, as her brother would be king over Ylesuin . . . and when this child reigned, Ylesuin might well award her the title of queen, the first ruler in her own name since the Sihhë kings. The peace he and Ninévrisë had tried to make would be all at risk in the generations to come, and everything rested on these two children and their affection for each other.

He hoped for reason. He hoped for a generation, in his two legitimate children, to knit their two kingdoms closer, so that there would never again be war between Quinalt and Bryalt, between eastern, fair-haired Guelenish folk, and the stubborn remnants of the Sihhë reign over the west.

And maybe, in this illegitimate son of his, this son whom Lord Tristen had advised him to hold easily in reach and treat generously—there was some unguessed key to the matter. If the boy they called Otter *did* make a good scholar, he might become an advisor, traveling between Elwynor and Ylesuin, to counsel both a queen of Elwynor and a king of Ylesuin how to make that peace.

Maybe, with that honest goodwill of his, Otter who was Elfwyn, that unlucky name, would gain the trust of both kingdoms, or at least learn to walk the sword's edge of policy and politics. Tristen's advice always ran deeper than seemed. It came of seeing connections most eyes never saw, Seeing into things yet to come.

Am I right? Am I being a wise king at the moment, old friend?

Will my daughter be the queen we hope for?
What next, for my two sons?
Gods, that they be, none of them, like me . . .

He had had his misspent youth, out of which Elfwyn had come. He had been, himself, no great scholar, only adequate for a young gentleman. He knew his ciphers only because the Quinalt father in charge of his earliest education reported regularly to the king his father, Ináreddrin. Ináreddrin, a true Marhanen, had had his own temper—and his son had had his own to counter it. A king, being king, could have his son confined to his room if his son did not get a better report on his math—

And he had escaped out the scullery doors, gotten caught, and beaten. And did it twice and three times more, finally enlisting his brother in his schemes and driving off his tutor in as elaborate and long-fought a series of maneuvers as he had ever contrived.

Then his father had found Master Emuin for his two sons' betterment. Emuin, a gray-robed Teranthine priest, had let him get by with nothing and had his own ways of getting a prince to pay attention to his books. Cefwyn, having found someone who listened when he asked that question that doomed him with other tutors, that deadly dangerous word, *why?*—and equally perilous, *why not?*—had launched off into old records and acquired a habit of citing them whenever he was angry at priests or nobles.

Contrarily, his father had then decided his elder son was too studious by far, that he had all the bookwork a Marhanen prince could possibly need. Ináreddrin had decided it was time for his heir to get the other half of a practical education, to learn not the theory, but the practice of the law, to understand not how bees made their hive, or what made the moon change her shape, or what the Quinalt practices had been before they limited the gods to five—but what the oaths were between the king and each province, and how to provision an army—he wanted his heir to have a practical understanding of how to keep his quartermasters from pilfering the stores, how to break a rebel or train a horse, how to read a map and, from his father's example, how to hold an angry, unruly people in fealty—thank the gods, in those days, for his bodyguard, who had kept him alive, and for Emuin, who never left him, even when the lessons turned darker and more dangerous and less to his liking.

His younger brother, Efanor, however, had seen the storm clouds flashing with paternal lightning, and Efanor, having a religious bent, had become more religious before their father's attention turned to him. For a few years Efanor had been insufferably righteous, estranged from sin, sinners, *and* his elder brother. The army, subsequently, had sent back an angry elder prince with the habit of command, with less patience, not more; and things had only gotten worse between him and his father. Efanor had, at the same time, made himself the dutiful, the proper son, favored by the priests and ultimately by both their father and certain lords, sycophants who had had their way with the law and their father. Their father had formed a desire that Efanor should succeed him, and sent his heir to Amefel, a province rife with Elwynim assassins, in hopes of losing an argumentative heir and gaining an excuse for war; but it was Ináreddrin who had died, instead, trusting the wrong men.

Now Ylesuin was under his rule, Efanor was his right hand, and he had gained Elwynor not by war but by treaty and marriage. He had the difficult south bound closely to the Amefin, and the rebel Amefin, who were nearer Elwynim than not, bound to him in fealty and friendship, in the person of Lord Crissand—it was all a web of fragile threads they had made.

But in order to keep it together after him, Aewyn had to follow him, as Aemaryen would follow her mother, neither of them having seen the realm take shape, and they would have to learn their own lessons, how to mollify both sets of priests and how to keep their outer borders safe without letting any provincial lord build up a private army or exercise private ambitions.

Most of all they had to have the wisdom to understand who was honest, who was paying his taxes fairly, and who was skimming a bit off, that old pitfall of human wickedness. Blindness to corruption, thinking that just a little convenient corruption would do no harm, had led his father to disaster.

History. History, ciphering, and enough catechism to keep the king-to-be from saying the wrong thing to the wrong priest . . . this much he had gotten a priest or two to teach his unwilling son, thus far.

But now—now, too, remembering what a watershed the education of princes had been between him and Efanor—at the same time as he settled his illegitimate son in some useful and scholarly endeavor, he could not ignore this sudden bloom of interest in books that Otter had raised in Aewyn, this raiding of the library. He must not let that bloom fade or be the one to kill it, by stealing Otter away too abruptly. He knew Aewyn's temperament, he knew its angers and its schemes and the softer elements of it, the vulnerable heart Aewyn guarded so secretly, and he knew he had to steer that stubborn Marhanen will in the right way and get him to copy Otter's virtues . . .

Virtues acquired in a much harder situation, with far fewer prospects than the dazzling horizon of a prince. He had to get both his boys to ask the right questions, the whys and why nots of the world, and to come up with answers his own generation had failed to find.

Emuin would be the ideal tutor, once Otter went . . . wherever Otter must eventually go, for his own sake, and for his own happiness, for a few years. Emuin would be ideal. But Emuin, alas, had passed from the world years ago, simply, quietly vanished, before Aewyn had a chance to benefit by that wisdom. Emuin had been, even among the religious, that excellent thing in a royal advisor—too slippery to raise controversy in what he taught, no matter he belonged to neither major sect, simultaneously turning out a cynic of a king and a devout and cannily religious man in his brother.

If he knew where to lay hands on a Teranthine father these days, he said to himself, he'd hire the man on sight, unexamined. But he had no such resource. The Teranthines had quietly disappeared from their monastery and left a vacant shrine in Amefel.

He sat alone in the chair in front of the fire, watched it devour the wood, and waited for a particular coal to fall—if Emuin were here, they could lay wagers on it, and the old man would cheat. He was sure Emuin had cheated in such bets, having a Sight he lacked.

Whomever he found now to teach his son, it must be someone he could bring here, because it was impossible to send Aewyn away to study, twice lonely, parted from Otter and settled somewhere, worse, where he could have no idea what the boy was learning—or doing.

Surely there must be, in all the kingdom, some reasonable learned man he could hire to keep the boy's nose in the right books.

Let them go together to Elwynor? The Quinalt priests would howl . . . *their* Marhanen prince gone to learn from heretics.

There might be other disadvantages to that idea. Boys changed into men, and granted he could sunder them now by a decree, he was by no means sure yet what this stray son of his would become when he was a man.

Otter, now, the determined scholar—the Bryaltine fathers in Henas'amef had taught him his letters, but not Bryalt catechism: a royal order had settled that. And a royal request, once he understood the boy's growing need, had had books sent down from Duke Crissand's library, on loan for Otter's studies in the Bryalt shrine.

If he did, however, let Otter slip to the Bryalt side and learn the catechism, the liberal scholars over in Ilefinian would feed that keen mind with a bolder understanding of the world than their timid brothers down in Henas'amef would have done. The Elwynim Bryaltines would, oh, so gladly make him one of their own—fit him for an orthodox Bryaltine priesthood in Elwynor, or, contrarily, fit him for some high administrative post in his half sister's court in Elwynor, his half brother's court in

Ylesuin, or a trusted post in either treasury, or in law or even in the Dragon Guard or the Elwynim army. A bastard son could rise very, very high, by merits and wit, given the goodwill of his legitimate siblings, and given a clever mind, such as the boy had: incapable of rule, if his ambitions were still tied to the house of his birth, incorruptible, if those ambitions were adequately satisfied . . . he could be of great use. His own Commander of the Guard was a case in point.

Though Ninévrisë was right: sending the boy to Elwynor this summer might bring him under priestly influence, but it would remove him from Paisi's gran, who had been a stabilizing force: lay it to the old woman's account that that the boy had grown up knowing right from wrong and caring to do right.

Practical things the old woman had taught him, too: how to mend and make, how to judge the weather, how to feed himself off the land, things profitable for a young man to know: Paisi's gran was an estimable woman, and not the least of her virtues had been her silence, keeping discreet silence on those things that, the more Otter went into the world, the more it was inevitable he know—those deeper details of his mother's ambitions and the history of the Aswydd house of which he was the last direct descendant.

Of witchery, of her own craft, the old woman had likewise taught him nothing. That had been her choice, he supposed, if it had not been Tristen's specific instruction, but the course she had chosen had kept Guelen doors open for the boy. She had also kept very much to her small grant of land, had kept the boy remote from the Amefin court—and consequently remote from the bitter sort of gossip the boy was otherwise bound to have had flung at him, where protection from higher authority was not so evident.

All credit to Paisi's gran—where Emuin had not been available, Gran had done her best.

And best it was, or had been, until now, until it was time to settle a future on him, whether Otter would live the rest of his life in the country tending goats, a lad with a rare bent for scholarship—or whether he would stray out of those bounds when he had grown another few years. It was not for the boy himself to make all those decisions. It was Cefwyn's obligation.

The slide toward decision had already started: Aewyn had started it, with his invitation. He had watched and made others. The first and easiest courses for a royal bastard were already unlikely: the military was not a likely choice: Otter was slight of build, not the soldierly sort, and he had never learned weapons or horsemanship, years behind other boys. Religious orders were less and less likely as a solution, once one understood that keen wit was prone to question what he was told as dogma: that curiosity would be troublesome for him, even for the Bryaltines.

The time for absolute decision might not be on them yet—but it was surely coming soon. The old furor about wizards and orthodoxy had died down, so reports said. The town of Henas'amef was quiet, mostly forgetting the prisoner lodged in its tower. Otter's peers were not old enough to have witnessed the events around his birth, and their seniors had more discretion than to shout out the details in the streets. Lord Crissand sat in power in Amefel, with heirs to follow him, and there certainly was no desire on his part to disturb that situation. Time had healed all it could heal in Amefel and kept secret all it could keep. Nothing untoward had happened for over a decade in that province, and that was to the good, was it not?

Lord Crissand had interviewed the boy annually for the last decade and more, reporting him a well-spoken and earnest young man, grateful for his tutoring, anxious to please, asking only for financial advantage to the woman he called his gran. Otter had never once asked for gifts for himself, though he received, annually, at his birthday, a single small and well-chosen remembrance each year, be it a pair of boots or a new shirt from his royal father. Asked what he needed, the boy had said, from year to year, a new axe head, or a cooking pot, or a pair of geese to keep Gran's yard weeded.

Gran now owned four goats, twelve geese, and, occasionally, though un-successfully, pigs, all the modest farm would support, and had avowed her-self remarkably content with her wealth and with what she called her two boys. The offered cow the old woman had turned down as far too grand and eating too much for her household, and if she had any complaint, it was about the goats, which had been an occasional trial in her herb garden. That latter asset had brought her most notoriety and profit . . . he smiled, think-ing of the meeting before last and the issue of the goats and the garden: the goats had left the bean rows much faster than goats ordinarily abandoned their intent, startling the Guard's horses in their escape, and the old woman had been embarrassed.

A witch, a wisewoman in every sense of the word, she was kindly re-garded by her neighbors and consulted not infrequently by Duke Crissand himself. Such practitioners and makers of charms were part and parcel of the old beliefs of Amefel—not quite officially countenanced by the Bryalts but not often spoken against, either. An honest and good hedge-witch she remained, despite royal attention, a witch whose cures worked. She probably carried a bit of the old Sihhë blood in her veins. And a peculiar advantage, that would be, in keeping Otter safe from his mother, and keeping Lord Crissand safe, to boot.

So complain as the Holy Father might about witchcraft rampant in Amefel, Paisi's gran and her connection to the duke of Amefel remained none of the Quinalt's business. The Quinalt in Amefel had indeed complained, all the way to Guelemara, incensed that a royal bastard was in Gran's keeping—more incensed that the royal bastard was alive at all if they had told the truth.

But the Otter he had brought to Guelemara late in the year was the very best proof of the old woman's good teachings, and he was well content with his choices throughout the boy's life.

Sending the boy to Elwynor to study was the most probable course. He would have to hear Aewyn's protests when he informed him. Worse, he would have to fend off Aewyn's demands to go with his bastard brother, to whom he had attached such sudden affection, and who, as best anyone could tell, reciprocated.

He would grant permission for messages back and forth—maybe even allow the use of his couriers. There would be summer visits, holiday visits. He could promise all that. Boyish rivalry and Otter's frequent letters from Elwynor might, who knew, habituate his heir to the Guelesfort's library. He could imagine the growth of wisdom in both his sons. And Ninévrisë, whose virtue, whose compassion for her husband's foreign bastard had made it possible, would be the boy's official guardian while he was in her kingdom.

Oh, that would confuse the clattering tongues in the bower. His queen was fierce and forthright—oh, never challenge Ninévrisë in a cause she supported; and her simple goodness—

The bloody Marhanen, his grandfather, had taught him how to take and hold, had he not? But Ninévrisë had shown him how to loosen his grip and gain loyalty. It cost so much fear to trust anyone. It challenged his furthest limits of experience.

But two people had shown him how to loosen his hand and let things free to take their own course, and one was Lord Tristen, one was Ninévrisë Syrillas, and he knew he was the luckiest man alive to have had them.

The boys—the boys would benefit, would not lose their friendship, would grow well, even separate. Would become men of sober purpose—sooner or later.

Not too soon, he hoped.

iv

SLEET HISSED AGAINST THE WINDOWS—BARE DARK WINDOWS THAT SHOWED A storm haze above the spine-backed roof of the Quinaltine. Light from the banked fire, a warmer hue, sifted in from the other room, touching the edges of things, spilling across the wooden floor and the vine-figured rug.

It was a good night to be warm abed, and Otter had made himself a warm spot in smooth woven linen, when coarse wool and rabbit skins had kept them warm at home. The sheets had a wonderful feel to them; the pillows were several and soft. Paisi snored beside him, and the Festival and duties seemed far and unthreatening, part of the daylight, not the windblown dark. The windows held their own fear: such an expanse of glass, in little diamond panes, such a wonder to behold, from such warmth and softness.

In the cottage they would have had the shutters closed tight and barred against such a storm, and they would have stuffed the cracks besides, but the thin glass held out the wind and the cold alike—or most of it: the servants had advised they should shut the drapes to keep the cold out, but the glazed windows were such a delight to them both that they kept opening the drapes again and keeping them open at night, which they never would the shutters, except in summer. The sleet that fell now was too fine to see from where he lay. But if one defied the cold to get up and stand near the window, he was sure he would find the sill all snow-covered, and a ghostly snow coming down beyond, the whole sky aglow with it, and it haloed about the torch he could see from that window.

The floors were too cold tonight to tempt him. If he wanted to leave his warm spot, he ought to throw a log on the fire while he was at it—but he stayed right where he was.

When he shut his eyes to the window he recalled the high walls of the courtyard that afternoon, remembered soaked gloves, cold fingers, horseplay, and snowballs. He had caught Aewyn with his head up and gotten snow down his back, then Aewyn had pelted him with two, hard and fast, never minding being hit. Before all was done they were laughing too much to make more snowballs, and only raked it up and threw it with no art at all, showering each other at the last in a flurry of white.

It was the best winter, the best winter ever. All his life he had thought, what if my father should send for me? And what if he wanted me to serve in the court?

He had imagined being a servant, a clerk. He had never dreamed of such fine clothes, wonderful clothes, like holiday every day, and delicate food, as much as they ever wanted, with no chores to do. It was a strange feeling, to be at play all day long, every day, with no water to carry . . .

Except Paisi directed those who did, boys who trudged up high steps with full buckets of steaming water or pitchers of plain; or servants who carried up the trays of food and took the scraps down. Paisi had no chores of the ordinary sort, but it troubled him that his father's largesse did not altogether encompass Paisi, for his sake. He wanted to protest that state of affairs. He tried to think what he would say to his father on that matter, if he had a chance, and feared he would lose all the words—and feared he would incur his father's wrath by trying to tell him what to give and to whom.

As it was, Paisi had no chores, except to tell others what to do, which Paisi seemed to enjoy for its own sake. There was that to make him happy.

And Aewyn—Aewyn was every bit his friend, as he'd always been when his father would ride by Gran's farm, and a blond, frowning boy would get down from the saddle—frowning, that was, and quiet, only until they could get off by themselves by the side of the cottage and get a few words between them.

"Papa says you're my half brother," Aewyn had said, in the first days when their voices had been high and childish: he could remember that curly blond head, that fresh, rose-touched face, and those blue, blue eyes staring at him. Otter, dark as Aewyn was fair, had dug his toe in the dirt, and said, faintly, conscious of the king talking to Gran around by the front door: "The king is my father."

Aewyn had frowned, thoughtfully, and he had thought the blond boy would be angry to hear that, though it was the truth he told. He had been six, and Aewyn was still five, so he understood.

"So you are my half brother," Aewyn had said again, then proceeded to show him his particular treasure, a toy he had picked up in town, a horse whose legs moved.

Otter had never held a toy Gran or Paisi had not made. Aewyn had given it to him, and left with one of his, a carved boat, which Aewyn said next year that he had lost in the brook while his father was hunting, and he was ever so sorry to confess it. So Paisi had made him another, which Aewyn still had, locked away, and never had sailed it.

Aewyn was in every regard like his father: athletic, blond, tall, and easy to love, even when he had done something he ought not. His father loved him, that was ever so clear: the king laughed, lifting Aewyn down from his pony on that visit, in vast and easy strength. Then he had turned sober and frowning, looking down at him, looking him straight in the eyes, until Otter remembered to duck his head and look down and bow.

"Elfwyn." His father had used his real name, though no one ever did. "Are you a good boy?"

"I try to be, Your Majesty." His father asked that question every year. It had sounded foolish even to a boy of six, seven, and eight.

By then he had learned to be jealous, and for all his eighth winter he was jealous of Aewyn: he had stood before Lord Crissand, every year, to be asked much the same questions, and, true, to be given something fine for a gift, then asked what he needed. He rather liked Lord Crissand, in the way he liked sunlight: it was always there, and so was the lord in the great keep, watching over everything. But long before then, he had been taken to the priests, and taught his reading and writing, and that year was given more advanced books to read, which the priests—one in particular—said was as useful as teaching a dog to cipher. He had been certain then that they would never say that of blond, tall Aewyn. Everyone loved Aewyn, just because he existed.

So that year he had turned glum and quiet, and had not been sure he wanted to talk to Aewyn at first after Aewyn had gotten off his horse, but Aewyn had nudged him with an elbow and almost started an argument, which Paisi had stopped, and the two of them had run away to see the new lambs, and hid when Paisi had come looking for them. The king and all his men were waiting on their horses, and had been waiting, as Paisi said, and he had said to Aewyn, "We have to go back. Your father will be furious."

"Oh, he might be," Aewyn had said. "But not that much."

And by that time Aewyn had gotten tall and strong enough to hold him, and hurt his arm, keeping him from running back to the house. He'd been terrified when Aewyn ducked him back into different cover. And the king of all Ylesuin had gotten down from his horse and come searching with Paisi and Gran. He had been too frightened to open his mouth, though he could see them through the leaves of the bush where they were hiding.

"Aewyn!" the king had shouted, and Aewyn had come out, laughing because no one had found them, and insisted he come out, too.

"That was damned dangerous," Paisi had said that night, after the royal procession was long gone. " 'E ain't to trifle with, Otter. 'E ain't."

"I know so," he'd said, and Gran, her shuttle flying and the harnesses clacking, had said: "Someday the Otter's going to go down that road. Someday he'll go find his own way in the world. He's got to be wise when he does."

He'd understood then that something had passed between Gran and the king, and ever after, Paisi talked about him going to seek his fortune in Guelessar, in service to the king. Paisi had said that one day his father would call him over, and ask how he had grown, and if his father liked the answers he gave that day, he might find him a place in court, maybe to be a clerk or minister, or to serve with the army, to ride a horse and carry a sword as an officer of the Guard.

"As I can't teach ye too much about horses that ye ain't learnt of goats, but I can show ye the sword," Paisi had said. "I don't know it well, but I can show ye some."

They had practiced to be the king's soldiers, then, with sticks, and with the quarterstaff, which Paisi could indeed use very well, and which had raised no few occasions for Gran's poultices. He had had no great skill at the staff, when all was done. Paisi kept knocking him down, and once knocked him senseless, to Gran's and Paisi's dismay. So he applied himself with greater zeal to the books.

This year, however, after the king's riding by and Aewyn asking him to come visit him in Guelessar, the King's Dragon Guard had come, the captain of the Guard detail bearing a letter, and two grooms bringing light horses, for him and for Paisi to ride to the capital.

He had never ridden a horse. He managed not to fall off on the way. His was a bay gelding named Feiny and Paisi's was a piebald named Tammis—and he had learned from the grooms how to see to the horses' feet and what a horse needed, the same as he knew for the goats and geese. He was delighted to get along fairly well with the horse—he had grown less and less sure he would manage as well with people in Guelemara, and by the time he saw the walls of the city he had been terrified. He had looked forward to a summons from his father, and now faced the reality with deep trepidation, the more so as he rode into a Quinalt city, where witchcraft meant death by fire or hanging, and where, now, he had to face a brother who'd been his friend in the farmyard, where *he* was the one who knew all the places beyond the fences. Now he knew nothing at all.

He had been so scared when he rode into the courtyard of the Guelesfort. He had been thinking for the last two days of the journey that Aewyn might think differently about him in his own yard, or might even forget that he had asked for him, or grow bored with him after a day or two. But all that fear had flowed out of him when Aewyn had run down the steps to the stable yard and held Feiny's bridle for him, despite the hovering grooms.

It had been that way between them from that day forward. Aewyn had been so looking forward to a brother. He had gotten a sister instead. He loved baby Aemaryen, to be sure. But, as Aewyn put it, even a brother wouldn't have been that good, lying around most of the time, and crying and wanting all his mother's attention whenever he tried to talk to her.

Besides, Aewyn informed him, his sister would grow up to be Regent of Elwynor, and maybe queen of that kingdom, and would never even live in Guelessar at all once she was of age: it would not be her choice, when it happened, but it meant she would go away. The lords' sons let Aewyn win at every game, and their fathers were always looking for advantage and gathering gossip. So a brother was his heart's desire, and when he had put it to his father this year, his father had agreed.

It was the happiest winter. The very happiest of Otter's life, little of it as he had had yet. He had expected to leave before this. He was sure he would have to leave in spring. He would ride back to Gran's in time for him and Paisi to do the planting, then—

Then—would come a difficult question. He would want to come back to Guelessar. He would want to go riding with Aewyn, and just—be here and live here the way things were now. But he missed Gran, too, and Gran needed him, and especially needed Paisi. Even if the king wanted him to stay here, the way Paisi and Gran had always said he might do, he still had to get home when he was needed—and that meant leaving Aewyn, the thought of which had already begun to hurt.

But he did long for home, too. He could see the cottage with his eyes shut.

He could see the thatch snow-covered as it would be, now, since the recent snowfalls, and the yard and shed roof alike under a thick white blanket. It had that clarity of a true dream, the edges unnaturally fine and clear in the night, just as if he were looking at it tonight. It comforted him.

But there was no smoke from the chimney, and there ought to be: there was always a little smoke, even at night. Certainly the snow never collected atop it. And he tried to dream of the inside of the cottage, and to dream of Gran, to be sure she was safe. He imagined her asleep in her bed, under the patchwork quilt, but imagine as he would, the only thing he could see, more and more insistently, was the chimney, the very top of the chimney, as close as he had seen it when he had climbed up with Paisi to mend the thatch last fall. A thick rim of snow lay about the vent. The warmth should have melted it, as fast as the snow fell. But it had snowed the chimney almost shut.

Something was wrong. Something was very wrong, and he could not find Gran and he could not wake up, not without a great struggle, as if the dream did not want to let him go.

He reached out with his hand. He found the bedclothes cold. Paisi was gone, nowhere to be found. He was alone in the bed, and he sat up, flinging the covers back.

A strange sight met him, Paisi sitting on the hearthstones in the other room, a huddled shape just sitting on the hearth between two good chairs. The light of dawn was in the windows, a gray and icy dawn.

"Paisi?" he said, but Paisi didn't move.

He fought his way to the edge of the thick feather bed and rolled out and down, his feet meeting the icy floor. He dragged a coverlet off, wrapping it around him as he went.

"Paisi?"

Paisi still didn't move. Otter sank down to his knees and shook Paisi by the arm. Paisi was cold on one side and overly warm on the other.

"The fire ain't lit," Paisi said, gazing into the coals. "She's abed sick, an' the fire ain't lit."

He felt chill himself and thought to wrap the coverlet around Paisi, who let it fall.

"Paisi?" He closed Paisi's hand on the cloth. "Take it."

Paisi's hand closed and he held on to it, still looking into the coals, shaking his head slowly. "I can't see 'er, Otter. The cottage is dark, an' the fire ain't lit."

"I dreamed, too, about the chimney being out. I dreamed it just now."

"She's fevered," Paisi said. "She's got the fever, she ain't fed 'erself since yesterday."

"What can we do, Paisi?"

"I don't know, I don't know what to do." The note of unreasoning fear in Paisi's voice would have sent a chill through him if none had been there to start with. "You dreamed it, too?"

"I dreamed about the chimney."

"The fire," Paisi said. "The fire not bein' lit, in this weather—"

"We can tell the king!"

"About what, Otter-lad? Can we tell him we *dreamed* it? Can we talk about dreams wi' these Quinalt priests hoverin' near? She's sick abed, is what. That damn chimney's choked up again, and it never were right. I wanted to tear that crooked thing down this summer an' build it anew, an' she wouldn't have it, no, no, the fields wants weedin', the shed wants the door fixed, it ain't no great matter, run a stick up it, and it'll do, it's always done. If the smoke don't kill us in our sleep . . . Damn it, Otter-lad!" Paisi ran his hands through his hair so it stood on end. "Maybe I'm makin' trouble that ain't trouble. Maybe she'll wake up and take one of 'er potions, won't she? She'll poke the broom handle up an' unstick that chimney."

"If she can reach it."

"Oh, I was worri't leavin' her! We stacked that firewood high as she could deal with, but the rest in the shed, it's all big pieces, an' if her coughin' starts up fierce . . ."

"Look, she can bring the animals inside. Remember the winter we did that. They'll heat a room."

"That don't *feed* them. Or her."

He drew a deep breath. "Paisi, it's just three days back there."

"It ain't three days wi' this storm."

"But wouldn't you go?"

"Aye," Paisi said. "Aye. I would. *I* would. But she'll skin me. I swore I'd watch over ye!"

"We could tell the king, all the same, and he'd keep secret how we knew. He was Lord Tristen's friend. Wizard-work isn't any surprise to him."

"There is that."

"He could just write a letter to Lord Crissand."

"Oh, aye, and they'd take their time, and some soldiers would come out t' th' house an' ask if she was well, and she'd swear she was well if she was dying."

"Then go, go right this morning and see how she is, and fix the chimney. And then I'll tell the king what's happened, and I'll come after, soon as I can."

"No, now, me lord, don't be foolish."

"I'm not 'my lord.' "

"Ye're his son. The king give ye them fine clothes for holiday. He's got 'is mind set, is what. It's what you got to do. I'll go see to Gran, and you stay an' do as ye have to."

"And what will I do if Gran died?"

"Don't say it!" Paisi said, and made a ward sign against the thought. "Oh, I should 'ave prepared better! I should ha' fixed that damn chimney . . ."

"You did everything you could! We didn't reckon with the snow just keeping on and on like this. We didn't plan on Gran needing help, but you know what she says: some dreams are a warning, is all, and it's what may happen, not what *is* happening."

"Oh, aye, an' I'll walk in and she'll curse me for a fool. But if it is a warning-dream, we're summat ahead of it, ain't we? But ye're right. I'll see to that chimney, then come on back, wi' no delay."

"You'll get there before the Bryalt holidays start, as is. And if it's nothing, Paisi, you should just stay the whole holidays with Gran. This isn't going to be like ours."

"Oh, that ain't fair, an' you wi' nobody to see ye get meals . . ."

"I can perfectly well see to myself! And you can be there to spend holiday with her, so she's not alone."

"I ain't at all sure."

"Have a cake at the shrine and think of me. I'll be perfectly safe, and you can write to me straightway as you get there and let me know how things are."

"Now 'ow will I get a letter out?"

"Well, they change out the Guard every month, don't they, even in bad weather. And if it's a message to somebody in the Guelesfort, they'll carry it. They will. And coming home, you know they'll go as fast as they can." He took comfort in the plan. It was one of his best. "Which is as fast as the king sending somebody, isn't it? That's how the merchants send things."

"Still," Paisi said.

"If it turns out I have a place here through spring, you know, you'd only have to go back when the garden goes in. You know Gran can't do the heavy plow—she'll put the garden in, but the rest will take the push-plow, won't it?"

"Farmer Ost'll bring his oxen over. He'd do it for her. That were the plan, that were what she said, if need be."

"Well, but then Gran will have your help doing the other things. So you could just stay on a little."

"You're trying to make me stay there the spring, and I said I wouldn't!"

"I'm not."

"Are so. You and Aewyn are having a rare good time—as should be, m'lord, don't mistake me."

"We'll be perfectly well."

"Only so you stay friends while I'm gone and don't get in any trouble. Boys is apt to quarrels."

"I shan't, with him, Paisi. He's my friend, he's my true friend, besides being my brother."

"Gods hear that 'un, Otter-lad. But I'll feel better if I know Gran's set."

"And you come back to me when the chores are done and the planting is in."

"But if I go—if I go, how's you even to draw your bath or get your food in this great place? You don't know the ways . . ."

"Once you're well away, and they can't stop you," Otter said, "then I can tell the king, and he'll see I have someone."

"Oh, somebody in my place, will he be? I won't like that!"

"Never in your place, Paisi. You're my brother."

A grunt. "Which I ain't, an' that's the fact an' ye know it. Nor be so cheeky wi' 'Is Majesty, neither, wi' askin' for help as if ye're due the sun an' the moon besides. It's dangerous to assume about lords at all. They can be generous, but they got their moments, too, an' they think thoughts we don't know about, so don't be cheeky an' don't tell 'im too late."

"He won't be angry. He'll just be glad we saw to matters ourselves, and it's not as if I'm going to starve here for a day."

"Well, ye may, if ye ain't careful. Ye can't store food here, not on Fast Day. Ye got to clean the place out an' go without food in the premises, dawn to dark."

"I'll find my own way to the kitchens perfectly well, I'll follow every rule, and I promise, Paisi, I promise no one will ever, ever take your place. I'll wear my Festival clothes and sit and listen to us being cursed, being ever so quiet and good, and you—you take your holiday clothes home. You can be quite the sight in the Bryalt festival, won't you? You'll have the Guelen Guard saluting you."

"Oh, m'lord, I'd look the fool. They'd arrest me on the spot!"

"Well, then, but Gran at least should see you in your fancy clothes, shouldn't she?" Otter flung himself to his feet and pulled Paisi up to his. "And we sit planning when we should be doing. Get what you need. Take the short sword with you. It's just getting light. We can get out to the stables."

"What's to do at the stables? *My* horse is way down in pasture."

"Feiny's here."

"He's the king's gift!"

"He's mine, and you can borrow him. Now, now listen. There'll only be the one boy in the stables until after breakfast. You dress in your livery, so's you look important. I'll ride down to the gate, you walk with me, and then we go out the gate and get your Tammis out of pasture, and there you'll be, on the road . . ."

". . . lookin' rich as a lord and ripe for robbers. And where's a bridle nor even a halter for me horse?"

"Well, but you can wear your plain cloak, then, after you're away, and change later. And I'll get a bridle for Tammis when I get Feiny. You can take Feiny's saddle for Tammis, and there you are!"

"Feiny's bigger n' Tammis. And look at it comin' down, out there, even yet! Ye're apt to fall off wi' no saddle, ye'll come back half-froze, if ye don't get lost out there, and wouldn't your father hear about that?"

"Well, well, then take Feiny once we reach the gate."

"Oh, now I'm ridin' 'Is Majesty's own gift."

"He's mine to lend."

"Oh, aye . . . an' how am I to feed that tall great horse once I get home wi' 'im, for that matter? We never did know that bit, when your father give us them horses—wherever's food for them? Gran don't have it."

"Well." It was a question worth thinking about. "You'll just have to go to the duke and ask."

"Just go to 'Is Lordship an' bid 'im feed my horse, please."

"Exactly that."

"Oh, gods."

"Lord Crissand will understand. He knows you come from me. He knows I went to the king."

"If the king ain't sent to 'im by then, askin' a horse thief be hanged on sight!"

"Lord Crissand won't be angry. Neither will the king. I swear he won't. Don't hesitate to go to the duke. Ask him what you have to ask for, for you and Gran, and say I told you to do it. I'll tell my father what I've done long before any message can get there."

"And if somehow you need a horse to get away?"

"Tammis is a perfectly fine horse for me, and he's still in pasture, isn't he?"

" 'E's a piebald, and lords don't ride piebalds."

"Well, I'm not really a lord, then, am I? And if you're not back, and Aewyn and I go hunting after Festival, I can perfectly well go down to the pasture and get him, and bring him up to stable for the trip, and feed him apples the while so he'll be fat as a pig."

"Oh, aye, them damn apples!"

"We can't get them. That plan is done, Paisi. You just have to go."

"Well, I thought of something to think on. Your horse is a stable horse, and he don't have his winter coat. He ain't fit for the cold."

"He has the barding, doesn't he? I'll have it on him. Just keep the blanket on him most times at Gran's, and at night while you're on the road."

Paisi looked at him long and hard. "I don't like it, m'lord. I don't like it. I swear the king is going to be huntin' a stolen horse, an' me on 'im."

"Well, they aren't even going to feed him up here on the holy day, with all their fine care, are they? With you he'll have something to eat on Fast Day, and we'll take care of Gran, which is what we have to do, no matter what. You do it, Paisi, you do it for me. Let me deal with matters here."

"All the same—"

"Do you trust me?"

"Aye, aye, I trust ye. I trust 'Is Majesty, and probably I trust Lord Crissand."

"You know how to do these things."

"Steal, d' ye mean, little Otter? Aye, I can do that. An' me sense is tellin' me go plain and go quiet, an' not wi' any lord's horse, if I had a choice."

"But he's the only sure horse we can get to in this weather."

"Aye," Paisi said reluctantly and with a deep heave of his shoulders. "Aye, that's so."

V

OTTER REACHED THE STABLES AND SLIPPED IN BY THE LITTLE SIDE DOOR. IN-side, there was only the one boy, dozing in a stall. Otter padded softly past that gate, with the bundles he brought from their chambers—two blankets too fine for rough use, good woolen blankets to keep one warm; and Paisi's razor, and his working knife, all wrapped in Paisi's heavy outdoor cloak, along with the short sword Paisi had had since the war. Paisi was making his own trip to the kitchens, in indoor clothing, saying he was to fetch up a breakfast for a peevish young master, but in fact taking a spare shirt to wrap up several rolls and a sausage from whatever tray they provided.

Otter's mission was to provide grain, a lot of grain, against the cold and hard going—they had learned on their journey here what an appetite a horse had when there was no time nor chance for grazing, and this snow, covering what grass there was, would make matters worse. He carefully eased up the latch on the granary door—it was well gated against hungry strays. He had brought a sack of sorts, a fine handworked pillow casing; but he discovered instead several rougher, sturdier bags on a nail beside the door, and took two of those for the purpose instead. He slid up the little slat and filled the bags as full as he dared, as much as he hoped might see Feiny and his immense appetite down the road. He tied the two together with twine saved on a peg, the stable's thrifty habit.

Then he slipped back out and latched the granary door, having by stealth filled every need that might raise particular questions. He soft-footed it back to the outer door and this time let it thump loudly shut, as if he had just come in, setting the grain down in the shadow beside him.

Horses stirred in their stalls. The stableboy waked. Otter couldn't quite see Feiny, whose stall was down at the end of the row. He waited, grand as any lord, and the stableboy came out, straw clinging to his hair and his coat in the white light of dawn.

"Your lordship?" the boy asked.

"I need my horse."

A little stare. The boy scratched his head, and his ribs, still sleepy, and not as inquisitive as Otter might have been in his place—but he had often enough come here at odd hours to see Feiny, he and Paisi both, they being farmerfolk and missing the goats and geese. Having Feiny to fuss over and feed had been a warm and familiar thing for them, and the stableboy never minded their doing his work, once he'd understood they truly wanted to feed and water and curry one of his charges. It was surely only a small step more to say he wanted to ride out at this gray hour, and it would not pose a problem, Otter hoped, that would make the stableboy wake the stablemaster.

"Aye, your lordship." Still scratching, the boy walked on toward Feiny's stall and the tack room, in a murk so thick at that end of the stable that only the posts and fronts of the stalls were visible. Otter picked up his heavy sacks and followed after.

"All his tack, if you please," Otter said. He had learned that word.

"The bardin', too, your lordship?"

"Yes," he said.

"Aye, your lordship," the boy said, never asking where they were going, or why the odd hour, or any such thing. It was all too easy, and Otter restrained himself with difficulty when the boy went after the tack and hauled it back to the stall-side, piece by heavy piece. On any other day he would have found it hard to stand and not help, but now the safety of their plan rested on the boy's doing what he asked with no asking questions in return, and standing in the shadow assured the boy had no one to ask. The boy gathered everything, the heavy quilted-felt barding and all. Then he led Feiny out, Feiny with his rest disturbed, and in no particularly good spirits at this hour.

The boy simply put on the bridle and left the halter hanging on the fence, whence, when the boy ducked down to get the saddle, Otter simply lifted it and tucked it and its lead rope up with the blanket bundle he carried.

The saddle went on, all in silence, the boy quite content to be let alone at his work, and the buckles were buckled and the cinch was tightened—Feiny let out a deep, discontented sigh and shook his neck until all the loose parts flew.

"That's good," Otter said, and took Feiny's bridle. "That's very good." He began to lead Feiny about and down the aisle toward the outside, hauling everything he had under one arm and with one straining hand, under his cloak, and trying not to let his burden appear heavy. The boy murmured a courtesy and went to open the door for him, letting him out into the breeze and the gray dawn. Feiny put his ears up and back again as the cold wind blew into his face. He began to dance about on the cleared and sanded cobbles outside.

"Shall ye need a hand?" the boy asked.

"No, no, it's quite enough, thank you. Go back in and stay warm."

"Thank ye, your lordship." The boy bowed and ducked back into the warmth, and Otter drew the reins close and steadied Feiny by the old stone border that gave him a convenient step for getting up. Feiny decided not to stand at all, nor give him a convenient way to get the baggage onto Feiny's back. It became a circular chase, him and Feiny, until from around the corner Paisi showed up, himself cloaked and laden with improvised baggage, to lend a hand.

"Did you have any trouble?" Otter asked, trying to get the heavy grain sacks across Feiny's neck.

"None," Paisi said. He was wearing his field boots, and his good heavy cloak, and showed a flour sack he had gotten. "Sausages, a good white loaf, and cheese, white an' yellow. I said ye was fussy an' out of sorts, so's ye know your state when ye get back to your rooms, m'lord."

"Hold him," Otter said, and with Paisi's help got the grain sacks across the saddlebow, at which Feiny sidestepped and threw his head, stamping one shod rear hoof like the crack of doom.

"Stop it," Paisi said, shortened up the reins, and slapped Feiny sharply on the shoulder. "Don't you kick, ye rascal."

More baggage went up. Otter struggled with the saddle ties atop the quilted barding, hoping not to have the blankets and sacks spilling in opposite directions, and he stood on the stone curb to tie the knots. It was a poor job. It made no orderly bundle, but it stayed, at least, until he could get his foot in the stirrup and get into the saddle.

Paisi handed him up the reins. It was their plan to go out like man and servant—young lords were prone to errands at the edge of dawn and dark, not the sort, Paisi said, that the gate-guards were apt to question, and if asked, he had to say he was visiting a friend.

Lies, again, but the sort that would get Paisi on his way. Beneath his cloak, Paisi had all the coin they had but his lucky pennies, the small hoard that Gran had given them—"Which I won't need," Gran had said, pressing her savings on them, "but who knows, in the city?"

Who knew, indeed? But with the pennies, Paisi could stop at farmhouses and buy a place for him and Feiny to sleep, out of the wind, and perhaps buy more grain than what he had, if Feiny ate it all.

Feiny started to move—the horse was inclined to move the moment he had someone on his back, never mind where, and frequently in an inconvenient direction. Otter anxiously drew the reins in to the least freedom Feiny ought to have, and pressed him with his knee, and turned him toward the gate, a direction not to Feiny's liking. But he let Feiny know with his knee and his hands that he was bent on that gate ahead of them, and that Feiny shouldn't throw his head and try to shoulder Paisi down. He had never been inclined to hit the horse, as the grooms said he should; but this morning he desperately gave Feiny a sharp kick and a short rein, and with a sigh, as if it had been a mere annoyance, Feiny went toward the gate.

It was shut at this hour. Paisi went first to the gate warden's post and rapped at the little oaken door. "The watch, there!"

Otter bit his lip and kept Feiny still while Paisi talked to the gatekeepers and requested the gate open. The gatekeeper came out, carrying a lantern nearly useless in the growing dawn, and held it aloft for a passing look at Otter's face. Then: "Ye better watch that 'un," the guard muttered, he hoped regarding the horse, which was backing and stamping a hind foot, and signaled the other man to run the chain back on the iron gates.

The gates moved quietly on their hinges, well-kept gates, opening just a little earlier than ordinary, and Paisi walked by Otter's stirrup as they moved briskly through, Feiny turning a wary and misgiving eye to the gate wardens.

They went out onto the high street and along the stone wall where the great Quinaltine hulked against the dawn sky ahead of them. There, under that vast and disapproving stone presence, they crossed the square and took the downward street as the light grew. Merchants opened their shutters and began to set out their wares. Housewives swept their steps clean of snow, and stared at their passage with more curiosity than Otter liked.

Perhaps the stablemaster would wake and ask where Feiny had gone. Perhaps soldiers would come to stop them before they got to the gate.

But no one spoke. Merchants stared as they passed and looked up the gray and lonely street as if they expected to see more than two riders.

Paisi, walking briskly at Feiny's head, said not a word, not all during the long way down, not when they began to see a few other people coming up the hill toward the market square, one man with a mule, several men carrying bundles behind him. There began to be more such, and Otter breathed more easily. They had passed the delicate moments in which they were the only travelers on the street, and become less conspicuous, to Otter's way of thinking.

It was the western gate they chose, the lower end of Market Street, where a sparse weekday market was spreading its canvas, only three merchants as yet beginning to offer wares on a threatening and snowy morning, and those the sort of goods that might fare best on such a day: knit goods, dyed wool, and hot cider.

The city gates beyond were open, now, a fresh scrape in the snow to show where they'd moved, not long ago at all. And blocking those gates, a small outbound company of pack mules and packhorses milled about. A pair of merchants, wrapped up in cloaks, were talking with the gate wardens.

Here was the place Otter chose to get down, screened by the small caravan, the two of them afoot and anxious.

" 'Ere might be a lucky thing," Paisi said in a low voice. "Wait an' look wise."

Otter opened his mouth to ask what Paisi intended, but Paisi ducked away from him, walked in among the mules, and a few moments later came back with one of the merchants, a respectable-looking graybeard hooded against the snow.

"This is indeed your man, your lordship?" the merchant asked.

Look wise, Paisi had said, and Otter had stood lookout for Paisi in little mischiefs before, in Amefel. His part was to be the lord, and he stood as tall as he could and pretended he was Aewyn. "He is, sir."

"As they're goin' by way of the monastery at Anwyfar, m'lord," Paisi said, "an' they'll feed me an' the 'orse for as long as I ride alongside, it bein' safer wi' another rider in the company. A pack train, an' all mounted, can move right along in this snow."

There were now and again robbers to fear on the roads, when the weather made men desperate. It was a handsome offer, good for both parties, and the merchants clearly took Paisi for a lord's personal messenger.

"As they'll break any drifts wi' them big mules, and switch the lead about," Paisi said, "an' it'll be far easier an' faster."

Far faster. Otter found his heart beating hard, perhaps simply because their plan was finding great good luck, and he nodded. "A good idea," he said, taking Paisi's word as law. He handed over Feiny's reins. "Excellent." It was one of the king's own words, in the king's tone. "Be safe."

The last words were not lordly: they were desperate. Paisi's gloved hand took the reins.

"M'lord," Paisi said, with a huskiness in his voice. "I'll be quick as I can."

"Do," Otter said, then it was the plan, clearly, that he keep on being the lord and simply walk away, leaving the details to Paisi, who would travel far, far more safely by reason of the merchants.

Luck. Happenstance. Everything had fallen into place so neatly—everyone who could have opposed them had just not happened by, had not looked out their windows, or turned up in the stable early, and the gate wardens had showed no suspicion at all. It was done, and now Paisi would do what he promised and see to Gran, in the hopes that all their good fortune was just that.

Gran could bend luck. She claimed to bend it ever so little, being only a hedge-witch, but that they had been so lucky might be good news, that Gran's witchery was working; or bad news, that Gran was in direst need and bent luck around them, who were hers, in great desperation to get help.

All Otter could do now was to wrap his cloak about him, keeping the hood up, and trudge uphill in an increasing snowfall that misted the high hill. White made the great Quinaltine into a hazy ghost of itself and all but obscured the Guelesfort and its walls and towers. Only the streets were real, and those cold, snow-edged brown beams and gray stone. The walks and cobbles were all snowed over in a sheet of scarcely tracked white, except the few open shops, and traffic down the center of the street. Newly swept and sanded porches began to be covered again. People were at breakfast, generally. Only the baker enjoyed a brisk traffic of young boys and housewives, an area which he skirted, unremarkable, brown-cloaked, and curtained by the snow.

He was lonely already, but—he said to himself—he had to be a man. For the first time he was altogether on his own, and for the interval between now and having the king's help, he would not have Paisi telling him do this or do that. Manhood began with getting through the day without giving anything away, sleeping alone for the first time in his life, and seeing himself fed and bathed and dressed for Festival tomorrow.

Manhood meant explaining what he had done, as soon as he could, as soon as Paisi was inconveniently far away, and it meant taking whatever blame might fall on him, from the king, from his father, who had invited him here and given him Feiny for his own.

That he did not look forward to with any pleasure at all. He would do that when the time was right, but well before any accusation got to his father, who would pay little attention to the ordinary running of the Guelesfort and ask no questions of the various staff and guards until someone grew troubled enough to pass a report up the line. Once Paisi was too far to overtake, he thought, the king might frown and be angry about it, but he would let Paisi go on to reach Gran.

That was the essential thing.

vi

THE LUCK CONTINUED. THE GUELESFORT GUARDS ASKED NO QUESTIONS OF HIM except, "Are ye well, m'lord?"

"Oh, yes," Otter answered them, and added, perhaps foolishly: "I sent my man on an errand."

"Aye, m'lord," the captain said, as if a little surprised to be told that, and that was all he said.

Otter avoided the stable precinct entirely, skirting all the way around the yard to a side door that mostly servants used, inside and up a scantly lighted stair to the main floor, and upward again.

He was hungry now. His breakfast was on its way to Amefel with Paisi, and he was not foolish enough to go down to the kitchen asking for more. He took off the cloak and slung it over his arm as he climbed. The next was the floor where his rooms were, but that was also the floor where the king's and the queen's chambers were, with their guards, and where Aewyn's was, more to the point, guards who regularly dealt with him and who might tell Aewyn he was behaving oddly. He climbed up yet one more level of the Guelesfort, and yet another, up where the household servants lived in far less circumstance and far narrower rooms. The dim upper hall was the regular means by which he and Aewyn had skirted watchful guards and gotten past the central stairs, and he used it this time, passing this and that servant, who bowed or bobbed and gave him the whole hallway as he went, not unaccustomed to see a youngster here.

At the farthest end of the servants' level was another narrow stairs that led down past a narrow slit of a window, which dimly lit the passage above, and by this stairs, he descended back to his own hall—a long, polished hall largely untenanted in winter, except for him. At this end of the hall, the last watch-candles had burned down to guttering stubs, overpowered by the light of the tall windows at the landing of the central stairs.

His part of the hall was in shadow, and with a considerable agitation he opened his own door and slipped into his own empty rooms.

Their fire was all coals, lending heat to the room. The tall windows, on which the curtains were drawn back, were milky with frost but gave their cold, dim light. The last remnants of Paisi's preparations remained on the little table, the things he had thought Paisi should take, like bits of cord and the fine new boots, which Paisi had declined. Paisi had worn all his shirts, and both his pairs of trousers, for warmth. The good boots, he said he would not take, but he had worn his second-best.

And all was done.

Now Otter had only to wait, and delay notice of their conspiracy.

He started to sit down on the fireplace stones, in the homey way, but he took the chair instead, constrained to be a man, and a lord at that, and to command the servants and maintain a young lord's dignity—if he had to order servants about, it was hardly the time to have soot on one's knees or scuffed boots. He shifted his feet down when the soles grew too hot, watched the line of moisture ebb on the darkened leather: lord he might pretend to be, but he had to tend his own soaked boots and rub the luster back into them to cover the evidence—he was obliged to put away their leavings and make his bed and do all those things Paisi had been doing since he came here, things which he very well knew how to do. At Gran's, bedmaking was a matter of throwing a coverlet over and making a sitting place out of their sleeping place. Here, all the bedclothes were ordered, and precise, and immaculate.

If he could keep up the pretense for three days, he thought, and not let slip to Aewyn that Paisi was gone, then Paisi could get as far as Averyne crossing, where he would pass into Amefel, well, granted the snow might make his passage somewhat slower—but close enough.

There was a flaw in their plan, which loomed perfectly clear now that everything was beyond recall: the stablemaster, and Feiny, and Feiny's empty stall. The stablemaster would ask the stableboy, the stableboy would say that Feiny had gone out in the earliest light, then—then the stablemaster, who knew who Feiny belonged to, would start wondering what the king's bastard son was up to and when he would come back. He might waste a little time inquiring down the hill and asking someone to find out whether Paisi's horse was still in pasture, but possibly not.

Despite all that luck could do, by dark, perhaps even by noon, the stablemaster might ask questions of the gate wardens uptown and down, and the gate wardens were attached to the Guard Commander, and the Guard Commander might start thinking that perhaps he should tell the king's personal guard or the seniormost of the king's servants that the king's son had failed to bring Feiny back from an early-morning ride.

But he had told the gate warden, hadn't he, that he had sent Paisi on an errand, so there. That might bring the question down to Feiny's being missing, with all his gear, and the stableboy having been part of it, the boy might be in for punishment for having helped them. He was worried on that account, but he knew nothing he could do that would not put their plans at risk and possibly have Paisi in trouble. He would have to make it up to the boy if he took a beating.

The word would eventually get to his father, however, by whatever route, and he would do well to tell his father first, would he not?

He hoped that all the luck that had run with them was now going with Paisi, because it suddenly seemed to be quite precarious, where he sat.

He could run down the hall and beg audience. But the king was busy with important things, and news of his misdeeds would not find sympathy with anyone in the king's entourage. The king surely wouldn't be too concerned if a servant ran an errand home, with the intention to come back.

And hadn't the king given him Feiny outright? Better if they could have used Paisi's horse, who was coated for the weather, but they had all Feiny's gear, and had him warm, and assured him being fed, and if Gran's luck was moving Paisi home—he just had to hold out.

He stopped dead on that thought, stopped so long that his boot soles scorched and stung. He imagined the moment he would face his father. "Sire," he would say, "Paisi went home to see to Gran." That was certainly the truth.

But then, inevitably: "Why?" his father would ask.

And what could he say? They were all Quinalts here, except the queen, who had no reason to love him because he was the king's bastard, whose presence here had to be an embarrassment to the family; and it was the Festival, when everybody was confessing sins and being particularly holy—

And what could he say to excuse his actions? Gran sent us a dream? Or: because we dreamed the same dream, Paisi had to go?

They hadn't quite thought that part through. Thinking of Gran, it seemed so natural and reasonable, what they did, even the unnatural run of luck that had guided them, and guided Paisi. But the moment he thought of explaining his reasoning to his father, things appeared in a Quinalt, Guelenish light, and it was neither natural nor reasonable, as Quinalt priests would look at it. It was a Sending that had called out in their dreams. It was witchcraft, pure and simple, which was the same as wizardry: Gran was a witch, and he the son not just of a witch, but of an Amefin sorceress—he was the lasting embarrassment of his father, who never should have slept with such a woman.

So above all, he couldn't just confess about the dream—his father might understand, but the moment it got to a servant's ears, there was no telling where the news would go next or how it would take new shape. He could plead for understanding, that he never had had any sorcery about him, not once in his life, nor wanted any, and he could say that Gran must be desperate to have Sent that dream. He could hope that his father, who had known Lord Tristen himself, would look on the matter with complete sympathy— and overlook the horse, and Paisi's going off. They had been lucky about their misdeed. He might argue they had been under a compulsion—he knew from Paisi's stories and Gran's that sometimes, when wizardry or magic was working, things couldn't be helped falling into place, and even people who ordinarily didn't have a smidge of wizardry might just go along with things, cooperating more slowly than some, but move they might, not thinking as clearly as they might.

And now the stableboy might be beaten, and the priests might get wind of his having heard Gran and remember, if they had ever forgotten, who the king's bastard's mother was. And he still had to ask Aewyn about the red coat, and ask if that was right, and now it was all tangled together. He couldn't lie to Aewyn and ask for his help at the same time.

Luck, when it ran so strongly and so suddenly, could be bad luck as well as good: it could be sorcery as well as wizardry. It could even be magic, which he didn't understand, except that it was Sihhë-born, Sihhë-made, and sometimes inherent in things, and a foolish boy could pick up something with magic about it and have very little choice or sense about what he did next. He might not be making it up about a compulsion.

He hadn't acquired anything he could blame for his folly, had he; and he had assumed the dream had come from Gran . . .

That was the problem. He and Paisi had assumed it came from Gran, when his mother sat there in Henas'amef in her tower, silent through all his life.

But his mother's son had been called away to his father's palace, and his mother hated his father, did she not? She hated him beyond all measure, and all the magic that bound her to her tower prison had kept her spells inside. They had never been able to get out. Gran said they couldn't: Gran said that it wasn't her witch-work that kept his mother in her prison, but Lord Tristen himself, with magic no wizard or sorcerer could bend, let alone break.

That was what Gran had assured him when, after the earliest visit to his mother he could remember, he had had nightmares, terrible nightmares of her breaking out of her prison and turning up outside their window, in the dark.

She could not get out, Gran had assured him. "Not her nor her wishes, neither."

And was that not still true?

If his mother found out he had gone to his father, and if she grew very, very angry . . . who knew what strength she might find?

It became more and more urgent to tell his father, and to get an older, wiser head to work on the matter. Aewyn would, he had said it to Paisi, likely sleep until noon. And maybe he didn't even want to see Aewyn yet. He had to find the right time to tell his father and make sure no one heard . . . not easy, to gain a completely private audience with the king of all Ylesuin, but he had to try. And meanwhile if bad luck started showering around him, he would know it was his mother; and if good, then he would be more hopeful that it was Gran's work: that was one clue he might have to the origin of it.

The best thing to do, in any event, was take care to have a clear head and a calm heart, to tell the truth where it did good, and to say nothing to anyone at all until he could reach the king.

First was to satisfy the hunger pangs and settle himself to live alone. Paisi might be on the road with their breakfast, but there was a pitcher of drinking water in the bedchamber, and Paisi had left behind the food they had in the room for simple moments of hunger. There was a stale end of bread from two days ago, though the sausage he had thought was there, was not. There was the fireplace poker, in the absence of a toasting stick.

He wiped down the poker, skewered a stale bit of bread, showering crumbs on the hearth. The toasted bread revived itself, there was indeed water in the pitcher, and it made a fine, even homey breakfast, making his thoughts happier, for the moment. He was warm and dry, he had found his breakfast, and ill seemed at least a little further removed from the day's doings. Afterward he sat waiting, holding on to the three-coin luck piece that Gran had blessed and watching the snow come past the windows.

Paisi must be beyond Guelemara's farms soon. He would be chatting with the merchant as they went, finding out all the gossip—Paisi was good at that—and tonight Paisi would be warm and safe by a fire, helping with the mules. Feiny would be warm and safe, too, with other creatures about, if he would only get along with the mules.

And when Paisi did get home, he would see that Gran had what she needed, and cook her meals, and renew the indoor wood stack, just about in time for the Bryalt festival to start, with its dances and its feasts and all the merriment in town. Paisi deserved that. Lord Crissand was a kind lord, who would understand perfectly well why Paisi would have come home, and he would, by the king's own order, see that Gran had everything she needed before Paisi rode back again.

He could, perhaps, tell his father that Paisi had been so homesick for the Bryalt holidays he had sent him home. That would save him having to admit to the dream.

He could say that Paisi and he both had grown very worried for Gran, considering the storms this last several weeks, and that they had not been sure they had left enough wood, and they had not wanted to bother the king or have soldiers going out to do what they should have done in the first place: the first was almost the truth, and the second fact was that Gran would never tell the truth to soldiers. Paisi was right. She would meet them at the door and say there was nothing she needed, no matter what.

Blaming it all on their worry about the weather might be a very good lie, maybe even a white lie, since it would protect everyone from blame and even save the king his father from having the priests all in a flutter. It wasn't that bad a lie.

And Paisi had only come along with him to Guelemara in the first place to take care of him, and he had never been forbidden to send Paisi back—because no one ever thought he would be sending Paisi anywhere else, he was sure, but it was so. The horse, now, being his—he could argue that he thought the horse was his to send, though it was unlikely his father meant him to keep so fine a creature when he did go home again.

At least, he said to himself, at least if his father was angry, the anger would not fall on Gran's head or Paisi's: it was his own at risk.

And, while truth was at issue, he would learn essential truths about his father when the first truth came out. He would discover, for one thing, whether his father would forgive him as readily as he forgave Aewyn, and laugh—Aewyn had always said that their father wouldn't be annoyed at this or that thing, and Aewyn defied the rules with blithe unconcern. All he wanted for himself was one grace for one solitary misbehavior. It seemed within reason . . . if the king really did care what became of him.

All those years that the king had stopped to talk to Gran—he had always taken for granted that it was about him; and then he had begun to believe it was concern for his welfare. The annual gifts had persuaded him so.

But had the conversation really been regarding him?

His father had other concerns in Amefel: the cold light of day had made him reckon that into the balance. His father might have been stopping to ask Gran about his mother, not about him.

If that were so—maybe he would have far less patience with his misdeed.

Well, there was the truth to learn. At worst, his father would send him home and never want to see him again. But at least he would have done the right thing by Gran, and he would not have built up fond hopes about his estate in life, hopes which, if followed too far, could do greater harm to him and Gran and Paisi than he could manage now. Maybe he was meant to be a goatherd, or maybe learn Gran's craft, if he had a smidge of his mother's talent. He was never a wicked person. It was a choice, was it not, whether to turn wizardry to sorcery? It wasn't a taint born into him, was it?

And if his father turned out not to want him here, then he could only make things worse for himself and Aewyn and everyone by staying too long. If his father cast him out, there was still a hope that someday Aewyn would come visit him . . . there was their friendship, which above all else he wanted not to betray. And he didn't think he had.

He almost wished he had gone with Paisi, back to his life in the country, where he could help Paisi on the farm and live a quiet life in a place he loved until the king and Aewyn rode by again. That was no bad fate.

Well, and if that was all done and gone—it never had been much. And if not, and his father did forgive him as freely as he would forgive Aewyn, on whom he clearly doted—well, then he'd know Gran's extravagant hopes for his fortunes were justified, and he could trust a little more to that fragile ice.

If his father did forgive him, then he would give his father what a good father might hope to win from him . . . like trust. And love.

He would so very much like to love his father. He had come here hoping to find his fortune, to be given something to do, or be, and so far he had found that it was Aewyn who had bidden him, to give him friendship—not inconsiderable at all, by no measure insignificant, but not altogether what he had come hoping for.

If he found a father who could love him, that he could love in return, and trust . . .

Oh, it was a giddy, soaring hope. And he had just done everything a fool could do to make things go wrong, had he not? He deceived, and stole, and lied.

So here he sat on the very hinge point of his life, gifted with his new clothes he was now afraid to question with Aewyn; with new obligations—and overwhelmed with the possibilities—and having a secret he had to keep for at least a day.

Maybe, he thought, after he put on his best show of manners in the Quinaltine on Fast Day, maybe after he proved he could do well and be dutiful, that would be the best time to tell his father what he had done.

If he could keep the secret from spilling out of the courtyard and the stables.

From now on he must make no more mistakes, none at all. He had been Otter all his life, and that was a safe name. The one he was born with—Elfwyn—he knew was an enemy's name, a king's name, the one the Marhanen kings of Ylesuin had betrayed and murdered. If only his mother had given him a name out of her own Aswydd house—a name like Heryn, even, her brother who was hanged—that would have been bad enough for his fortunes. But she had named him after a remote relative only she claimed, the last of the Sihhë kings and the source of her abrogated rights and titles as well as the Gift she had. The name had insulted his father, whose house had succeeded the Sihhë kings, it had threatened Lord Crissand, who had gained her titles, and it had outraged the Quinalt priests. It had been a wicked stroke on her part: it was clever, and it made everyone around her as uncomfortable as possible: that meant his mother was happy.

Gran had stepped in, then, and called him Otter, a country name, from a countrywoman, and it had served him all his life. But it wasn't a city name, or a name to go about with, and among the hopes he had had in coming to Guelemara, he had hoped his father would give him a new name, a Guelen name, one the Quinalt priests would accept, one he could wear in public, and stop people whispering about him.

"There's the king's son," they would say, if he had a Guelenish name like Gwieden or even Wynsan or Feisun, which every third person in town seemed to be called. He would settle for Wynsan, not—"There's the witch's brat."

He didn't know what he was going to be once he went into the sanctuary of the Quinaltine with the rest of the family. Probably nobody else had thought of it, yet. There was a book there, that the priests wrote names in, when a person was blessed and sealed, whatever that meant. But if they wrote him in the Quinaltine book, what would they write? Otter from Amefel? Not next to Aewyn Marhanen. His father would find it entirely uncomfortable to have a son named Elfwyn or Aswydd, would he not, and he was both, and those fine clothes were trying to say Marhanen—if he was meant to have them.

Oh, he wished he had gone with Paisi when he'd had the chance. He still sat waiting, waiting to gain what Gran had always told him was his fortune . . . and dreading some shout in the hallways: The Amefin brat's stolen a horse and lied to the gate wardens . . .

Why, oh, why had he stayed? He had settled into certain appurtenances of this princely life: Aewyn's comradeship above all; and books, as many as he liked; and bread with no mill sand in it; spiced foods; clean sheets and warm fires and glass windows—all these wonderful things he still looked on with wonder and yet could not imagine now being without. The priests always said wealth could never make anyone happy: but it seemed to him, where he sat, that these things were a reason for great contentment, if he could continue here.

Wealth, and a righteous name that Guelenfolk could say without blanching, if he could only attain it, could do one other thing for them. If he gained a name he could wear comfortably among Guelenfolk, and be in the king's house, and if he had gold, then he could help Gran and Paisi, and provide for them handsomely to the end of their days. Paisi should not be his servant. Paisi was Gran's true grandson, was what, when he himself had had no right to a place under Gran's roof until Lord Tristen had asked Gran to take him in and keep him away from his mother. Paisi's real place in the world was to take care of his gran, not him, and to inherit her farm someday, and to have a fine herd of goats and another of pigs and enough money to hire a helper. Paisi could be a substantial man, with property.

His wealth was their answer. He would get through this. He would do all he could to send Paisi home for good. He would find his own way in this strange place, after making peace with his father. He might be terribly lonely, then, bereft of the family and life he knew.

But there was Aewyn. His absent brother. His friend. His model of what it could be, to be King Cefwyn's son.

At the moment he dreaded going to Aewyn: he was by no means sure Aewyn would not immediately see that something was wrong, and if Aewyn got the truth out of him too soon, he might take offense at not being told from the start—gods, he was supposed to be helping Aewyn with the apples this morning, and he hadn't, and now Aewyn was going to ask questions for sure, where he'd been, what he'd done—

Aewyn might be angry with him, and might tell his father, and the soldiers might catch Paisi before he had reached the first way stop.

That was no good. He'd let Aewyn get worried about him, that was the way. He'd tell Aewyn he'd been hiding out and confess the whole truth right after services tomorrow. By then Paisi would be much too far to catch, and Aewyn would have to feel sympathy for him. Likely the clothes were exactly what he was supposed to have, and he would just have to show up for services and not say anything to Aewyn before tomorrow morning.

It was dangerous. Aewyn did have a temper. But that way, if his father did let fly, Aewyn would intercede for him until he had the story, and he could talk his way past Aewyn, after it was too late for a report to do anything to catch Paisi or thwart that—Aewyn might be angry, but he would not likely want to have him sent home, and knowing his father that much better, and being able to say things a bastard son wouldn't dare say in his own defense, Aewyn could talk his way out of trouble for him—it was going to be unpleasant, but if he knew Aewyn, and he thought he did, the storm would blow over, if he just didn't have to lie to Aewyn beforehand.

So long as he didn't lie, everything would be patched up and cobbled together. And Gran's gifts—those would go on. She needed them.

He'd once thought Lord Crissand was the sole source of the good things that came to them in their cottage, and that of course lords naturally gifted old peasant women with goats and hay and good blankets. When he had learned a few years ago that it was his father the king behind it all—his father the king, and, long ago, Tristen Sihhë—

Surely, whatever else happened in Guelemara, those gifts might continue.

Oh, he wished he knew what to do.

Maybe, please the gods, it was Gran's Sending that had reached out to him, and he had done the right thing. Gods forfend it should be his mother's.

Act on a piece of wizardry, cooperate with it ever so little—and it spread and developed branches.

Wasn't that what Gran had always warned him?

vii

AFTERNOON CAME, AND WITH AFTERNOON, A PATCH OF BLUE SPREAD IN THE sky, while the snow had stopped for the last hour. Whatever Aewyn had done about the stables, Otter was sure Aewyn had done by now, and he might be angry, staying in his room, waiting for him to come and apologize.

He would have to wait. Otter put away the strayed items about the room, dined on more toast and water, while thus far, so far as he could guess, the question of a missing horse and a servant's mission somehow had not gone beyond the courtyard, nobody had mentioned it to Aewyn, and Aewyn had not come to his room, which meant, probably, that Aewyn was put out with him.

But there was still the likelihood of the stablemaster asking, when Feiny never came back. As the afternoon lengthened, worry wore a deeper spot in his imagination. Otter finally gathered his courage and decided he should go down to the yard to head off questions and prevent any difficulties from reaching the inner halls and complicating matters with Aewyn and his father.

He put on his better brown cloak, to look as much like his father's son as he could, and walked down the hall, this time to the central stairs, keeping a slightly worried eye out for Aewyn or his bodyguard. He saw no one, which indicated Aewyn was somewhere other than his rooms. He went down to the main hall and so on to the stable-court door. Past soldiers busy with their own concerns, he walked out into the crisp air and sunlight of the courtyard, and, descending the steps at an idle stroll, he walked through the yard.

"Your lordship."

He looked aside. The stablemaster had seen him, and diverted onto his track straightway with the air of a man bent on business.

His heart beat hard. "Sir," he said respectfully and as innocently as he could manage. The stablemaster had the look of an old soldier, weathered and white-mustached, with no nonsense about him, and Otter's every desire was to bow and look at the ground—but he had known, coming down there, that he might be caught and might have to try out his story on the stablemaster or the gate warden or worse.

"The boy says ye went out by dawn an' took Feiny out."

"I did, sir," he said, light-headed with fright. "Paisi had to go home." The story started to change its order, and its pieces, coming hind end first into the world. "Our gran's taken ill. He had to go, and with the drifts and all, we couldn't get down to the pasture. So I sent him on Feiny, with grain enough, and cover from the weather. He'll be back, Paisi will. With Feiny safe and sound."

The stablemaster's brows drew together like a gathering cloud, and the frown deepened. "It's a hard ride, at best. And that man o' yours ain't up to that horse, your lordship, forgive me. The boy's a fool that didn't ask what you was about. If we'd ha' knowt, we'd ha' provided a gentler horse."

There it was. The boy had the blame and might take harm for it, and in the face of such bluff goodwill from the old stablemaster, he lost all resolve. He could scarcely track the story that had fallen out of his mouth already.

"It was my fault," he said. "It was my fault, Master Kei. But Paisi is much better than I am on a horse. And he's traveling with merchants."

"Ha," the stablemaster grunted, eyebrows lifting at that comforting news. "A message come, was it?"

"Yes, sir," he said. The lie fell out of his mouth and took solid form. "From Amefel."

"An' this messenger, did he ride back wi' your man, wi' no change of horse?"

"Yes, sir." It was the quickest way he could think of to dispose of any messenger, to have him go away with Paisi, and be with him, and keeping Feiny safe. "And he'll be back as soon as he can."

"Aye, your lordship." The stablemaster let him go with a doubtful look, and Otter took the chance to escape, knowing that he had not done well. Now his tale had added a message, a messenger who hadn't stopped to care for his horse in the Guelesfort stable yard, and no word how the message had gotten upstairs to him without passing the guards who watched everyone come in and out. He hadn't thought about such details until the words were out of his mouth, and now the lie had more pieces. Which pieces ultimately couldn't fit. And before too long the gate warden and the stablemaster might have a cup of ale with the Guard officers, and it was all going to break loose before he could talk to his father or Aewyn.

He didn't know what to do, now, except to go on holding to the lie long enough to let Paisi get as far as possible, because if his father turned out to be angry, he could arrest Paisi, who might try to run, and the gods knew what could happen to him.

Toast and water had worn thin, by now, so very thin that his stomach hurt.

Fast Day was tomorrow, when he had to go without food or drink all day long, and when he would have to face his father and Aewyn and confess everything: he didn't know if he could face it on bread and water. And he was near the kitchens, where he might not have too many chances to come today. Getting food was Paisi's chore, but now Otter had to do it if he was to have any food at all; and he had to get himself ready in the morning, and not oversleep, not if he had to sit up all night. If his argument for sending Paisi away was that he was so sure he could manage without him, he had to do for himself and prove it.

So he turned toward the kitchens and climbed that short stair by the scullery, into a hall lit by a steamy little glass window, then into the huge arch of the kitchen.

The air inside was thick with steam and smoke, with the smells of wood fire and bread baking, the bubbling of meats and pies and cabbage, every sort of food one could imagine. A thick-armed maid spied him and fluttered him away from a floury counter edge, crying, "Oh, young lord, ye'll have flour on your fine cloak, there. What would be your need?"

"Bread," he said, relieved it became so easy. "Brown bread. Cheese and sausage, if you will."

"Aye, your lordship. Don't touch nothing, pray. Ye'll get all floury. Stand there an' I'll fetch it. Is one loaf enough?"

"One black, one brown," he said, giddy to find things suddenly falling his way and hoping it was an omen of Gran's Gift taking care of him again. He stood in the rush and hurry of the kitchen, avoiding floury and greasy edges for the few moments until the maid came back, bringing him a small basket with a round loaf of crusty dark bread, a long one of brown, a small sausage, and what was likely the cheese wrapped up in oily cloth. "Thank you," he said fervently, taking his leave, and edged his way back into the little hall and on up to the servants' stairs, which led to the main floor.

He was just setting foot on the first step up that grand stairway when someone hailed him from behind, and not just any voice.

"Nephew?"

He turned back reluctantly, holding the silly basket, caught, plainly caught. The Prince, his father's brother, who held his offices in the lower hall, had come out to overtake him and clearly meant business.

"Come," Efanor said. "Can you spare a moment?"

"Yes, Your Highness." He had never spoken two words to this man in all his time here, nor had Efanor ever addressed him. He caught his breath and tried to gather his wits as he made a little bow and followed Prince Efanor back to his writing room, a narrow, book-laden venue he had never entered. Books balanced crazily on the counter, and several, open, overlay the writing desk, sharing the surface with an inkpot and a quill left in it, writing interrupted. The Prince had chased him down on the instant, hunted him to the foot of the stairs, and all he could think was that a report had come in. The gate wardens must have reported to the Guard, and Prince Efanor had heard about it—which was the worst thing he could imagine. Efanor, who went habitually in black, and wore a silver Quinalt sigil as if he were a priest, was always so solemn and royal—Efanor advised Otter's father, and judged cases, and handled the accounts, besides. He was as good as a priest, to Otter's eye, a priest with the very strictest notions of truth and proper doings; and all he could think of now was to confess—to confess every lie, every sin he'd committed or thought of committing before this man could ever accuse him of his misdeeds, and maybe—maybe, because Aewyn had told him Efanor was not in fact as strict as he looked—to find some absolution, some penance, some way to mollify this man before he went to the king.

"Sit down," Efanor bade him, and as he was about to sit down, whisked the basket from his hand. "Food for tonight?"

"Yes, sir." He sat, and Efanor set the damning basket on the edge of the writing desk, behind which Efanor took his seat.

"You're of the Bryalt faith."

"Yes, Your Highness." He wished he could sink through the stones of the floor, right on the spot.

"Are you a good Bryaltine?"

"I don't know, Your Highness. Not as good as I could be."

"Have you ever attended a Quinalt Festival?"

"No, Your Highness."

"This is not Henas'amef, and the Quinalt holiday is not a time for frivolity of any sort."

"Yes, Your Highness. No, Your Highness."

"Nor a time for leading your younger brother into mischief."

He was completely taken aback.

"I hope I have never—"

"Not yet. But boys being what they are, and two boys being twice one, it seems worth mentioning in advance of a public occasion."

"I would never—"

"No, being a clever Otter and hard to catch, you would not. Your half brother is less cautious." Efanor waved a hand toward the ridiculous basket. "Palace manners, however—you have a servant. You are not in the country. Let him carry such things. People note such behaviors as out of the ordinary, and they gossip. People will all too readily note *you* as out of the ordinary, and gossip about every little item that suggests oddity or scandal. Give them nothing. Be as unremarkable as possible, and be very wary about entraining your half brother in any schemes in public view or out of it. You have none such in mind, I hope."

"No, sir," he said faintly, desperately, and knew that he had lied, simply by failing to confess the truth, twice in the same hour. Was not three wizardous, and binding, if wizardry was possibly in question?

"Keep your chin up. Look all men in the eye. You are my nephew, in whatever degree, and my brother's son. *What* is that hanging about your neck?"

His heart skipped a beat. He clutched the object in question. "A luck piece, Your Grace. My gran gave it to me."

Efanor silently held out his hand.

He didn't want to give it up. It was his luck. It was his tie with home and

Gran. But he reluctantly fished it out of his collar and past the fastening of his cloak, and lifted the leather cord over his head.

Efanor took it, and looked cursorily at it as he laid the cluster of cord-bound pennies on his desk. "The queen herself is Bryalt, to be sure, but your gran's form of the Bryalt faith verges just a wee bit closely on hedge-magic. You do know that."

"Yes, Your Highness." It was no more than a whisper he managed.

"You have been exemplary. I know. You are my brother's, the result of one night's youthful indiscretion. You carry Aswydd blood. You are taught by witchery—all these are matters marginally acceptable in Amefel, but I need not warn you, they are anathema in Guelessar. Yet my brother wishes to do you justice, so far as he can, and my nephew has taken to you and become your companion, so far as he can; and this places you under certain constraints of behavior—do you follow me?"

"Yes, Your Highness."

"You will be under close public observation. No one can foresee how grievous might be the outcome if you were to be seen to violate propriety in services in the least degree. Do not fidget, do not cough, do not sneeze—and do not above all be seen to wear any charm, particularly to services, particularly within the premises of the Quinaltine."

"Yes, Your Highness. It's only a keepsake."

Efanor gathered up the charm Gran had given him and gave it back to him.

"Tuck it away and do not wear it publicly until the day you cross back into Amefel. There is virtue in the piece, and that will not do, that will not do at all, inside the sanctuary. Most of the clergy is dull as stones, but there are reasons. Trust me in this."

"Yes, sir," Otter managed to say, and clenched it fast. Virtue? Could his uncle possibly feel witchery in it?

Efanor asked him, "Do you truly believe as the Bryaltines believe?"

"I studied writing with the brothers."

"That is not what I asked."

"I don't truly know what the Bryaltines believe, Your Highness. I never had the catechism."

"Indeed. Does the Quinalt service frighten you?"

"I heard—I heard somewhere, Your Highness, that they curse the Bryaltines. That scares me."

A sigh. "An obscure part of the service. A nuisanceful point we oppose, but—" A shrug and a shake of his head. "Be patient with us Guelenfolk. The queen herself endures it. The liturgy is under review . . . under close review, considering the succession."

Considering the succession. What did that possibly mean?

Then he thought of Aewyn and Aemaryen, whose mother was Bryaltine, and one of whom would grow up Bryaltine.

"Your quiet acceptance, like the queen's, will be noted. Your presence with the family will disturb some folk, but, more important, it will reassure others that you can enter under that roof without fear. Your quiet, respectful attendance, your observance of Quinalt forms, will answer important questions and provide your father with answers to questions."

"Questions, Your Highness?"

"About your mother's influence."

His cheeks flamed hot.

"Take no shame in my saying so," Efanor added gently. "That influence may pose critical questions in certain minds, but not among us who understand the circumstances. Certainly your birth was none of your choosing. We hope to have a quiet, a decorous service. Servants do gossip. Be scrupulously observant. I see you are stocking up on food."

The blush surely grew worse.

"You know you must consume all this food tonight," Efanor said, "or cast it out before sunrise, to have no sustenance nor drink in your room . . . if you are observant."

"Yes, sir."

"Rise before dawn. Dress in the clothes provided you. I trust they do fit."

"I'm sure, sir." He was no such thing. He had had no time to try them. And he was too distressed to ask if what was provided him was proper. The very last thing he wanted was His Highness inspecting them in his room and finding Paisi gone.

"Join us in the lower hall just before dawn," Efanor said. "Join the processional with the family. Sit with us, walk and sit in order just behind me, not next to Aewyn, and do not exchange glances with anyone. Have a pleasant look, however. A smile is not in order during the processional into the sanctuary, but you are permitted to smile after services, when you walk out in view of the city. Do you think you can observe all that?"

He attempted a smile, uncertainly, obediently, and, he feared, unsuccessfully. "I can, Your Highness."

"Leaving the Quinaltine by daylight, one may smile. Smile, and never frown; but laughter—laughter should occur only when you are back well within the Guelesfort gates, no matter what your half brother provokes. This is a very grave matter: I cannot say that strongly enough. Mind, if any priest or His Holiness speaks to you directly within the sanctuary, look down when spoken to and answer him modestly and clearly. Especially try not to frown at any particular people. One notes you do this at times."

"I never intended so, Your Highness."

"Thinking, perhaps? A lad of deep thoughts?"

Another blush. "I never meant to offend anyone."

"Well, let me see your cheerful face again."

He tried. He tried with all his heart, then he thought it was the third lie, and the smile died a sudden death.

"Good lad," Efanor said somberly, and gave him back his basket, a dismissal. "Don't take this meeting as a rebuke. Take it for concern. I am concerned, young Otter, as a close kinsman."

He felt a sudden urge to confess everything, to pour out all his sins to this man—it seemed for that one moment that he might make Efanor understand everything that had happened. But he hardly knew this priestly elder prince. He had always found Efanor a cipher, a stiff and formal sort servants skipped to obey and facing whom soldiers snapped to attention, even if he was notoriously holy and very scholarly.

"Your Highness," he said instead, and stood up, with the silly basket in his hands.

"I'm told you read quite well."

"Yes, Your Highness, I hope I do."

Efanor handed him a little roll of parchment, tied up with brown cord. "This will explain in some detail the days of the Festival, what you should do on each particular day, and when you should rise and sit and expect to depart services."

He took the little scroll and tucked it, along with the charm, into his bosom. "Thank you. Thank you very much, Your Highness."

"And you won't really need all that bread," Efanor said. "My royal brother is hosting the family tonight in his chambers. It's a custom we have. Your man will dine with the royal servants, where one trusts he will remain sober. Wear your second-best for the occasion. And appear at sunset."

"Your Highness." He hardly had breath left in him. And Efanor clearly had no idea Paisi was gone.

He bowed. Efanor favored him with a small smile, and stood up, and offered him the door.

He bowed again. He went out into the hall, on his own with the basket, and with the instructions, and with his charm, and his lengthening chain of fabrications, and went back toward the stairs.

He had lied the third time. Everything had, on the surface, gone well and smoothly. He had only to wear his second-best clothes and have supper with his father, and smile at the right times and not the wrong ones when they went in public. But his heart kicked like a hare in a trap. Was it tonight, not tomorrow, that he should tell his father the truth?

It had no certain feeling, the way his luck ran now.

Paisi, oh, Paisi, he thought. *Be careful. Be ever so careful.*

It might still be my mother's working.

viii

IF PAISI HAD BEEN WITH HIM AS SUNDOWN CAME, HE WOULD HAVE LAID OUT all the right clothes for the dinner. He would have called for a bath well in advance and had the house servants carry the water up, and Otter and Paisi would have dressed in good order. But Paisi was somewhere on the road south now, perhaps approaching some village, or at very least one of the windbreak shelters they had used on their way, with a good stone wall for protection and a place for lawful fires.

So as the day dimmed in the windows, Otter did as Paisi would have done and laid his second-best out on the bed. He had no idea how to get a bath, which required informing someone: he had no idea who that person was.

He did know the source of drinking water, however, down by the inner well, where the whole Guelesfort got its water from a spring unstoppable by drought or hostile attack. It was cold as old sin when it came out, that was what Paisi had said, and miserable for washing, but it would serve in present circumstances. Otter carried it upstairs in the drinking pitcher, and none of the servants, lowest of the low, asked him his business.

He warmed a little water in the fireplace, for which wood was running somewhat low, and he used the washing basin for a bath, there on the warm hearthstones. He took pains with his appearance as he dressed, and found himself, as far as he could tell, acceptable. He had put the basket of food by the hearthside, to burn before morning, as Efanor's little scroll informed him he should do. He had put the amulet in the clothespress in one of his gloves, where it would rest, safe from prying servants and accidents.

And he had on his fine dark brown, modest and plain, but very, very kind to clean skin. He thought he must look very fine, not as showy as he was sure Aewyn would appear tonight, let alone their father and the queen. But he was ready. His hair was combed. His linen was spotless. He hoped he would find the courage he needed. He hoped Aewyn was speaking to him and that he could signal the need to talk to him in private, when he could make peace.

He had been alone since dawn, and trembled at the thought of trying to confess his sins tonight, at least to Aewyn, as quietly as he could, and maybe, if he could possibly catch the king in private and without servants or guards—maybe he should just take the chance instead of waiting until tomorrow.

Tonight was sure—well, almost sure. Tomorrow—he had no notion whether he would have a chance then, either: it was only Aewyn and his mother, so far as he knew, who could get to him completely in private.

But there was still Aewyn to face. And that came first.

He left his rooms at the very edge of dusk and went down the hall and across the landing of the grand stairs, a long walk to the opposite wing that the royal apartments occupied. The guards here all knew him, and ignored him as someone who had leave to come and go, and the fact that the guards were still at Aewyn's door informed him that Aewyn had not yet gone to his father's chambers. He saw that with a sudden rush of hope.

The guards had to announce him: they did that when he simply appeared at the door and waited, and it was no delay at all before they let him in.

"There you are!" Aewyn said with a frown. "*Where* have you been?"

"I—" he began, then lost the thread of everything.

"I tried to find you early this morning, and I couldn't, so I took a sack of apples from the kitchen storeroom, and I took them down and paid the stableboy to lay them out tomorrow. Then the tailor showed up, and Master Armorer, and that was hours of standing." Aewyn's face grew worried, then, reflecting his. "Is something wrong? Where have you *been* all day?"

Otter lowered his voice to its faintest. "In my rooms. I had to send Paisi home, on my horse."

"Why?" Aewyn asked, hardly lowering his voice at all, then seized him by the arm and led him over near the tall diamond windows where there was a modicum of privacy from the servants. "Why? What happened?"

How did he know about Gran? That was the burning question. And he chose not to lie—but not to tell everything until Aewyn thought to ask him.

"Gran's taken ill. And we didn't count on the storms being so bad and there might not be enough wood small enough for her to carry, and sometimes the shed door freezes up with ice, so you have to take an axe to get the ice clear."

"So Paisi left, and you helped him?" Aewyn's eyes were wide. "I didn't see you down at the stable when I was there."

"We were out before it was more than half-light, and I rode and Paisi walked as far as the gate. We found merchants for him to travel with, so he's safe. But I had to lie to the gate wardens up and down, and then the stablemaster's boy, and then to your uncle . . ."

"To Uncle Efanor? How did *he* get into it?"

"He stopped me in the hall to tell me how to behave in Festival, and to tell me to come to dinner tonight."

"But you're completely by yourself now! Who helped you?"

"I had a bath, and I always dressed myself. And I had already gotten food for supper, except His Highness said I was to come to dinner."

"Well, but you're all alone! You can't be by yourself. Come stay with me tonight!"

"I can't. They'll know, and they could still catch Paisi if they know too soon." He hadn't made up his mind, but all of a sudden what he told Paisi he would do seemed the best course. "I have to pretend he's still here at least until tomorrow; then they won't bother to chase him."

"You think they *would* chase him?"

There was the hardest part, the part he hoped would get by. "We aren't supposed to know about Gran, and we do, by a way that we're not supposed to, and if we weren't supposed to know, then we weren't supposed to go, either, were we?"

"How *did* you know?" Aewyn asked, and Otter took a deep breath and told the truth:

"Dreams. We both had the same dream, and Gran can Send a dream if she has to. She needs us. And Paisi had to go, and we can't take a chance of Paisi getting caught. He has to get through."

"But he *is* coming back, isn't he?"

"He will, as soon as he can. It's three days to get there. Longer, with the weather. And he won't try to come back until it's safe on the roads. I told him not to try. But I'll tell His Majesty tomorrow, after Fast Day, after Paisi's had time enough to get clear away. And I'll do my best to explain everything. I hope His Majesty may forgive me."

"He won't be angry."

"I hope he won't be. I was so scared your uncle knew—"

"Well, but he doesn't, then, does he?" Aewyn loved plots above all things:

his eyes sparkled. "And if you don't have anybody to do for you, well, I can send you gifts, can't I?"

"Can you send a whole bath?"

Aewyn laughed. "I can! I shall! And with the family dinner tonight, you won't starve."

"So. See?" He feigned complete confidence. "It's all perfectly fine. And I'll confess what I did, when I have to. But maybe nobody will ever notice Paisi isn't here!"

Aewyn's eyes fairly danced. "*How* did you get away with the horse?"

"I asked the stableboy to saddle him."

"And just took him out?"

"Paisi got breakfast from the kitchen, and I got Feiny out. We rode down to the gate before anybody was much on the streets, found some merchants who wanted a guard, and there we were. They promised to feed Paisi and Feiny both until they reach the crossing. And I sent Feiny out in all his gear, so he'll be warm enough, especially with the traders' mules and enough to eat."

"That's clever!"

"And I still have Paisi's horse, if I need him."

"He's a piebald."

"He has all his legs, last I saw."

Aewyn laughed. "Well, he can't keep up with mine. We'll tell Papa what's happened and get you another horse."

"I can't feed the one I have!"

Aewyn took on a quizzical expression. "The boy will feed him. He always does."

"But at Gran's . . . Gran can't feed a horse. We'll have to give Feiny and Tammis back when I go home for good and all."

"You're not going home!"

"I don't know. I suppose that depends on whether your father sends me home for stealing Feiny."

"He won't! You'll be here forever."

Aewyn clearly had his mind made up on the point, and it was good to hear, but equally clearly, it was only Aewyn's opinion, not the king's.

"I hope to be here," Otter said. He wasn't sure about wanting it through spring planting, when Gran needed him, and once he'd said it the very ground under him felt shaky, as if nothing before him was the same as before. "I don't know where I'll be once the king finds out."

"I'll go with you to tell him."

"After Fast Day. To give Paisi time enough. If soldiers came after him, I don't know what he might do."

"After Fast Day," Aewyn said. "So we should go to dinner now. And we'll have our secret."

ix

OTTER HAD ONLY ONCE STOOD IN THE KING'S PRIVATE CHAMBERS, AND HAD NO idea where he was to go, beyond the little room he knew, but Aewyn knew the way to the inner halls, quite confidently. He marched them past all the guards, all the servants, arm in arm, at the last, a terrifying lack of manners, right into the room set for family dining.

The king was there, and they disentangled themselves and bowed respectfully and properly—bowed, likewise to the queen, Ninévrisë. Aewyn came to her for a kiss on the cheek.

"Mama," he said, and returned her embrace.

Then Ninévrisë reached out a hand toward Otter, too, beckoning insistently. "Come," she said, "come here, young man."

Otter advanced ever so cautiously, his heart thumping. His vision was all of white and gold, beautiful furnishings, beautiful table, beautiful pale blue gown and a nearer and nearer vision of dark hair and a golden circlet, with the most luminous violet eyes gazing right at his. He was caught, snared, drawn forward, constrained to offer a hand, and to touch and be touched.

"Welcome," the queen said, when he bowed and looked up. "Welcome, Otter."

They said the queen had been with his mother the hour he was born. They said the queen had held him in her arms. He had never been able to grasp it for the truth—that she could be so kind to her husband's bastard. He was utterly dismayed when she drew him forward and kissed him lightly on the cheek, in the way gentlefolk kinsmen did.

"Your Majesty," he murmured. She was that. She was a reigning queen in all but name, in her own kingdom of Elwynor. And wizardry and witchery were not at all dead in Elwynor: her title, Regent of Elwynor, held place for the return of a Sihhë king. The Gift, Gran had told him, ran as strong in that line as it did through the Aswydds. He felt it tingle through her fingers, through the touch of her lips, so potent for the instant that it sparked through his bones and left him addle-witted and dazed, staring at her.

"Come, oh, come," Aewyn said impatiently, dragging him by the arm, past Prince Efanor, and past the king himself, to claim a seat beside him at table, standing. They were only Aewyn, and Efanor, and the king and queen, and it was impossible to think only five people could eat at that great table, with all those plates and cups. There was holiday greenery, just as Aewyn had said, and birds served under their feathers, and pies, stacks of pies. It hardly seemed so grim, the Quinalt holy day, as it had sounded in Efanor's little list of instructions.

King Cefwyn pronounced the prayer: "Gods grant us peace, prosperity, and our heart's desire. The gods look down on us and bless us all."

"So be it," Efanor said quietly, "and bless them that serve and them that guard."

"So be it," the queen said.

"So be it," Aewyn said, and dug his elbows into Otter's ribs.

"So be it," Otter breathed hastily, and everyone smiled and looked pleased with the occasion, while the whole room and its colors and smells seemed a haze around him. For an instant all he could think of was how to traverse the length of that table and speak to the man who had fathered him. He had no idea now what he would say or where he would start once he did start to explain; but now he remembered how he had lied to Efanor, who had been nothing but kind to him. The queen had just gone out of her way to be kind. And Aewyn—Aewyn, who was entitled to everything by right—he had involved Aewyn, delaying telling him what Aewyn now knew, and now expecting his help. He sat in the heart of the family, Aewyn most of all having brought him here. Aewyn and his mother had each had more than a slight choice about welcoming him under this roof. Aewyn had poured out his affection and his wealth and his kinship on him as thoughtlessly, as generously as breathing. And the queen, who most of all had every right to wish he never existed—he still felt the tingle of her lips touching his cheek and the warmth of her hand.

No group of people in his life had ever had so much cause to wish he had never been born, and no one had ever been so generous toward him, except Gran and Paisi. What had he done to deserve such trust, and what did he do to repay it but a piece of mischief growing worse by the hour: it was what Paisi had said—it was not the obvious thing that was the crime: it was not taking Feiny; it was the Sending and the Seeing, right in the midst of their holy days.

Aewyn was not distressed, he told himself, over the soup. Aewyn would choose the best time, and broach the matter, and all he had to do was bow his head, beg forgiveness, and promise never, ever to cause any difficulty in the house again.

But for tonight, the way he had arranged with Aewyn, the matter stayed unbroached, throughout a lengthy dinner, course after course. There were small mince pies for dessert, with fantastical designs in the crust, and the centermost built into little towers. Otter could scarcely eat his.

"You mustn't save it," Aewyn said, nudging him.

He ate it. He wished he hadn't. It brought him to an uncomfortable fullness, and he had his mouth full when the king and queen rose and announced they were retiring for the evening, together. It was his last chance to bring up the matter of Paisi—to blurt out, "I've done something terrible." He swallowed the too-large bite. And he still couldn't say it.

Everyone stood. Aewyn's mother said it was time two boys should get themselves to bed, Prince Efanor concurred with the queen, and there was nothing to do but bow the head and accept it.

"And everyone to their own rooms," King Cefwyn said pointedly, "or you'll talk all night and be sorry in the morning."

"Sire," Aewyn said, bowing his head to a direct order.

So there it was. Aewyn was obliged to go off with his guards, and Otter walked beside him in the short distance to Aewyn's room. After that he went on alone, down the hall, across the lonely gap of the grand stairway landing, and on into his own, less-lighted hall.

A few of the residents' servants were out and about, carrying this or that. They paused and bowed to a boy in fine clothing. But no one stood guard at his door, and when he pushed down the latch and entered his rooms, they were almost dark, having only the light of a banked fire. There was no Paisi to have the candles lit, or to have stirred up the fire. The place was full of shadows, and they lurked deepest in the bedroom.

He put a few more sticks on the coals, to make a brighter light, and took the night candle and lit it—they had a jar of waxed straws by the fireside for that purpose. Then he gathered the courage to venture into the bedroom and light a pair of candles there.

The end of his straw burned off and tumbled as he lit the last. It aimed right for his sleeve, and he dropped the straw and stamped it out on the floor as he furiously wiped at his elbow, hoping it hadn't just burned a hole in his second-best clothing. Close inspection under candlelight showed only a little black about the elbow: it was a narrow escape.

He took off all his finery forthwith, to hang it up in the clothespress. To his dismay, there was a gravy spot, or a touch of greasy fingers, on his coat. He tried, with the washing basin, to wash it out, shivering in the fireless cold, but he feared he only made it worse.

And he dared not oversleep in the morning, that above all. To save time in the morning he laid out his Fast Day finery, disposing it on the small dining table, and on the chairs. Then, shivering and unable to feel anything in his feet, he snatched up the chill coverlet from the bed and wrapped himself in it, heading for the fireside where the warmth was.

He poked the fire up a bit. He decided to burn the last of the bread and cheese he had laid here, all proper, not taking a chance on being late in the morning and forgetting it. It stank as it turned to ashes, and the cheese caught fire and ran over the coals before it turned to ash; the sausage became a little log, smaller and smaller, but the fat in it lent light and warmth right along with the wood.

It seemed a sin to burn food when there were so many hungry in the world.

And tomorrow they and all their beasts would go hungry to remember the poor, he supposed, and to feel what it was to have an empty belly.

But he had rather have given the food away to someone who hadn't any. And he wagered the kitchen stores were still full, so what provision had the Guelesfort made about that? Did they carry it all out and bring it back to-morrow? Surely they didn't throw out all the barrels and barrels of goods, or burn all the bread.

Fire, fire to light the night. He warmed himself enough, finally, to get up and scurry back to the bedchamber to douse the candles, and then, hating the dark, he came back to his warm quilt and warmer stones, all tucked up and very weary now. It seemed days ago he and Paisi had sat by this very fire, but it was only this morning, and they had made their theft and gotten away with it, and he had trudged up the hill and met Prince Efanor, which had led to tonight at the king's table . . . all, all in one long span of hours that left him very tired, very relieved Aewyn forgave him, and very prone to drop off to sleep.

He daren't, he told himself at first, and then thought he could risk a little nap, sitting up by the fire, his head on his arms and the blanket close about him. He put a new stick of wood on, then let his eyes shut, if only for a very little time, and listened to the snap and crackle of the new wood.

X

FIRE, FIRE AND WAILING, FIRE THAT LEAPT UP AROUND GRAN'S ROOM, AND sealed the doors and the windows. The wailing was of a soul in pain, and the fire became a roar, burning face and seared eyes . . .

"No," Otter cried. "No!" He flung off the blanket to wake up, and scattered coals, and put his hand on an ember, which made him cry out and flinch.

He had flung the corner of the coverlet into the firebed, and he snatched it back in pain and fear, putting out the smoldering fire on the fine blanket with his bare hand. Pain and smoke alike made his eyes water, and he sat bare-shouldered in the chill, cradling a burned hand. The fire had gone nearly out, which had saved him from setting the whole coverlet afire. He sat and shivered.

He had put out the candles and let the fire die down to embers, and in doing so, he had thoughtlessly lost all markers to tell him the hour. He looked at windows which showed a haze of light, but when he got up, shivering, and tried to see whether that was approaching dawn, no, it was only snow haze around the two torches that burned all night, and a few more about the Quinaltine, obscured in a brisk snowfall.

There was no knowing what time it was, and he had to be up and dressed on time, above all else. The nightmare and the burn had his stomach upset, and his limbs shivered as he went out into the little hall and listened at the door for anyone stirring outside. He opened the door to the outer hall and looked out, wondering if there might be a passing servant, but the hall was eerily dark, with only one watch-candle still burning far down by the landing, and none in his wing. He shut the door and retreated back to his fire, lost, with no idea what hour it was and not daring go back to sleep now.

He built the fire up again, shaking so from the fear of the nightmare and from the cold that his knees knocked against each other. He thought of how Paisi might be sleeping in fair comfort by the merchant's campfire, in some wayside shelter. And then he wondered if Paisi had dreamed the same nightmare.

That was the most terrible thought, that it was another warning, and he could not confirm it to Paisi, nor could Paisi tell him what he had seen.

Danger, it foretold. Danger of a terrible kind. Sickness, and then fire in the night, cutting off all escape for an elderly woman fevered and abed. He sat shaking from a chill he could by no means banish, watching the tame fire in the hearth leap and jeer at him. The crackling and snap of the fresh wood sounded loud in his ears, and he sat there listening to it, finding it more and more ominous.

Best he get up and get dressed and not compound his faults in the household. He heated water in the little warming pan, washed, and dressed in the colors that, in the grim firelight, were red made more red. The shield with the gold Dragon glittered with fire, and the Dragon's eye glinted with it. He pulled it on, piece by piece; he combed his hair, and put on his fine new black boots, and sat down, this time like a city lad, in one of the two chairs near the hearth, arms folded tightly across the Dragon, his eyes on his boot toes, then on the fire that leapt and menaced in the hearth, a dragon of its own kind.

His eyelids grew heavy. But he was ready for the morrow. The moment he heard a stir in the hall he would go out and go downstairs to wait, even if it was only the servants going about their business. Better early than late, he said to himself. If he turned up in the lower hall an hour early, as well wait there as here.

Supper with the royal family seemed a distant dream, something that, like these clothes, never could happen to Gran's boy, like the life that never could happen to Otter, just Otter, who drew the water and tended the goats—Gran's foundling, the witch's brat.

His eyes shut. He fought them open once, twice, the third time, or perhaps failed, for just a moment. He saw a slit of firelight, and then more, and the fire roared up, thundering around him. He saw fire in the goats' eyes as they fled in confusion; he saw fire shooting up the little berry bushes by Gran's door, the ones that grew close and snagged a cloak if they weren't careful. He saw fire eating up the thatch of the roof, and he was inside, and Gran slept in her bed under her patchwork quilt, and he couldn't wake her. "Gran," he cried, shaking her. "Gran!" He lifted her, blankets and all, and tried to shoulder his way out the door, but a beam fell down to block his escape, and fire rained about them.

"Gran!"

He waked so violently he nearly fell out of the chair, and clung to its arms, sweating, not daring move until he knew for certain where he was.

He made his feet move then, just to prove it was no longer the dream around him. He unclasped his hands from the arms of the chair and stood up and walked about a bit, while everything rippled and leapt with fire-shadow and firelight. He reached for the amulet he wore, that luck piece Gran had given him, and for the first time since she had put it about his neck, remembered it was not there. He wanted to touch it, to hold it, and find that warmth of memory it always had. It might, he thought, tell him that Gran was safe and assure him that it was only an empty dream.

He lit the watch-candle and went to find his luck piece, down at the bottom of the cabinet, in the glove where he had hidden it. He shook it out, gathered it in his fist, and it comforted him to have it, but there was no great sense of presence in it, and it failed to ease his fear.

"Gran," he whispered, holding it in one hand before his lips. "Gran, do you hear me? Be careful of the fire. I had a dream. Are you all right, Gran?"

It grew cold in his hands, cold as the room around him.

And everything was still, everything but the fire crackling in the other room.

He shut his eyes tight, and saw flames and felt the pain of the burn on his clenched hand.

His stomach hurt with fear. Shivers took his limbs. For a moment he thought of slipping down to the stable and escaping onto the road to find Paisi, going home where they both belonged. But he had given Paisi the only horse easy to reach, and the gate wardens would stop him this time. He was trapped, and all he could hear in the world was the crackle and snap of the fire, while the amulet stayed cold in his fingers.

There was one way to know. There was a thing Gran did, when she needed to foretell for a neighbor or, once, for Lord Crissand, when he came to her cottage at night and in secret.

The Guelesfort was still and hushed, with no one to see him. He could do it: he knew what Gran had done. If Gran wouldn't listen to him by way of the amulet, then the amulet itself might gain her attention . . . if she was all right. There was that dread, dire chance that the dreams hadn't come from Gran. There was the chance they had come from the tower in Henas'amef.

And if that was so, if dreams from that place had reached them, disturbed their sleep and sent Paisi out into danger on the roads, then it was possible he could tell Gran that, and if he did—then Gran would be able to deal with it. Gran would go into town and tell Lord Crissand, was likeliest, who would realize what his mother was up to and put a firm stop to it.

He just had to be quick, and do it now, if he was going to do it, and clean up before he ever heard a stir of servants in the halls.

He needed a string—the cord from a shirt tie served for that. He had the washing bowl. He had clean water from the pitcher. He had oil, from the little bottle they had on the dressing table, for chapped hands and cold-stung faces. He had a candle and a writing quill, which was the feather that would disturb the water.

He hung the amulet from the string, a bond between himself and Gran, so the Seeing would go where he wished. He threaded the feather through a knot in the string and held the string so the tip, hanging down, just touched the oiled water in the bowl. He waited while the draft in the room breathed warmth on the feather, and it trembled as it just touched the water, only slightly disturbing the film of oil.

On that watery surface he looked for his vision, and if he looked at the curls of oil just so he tried to convince himself he could see a fence, and a cottage, and a chimney, that beloved, crooked chimney, perfectly safe.

"Gran?" he said, and his breath disturbed the feather, and made new ripples on the oiled water.

He tried to see her. He tried to see her sleeping—or sick in her bed if that was the case. He tried to make his voice reach her dreams.

"Gran? Paisi is coming home. Paisi is on the road tonight, safe with some traders. We're both well. Oh, Gran, be careful of fires. Be ever so careful. I had a dream that worries me . . ."

He heard a step in the other room. He looked up and saw a shadow between him and the fire: Aewyn's serving-maid, with a tray in her hands.

She saw him. Her hands flew up to her mouth. The whole tray crashed to the floor, in a ruin of pottery.

He seized the cord, took the basin up to try to pretend it was something else. A flood of oiled water slopped out over his arms, down his body, and the maid squeaked and ran back the way she had come, leaving tray and all.

He clutched the amulet fast and took the bowl, to dispose it back on the washstand, his floor awash in spilled water, spilled oil, and spilled porridge.

Aewyn's maid, the one the guards had teased, had been bringing him breakfast.

He tried to mop the oily water off himself. He went to the fire and tried to blot himself dry, but the oil clung, and would stain when it dried, like deadly sin. Word of that sin was running down the halls by now, unstoppable, on the lips of the one servant who was devout Quinalt.

CHAPTER TWO

i

THE WHOLE FAMILY WAS ASSEMBLED, ALONG WITH THE LESSER LORDS AND OF-
ficers who lived in the Guelesfort, down in the lower hall, with all the candles
lit. Some of the lords who had the grand houses about the square had come
in, to walk in the procession with their banner-bearers and their households.
The crowd grew. Still there was no Otter, and Aewyn fretted, standing at the
foot of the grand stairway, positioned so that he could see and signal Otter
the moment he appeared on that stairway.

He had sent the girl with breakfast, to be sure, for one thing, that Otter
didn't oversleep. And he knew above all other things that Otter was shy of
the maids and would have hastened her right out after she delivered it. It had
been a little joke, a prank on Otter and on the maid alike: he knew it would
send a fine blush to Otter's face if he was caught abed, and the maid would
set down the breakfast and run like a deer. But it had a practical reason, too.
One of the men might have lingered, asked for Paisi and asked more questions—so the maid had been the best choice.

But it was the verge of dawn, Otter still hadn't come down, while the
family was all bundled up against the cold and much too hot, standing and
waiting. Everyone was preparing to leave, and it was surely only Otter who
kept his father waiting this long. Aewyn fretted in silence while the lords
talked together in the solemn, irritable way people did on Fast Day. No one
was in a particularly good mood, having been awake an hour or so ago, in
the dark, to get something on their stomachs. Now breakfast and tempers
were wearing thin in the anticipation of a day of no food, no comfort, and
dreary sermons about sin and damnation.

Oh, he wished now that he hadn't been so clever, that he'd just taken
Otter's breakfast down the hall himself and let his servants and guards fuss
about it. The maid was a skittish fool as well as a prude. Everyone knew
that. She was not only scared of men, she was scared of Amefin folk, scared
of everyone who wasn't Guelen. It was even possible she'd never taken the

breakfast there at all and that Otter was still asleep in his bed, with no one to wake him. If that was the case, he swore he would have her beaten.

"Where is he?" his father walked near to ask him.

"I don't know, sire," Aewyn said faintly. "He should have been here. I sent my maid with breakfast, to wake him. Shall I go up and find out?"

"We have to leave now. We have no choice," his father said, vexed, then turned and dispatched one of his own bodyguard upstairs on the spot, with orders to rouse Otter.

No choice. No choice, now, and no Otter with the family, Aewyn thought, as his father waved a hand and set the whole processional moving toward the doors. And it was the worst outcome: his father's men were apt to ask close questions, particularly if they did find Otter abed, and Otter *was* a godless Amefin, in the reckoning of all too many Guelenfolk. This morning was to be Otter's chance, his moment to make his best appearance before all the people, nobles and commons, to be written in the book and quietly mend so many things that had been wrong as long as they had been alive.

It was Otter's chance, and if he didn't come down the stairs in the next few moments, it was worse than a missed chance: it was a disrespect to the Quinaltine and to the family and most of all to their father . . . only the family knew it, of course, at this point, but that meant the family servants and guards knew it, and *that* meant kitchen staff was going to find it out by noon, and half of Guelemara was going to know it by nightfall.

The great doors opened on the dark. Lantern-bearers went downstairs and out first. The snow fell in a fine sleet outside, hazing the lanterns and the torches, as a wave of cold gusted in at them. A priest and two acolytes met them at the doors—doubtless they had been freezing quietly for the last half hour. The priest walked ahead, chanting about sins and atonement and ringing a bell, the acolytes swinging censers, which glowed with inner fire.

The family walked first after that. It was too late, too late, now, for Otter to make his appearance; and with a backward and despairing glance at a vacant stairway, Aewyn fell in with his mother.

Incense could not linger in the wind. It left the censers as fast as it rose, leaving nothing but the faintest impression. That walk down the Processional Way and into the Quinaltine square was even more exposed to the wind, and the steps of the Quinaltine itself had gotten slick and treacherous despite the boys generously sanding the treads. Aewyn stayed close to his mother, who had refused to relinquish Aemaryen to the nurse this morning and was in no cheerful mood.

Inside, the incense was thick in the comparative warmth, the dim sanctuary packed with worshippers who rose to their feet, a thunderous echo as the family walked in. Anyone who might have thought to see Otter with the royal family this morning looked in vain . . . an absence that would signal something in itself. Aewyn walked by his uncle's side, his mother and father walking together down the aisle, with his little sister in his mother's arms. Trumpets sounded, startling the handful of pigeons who always seemed to have found a way to settle on the lofty cornices inside, and the choir broke out in a hymn of repentance and sorrow, while the birds flew about in consternation. In his heart, Aewyn wished he could fly up and sit elsewhere—up in the dark rafters would be nice, where no one had to look at him, but the family was destined for the very front row, up by the railing that seperated the priests from everybody else.

They reached their seats. When the king sat, then the nobles and the commons could sit down. The skittish pigeons flew into the sacred place and out again, and the priests arrayed themselves behind the altar that divided the railing.

His father's bodyguard was always right behind them. So was the Prince's guards, who still attended Efanor, and Guelen guards stood at intervals by the pillars as the Lord Chamberlain and the Lord Marshal of the North reached their seats. The majority of all the seats went to the nobles, the rest to the richest burghers of Guelemara—the poor were obliged to stand out in the dark as the sun came up and the snow came down, for the whole length of the services, while the priests talked about sin and repentance.

Do the poor people get a service, too? he'd asked his father, a year or so ago, and his father had said, No. The sermon is on sin. Rich sinners contribute more. And probably, with the nobles and the burghers, His Holiness has the right audience.

Hush, my lord, his mother had said, looking about at the servants.

And his father: Rich men give power. That's the offering the priests most covet. The boy should learn that. He's of an age to know how the world goes.

The priests shouldn't hear you say it, his mother had said, and his father had said:

See? Power. Power is what they want most. And, mark me, son of mine: they shouldn't get too rich a diet of it.

He was supposed to be meditating on his sins, not on the priests' bad behavior; but there it was: he meditated on that exchange with his father instead, every word of it brought fresh in his memory by present circumstance. He meditated on Otter, and their plot to feed the horses, against the priests' will; and on Otter's absence this morning, which worried him no end, and was probably because Otter, who was shocked that people lied, had decided he didn't want to be lied to when he was as upset as he was about his gran. His father's guard had failed to turn him up; he had heard no late arrival coming in.

He hoped Otter had just gotten upset and hidden away when the search started—Otter would do that: he had no great trust of soldiers. He knew all the hiding places Otter could use, all the secret places he had shown Otter in the Guelesfort, and if Otter was hiding, he would be deeply hidden, where his father's guards, not having spent a childhood in the Guelesfort, would not likely look—or fit into.

The Holy Father got up and talked about sin, sin of thoughts and sin of deeds, sins of omission and sins of commission, in clerkly detail. His Holiness said they had to examine all they did and failed to do, all they thought of doing and all they refrained from doing. It seemed to Aewyn that if they did all that, they'd never budge from where they sat, and he was otherwise inclined. His thoughts were already winging through the Guelesfort, impatient to act the moment they escaped the sanctuary.

Aemaryen began to fret, a thin, plaintive cry. Other babies took to crying, which roused still others, so that it was a wonder the priest could remember what came next. But crying babies led him to talk about lamentations for sins: lamentations, as if babes in arms had committed any sins. End to end of the dome it racketed, unfed babies, unhappy mothers and fathers, fretful two-year-olds, who had to be admonished not to fidget, and toddlers, who only knew they were hungry, too, and kept swinging their feet or squirming.

Aewyn sat and clenched and unclenched his hands, clenched his toes in his boots, bit his lip and counted the rosettes on the railing behind the altar. When he was done with that, he counted the orbs that decorated the screen behind the altar; and then he counted the intersections of bars that screened the choir.

The choir stood up and sang, a high, piercing wail, lamenting the sins of the world. By now every baby in the sanctuary was crying—crying for the sins of the world, the priests said, like the dumb, unfed beasts. His mother spent her service trying to comfort the baby, while his father sat stone-faced and unmoving at this comparison.

And somewhere in the halls of the Guelesfort, themselves missing services, his father's guard kept searching, he supposed, to no avail yet, since they hadn't dragged Otter into services like some escaped felon.

But, oh, gods, he thought then: if they had started looking for Otter, they were likely looking for Paisi, too—and that trail went clear to the town gate and on.

It certainly wasn't the way they'd hoped for their father to find out about Paisi's escape. Otter might think of that, too, and just run for it, being a skittish sort.

Lamentations for sins, and a spate of long, long singing. Aewyn made himself sit still, working his toes to keep his feet from going numb on the chill floor. He lost track of what the Holy Father said, wondering how far Otter could get in three hours, if he had suddenly decided to follow Paisi, and run.

If he had . . . their spring was ruined. Everything was ruined.

If he had . . . maybe he was as far as Esbrook, by now, but not if the snow was still coming down outside. It had been snowing before dawn. But in the shadowy bowels of the Quinaltine there was no way to for him to know now whether the snow had stopped or whether it had come on a blinding blizzard.

Third long lamentation, and a prayer for which they all must stand, even the king and queen. Aewyn stood up in his new boots, working his feet to bring the blood back to his toes. The sanctuary by now smelled of musky incense combined with wet fur, furs that had come in snowy and then, soaked from snowmelt, now overheated. Everyone stank, stank of fur, stank of perfume.

He wanted desperately to be back in the Guelesfort. If he was there, he could find Otter. He knew where to look, and he could talk to Otter and get sense out of him—if he hadn't gone for the gate.

At last, at last, the singing drew down to the final hymn, the one that cursed the Bryalts. Aemaryen had long since exhausted her outrage and dropped off to sleep, one small arm trailing from his mother's arms, and he saw his mother's weary and angry expression, her impatient side-to-side rocking of his little sister. Nurse, who was in the row behind, leaned forward and mutely offered again to take the baby, but his mother doggedly shook her head and kept rocking Aemaryen, her lips grimly set.

He had never taken the service seriously in his life. Now the words embarrassed him, angered him. He accidentally met his mother's eyes. Not that much longer, that expression said. His mother meant to endure the insult for his father's sake; and his father knew, and his father's jaw had a muscle jumping. He realized for the first time how very greatly this annual show upset everyone, how his father himself didn't have the power to prevent the Holy Father doing this; and he told himself that when he was king, he would find a way. He might have to be Quinalt all his life, but he would find a way to get the better of the priests. His sister would have to grow up Bryalt, and leave them, and go to Elwynor to live, none of it her choice, either: that was the way of kings and queens. But they had much happier festivals in Elwynor, the same as in Amefel, and he and Otter would go there and visit his sister when they liked. He would do all of that when he was king.

But when he was king, he would have no father to guide him, and he couldn't at all look forward to that day. So he would be patient, oh, so patient, standing here every year for years and years and years if he had to. He would grow angrier, and angrier, like his father, whose feelings toward the priests and whose occasional blasphemies he began to understand entirely. He would store it all up, for his mother's sake, for his sister, and for Otter, too. He would make himself strong, and clever, like his uncle Efanor, but, unlike Efanor, he would not work with the priests, to manage them, but against them, one and all, head-on and headlong, as his father would say.

Finally, finally, the Holy Father held up his arms, invoked the gods for mercy, and dismissed the congregation.

Thank the gods, he said to himself, not half-reckoning what he was thinking. The royal family at least had the precedence in leaving the sanctuary, and he followed his father and his mother down the aisle, Aemaryen suddenly yelling with might and main.

The great doors opened on a white, snowy morning, and they walked out into the clean, cold air, down the sanded steps, and past the lines of Guelen and Dragon Guard who made a barrier against the general townsfolk. They walked, Aemaryen hiccuping and furious, and kicking, now, so the nurse finally intervened, for decorum's sake. Trumpets blew, and the great iron gates of the Guelesfort swung outward to receive them home again.

All Aewyn was thinking of by now was to slip away from the family and go to Otter's room, by the first, not the grand, stairway. The moment they passed into the warm, close dark of the Guelesfort he dived aside and ran up the stairs the servants used, with his own guard in confused pursuit.

The upper hall had all the candles lit despite the light from the windows. He hurried to the room Otter had, where guards stood.

"Have you found him?" he asked his father's guards.

"No, Your Highness," the answer was. "We're still searching."

"Your Highness," his own guards tried to remonstrate with him, but he ignored their protests and hurried on, then, across the landing for the grand stairs, wickedly racing ahead of his father's procession upward. He dived into his room and met his own servants' startled faces.

"Where is he?" he demanded. "Where is Otter?"

"Your Highness." Captys, senior of his servants, was there. Two others were. And Captys was clearly distraught.

"Where is Otter?"

"Your Highness, the maid, Madelys, saw him at witchcraft, and when—"

His heart turned over on that word. "Who said? Who said so? Madelys?" The girl hovered in the doorway beyond, knotting and unknotting her apron. "Fool! Where is he?"

"He seems to have vanished, Your Highness," Captys said.

"Useless!" It was what his father would say, when he was at his wits' end with the servants. "Stay here, the lot of you! You, too," he added, stabbing a gesture at his guards. "Stay here and tell my father that *I* shall find him."

"Witchery!" Madelys cried. "Your Highness, you might put yourself in danger!"

"I want *her* gone before I get back! Banished from these rooms, forever!"

"Your Highness!" Madelys wailed.

"Fool, I say!"

"No, Your Highness, I saw it! He had the water and the feather and a charm, and he was at it, plain as plain!"

"And you know so much about witchcraft I should be suspicious? Go down to the kitchens, and do not you say any word of gossip, girl, not one, on your life! Count it lucky I don't send you to the Guard kitchens! Damn it!"

He spun on his heel and stalked to the door, and out it, with one furious look at his senior guardsman, Selmyn, who attempted to follow. "My orders!" he said. "Carry them out!"

With that, he slammed the door and ran, ran, ignoring his father's party, which was just going in the doors: little Aemaryen, starving, sleepy, and furious, made noise enough to cover any commotion. He ran right past them for the servants' stairs, up and up, past even the level where the storerooms were, and where his father's men always searched if he was missing.

Upstairs, however, farther upstairs—one apparently useless little set of steps in the high end of the endmost workroom, if one got up on the counter, and above, there was a little trapdoor, an access to the eaves. He had shown it to Otter, the two of them up in the very highest part of the Guelesfort, looking out the littlest windows of all and watching people come and go in the yard, while they ate stolen sweets.

He had no candle, this time. He stopped still, standing right over at the opening of the trap, knowing by memory what was next, which was a lot of beams, but if he went farther, he would be utterly blind in the dark, with only the dim light from below to mark where the trapdoor was. If it were to be shut, it might take searching on hands and knees to find it again.

And Otter, if he was here, had shut it.

"Otter!" he called out, fearful to go too much farther without a light. "Otter, it's Aewyn! Where are you?"

ii

"AEWYN WILL FIND HIM," CEFWYN MUTTERED, HAVING SEEN HIS SON RUNNING in the hall and knowing very well what he was about, given the report from the guards. "If he's not away out the gates. Damn that girl!"

Ninévrisë set a hand on his shoulder. She had stayed by him. Efanor was elsewhere in the hall, tracking precisely where and to whom the maid had already prattled her tale of witchcraft and trying to forestall a priestly inquiry.

"The court will not have truly expected his appearance," Ninévrisë said.

"They had rumors of it. And not a sign of him, nor Paisi, either. If they're anywhere, they're in the loft. Why doesn't the Guard ever search the damned loft? We hid up there, in our day, there and the stables, but no one ever searches the loft."

It was close quarters up there for a man without armor, let alone a guard in full kit, that was one reason. The juniormost servants had to perform that search, if needed—now and again an investigation went into that precinct. But it was a maze of timbers and nooks, and one boy determined to burrow deep into the eaves would not be found until he grew desperate from thirst.

And damn Otter for a fool—damn the circumstances that had sent a hare-witted girl to his rooms to spy on him. And where in the gods' own name was Paisi?

Things had gone wrong, and gone wrong at several points, and it was not only the serving girl who fretted about magic. The king of Ylesuin had attempted to slip his sorcery-gotten son into respectable notice at court, attempted to gather up all the misdeeds and tag ends of his misspent youth and to do justice by those who hadn't had it. Most of all he had tried to ignore the old connections, thinking he could just ease the whole untidy situation past the jagged edges of old magic, Sihhë magic, and Tarien Aswydd's outright curse.

He wished, not for the first time, that Tristen had heeded his invitations and come to visit. He wished that, well before this day, he had risked the notoriety of the deed and ridden into the west himself, to visit his old friend. "Help me," he might have said, had he had the chance to plan this visit for himself.

You left me this boy. You advised me to treat him kindly and do justice by him.

Now look. Now look, my old friend. He can't come to the Quinaltine. He more than will not: there's been this maid, this silly maid, it turns out, who spied the young fool doing what his Gran doubtless honestly taught him, and runs gibbering the news through all the Guelesfort.

And who sent the maid?

My youngest son did, Aewyn, who meant the boy no harm, no harm at all. I'm sure of that, among other things far less certain.

Are you aware what's happened here, my old friend? I fear this is not just bad luck. It can never do so much damage and be nothing more than bad luck, can it?

But you told me once that luck was a sort of magic in itself, did you not? Or the workings of magic, was it?

Well, luck has run completely against the boy you bade me preserve, when it involves the Quinaltine. You told me yourself there was ill in that place, grievous ill, and old harm. Efanor confirmed it. And was it only my desire to be ahead of the priests and the gossip that made me force the boy into this appearance?

I mislike what I've done. I mislike greatly what has happened here, old friend. Be careful, you said. And was I careful enough, in my haste to see this through?

Clearly not so. Not nearly careful enough.

"My love?" Ninévrisë said, in his long silence.

"Do you perceive anything untoward?" he asked. The wizard-gift was in Ninévrisë, from her father and his fathers before him. Perhaps he should tell her about the writing there in the frost. He knew he was blind and deaf to such stirrings in the world, deaf as a stone; but something for good or for ill made him reticent, and her son, her son, Aewyn, who had always seemed as blind and deaf as his father—where was he, this morning, after fidgeting his way through services?

Their Aewyn had become as slippery as Otter, and sped off on the hunt without a word to his parents, bent on solving matters himself.

A father was the point the boys shared, the blind and deaf heritage. He had always assumed his blond, bluff son was like him; that if there was any witchery to turn up in his children, small, dark Aemaryen would have that perilous gift, and fair, tall Aewyn would be as deaf as his father.

"Otter is afraid," Ninévrisë said softly. "Be forgiving of him."

Another woman might take satisfaction in a rival's child's difficulty. Not Ninévrisë. Another woman might have been blind to the risks in the boy coming here, and equally those in his never coming here at all. Not Ninévrisë. She knew what was at issue and where it began.

He laid his hand on hers, where it rested on his shoulder. "Forgiving is all I can be. He is what he is, and I brought him here on Tristen's advice."

"None better," Ninévrisë said. "And I will warrant the boy conjured nothing." A little contraction of her fingers against his shoulder. "Whatever he did, did not pass the wards. I would feel it if he had."

"Good for that," he said, watching the snow fall and hoping he didn't have a son out on the roads at this moment.

"Your Majesty." The Lord Chamberlain himself entered the room. "His Highness Prince Aewyn, with Otter."

Oh, indeed? That quickly?

He turned a serene countenance toward his staff, slipping Ninévrisë's hand to his arm.

"Admit them."

Bows, courtesies, ceremonies of approach and departure delayed everything in his life, and never the ones he wanted delayed. The Lord Chamberlain, an old, old man, went out to the foyer, doors opened, doors closed, opened again, and Aewyn finally came through them with Otter in tow, Otter wrapped in Aewyn's cloak, the one puzzle in the sight, and Aewyn and Otter both a little cobwebby about the shoulders, which was no puzzle at all.

"He didn't mean to," Aewyn began, the immemorial beginning of excuses.

"One is very sure," Cefwyn said.

"It was that fool Madelys, my serving-maid," Aewyn said. "I sent her with breakfast, before the hour, and she screamed and Otter spilled oil all over himself, and he'd ruined his clothes. Paisi's in Amefel."

Now there was a model of concise reporting.

"Paisi's in Amefel, you say."

"He was worried about Gran, Your Majesty," Otter said faintly, "with the weather, and all."

"So I was going to have my staff look after him," Aewyn said, with no space for a breath between them, "and see he had breakfast, but that fool maid walked in without a sound and thought she saw what she didn't see."

"Was there magic?" Ninévrisë asked, dropping her hand from Cefwyn's arm. "Otter, tell the truth."

"I tried, Your Majesty," Otter said in the very faintest of voices. "I'm very sorry."

"Why would Paisi go home?" Cefwyn asked.

"A dream, Your Majesty," Otter said in anguish. "I had a dream. So did Paisi. So I told him he had to go."

"When was this?"

"Yesterday."

A full day on the road, in this weather. Fool boy, Cefwyn thought, hoping Paisi was not frozen in a snowbank somewhere along the road. He made a little wave of his hand. "Let us see. Let us see the damage. Unwrap the cloak, if you please."

Otter had clutched it tightly about him. The boots were not auspicious. He opened the garment, and showed a wreckage of good tailoring, from oil to attic cobwebs and dust, head to foot.

"Oh, dear," Ninévrisë said.

Otter looked as if he wished he could sink through the floor.

"It's not his fault!" Aewyn said.

"No, now, be still. Let Otter answer for himself. Paisi left yesterday, alone, one presumes."

"Yes, Your Majesty. Well . . . not alone. I sent him with some traders."

Cefwyn raised a brow. There had been a certain resourcefulness in the plot. There was a likelihood Paisi would get through.

"And being without wiser counsel, you took to witchcraft to see his progress? Or was there more to it?"

"I dreamed again. But I don't know who Sent it."

"A very prudent thought," Ninévrisë said, with a look at Cefwyn. "Paisi's gran might have Sent to him: there is that special connection. But Sending past all protections? I never felt it."

Wizardry had passed the wards no less than Tristen Sihhë had laid about the Guelesfort windows . . . there was a troubling thought. An ordinary mouse could have made a new hole, a way into the walls, who knew? Ninévrisë saw to such things, quietly, in her own way, but there were ways to make a breach.

And there was—he never forgot it—one ready source of bad dreams in Amefel.

"So you sent Paisi away," Cefwyn said deliberately, in the tone with which he daunted councillors. "And told no one."

"He told me," his younger son said.

"So you joined this conspiracy."

"Paisi was already gone," Aewyn protested, "and he wanted to tell you, but there was the dinner, and uncle was there, and he had no chance to, because of how he knew, and the servants coming and going; and he was going to tell you after services today, but the fool maid ruined everything."

"Indeed. And where is the fool maid at this moment?"

"I sent her to the kitchens and told her not to talk to anyone."

"In the kitchens, not to talk. Gods save us, boy!"

"I threatened her life," Aewyn said.

"Of course," Cefwyn said, ignoring Aewyn's protestations, and looked straight into Otter's eyes. "A problem broadening by the hour. Do you understand that?"

"I am the only one to blame, Your Majesty."

No excuses, no temporizing. And, alas, no ready excuse that would cover it. The pale gray eyes that damned the boy in the observation of honest Guelenfolk stared back at him, incontrovertible heritage.

"Don't use magic," he said bluntly. "Am I asking a bird not to fly?"

"No, Your Majesty," the boy said, and in the silence he left for further comment: "I didn't want to use it. I won't use it. I won't, again, Your Majesty."

A damned cold word, that. *Father* might have carried more intimacy, but the boy had never used that word to him. The exchanges between himself and his own father had been that remote; the tone recalled that fact with an unpleasant chill about the heart, remembering where that bond had ended.

"Well, well, we have to repair the damage as best we can. Tomorrow, dress in your second-best, that's the way of it. More clothes are coming."

A hesitation. "There's a stain on it, Your Majesty."

"Gods save us, dress in your third-best tomorrow and walk with us. We shall find you staff—who will not, hereafter, see you practicing witchcraft, if you please."

"No, Your Majesty. Witchcraft, that is."

"You're confusing the boy," Ninévrisë said, holding out her hand. "Otter. Elfwyn. Lad. Come. You shall have servants, if you please, and you shall walk with us in the morning to the services, if you will, and mend things with the Quinalt, the gods willing. Here. Give me your hand."

Ever so gingerly Otter gave his hand, and Ninévrisë took it, kindly drew him close. "Don't ever fear to approach your father, or me. It was a mistake, is all, a simple mistake, was it not? Your father will send men to Amefel to be sure Paisi is safe—will you not, my lord?"

Cefwyn cleared his throat. He had not yet thought of it, but it was the sensible thing to do.

"Bryalt as I am," Ninévrisë said. "At least say that you are. Unaccustomed to Quinalt holidays, are you, lad? You shall have one of my candles: it smells of evergreen. You may light it in private, and no one will dare say witchcraft, only so you don't do it in the halls. And you shall have holiday cake, after Fast Day is over. I shall send you some spiced cake, with honey, just the same as in Amefel, even if it is a little early in the season."

Were there tears on those lashes? "Thank you, Your Majesty."

"And I shall have my own servants look in on you in your quarters, and draw your bath, honest Bryalt folk who won't take alarm at a holiday candle."

The voice grew fainter still. "Thank you ever so much, Your Majesty."

"You could indeed have reported the dream to me or to your father, you know. You could have told it within this chamber, and even within our servants' hearing."

"And within Efanor's," Cefwyn muttered. "There's no doing in Amefel that will affright any of this household. Be sure of that."

"Yes, Your Majesty." The barest whisper.

"So Paisi left for Amefel," Cefwyn said. "Afoot?"

A little hesitation. A look of dread. "On my horse, sir. We couldn't get to Paisi's. But Paisi will take good care of him. And Feiny went in all his gear."

An interesting notion. "If he isn't hanged for a horse thief, clever lad."

"My lord," Ninévrisë chided him.

"Well, he should have come to us early," Cefwyn said. "Have I ever done anything but good to your gran? Could you doubt I would send someone to inquire?"

"It was just a dream, Your Majesty."

"Adequate to send Paisi out in the snow."

"But if I did say, and you sent your guard, and they came to her door, Gran would never tell the truth, not if soldiers came asking after her. We cut all the wood we thought she might need, but this storm's been going for days. She needs Paisi; she really needed him from the start, but she insisted on sending him with me. She's all alone, now, and we had the dream, and she can't haul the wood in if she's sick."

"Do you believe she is ill?"

"We both dreamed it, that she was sick."

Otter's behavior encompassed a wide maze of young thinking and young solutions, and with it, a fair amount of adult enterprise, slipping a highbred horse out of the stables, down the hill, and out the city gates in full kit. In the scales of magic active and passive, it was worth noting that after two days, there never yet had been a report the horse was missing, none yet that Paisi's absence forecast Otter's adventure in the Guelesfort rooftrees. No less than the Dragon Guard, skilled at uncovering miscreants of every sort, had been turning the Guelesfort upside down for hours without discovering either fact, let alone sending a boy into the heights.

Slippery and clever: that was one troubling attribute; and as glumly unexpressive toward his king as a habitual felon toward a familiar judge: the one might be a useful skill, even a princely one, but the other would not serve at all, not unless the boy found employment as a bailiff or a town magistrate.

"Well," Cefwyn said, trying to provoke a happy spark in those gray eyes, "well, take care hereafter. And pray be caught by the servants in some Quinalt rite and stand with the family tomorrow dawn in services. If there arises any question you have observed the Fast—you have observed the Fast, have you not?"

"Yes, sire."

"Well, well, much to the good. We'll have a priest to declare it, and record your name—your true name, Elfwyn—in the Festival Record tomorrow."

Otter brushed—uselessly—at his cobwebby, greasy finery, as if that could erase the oil. "Yes, Your Majesty."

"And there remains the welfare of that rascal Paisi now as well as your honest gran. I shall send men down the road to be sure he got there and see that your gran receives all necessary attentions and supplies, without asking if she needs them."

"Thank you, sire." Gratitude shone out of those gray eyes, utterly clear and bright, lightening all about him for the moment it lived.

"Well, well, get on with you." He gave a wave of his hand, dismissing the boys. A dark presence had come in by the door and deserved immediate attention. "Do as you please until morning. Then, gods save you, be on time in the morning! Nevris, I have a message waiting, doubtless. Your patience."

"I'll see the boys to the hall," Ninévrisë said, understanding, and pressed his hand and swept the boys and the commotion out, doubtless to direct her maids to take certain action. A maid swept a candle and an evergreen bough from the mantel, then hurried off in a flurry of skirts.

He, himself had business with the shadow that, after due courtesy to the departing queen, had reappeared in his doorway.

iii

"WELL, MASTER CROW?" CEFWYN SAID, AND THE SHADOW, A MAN ALL IN BLACK whose appropriate name was Idrys, entered the room. Lord Commander of the Dragon Guard, Idrys was, and in no happy mood—but that might be due to arriving from a long ride on Fast Day noon: no food, no drink to be had, and hours yet to wait for both.

Idrys gave a cursory nod, a weary nod, and sank into a chair. He had that privilege, in private as they were, and Cefwyn took the seat opposite.

"Lord Piram is buried, the old scoundrel," Idrys reported. "With appropriate honors. And his nephew has overcome the son to take the lordship. The will was oddly found to confirm it—subject, of course, to royal approval."

Never ask how that happened. But the son was feckless and a bully, the nephew worthy. At times Crow's attendance on a scene improved matters immensely.

"I cannot offer you drink today, alas."

Idrys shrugged, long-faced.

"I have, however, a mission, which you may undertake yourself, or commit to a man you favor."

Eyebrow lifted.

"A mission of mercy, as is. Young Otter has had a vision. His man Paisi has gone haring off to Amefel to see to his gran's safety—never ask why the boy became uneasy; but Paisi took a good horse and left. Search for Paisi along the road and make sure he gets to Amefel safely. In any case, the old woman is to have the best of care."

"I'm to go chasing after the servant in a blizzard?" Idrys frowned, weary and out of sorts. "And this is my great benefice?"

"Yes, after the servant, Crow. Tristen set him to his post, so far more than a servant, and one I would not have missing in a snowbank, thank you. Nor would I see harm come to the old woman, with *her* connections. He's taken my son's horse, and he's had two days' start."

"A horse thief, to boot. Do you hint I should go personally, or shall I indeed send a man?"

"Use your discretion. I am uneasy about this. I cannot define why, but it seems remarkable to me that Otter's conspiracy could steal a highbred horse, escape the gate, and elude all detection for two days by the best of your men."

The eyebrow rose a second time, and stayed. Master Crow understood such things, and knew that a run of luck where Aswydds or Sihhë blood might be involved was worth a closer look. He had fought in Elwynor and seen what he had seen.

"They'll be coming to holidays in the west," Cefwyn added slyly, "by the time your man could reach Amefel. There is the benefice."

"The boy is here. Consequently I worry for things here, my lord king. I'll send a man."

"Cakes and ale," Cefwyn said wickedly.

"They can be had here, today." A man on Fast Day was not even supposed to entertain such thoughts. "A little removed from the heart of noble sanctity."

"Blasphemy."

"Yet the boy stayed behind and sent his man to Amefel. Duty to his sovereign, do you think, m'lord king? Filial affection? Ambition?"

"Or friendship."

Idrys' lips pursed, thoughts held silent on a pairing that had been Lord Tristen's advice, the Prince and the bastard son. Idrys had made clear his personal doubts about this pairing, long, long ago.

"Friendship, I say, Crow."

"Be it so, my lord king. Be they the most devoted of friends. But there are things I should look into."

"The lad is slippery as the otter he's named for. That we have seen. And, granted, I by no means like this claim of visions. But I do not think the source of ill resides in the boy. Not in him, nor even in Gran, if you take my meaning. Another reason to have a good man in Amefel."

"Certainly things someone should look into," Idrys said. "Or askance at, granted either man gets to Henas'amef through this weather. Questions my man should ask directly at the source, by your leave."

Lady Tarien sat imprisoned in the Zeide tower, in Henas'amef.

"Have him ask them. His mother is not likely pleased with her son's being in Guelemara. But that she could get past Paisi's grandmother, with Tristen's seal on her imprisonment . . . and again past wards here, that I would not expect."

"Whence came the amulet in question?" Idrys asked.

His turn to raise an eyebrow. The snow on Idrys had scarcely melted, and he had gathered up the essentials of the scandal since his return. No one had mentioned amulets.

"One assumes . . . from the grandmother."

"And the urge to deception?" Idrys asks. "From which side of the blanket came that gift?"

Master Crow had his ways, and annoyed him with impunity.

But Lady Tarien's involvement in this was likely. If indeed an unhappy Lady Tarien down in Henas'amef had mustered both the will and the strength to make trouble, and found in a solitary old woman a boy's vulnerability in which to do it . . . then the boy himself was, as Tristen would call it, a gateway within the Guelesfort, warded and guarded by the grandmother, it might be, but locks could be picked, with patience and skill.

"The boy has ample reason to be worried," Cefwyn said. "And so have we—not least am I concerned about the grandmother. If she should pass from the world, young Otter is bereft; and I am not the one to deal with his less common abilities. He dreamed, do you hear, Crow? He dreamed. His man dreamed the same dream. He has the Sight, and he is no kin to Gran. That fact has come out, and will be whispered about in the kitchens."

"No mystery whence the Sight came. He is half-Aswydd. But, alas, you would not be rid of him."

"And Tristen, again, hear me, Crow, said take him in! Read me no sermons. Go or send to Henas'amef, and advise Crissand to watch his prisoner particularly closely this season."

"Perhaps a poisoned cup? There would be a certain justice."

"Lord Tristen advised against it," he said, and it came to him when he said it that death, with wizards, was not always a guarantee. He had never thought of that, not in all these years, but a little chill went over his skin now, a confirmation.

"Well, I shall get to it." Crow rose, bowed, a slight parting courtesy. "My lord king."

Loosing Idrys was like loosing an arrow from the bow. Best give him a target and aim him carefully, or the wrong man could die, or the wrong events launch themselves irrevocably—not foolishly, but not always what one wanted.

"Tarien," Cefwyn said, before Idrys could reach the door, "is not to be harmed or coerced. Nor is Paisi."

"My lord king." A second bow, a look as blithe and innocent as a black-hearted Crow could muster. "My man will carry your message faithfully. Have I ever failed you?"

iv

"SEE?" AEWYN SAID, PERCHED ON OTTER'S BED, WHILE THE SERVANTS WERE busy cleaning and brushing his clothes and the royal bodyguards stood uselessly by the door. "He was not so angry as all that. And did I not say Mother would take your part?"

"She was very kind," Otter said faintly.

"So be cheerful! All you have to do to make everything right is attend tomorrow morning and the next three days as if nothing has happened at all. The servants will clean your cloak. The tailor will have clothes ready tomorrow. And you have your own holiday candle. We can burn it on First Night of the Bryalt festival, the same as Mother does."

"It does smell of evergreen."

"Some of evergreen, some of bayberry. And I'll wager Mother sends you more cakes on the night, too."

"Was the king too angry?"

"He fretted. He scowled all through services. He was worried, mostly. I feared you had had another dream and run off after Paisi. Papa didn't know what I knew. But I thought if you were still here and hidden, I might find you upstairs, in the hiding holes, where I did find you. Whatever *were* you doing with a bowl of water that scared that goose of a maid?"

Otter put his hands behind him and his head down—sulking, or at least he had that look. One never could be sure in Otter's dark moods, when, like his namesake, he dived below the surface of his thoughts and not even the most persistent questioning could find him.

"Looking in the water," Otter said.

It wasn't at all an informative answer. Aewyn waited. Then Otter said:

"I miss Paisi. And I do worry about Gran."

"Well, Captys can stay here tonight," Aewyn said. Captys was his own chief servant. "You like him."

"I suppose so. But I don't truly need him."

"Well, you certainly need someone. Or you can stay in my quarters until Paisi comes back! Father didn't forbid it, did he?"

The spark showed in Otter's eye, then faded. "No. No, I shan't cause any more trouble. And I daren't have you caught in it."

"Me?"

"The girl ran. I have a sorceress for a mother and a witch for my gran. Everybody already thinks what they think, and I never want them to think ill of you. That would be the worst thing."

"Well, let them try to do anything! You shouldn't be afraid."

"They burned Bryalt folk here."

"They never did."

"They burned your mother's priest. Paisi told me."

Aewyn was taken aback. He never had heard that, but Paisi had never told an untruth, either. It must have happened before he was born, in the trouble in those years. "Well, a good many things happened before us. They never will do it again. Father won't let them."

"Maybe not. But people here hate witches. Quinalt priests do."

"You're not a witch."

"Wizard. Men are wizards. Women are—"

"Well, I wish you were. My father's favorite tutor was a wizard, for what it matters. Emuin Udaman was a Teranthine, and Teranthines can be wizards, just like Bryaltines can be, with their priests saying not a thing about it, so there you are!" Aewyn swung his feet. "Father says if he could find another Teranthine, *he'd* be my tutor and I'd learn some sense. I almost remember Emuin. I think he should look again."

Otter gave a grudging laugh, finally.

Aewyn asked: "So what were you truly doing with the water and the charm?"

"I was trying to see Gran, or Paisi. But I failed."

That was disappointing. "I wish you *could* do magic."

"Wizardry. Magic is born in you."

"Well, whatever it is, I wish you had it. I wish you could show me. I should like to see it."

Otter looked about them. The servants were all in the other room, and it had been a foolish thing to say, Aewyn knew it: but there, it was said.

"I wish I could," Otter said. "It was the first time I ever really, truly tried, and it was no good."

"But you had the dream."

"I dreamed, but that was none of my doing, the dreaming, I mean. It would be a Sending. And we shouldn't at all be talking about this."

"Well, it is all nonsense, is it not?" The candle still sat on the table, where Otter had set it down. Aewyn slid off the bed and went and set it on the mantel instead, amid its evergreen bough. "See? Now we shall have a proper holiday, just like in Amefel and Elwynor. Change your mind and stay in my rooms!"

"I think I should stay here. I have trouble enough. And you should let the queen send her servants. Keep Captys. Thank you—thank you for rescuing me."

"Piffle." That was what his mother said to nonsense. "Piffle. I'm going back to my rooms, I suppose. But come after dark. Then we can have supper. Right after services tomorrow we can eat, and you can come to my rooms for supper then, too, do you agree?"

That drew a brighter look, a hungry look. Otter nodded yes, and Aewyn winked—his father's wink—before he walked into the other room and gathered his servants.

V

THE WORLD SEEMED MUCH BETTER IN OTTER'S EYES: HE HAD THE KING'S FORgiveness, his brother's invitation to supper tonight, the noon meal, and supper tomorrow, and the promise of the queen's servants' help if only he could keep out of trouble.

His brother had taken away his own servants and the guards. The rooms were neater than Paisi had ever made them, and he would like a bath. Baths were a luxury he had gotten to love, with all the chill of winter outside the windows and creeping into the stones, and, filthy as he was, he longed to be clean. There was the way they did it at Gran's in the winter, a matter of soaking towels in hot water and scrubbing off; which was its own sort of comfort to wind-raw hands and cold-numbed feet, and he began to heat water in the bedwarmer to do just that.

He wondered how Paisi fared tonight: he would be well along to the river crossing by now, and he hoped Paisi was toasting his feet by a good fireside, with no constraints of fasting or praying in the merchants' company. He had thought a great deal about Paisi, and how he could join him, during his hours of hiding in the drafty heights. He had been so chilled and hungry he had thought he would never be warm or fed again.

But the king forgave him. No one even seemed that angry. And the queen . . .

He visited the candle while the water heated. He smelled its green scent but did not touch it: it had a tingling about it, a magical feeling that whispered of forces, kindly forces, he thought . . . but forces, all the same, and a power that was neither Gran's nor yet his own mother's, and he was sure that if it were lit, the fire would loose those things around him. He was grateful to the queen, but he dared not be ready to loose a force he didn't wholly know and let it have its way in his room. Gran and his mother alike had made him cautious in such regards, and Gran's sort of witchcraft had gone amiss this morning, whether it was his fault or the Quinalt's. He was not ready to try another pass at it.

Besides, the scent reminded him of home and weakened him, which was a spell unto itself; and had a power in its very nature. He felt it. And the queen was Ninévrisë Syrillas, of the old blood, the Sihhë blood, from long ago, like his mother's Gift, though light and not dark. And Gran had warned him, had she not?

Ye respect the queen, young lad, ye respect that great lady. The Sight is in her, no question, like in her da, him under the hill in Amefel, an' don't ye e'er doubt it.

He gave a little shiver, as if a draft had touched him.

Or a door had opened.

It had. His heart jumped, as he found Efanor standing in his front room, Prince Efanor, accompanied by a priest in black robes.

"Your Highness," Otter murmured, and achieved a small bow, trying to gather his wits in the process. And to the priest, respectfully, with another bow: "Sir."

"Well, Otter," Efanor said quietly. "You certainly had a cold, dusty day."

"Yes, Your Highness." Perhaps the king or the Prince might have disapproved of Aewyn's visiting here, after his misdeeds—or perhaps Efanor's forgiveness would not come as easily as his father had led him to believe. Perhaps they had come to punish him, after all.

"Sending your man away was one thing," Efanor said, "and whether that was wisely done or not remains to be known; but pretending otherwise, Otter, and deceiving your father and attempting matters which ought not to be undertaken here—by such small gaps in judgment other forces find their way where they ought not, getting into places where otherwise they cannot come. Have you any least notion what we tell you?"

"That I was a fool, Your Highness." Efanor was the most scholarly Quinalt of anyone he had met, except the priests, and while much that Efanor said racketed through his hearing and never stuck at all, he had the one matter clear, that there was fault, and it was his, and that what he had done was dangerous in ways beyond his understanding.

"Well, well," Efanor said, "you were that. And it was a boy's fault, not to be repeated. Loneliness at holidays brings dark thoughts, which we simply shall not allow. The true story will go abroad, that illness in your gran's house detained you this morning—that is the truth, is it not?"

It was, when he looked at it that way, a certain version of the truth. "Yes, Your Highness."

"Well, and hereafter you will not be alone. Brother Trassin will attend your needs, whatever they be, until your man finds his way back again, as I trust he will. Will he not?"

"He will, Your Highness." He was distracted, casting an apprehensive glance at the man in priestly black. This was a dour-faced and solemn man, his hands tucked up into his sleeves: Quinalt, very surely Quinalt—though a monk, by the title, and not quite a priest.

Still a spy, Paisi would say. A sneak and a spy set here to catch a boy doing what he ought not, and what word of protest would priests believe if this man reported mischief of any kind?

"Come." Efanor walked into Otter's bedroom, and to the white-frosted window. There, having beckoned him near, Efanor set a hand on his shoulder and looked straight into his eyes at close range. "This man is a servant of the Patriarch, and will search and spy to prove there is no harm. You understand me. Have you anything you ought not to have in these rooms?"

"Gran's amulet." He pressed his hand against his chest, where, since this morning, it rested beneath his clothes.

"Give it to me, for the while."

He was reluctant, but dared not refuse. He reached into his collar and drew it out, warm from his body, warm with Gran's protection. Burning cold flowed toward him from the window the while, chill enough to sting.

"Good lad." Efanor pressed something else into his hand, another warm object, on a chain. "Whatever gift comes in love is potent," Efanor said, "against all manner of ills. Keep this close tonight and tomorrow, wear it openly, do well, and by Festival end, this man will be gone from your premises with a good report for the Patriarch himself—a costly favor I ask you, understand; a penance for you, one that will pay for your indiscretion." Again the intimate touch of Efanor's hand, but a calming one, a peaceful one on his shoulder.

It was a Quinalt sigil in his hand. It had no liveliness such as Gran's coins had. But he obediently slipped the chain over his head and let it rest in plain sight, while his heart thumped away in fear.

"Good, good," Efanor said. "There's good sense there. Endure the brother. A necessary matter."

"Yes, sir," he whispered, and Efanor went away.

"Why is there an empty bedwarmer in the fireplace?" Brother Trassin asked.

It had boiled dry. "I would like a bath, sir," he said. "Will you arrange one?"

Trassin frowned but went and did that. Water arrived, hot water and cold, and he did bathe, letting Brother Trassin see the Quinalt sigil, but he did not want the brother in the little bath while he was bathing. He wrapped in towels, dried his hair with them, and hung things neatly. The clothes—he hardly knew what to do with. He hung them up, too, in the bath, and dressed in his most ordinary clothing.

"I need my clothes cleaned, sir," he said to Brother Trassin, and Brother Trassin, instead of taking them himself, went and called servants to do that, standing by in great disapproval until the dirty clothes and the towels disappeared.

"Were other clothes to come?" he asked.

"I have no idea," Trassin said, paying him no m'lord and no courtesy. He simply stood in the room, arms in his sleeves, the Quinalt sigil prominent on his breast, and that was that.

Brother Trassin stayed, no fount of conversation or pleasantry, and while he sat in his bedroom pretending to read, Brother Trassin pretended to clean the place again, opening all the cupboards and drawers and looking into everything in the process. Brother Trassin spoke never a voluntary word to him, except to give him certain long, long looks, as if he expected him to turn into a rat or a snake on the spot.

In those moments he felt very uncomfortable. Efanor had given him the other sigil he was wearing, a reminder that the Prince himself had contrived this and set a protection on him, perhaps for his father's sake, or Aewyn's.

Trassin continued his cleaning in the room where he sat. The queen's candle drew another such look from Brother Trassin, and a sniff. The man went his way then into the bath, into more nooks and crannies.

Otter went on pretending to read until the light failed in the window, and Brother Trassin fed the fire in the other room until that light was brighter.

"We may break our fast now," the lay brother pronounced, the only thing he had said, all day. "Shall I send down to the kitchens?"

"Do," he said, as he would have said to Paisi—though Paisi would have gone down himself, and so far as he knew, there was no one for Brother Trassin to send. But he remembered with great relief that he himself had somewhere to go. "For yourself only, sir. I'm bidden to the Prince's table tonight."

"Then I shall conduct you there," the monk said, and did just that—not lingering with Prince Aewyn's staff when they arrived. Trassin departed farther down the hall, on his way to the kitchens, or to report to someone, Otter had no notion which. He was greatly relieved to find himself on the other side of the doors, in Aewyn's receiving room, which smelled of a savory meal laid out.

"Ha! Just in time!" Aewyn called out, arriving in the other doorway, and came and flung an arm about him. "On time and hungry, are we?"

He took it for a reprimand and found nothing to say. He was in a glum humor. But Aewyn shook him in a friendly way and drew him toward the laden table—feast, as the long day had been famine—and poured a cup of watered wine. "Here, for a thirst as great as mine! I waited for you faithfully."

"You needn't have done that."

"Of course I needn't, I needn't *anything*, but I wanted to. How is the spy?"

The wine caught in his throat.

"Brother Trassin?"

"He's clearly the Patriarch's spy," Aewyn said, "the nasty old man."

Otter looked left and right, to see which of the servants was in earshot. "Don't say so."

"Oh, nonsense. Uncle knows exactly what he is, and His Holiness sent him over here after the rumor reached him. Papa doesn't like the fellow. He was *my* tutor for six whole weeks before Uncle found out he was the Patriarch's man, taking notes. He was the most boring tutor ever anyway. All catechism. He loves to read lists. Probably he's making one, in your rooms."

It was not encouraging to hear. "Lists of what?"

"Oh, horrid charms and things. Which you don't have."

"No. Your uncle took it."

"*Your* uncle, too. His Grace is not partial to Brother Trassin, I do assure you. Far from it. If he can get him in trouble, he'll be ever so happy. Cheer up. Have some pie. It's a wonderful meat pie."

It was, crusty brown and full of gravy. They sat down at table and everything seemed redeemed. Wiser, older heads had patched all the harm, and peace would prevail, if only he could do the things he should do in the morning and pass the next few days without fault.

"And when Festival ends," Aewyn said, "after all this is over and the to-do is done, then we shall have our hunting trip, even if your man stays on for festival in Amefel. We shall have my guards, my servants, so there's no fuss at all about your man being away. We can hunt rabbits." Aewyn popped a sweet into his mouth. "I can cook. Papa taught me how to cook on a campfire. I can at least do simple things. And we can bring most everything we need. Lots of blankets. It's quite cold out there."

The lodge seemed a sort of unachievable dream after this scrape. Otter could hardly believe the king would let them go off together to the country with no authority to keep them out of mischief. He kept his opinion to himself, however. If Aewyn was happy imagining the lodge and its wonders, and them turned out free to do as they pleased, then he was happy to agree.

And increasingly, he had no desire to go off somewhere until Paisi could send him news of Gran—good news. It must surely be good news, he told himself. Enough bad had happened, and now, this evening, and with a full stomach, his fortunes seemed to have changed.

vi

THE JUNIORMOST OF AEWYN'S GUARD WALKED OTTER DOWN THE LONG HALL TO his own rooms when Aewyn went to bed, and he was glad of the company. By that time the hall was on its fewest lights, and the shadows were deep and cold. He let himself in, saw his own fire banked for the night, and started violently when he heard a cough from the little side room, on his right hand, that room Paisi had never used.

Brother Trassin declined to stir forth, and he declined to summon him, only padded quietly past the fire and into his own chill and lonely bedroom to undress himself.

Paisi would have had a last log on the fire, would have warmed the bedclothes, would have shared his own warmth against the bitter chill, but he was satisfied enough to have Brother Trassin abed and invisible and by no means in the same bed with him.

The woodpile was greatly diminished. Paisi would have brought more wood up, with his own hands, without Otter's ever suggesting it.

This priest hadn't.

And clothes had, indeed, arrived; he saw that when he hung up the ones he was wearing. They were dark blue—nothing to provoke anyone. He had never seen queen's servants come at all: if they had, he had been absent at dinner. But likely, he thought, Prince Efanor's arrangements had replaced the queen's with more specific orders and new plans.

And the windows in the main room and here had the curtains drawn. He never liked the curtains drawn. He went and tugged and pulled at the heavy draperies to open them wide.

In the tall window, in its very center, there was a Quinalt sigil hung, a pewter talisman as large as his head. He went out to the main room, confronted those drawn draperies and hauled them back, each one, while the sounds of snoring came from the little room beside the foyer. In each, there was a similar circlet, with the Quinalt symbol.

It was a ward of sorts, he supposed. He hardly liked it. The place already had wards. The sigils aimed at witchcraft, at Gran's dreams, or his mother's mischief, or his own wondering, he supposed. They might as well have been bars on his windows.

The same sigil, on a chain about his neck suddenly seemed part of the same design, but remembering what Prince Efanor had said about it being given in love, he feared to cast it off or, more rash, still, to bid Brother Trassin take those emblems down and leave his draperies alone.

He lit a candle and went back into the icy bedchamber. And by that light he found the queen's candle and the evergreen gone from the mantel of the unused fireplace.

Dares he? he asked himself, indignation rising. *Dares he throw away* her *gift?*

Clearly the man dared whatever the Quinalt pleased.

He set the candle on the mantel, shivering with all this walking about. By that flickering light, he flung himself between icy sheets, gathered himself up in a shivering knot, and tried to warm a spot, breath hissing between his teeth.

He could not trust this man to wake him in the morning. If he understood Prince Efanor's warning, and Aewyn's, the man would like nothing better than to find him in the wrong. He couldn't trust the man for anything. He lay awake long, long, watching out the window, where the night sky made the Quinaltine roof look like the back of some great hulking beast, a predator lying in wait for foolish boys, and the Quinalt sigil hanging like a wakeful eye between.

Frost patterns had formed about the edges of the panes. He saw them in the candlelight, saw the evidence that the bitter cold he felt was no illusion. He thought of Paisi, afield on this bitter night, and hoped he was warmer than this and in better company.

He hoped Aewyn was right, that Brother Trassin was in no good grace with the king. He truly hoped so. Efanor himself both scared him and comforted him—he was almost sure of his goodwill, but had not quite warmed to him—Efanor being a very quiet, very thoughtful man.

He was glad at least the day had ended with his father knowing the truth, and Efanor trying to patch things, and Her Majesty on his side. That was a miracle in itself, a sign of things going much, much better in the world.

He shut his eyes on that thought. He held them shut, though the thought began to tatter and flow away from him.

He saw Gran's cottage, looking so forlorn in its little enclosure, so deep in snow.

But it seemed that as he came closer and closer, he saw that the shutters were hanging askew, and that half the thatch was missing, charred timbers in the opening.

His heart beat faster and faster.

"Paisi," he called out. "Paisi, something's wrong! It's all burned, can you see it?"

The house all fell in cinders, no more than a heap of stones and smoking ash.

"Paisi!" He cried. "Oh, Gran!"

"Boy," someone said somberly, and he waked with a hand on his shoulder, a harsh and demanding hand, and a face lit from below by a candle. *"Boy!"*

It was Brother Trassin shaking him awake, his face all harsh lines and frowns, Brother Trassin, who kept shaking him needlessly now, and ordering him to pray for the sins that troubled his sleep.

"Good gods deliver us," he said all in a rush, "gods save us." It was only what Gran would say when he'd been particularly bad or when she was startled. Gods save us from fools, was the rest of what Gran would add next, but he held that back, with Trassin standing above him. He recovered his arm from the brother, rubbing the sore spot the man's hard fingers had made. "It was only a dream, sir."

"You were chanting. You were calling out names in a trance."

"I was asleep. I dreamed. I called for my brother and my gran, sir, just that. It was only a dream. That was all."

"Mind how you dream, then," the brother said, "and what you invoke." With that Trassin walked away from him, taking away the candlelight, which leapt and flared and found strange edges to illumine as it left. It found edges of the clothespress, on which foxes were carved. It sparked off dark windows as the brother set the candle down in the other room and began to draw the draperies across the windows.

"Leave those, if you please, sir. I like the sky."

The brother left the curtain half-drawn, contriving to make even obedience disapproving, and turned, picking up the candle that gave his countenance the look of something carved and baleful. "The night is full of harm," the brother said. "It's nothing wholesome to look at. No wonder you dream."

"Good night, sir," Otter said, wishing the man would just go away. He was shivering, his bare shoulders exposed to the air, and he was embarrassed about the prayer he would not have tried to make if he had not been startled into it, and most of all he was worried about Gran and Paisi, in the dream he had had.

He drew the blanket up about his shoulders and sat there trying to keep warm until the man took the light away.

vii

"HIS HOLINESS' SPY'S INSPECTION TURNED UP ONLY HER MAJESTY'S CANDLE FOR a sin," Efanor informed Cefwyn, in the dim light before the dawn, before the procession downstairs. "I informed His Holiness whose gift it was, and we agreed there will by no means be any mention made of it in any record. The boy had nightmares. How not? I suggested that record, too, be expunged. Clearly the boy is distraught at his companion's leaving. *That* will be recorded."

Cefwyn regarded his brother sidelong and hung a dagger from his belt, discreetly on the side his cloak covered, while Idrys stood in shadowy silence, armed and waiting.

"So his indisposition and his innocence will both be in the record?"

"I have the Patriarch's firm word on it."

"Bad business, still, this messing with magic," Idrys said unbidden. "And no surety yet the boy won't bolt to Amefel, or spill another bowl of oiled water in his lap, if his bad dreams go on."

"He's done very well," Efanor said smoothly.

"For an Aswydd," Idrys said.

"Hush, Crow, damn you!"

Idrys inspected the back of his hand, on which a scar healed. "It is worth a thought, my lord king. The boy has arrived at a certain age, capable of passing on the Aswydd blood, never mind its own claims to royalty. As to what that blood does contain—did you not bid me ask about his mother's sorcery?"

"His wizard-work failed, you'll note."

"All the same, who knows? He's of an age. I'd not have his choice of bedmates influenced from the Zeide tower."

That was worth a cold, direct stare at Master Crow.

Efanor spoke, from the other side. "I talked with the boy that day," Efanor said. "He quite deceived me. He must have just come back from horse-thievery when I spied him, the cat straight from the cream, and not a trace on him. He has cold-blooded cunning. He has invention. He has a strong will. But he is not a thief, not a coward, and not, so far as I may judge, a sorcerer, nor even a wizard, considering the outcome of his efforts. Perhaps you should teach him the martial life."

"He scarcely knows the sword," Idrys said. "He can hardly manage his own reins or stay ahorse. So I hear. The lad's employment in the army is questionable."

"So he's no soldier. You're in no danger, Crow. Don't fear him so."

"Scion of a line you outlawed, my lord king, root and branch, living and dead . . ."

"And I rescinded the decree for Crissand, aye, for him and for Otter."

"Elfwyn," Efanor said. Otter's proper name.

"It was His Majesty's notion to declare that name to the people yesterday," Idrys said. "And he spilled oil on that notion, right handily. Did he not?"

"Damn it, Crow, is there no mischief elsewhere in the kingdom you can attend? Must you lurk about and annoy me?"

"The boy had no reason to avoid that name being proclaimed," Efanor said.

"We know who would," Idrys said.

"Her prison is secure," Efanor said, "or nothing is."

"Precisely," Idrys said.

"Idrys has a man riding in that direction," Cefwyn said to Efanor, "and will advise Crissand to take all precautions."

"Well and good for that," Efanor said. "But if there should be anything amiss with the grandmother . . . Write to Lord Tristen, brother. I strongly urge it."

"Get that weasel of a lay brother out of the boy's rooms. His Holiness has seen enough, heard enough, imagined enough. The spy is a feckless fool, and the boy is already upset. Withdraw all appearance of guards."

"To catch whom?" Idrys asked. "The boy, or the Holy Father?"

"Hush, damn you, Crow! Why," he asked Efanor, "do I tolerate this quarrelsome man?"

"Which one?" Efanor asked, smooth as milk. "The Lord Commander, or the Holy Father?"

Idrys opened the door for them, performing the office of a servant in this meeting without servants, with only Idrys' men outside, and at least one of their number, by Idrys' word, well launched on a snowy mission to Amefel.

"Come," Cefwyn said. There was worry enough, all considering. Ninévrisë would be waiting for him, with the baby, who was not a patient child, particularly when waked and dressed before sunrise. Aewyn would be fretting in the hall, or off looking for his half brother, to be sure, this morning, that Otter showed up for services.

He by no means liked the advice he had had from Efanor and from Idrys.

But if there were anything untoward in Amefel, Efanor was right: Tristen would know it.

Would you not, old friend? he asked the amulet he wore. *Would you not know if that vile woman had breached the wards?*

You promised us to watch over us. I've tried not to do foolish things.

I've kept my word to you. That was never foolish, no matter what Crow and my brother think.

viii

READY, READY, THOUGH OTTER WAS ALMOST LATE, AND BROTHER TRASSIN STILL fussed with his cloak pin and wanted to teach him the morning prayers.

"Please you, sir, I mean to learn, only His Majesty is waiting. I have to go downstairs. Gods bless us." He perceived it mollified the man when he said that, and he said it twice, breaking away. "Gods bless us, the Five bless us . . ."

It was the start of the prayer at least. *The Five bless us at sunrise and sunset, in sunshine and rain . . .*

And shall they bless us in snow, his rebel wits wanted to ask, and his terrors conjured worse than that. *And shall they, in fire? Save us from fire. Gods save Gran from the fire. Oh, Paisi, go, hurry as fast as you can . . .*

He escaped Trassin's attentions and hurried as fast as he could keep his footing on the polished floor, out the door and down the hall, past the doors from which the few other residents would already have departed, onto the grand stairs, with a quick grip on the balustrade, his feet skipping ever so fast.

He heard a gathering below. He was not too late. He saw the glitter of gold, a red cloak—Aewyn's. He himself wore his new dark blue coat, his good black boots, restored by the servants. Brother Trassin had insisted on helping him wash and dress, and, it turned out, had wanted to pray over him at every stage, while he tugged his shirt on and fastened his laces himself.

The blue cloak, accidentally pinned through his doublet, was crooked. He seized it in one hand and tried to straighten it as he reached Aewyn and the family, and Their Majesties. He bowed fervently, and intended to move toward the side of the hall, to keep from any conspicuous notice while he repinned the cloak.

"Here you are, on time, and you look grand," Aewyn declared, and turned to his father. "Doesn't he?"

"Perfectly fine," His Majesty said, laying a hand on Otter's shoulder, "and just in time. Move us out, if you please, Lord Marshal. Move us on, here, and let us get this under way."

The assembly began to move. The queen carried the baby in her arms, and Aewyn walked beside his father. Otter lagged back, finally securing the pin, hoping just to follow as quietly as possible, losing himself among the Guard and the officials who thronged the hall. Aewyn, however, turned half-about, caught his sleeve, and drew him forward without a word.

A gust fluttered all the candles and blew out half of them as the great doors opened on the dark outside. Staffs began to turn, unrolling banners that took increasing flight on that wind. Torches outside showed a world of falling white, and perilous steps, where Prince Efanor lent his hand to help Ninévrisë and the baby.

The way led along the center of the paved courtyard to those gates that were rarely open, tall iron gates with spikes along the top. Torches went before them onto the street, a war of fire and banners as the gusts battered both flame and cloth.

From there the way led beside the tall windows and high walls of the Quinaltine, and around to the broad, high steps where a throng of people had gathered. These steps were sanded, and easier than they looked. Having braced himself at the sight of them, Otter let go a wider breath and walked up with ease in among the columns of the porch, and, beside Aewyn and the king and queen, into the echoing dark beyond the great doors.

A shiver took him there. It was warmer inside, but only tolerable. The massive candles, posed at intervals, relieved only the dark immediately about their flames, cast light on the lower portions of towering marble pillars, while the space above and behind was lost in dark. Shadowy crowds of richly dressed people stood on either hand, having reached their seats before them. The end of the aisle was ablaze with light, a diffusion of a hundred pale candles of every size, like looking at the sunny world from the heart of some horrid, chill dark. The soul wanted to fly toward that safety, but the speed of the procession was set, and they proceeded at the same pace as on the steps. A choir sang, a mournful echo roused out of the spaces above the pillars; and priests swung censers, sending up clouds of incense that began to veil the light.

Otter wanted to sneeze. He wanted to very badly, and choked it back into an embarrassed hiccup as they reached their benches and filed in. His eyes watered.

The king sat. Everyone sat down, with a rattle and bump of the benches throughout the great sanctuary. Aewyn sat on the side nearest his mother, Efanor came next, and Otter sat at the end of the row. He watched as a bearded old man all in white and gold stood up in front of all the candles and the altar and lifted his hands. He began to talk about sin and dark, then the coming of the sun.

That last was comforting. Otter supposed this was the Holy Father himself, and found he had a persuasive, calming voice: he even agreed with what he heard, thus far; but then a pair of priests accompanied an even older man into the place of the first, and that old man began to chant in a reedy voice about sun and shadow, and the willfulness of Men, and the sins of the age.

It was not so pleasant as the other voice, and the reasoning eluded him, but Otter listened attentively, and stood when everyone stood and sat when everyone sat, and tried not to fidget as Aewyn did—Aewyn swung his feet, and his father had to put a hand on his knee and stop him. Aewyn heaved a heavy sigh, then, and meanwhile the old man had directed more incense be waved about.

Otter pinched a sneeze up his nose, and tried not to blink. Tears from the smoke shattered the candlelight. A baby began to fret, somewhere in the assembly, and other babies took it up, including the Princess, who let out a protesting wail.

Otter dared blink, finally, thinking the tears dry enough, and the light cleared into discrete, though blurry, points. There was a darkness between those points, and while the old man chanted, that dark in front of the front row, under the railing, seemed to move strangely, like spilled ink. The shadow began to run along the rail that seperated the choir and the other priests from the assembly. It flowed down from there like black water, and ran down the baluster at the corner, spreading across the floor right by the table where the candles sat. Otter leaned forward a little and watched in horrid fascination.

Gran could do things like that, making sparks march in a line on a straw, or making a puddle of water go silver, reflecting the light. But this trick with shadow felt quite threatening to him, like a rip in the world that swallowed in the light, and if it was a trick, Otter wished the priests would stop doing that, and they would just preach and be done soon.

But there was more singing, and more incense waved about, until at last the old man, with all the shadow now swirling about his feet, talked about sin and the wickedness of their forebears, about the world being divided into the gods' own and the others, and those trafficking in shadows, who were damned.

Maybe, Otter thought, it was a message, and now the shadow would disappear, driven away by the old man's power. Maybe they were all supposed to understand it as a trick and an illustration. But the shadow was lapping and leaping about the hem of the old man's robe, and he seemed not to notice it at all. He waded through it when he turned to the altar and poured a bowl of oil.

Otter's skin began to prickle. The shadow didn't go away. It coiled and sent out fingers up the old man's robes.

"We have to be blessed, now," Aewyn whispered, tugging at Otter's sleeve, and in fact His Majesty moved out, and Ninévrisë with the baby, and the priest dipped his finger in the oil and touched their foreheads each in turn, calling them by their names and titles. The shadow underfoot diminished under his father's feet and the queen's, but Otter felt a lingering tightness at the pit of his stomach, the feeling that he might at any moment be sick if he had to step in it. Efanor followed the queen, being called Prince, and duke of Guelessar, which he was. The shadow stayed away, hiding under the railing.

"Us, now," Aewyn said, dragging Otter with him out into the aisle, while the king and queen and Efanor filed back into the frontmost, vacant bench.

Otter caught a breath, stood still while the old man blessed Aewyn with the oil, calling him Crown Prince and heir of Ylesuin and forgiving his sins of the year.

Then the old man moistened his finger again, and Otter stared at it advancing toward him, not knowing what was happening at his feet, and had the terrible, awful, stinging urge to sneeze.

"Elfwyn," the old man began.

He had to sneeze. He did, startling the old man backward.

A crash resounded off the pavings, a priest moved to catch it, a censer dropped and hit the edge of the altar. Coals skittered across the altar as the pitcher of oil went over the edge and hit the marble. Fire spread in a thin sheet as the old man recoiled, brushing at his gilt-and-white robes amid cries of alarm from the priests, who ripped loose cloths and hangings to smother it and save the man. A great outcry swelled from the crowd, the crash of a bench, as people surged out of their seats to see or to escape the vicinity. Otter stood frozen in place, while priests fell to their knees and mopped and smothered the fire with banners and clothes. The shadow was gone. The fire died, leaving a stench of singed cloth, incense, and oil.

The old man cleared his throat, lifted his hands and signaled the buzzing crowd to settle again, slowly restoring quiet.

Sweat had broken out on the old man's face, and his hands shook as he turned and took another pitcher of oil. He poured a little into the bowl, atop the rest, and moistened his finger before he turned a sweating, disturbed countenance toward Otter.

"Elfwyn Aswydd," the old man said, his true name, his mother's name. "Do you stand to be blessed by the Holy Quinalt and written in the book?"

"Yes, sir," he said in a shaking voice, forgetting in that instant that he was probably supposed to say Your Holiness, as Aewyn had, but then it was too late. The old man touched the oil to his forehead and said, all in a rush:

"Sealed to the Quinalt. Your sins are forgiven."

The sins of Sight, and of running away into the rooftree and lying to Prince Efanor? Was he truly forgiven?

He walked away, glad to escape, at very least, half-blind to his surroundings as others, recovering from the commotion, got up to be blessed, the whole next row. It seemed a long, long way to walk before he found his place beside Aewyn, having gone all the way around the bench as Aewyn had done, to observe a respectful distance from the king and not to cross between him and the altar.

He breathed, every breath an effort. He shivered, trying not to let it be known.

"You did it," Aewyn whispered, nudging him with an elbow, while the blessing went on, and they all stood. They stood all through the ceremony, until the priest had blessed the last of hundreds of them, and the choir sang, and dismissed them all, and the royal family led the way out into cold, wanly golden daylight.

Clean wind chilled them. Otter's eyes stopped watering and his nose stopped stinging, but it still ran. He thought he would smell the stink of incense and fire for hours.

And the old man whose robes had caught—he had been so afraid the man was hurt, but he was not. He had gone on. And he was blessed. Forgiven. He was by no means sure he thought much of the Guelen gods, since Gran never had, but being forgiven was a good thing, was it not? And the shadow had gone. He felt as though he dared breathe again. He had done what his father wanted. They could write him in the book, with all the good people.

Today—he had figured it as best he could—even with delays because of the weather, Paisi should be across the river and onto the road on the other side, well on his way to Gran's.

And Brother Trassin would be waiting for him in his rooms.

ix

THERE WERE USUAL PROCLAMATIONS TO ISSUE, A ROYAL APPROVAL ON A FIFTH daughter's marriage in Carys—gods, was the man never out of daughters?—and the same from the current Lord Ryssand, no relation to the last, whose third-eldest son was the bridegroom: it required wax and the seal, but little thought. On this particular ill-starred day, Cefwyn wished there *had* been some distraction. At least the Patriarch had not gone up like a torch: he was, it was reported, a little singed, and in some pain, but nothing too serious.

"His Grace of Guelessar," a servant advised him.

News, maybe. Maybe an assuagement of anxiousness that, along with a too-bland, too-fatty sausage, sat uneasily on the royal stomach since noon.

"Admit him." Cefwyn blew out the sealing flame and tidied the unruly stack of stiff, beribboned parchments on his desk.

It was afternoon, verging on late afternoon. He had another dinner to face tonight, and could not imagine how he could get past the first course.

If Efanor reported matters in the Quinaltine solved, he might manage.

"Brother," Efanor said, closing the door at his back. "I've talked to Idrys. I've just come from the Quinaltine, inspecting the matter myself. There is a mark. No scrubbing will remove it. There are scratches on the altar, which appear to the eye but not to the touch, and I have seen them. They reportedly spell out blasphemies."

"Scratches that spell, for the gods' sake! The boy sneezed. The old fool jumped back, and a fool priest was standing too close with the censer—what more might there be?"

"I did everything possible to quiet this—"

"I know, I know. I knew it was difficult when I asked it. But a simple sneeze, good gods!"

"His body could not tolerate the holy incense. The oil burned the holy banners rather than purge his sins . . ."

"And purged them right away and forever in the next moment, once the old fool got his wits collected, damn it all. Did anyone notice he *did* receive the oil with no difficulty, after?"

"The fire mark on the floor cannot be scrubbed away. There's a permanent darkening of the stone."

"Well, pry it up and lay a new paving stone, if His Holiness wants it. The boy was a model of decorum and gentility throughout. Your spy was with him all night and all morning previous. He took the oil. He sat through services. He did nothing but sneeze, gods save the day! What does the good brother say? That he flew about the room last night and conjured rats?"

"The boy had bad dreams and waked calling on Paisi and Gran, who the brother was relieved to know are living relatives."

"Oh, for the gods' own sake, brother!"

"There is gossip running among the priests. The Holy Father now has a fever. The curious come to see the scratches. Some see claw marks. Others see blasphemies."

"Probably overzealous scrubbing," Cefwyn said. "Claw marks, for gods' sake! Claws that write. Do they observe good grammar?"

"The cracks are there, perhaps from the fire," Efanor said. "Or not."

Cefwyn shot back an angry look. "My son—my son, I say!—did not go there and scratch the precious floor. A censer fell. A priest dropped it. Fools have been scrubbing at the stone with all their might and now, lo! scratches appear. What a wonder! Gods, brother, you can argue with the arrant fools! Do it!"

"I have more concern than that," Efanor said. "Remember the wars. Remember the Quinaltine—"

"Long quiet, and long settled."

"It has been a battleground for spirits."

"Years ago."

"When the Sihhë last were abroad in the land."

"He's Aswydd, brother, not Sihhë."

"Thin blood, but that blood, all the same, brother, you know it. The censer indeed fell."

"The boy sneezed!"

"Or something there, once settled, does not like him there and wakes to notice."

"Oh, I'm sure something there doesn't like him. Someone among the priesthood doesn't like his presence or the Aswydd name, and I'll warrant there's been talk in the robing rooms. It takes no spooks, brother, no ghosts, no haunts, just one ill-disposed servant of the gods . . . maybe not even the man who dropped the censer, rather than set His Holiness alight. Maybe the scratches came from someone who cleaned it up, someone opposed to me who found a chance to do ill, in all this to-do."

"The boy has become a bone of contention."

"And dogs will worry at any scrap. I'd expected conspiracy among the lords, not the priests."

"Or the ghosts."

"The ghosts, for the gods' sake!"

"Ghosts, brother. I tell you plainly, it is not wise for him to go there again."

"And next the priests will bruit about the notion he dares not come back!"

"Better let them gossip old news than another incident, which there may well be if he goes back. Have him take ill, have him fall on the stairs. He should not cross that threshold again until we unravel this."

"Why don't we fault the fool who dropped the fire in the first place! What did *he* dream the night before, does anyone ask that?"

"The Holy Father has taken to his bed in pain and fever. He is not at his most reasonable this afternoon. Caution. Caution in this. Remember Lord Tristen himself . . ."

It had unhappy resonance to that other crisis in the Quinalt, in which a Sihhë amulet had ended up in the offering plate.

And no one needed remind him that riots had broken out in the town over suspected Sihhë influence, killing his wife's Bryaltine priest and no few others. Religious anger had divided the realm, had taken a war to settle . . .

And that war had roused horrid manifestations in the Quinaltine during the hour of the last battle. He had no reason to doubt Efanor's report of it. The place had its ghosts, unquiet ones. It was not the only place in Ylesuin so blessed.

"Let me remind you, too," Efanor said, "if the priests should begin to question his activities—the one item the Patriarch's spy did report in the boy's room was Nevris' candle."

Cefwyn turned a furious face on him, but Efanor, who was certainly no enemy of the queen, only set his jaw doggedly.

"I know you will not endanger her," Efanor said. "Or the treaty. And if this Amefin son of yours does begin to endanger her, or to threaten the peace we forged—no, hear me out on this, brother—I know you will use your wits to find another path. What you owe this boy, what debt you have to him, and all your heir's affection for him to the side—I pray you use your cleverness, not your will, in this case. Have your way and bring the boy along, but have it slowly. You knew the danger when you kept him here through Festival. You thought you could fly this young sparrow low and quickly past your enemies, have him entered in the rolls, and that the priests were in your hand. I had my misgivings. Yes, he is fair to look on, but he frowns too often. He has those eyes that some call Sihhë heritage. He is mysterious, and, forgive me, brother, your dalliance with the Aswydd duchess is—unfortunately—made new gossip by his arrival in a winter devoid of other topics."

"Good loving gods, Efanor, there is no trouble from the woman!"

"We suppose that there is no trouble from her. The people have been reminded most vividly, now, that there is still a prisoner in the Zeide tower. They remember the dead sister, Orien. They remember the fall of the As-wydds, and your lifting your own ban to raise Lord Crissand, which roused some debate at the time. Amefel had settled far from Guelessar's interest, until you brought this gray-eyed boy into the Guelesfort and made him your son for all to see. Now the people talk, and after this morning, they will talk in every shop and tavern."

"I did not plan for an old fool to back into a censer pot!"

"You certainly planned for someone among the lords of the land to raise an objection in audience, which you were prepared to silence by this little maneuver in the Quinalt. You insisted on Festival, on the sacred season—"

"My son asked him here."

"And you kept him on, full well knowing the delicacy of it."

"I didn't plan on fools!"

"Alas, fools grow like cabbages in Guelessar. But you know that, too. I can tell you nothing. I never could."

Efanor was water, to his clenched fist, and it was a tactic that had long infuriated him. Sometimes Efanor was right in taking the devious course; but sometimes, too, Efanor backed away too quickly and encouraged fools with momentary success.

"Damn it," Cefwyn said, "damn it, no, I refuse to send the boy home. Or to back off! Mend it! Find a stone, dead of night, replace the paving, replace the whole damned altar if you have to. Make a miracle. Let them chatter about that."

"Stonemasonry raises noise and dust," Efanor said, "and stonemasons talk. And one stone will not cure it. What has stirred in the Quinaltine, I fear, is beyond any mason to cure, now."

"You believe it!" he exclaimed. "Good gods, you *believe* it!"

"I believe in what I saw the day of the battle. I believe there is a haunt there that roused itself once. I saw it . . ."

"Once. The whole world shook, that day. There were manifestations from end to end of Ylesuin, nothing since, here or there. Oh, come, this was no encroaching shadow. This was no howling wind. It was a sneeze, gods save us! It was a boy's sneeze, and an old man's foolishness. No. One thing will buff the scratches into abeyance. A glittering substance. Apply it."

Efanor shook his head. "Be careful. Be careful with His Holiness, brother."

"We are the Marhanen. We have ruled since there *was* a Guelessar, in spite of idle gossips and busy opinions and drawn daggers. You know what to do and where to apply the gold. In all of Guelessar, there has to be one fit stone, if enough gold moves it. In all of Guelessar, there has to be an altar cloth wide enough to cover whatever marks may appear. And if there aren't priests willing to find a miracle in that, we can find more priests, too."

Efanor drew a deep, deep breath. "As you will, brother. I shall see what I can do. I do not promise success. And find some excuse for the boy to stay abed tomorrow."

"No, damn it, he will be with us in the morning. I don't put it past certain priests to have caused this with exactly that aim. Make that suspicion clear to His Holiness and tell him that as I made him, so I can unmake him."

"Not so easily, can you, and you know it."

"Yet I can, and by the gods I will, rather than disavow a son of mine because some priest dropped a pot, gods damn his connivance! Tell him I take this as a personal affront, an intended incident, abetted by priests, and tell him count his zealots—one of them is in the midst of this."

A second deep sigh. "I shall apply what suasion I can."

"Good." He caught Efanor's arm. "You are a true brother."

"I am also, and not by my will, the boy's uncle. The boy's honest and devoted uncle, brother of mine. I made my own mistakes in youth, less fortunate even than this one. I devote myself now to amends."

"What sin did you ever commit?"

Efanor turned one of those rare and pained looks that he had worn ever since a day in Amefel.

"Our father's loss? That was none of your doing. The fault is mine. By the *gods,* I refuse to have you carry my faults about. You are *not* to be that pure, brother of mine, without being a damned saint, and I won't have it, by the gods I won't!"

"Oh, we have each our flaws. Marhanen and Aswydd. I could never have achieved that. Gods save us, what a breeding!"

He glared. Efanor gave a little bow, a very little bow, and walked off toward the door, having had the last and telling word, which only vexed him the more.

Sometimes, however, the Marhanen luck simply held out against all odds, blind, deaf, and dumb. He had ridden to battle with it, time and again. It never worked in his favor when he retreated.

And was this boy, half of his blood, not due a share of that luck?

Otter would not be found hiding among the cobwebs tomorrow.

And if Efanor had to rouse out and bribe a score of stonemasons, there would be a miracle. Let the masons talk: let them proclaim in every tavern in town that they had replaced the stone. The people loved their miracles more than truth, and what appeared suddenly to set things right roused passions that paid no heed to rational explanations. He had learned the ways of the faithful, while the object of his own personal belief was across the border, beyond Amefel, and at present gave him no answers.

CHAPTER THREE

i

THE BOY WAS FEARFUL OF GOING BACK: EFANOR SAW THAT, WHEN THE FAMILY gathered before dawn for the morning processional. Aewyn attempted to cheer him, but the boy, Otter—Elfwyn Aswydd, as he was written, now, in the holy record—looked apprehensively into the shadows of the hall and started in every limb when a guardsman thumped a pike against the paving.

They moved, out into a snowy, breathless dawn, and across a soft new blanket of snow in the courtyard and on the street. Only a few earlier tracks marred the white.

They climbed the broad, sparsely torchlit steps toward the open doors and entered the sanctuary as they must do every morning of Festival. And here Efanor climbed a little faster, and seized Otter's arm and diverted him and Aewyn to the bench behind the king and queen, in much better view of the aisle, and of the lords who filled the benches. The Lord Chamberlain, flustered, filled in the next bench after with his family, and others moved smoothly into place, none noticing, perhaps, until the last row, when some might be left standing: no one sat in the king's row unbidden; and no one had dared crowd into the Prince's company in his appropriated row, either. Everything had gone just slightly out of joint.

But Efanor, nearest the aisle now, had placed the boys where he could keep an eye on both of them—Aewyn, he would gladly have sent forward with Cefwyn, so as not to taint the heir with his half brother's difficulties. He signaled so, but Aewyn, who had stuck like a burr when he had diverted the Aswydd boy, now ignored the urging to join his parents and stuck fast, publicly attached to the scene, making himself a hostage.

Well, Efanor thought, that was as it would be. The masons, paid for silence as well as labor, had done their work last night. A new stone, inconspicuous among the rest, lay in place, unblemished. The altar there was no replacing, but a broad white altar cloth covered the damages. Everything to the public eye was pristine and perfect.

He had gotten perhaps four hours of sleep last night. Otter beside him looked to have gotten less. The lad's face was white, lips pressed tight.

Cefwyn seemed perfectly happy, his requirements satisfied, his sons in place, the people quiet in the contemplation of the third day, the day of thanksgiving, happier than the day of fasting and the day of forgiveness. They had only the day of petition and the day of praise to get through, beyond this one—and if Cefwyn could draw an easier breath this morning, confident in his deafness to things that might move in the shadows—it at least kept his face serene as a monarch's ought to be.

Efanor felt no such serenity, nor would, he thought, until the sun rose on the world and shadows slunk back to their proper places.

It was always an uneasy place. Lord Tristen had said it was the Masons who had laid out the foundations, who had deliberately built on a place of power, and attempted—arrogantly—to contain it. But could anyone persuade the Holy Father to let Tristen Sihhë redraw the Lines beneath? No, a thousand times no.

Consequently the conflicting Lines were still there, more gateway than ward. They had flared into life that day of battle and outright broken, badly knit again by the persistent pacing of the Holy Father and other priests, back and forth, back and forth along that track before the altar. It was a ragged line they made, like loose scraps of yarn laid for a defense, not the bright, brave blue that attended Tristen's sure working—the mending of the Lines had started out as bits of red, then green, where they crossed, and a few, now, blue in the heart of the skein, showed a certain health.

But to Efanor's disquiet, if he looked in the right way, a shadow seemed to have fallen on the heart of the new paving stone, which the Masons had raised from the inner chapel floor and brought out here. Masons had trimmed it, chisels ringing in the dim, vacant hours; they had set it, pure and gray and polished, and cleaned away the dust.

Now a spot appeared, and spread like ink in water, right by the king's bench, right by Cefwyn's left hand.

It was not a spot such as ordinary Men might see, not yet: the choir sang, the congregation rose and sat by turns, but spread it did, and sent out tendrils of stain to touch other stones, running like ink in the crevices between stones. The white altar cloth seemed to glow with a red fire, as if coals were under the cloth, never blackening, only continuing to glow, a mis-set Line.

No one saw, Efanor thought to himself; *not a soul else noticed it.*

But when he thought that, he felt a strange thing: that fear sat beside him: not mischief, not a source of the darkness, but fear.

The boy was gazing at the floor beside the bench, his lips pressed to a thin line. Sweat stood on his face.

Efanor shot out a hand without forethought, gripped the boy's wrist, and pressed that cold flesh, gently, solidly, feeling, still, neither emanation of the threat nor an answering defense. It was a very mortal chill, the shiver of a soul completely vulnerable to the threat it perceived, and knowing not what to do.

He had force enough. Efanor had discovered it in him on that day, call it prayer, call it a Working, in Tristen's terms: he had prayed, then, not to the Five, but to justice, and fairness, and to the balance that kept the living in possession of the hill: he prayed now for the lives of all those present, all the city round about, for his duchy of Guelessar, for all the realm, all weighed against the dead, and whatever force tried to break those Lines that held the shadow back.

Shadow pressed back. The blue Lines turned red, and gold, and a few snapped. The boy shivered, and flinched, and Efanor loosened his grip somewhat, praying with all his might, lips moving now. The boy's other hand closed atop his, circle closed, force running through all the boy's being, and Efanor locked his left hand atop all, willing safety on the lot of them, on all present.

The Lines held. What he held, what he met, in that completed grip, tingled through him in a way he had rarely felt.

It held. It held through the singing and the Holy Father's sermon, the old man talking on and on about thanksgiving for deliverance from sins, and uttering inanities, outright inanities about birth indicating a soul's righteousness and rank being given by the gods.

What rank, this boy? Efanor wondered, distracted. *What holiness, this lad, the bastard, whose presence this place abhors?*

Whose life this place fears . . .

It fears him, fears the Aswydd blood. The old enemy, is it, you shadows?

The Marhanen lie buried here, Efanor thought: *my father, my grandfather, the queens, the forgotten princes, those who never reigned, and those who did—my grandfather who slaughtered the Sihhë-lords and overthrew their palaces . . . who suborned the Aswydds in the doing of it, but the Aswydds were never the object of the attack and never suffered what their lords did. The Aswydds ruled on, under special provision, with their own peculiar titles and honors preserved—the Aswydds still rule, by Cefwyn's own dispensation.*

Aswydd blood can't be the disturbance here.

Something else is.

A howling wind seemed to go through the sanctuary, up among the banners, but none of the audience stirred. The boy, however, looked up, candlelight reflecting in his eyes. The boy had heard it. The boy had felt it.

Had he heard some threat yesterday, when the censer fell?

There had been a thunderclap in that moment, in Efanor's ears. Thunder in the snowfall, that no one seemed to have heard, only the fall of the censer, the ringing of metal, the racket of the congregation all out of their seats, striving to see . . .

"Good lad," Efanor whispered, under the singing. "Good lad."

A desperate look turned to him. The boy's hands were like ice. Beyond, Aewyn had looked aloft, and cast them a worried look, as if perceiving some trouble beyond his ken.

"You should not come here," Efanor said to the boy in his grip. "I know that. I shall talk to your father."

"My lord." The boy tried to withdraw one hand, and Efanor let him, retaining only a hold on his wrist.

"I shall see you safely out of here, when the congregation rises. Walk quietly. I shall keep close by." Efanor let go the boy's wrist as the congregation rose. He slipped an arm around him instead, and when Cefwyn and Ninévrisë began the procession, drew him into the aisle, proceeding together behind the king and queen, down the long walk toward the opening doors. Aewyn came up on Otter's other side, and put his arm about him, the image of familial devotion as they came out the doors.

It was surely more familial devotion than Cefwyn might want displayed, making clear to all the witnessing crowd outside that here was the Aswydd sorceress's son, the family mistake, in the very heart of the family, embraced by both generations. Cefwyn might not see the shadows running the aisles like spilled ink, might not feel the bands of terror loosed from about his ribs as they passed the doors or see the sunlight as the cleansing force it was.

Otter must not go there again, Efanor said to himself, shaken. *He must not go there. Cefwyn's will or no, he dares not.*

He slipped his hand from the boy's shoulder then, letting Aewyn and Otter go their way in the mistaken blitheness of boys, the darkness inside now past. They made a game of walking together through the snow as they reached the bottom of the steps, kicking it into flurries.

Boys, still. Boys whose fates rested in other hands than their own—

In the hands of grown men, who had to act with the limited understanding they had; and Efanor turned back forthwith toward the Quinaltine, taking an untracked walk toward the priests' door, along the side of the building, where a wintry, snowy hedge concealed his visit from common view.

He opened the unlocked door, walked into the close, echoing warren that held the private chapels, the robing rooms, the wardens' chambers, and the storerooms that supplied the less public aspects of the Quinaltine services. He climbed up a flight of narrow steps, and into His Holiness' less public domain, where the Holy Father, the Patriarch, was shedding the heavy gold miter. His sparse white hair had wisped up into random peaks. He looked like any old man caught in dressing, except for the golden raiments, except for priests and lay brothers who raced up to him to ask questions and receive instructions, departing again at a run. It was a hive overturned, buzzing with distress and worry.

"Your Holiness," Efanor said.

"Your Grace, the spot is back. It's back, it's on the new stone, and it's larger. The whole city will see the mark!"

"Shut the doors."

"Shut the doors? It's Thanksgiving, the day before Praise. I have another service to hold in an hour, and the commons at eventide. We can't shut the doors!"

"We've other stones. We'll lay another stone. The services will be late today."

"What will we tell the populace?"

"Tell them anything. Lie. Decry excessive drunkenness in the crowd. Say you've taken ill. But shut the doors!"

He turned on his heel and left a royal order hanging in the air. The Patriarch might send to the king to confirm it; and he had to reach his brother beforehand.

He lost no time at all, crossing between the Quinaltine and the Guelesfort. Unlike his brother, he moved at times without guard or escort, and this was notably such a moment, in which his plain raiment and his haste was disguise enough, given the sifting fall of snow. The crowd in the square was waiting to be let into services that would, alas, be hours delayed. The guardsmen closing the Guelesfort gate realized who he was and let him pass.

He left melting snow behind him as he climbed the servants' stairs, up to the level of the royal apartments and straight down the hall . . . past the boy's rooms, and past Aewyn's, straight for his brother's.

But not without interception. A black-clad guardsman checked him with a hand on his arm, right near his brother's door.

Idrys.

"Your Grace," the Lord Commander said in a low voice. "I take it that it was not without disturbance."

"No," he said, "it was not."

ii

IT WAS A VISITATION OF ILL OMEN: CEFWYN SAW IT COMING—EFANOR, PASSING the guard at his chamber doors with no lingering courtesies, went straight to the point, just when the Lord Chamberlain had begun a report, and asked for complete privacy.

"The mark is back," Efanor said directly.

"No such thing!" Cefwyn said. "I looked. I saw nothing at all."

"Some see it. Some, among the priests, the Holy Father—as well as your Aswydd son—do. *I* see it. It will manifest again. I've ordered the doors shut, the stone replaced. Your miracle, brother, has failed; worse, it's gone wrong. All through the service, I was with the boy . . ."

"Who did nothing!"

"I will warrant myself, by deed or word or invocation, he did nothing— but what he saw, and what I saw, brother—"

"These Lines."

"You've seen them yourself. I know you can see them."

"I agree they're there. Once and twice, yes, I've seen them elsewhere, in darkest night. Why should we be so blessed this time? And why should it be the boy's fault? Why not one of the priests doing this?"

"I don't at all deny that it could be. But the fact is, other things manifest when the boy is there. They frighten him, and what I saw there this morning frightens me. Listen this time, brother. Whatever the cause, for the boy's sake, for yours, the boy must not go through those doors again."

Master Crow had come in, sole exception to the request for utter privacy, and stood by, arms folded, the last man on earth who might see mysterious Lines or give way to superstition; but he, like Efanor, had seen far more unaccountable things in his life.

"My lord king," Idrys said unbidden, "consider, not alone the boy's mother, but the mother's sister. Born at a sorceress's will—"

"You are about to offend me, Crow."

"Sorcery brought you into the Aswydd's bed, sorcery conceived a son you will not now disavow—on what advice, yes, has generally been good advice, but Lord Tristen never counseled you to bring that boy into the Quinalt, my lord king. I would wager heavily on that. This was your own notion."

"Damn you, Crow!"

"Oh, I'll deserve it more before I'm done speaking. What you do, you do broad and far. You were a wild and froward boy. You are a generous and occasionally excessive man, where it touches your demonstrations of the gentler sentiments: love me, love my boys, or be damned to you all. Do I mistake your intent to press popular sentiment to the wall? You appointed the Holy Father: you can unseat him if he crosses you—but you'll come to me to do the deed. Oh, I do serve you, my lord king, but His Grace has warned you, and I warn you. I *miss* Master Grayfrock. He'd mince no words. You find yourself hell-bent on a course that will destroy you—wizards are in it. And is there not a smell of wizardry about this boy? Say no, and I'll know for a certainty you're bespelled, my lord king."

It was one of Crow's better speeches. It left Cefwyn silent, except to say:

"You advised me drown him at birth."

"I don't think I specified the method, my lord king, but I did foresee this moment."

"So did His Majesty," Efanor said, "or he'd not have been so stubborn in this matter."

"Damn both of you! This is not for jest!"

"You brought this boy in," Idrys said in measured tones, "while I was otherwise occupied. You had no wish to hear my opinions on the matter. But being here now, I give them, gratis."

"If I'm ever cut, Idrys will bring salt, will he not?"

"The boy," Efanor said, "has no ill will, nor malice in him, nor practices anything unwholesome. He is innocent, and as Emuin would say, worse than that, he is ignorant. That said, this morning proves he has the Gift, in what measure I cannot tell—but enough: enough to make him a door through which Tarien Aswydd can look into this place, if not enter. The Quinaltine dead are roused . . . to what, I cannot say. It was no simple sneeze that hurled that censer to the stones. It was a struggle between what thin line protects the Quinaltine and what forces would bring utmost harm on you, on the queen, and on both your sons."

"No."

"Hear me. In him, Tarien has what she still lusts after: power. You always meant to take him from his mother. You snatched him from her at birth, you instructed him to fear her. But you had no power to break her desire for him."

"What would I, kill her and loose another ghost?"

"What will you? Disinherit Crissand's sons and install this boy as the Aswydd?"

"No. That is not my intent."

"No place for him, then, in Amefel, where he might live. What shall you teach him to be, then? A captain of the Guard? He can't ride, or fence. A *cleric*, perhaps! An Aswydd cleric!"

"If I wanted him a cleric, I'd send him to the Teranthines."

"If we could find one. Their shrines stand vacant. And even they would fear him. For what do you prepare this boy?"

"I am making a lasting peace between my sons, exactly the reverse of our father's intent for us."

"Sons defy their fathers' wishes. What, when your sons defy yours?"

He could argue with Master Crow. Crow only vexed him. Efanor had a way of cutting deeper, touching his fear for Nevris, for his daughter, and his son, in for the likelihood that Aswydd sorcery had indeed some purpose for his long-ago misdeeds, and revenge as its object. His stomach was upset, and for a moment he averted his face from the arguments, standing, arms folded, face to the windows.

"The boy should go home," Idrys said.

"Crow." The Marhanen temper threatened to get the better of him. "Time you left."

"He's done all you wished," Efanor said. "He's forgiven and blessed, and written in the holy record. And if his gran, as we have now established with Brother Trassin, is ill—if she should get worse—if there were a messenger to arrive with dire news, if the boy were simply to fly home to his gran, as a consequence of such a missive, it would be a great success he has achieved here. Would it not? There would be an explanation for his departure. And talk would die down."

Cefwyn let go a long, difficult breath.

"I like the boy," Efanor said. "He has admirable qualities."

"We are not burying him, damn it all! He will be back!"

"Indeed." Idrys had not gone away as requested. Cefwyn looked at him, where Idrys leaned, long arms folded, against the royal writing desk. "The stench of fire in the sanctuary is too evident, my lord king. And if we strip another stone from the chapel, and another, why, the priests will pray on bare earth by snowmelt."

"Aewyn will be in mourning," Cefwyn said.

"And what ever endeared itself to a boy's heart like the forbidden?" Efanor asked. "Separate them, and they'll fly together."

"And hate me for it."

"The boy is worried about his gran. This is my advice. Satisfy that. Let a message call the boy home now. Then bring him back in fat, lazy summer, when the streets are dusty and people are in more generous humor. Let the people see him out in the country, hunting with Aewyn, attending harvest dances, and playing pranks like boys, not—not visiting the Quinaltine at the hinge of the year, when everything is at odds. Let the people see his better qualities."

"Shall I tell you how he misled the stablemaster?" Idrys said smoothly. "Wit and guile together. Those are important qualities."

Cefwyn's fist hit the table nearest. "You have what you want, damn you, Crow. And if it's bad influence you want, you're sending him closest to it."

"You will be sending him back to Paisi's gran, with due warning, and a little wiser about the wide world. In all these years, he's been safe there."

"I'll want to know the rumors out of Amefel," Cefwyn said, "with no salt or sauce on them."

"That you shall," Idrys said. "But nearer at hand, there is the spy the Holy Father settled in the boy's rooms. That man should be fed a careful diet in the next few hours—for the Holy Father's benefit."

"I'll see to it," Efanor said.

"Feed him what you like," Cefwyn said to Efanor's departing back, "but get him out the Guelesfort doors within the hour. And you may tell the Holy Father that the Quinalt will resolve this matter, or their king will be offended. We are well certain that through lack of zeal on their part—perhaps even conspiracy against us, for political reasons—they have damaged the stones and attempted this threat to the Crown."

Efanor stopped dead. "I would hesitate at this point to declare war on the Holy Father."

"The Holy Father will not have my ear, I say, until this business is smoothed over. I'm sure you can state that position with sufficient diplomacy."

"Shall I advise the boy to prepare?" Efanor asked.

Cefwyn shook his head and cast a look at Idrys. "One of your men can contrive a message from Amefel. Do that first. Let him come into the hall, spread gossip in the kitchens, the usual thing."

"Whenever my lord king commands," Idrys said.

"He is my son, damn you. My *son*, who is nowhere at fault in this. Dispatch your messenger, let that damned spy see it when you deliver it—I fear the boy will have to believe it at least for an hour. I'll tell the boy the truth directly before supper. Arrange an escort to leave with him, before daybreak tomorrow."

"My lord king," Idrys said, grimly satisfied.

Efanor said nothing, only left.

iii

OTTER HAD NO APPETITE FOR FOOD. THE LAY BROTHER HAD SET A TRAY DOWN on the table and taken a certain amount back to his little chamber, where he ate and drank as if there were no spot on the Quinaltine floor and no shadow there.

Otter's stomach knew otherwise. Aewyn had dined with his mother this noon, and asked him to come, too; but he had no desire to sit at table with the queen asking him questions he would not know how to answer.

Was it better today? Her Majesty might ask.

No, he would have to say, if he were honest.

And: What troubles you? she might ask, which was worse, because the dreams were back, just behind his eyelids, whenever he shut his eyes at all, now. He saw fire, firelight on snow, and Henas'amef sitting on its hill, and a trail leading through snowy woods.

He saw Gran's house as all blackened sticks.

Doors opened and closed. He supposed Brother Trassin had taken his noon dishes out himself, though the man had done little else, and fed himself prodigiously, to judge by the size of the tray he had taken to his rooms.

In time, the man came back from the kitchens. Otter was reading at the time, and only noted it, and kept reading, trying to lose himself in the words.

But the poetry had failed to hold him. It was all about spring and flowers, and outside his windows, snow was coming down again, thick and wild, piling up on the sills—

Snow would be falling, likewise, in Amefel, across the river. Snow would put out fires. Gran was never careless with fires. She never had been.

Brother Trassin came to the doorway of the room with a rolled paper in hand.

"Pray to the gods," the brother said. "Bad news, poor boy. Very bad news."

He didn't understand, at first, what the brother meant. But he laid his book aside on the table. "Sir?" he asked, rising.

"This has come," Brother Trassin said, and handed him an opened document, its two seals already cracked, two shades of red wax. "I have the greatest concern, boy, the greatest concern for you."

He was puzzled. He understood he was to read the paper, and held it so the window's light shone through it. It was from a military clerk's hand. It said, beyond the opening and name of the Guelen clerk, that a guardsman who had visited Gran had come to the Guelesfort at midafternoon with a spoken message, which was rendered here as the guardsman said it and meant to be delivered to him.

The woman is very ill. She urgently wants her grandson at her side.

It was hardly Gran's way of saying things, or even a soldier's, but it had evidently come through a clerk, and the words would have changed. There was, appended to the bottom of the paper another statement, from the Commander of the Dragon Guard: *His Majesty excuses you from services.*

Somehow—not by the ordinary way messengers came and went—this had gotten into Trassin's hands. The broken seals—the first was plain, but the second looked like an official seal, with the Dragon on it, in red wax, said that Trassin had read it.

Fear made his stomach upset. He felt a profound shock and all the same, he was angry.

"How did you get this?"

"From the Lord Commander, in your name, boy, as in care of you."

"And read it? How long have you had it?"

"Dear boy!"

"How long have you had it?"

"Just now I got it. I was in the kitchens. The Guard is forming an escort for you, in the early hours. They are calling up the horses and packing for the journey. They will escort you out before the sun, back to Amefel, to deliver you back into Lord Crissand's lordship and lose no time about it. I heard this, and went to the Prince, who confirmed it, and I came here, to bring you the message myself, poor boy."

A message from Gran would have passed Paisi on the road and Paisi would be with her by now. Paisi would be seeing to her welfare. She would be well by now. There was surely no reason to worry—this was at least three days old. Or more than that. And his father knew it, and was sending him with an escort of soldiers—

"Your dreams," Brother Trassin said, "your dreams of misfortune must have some unhappy foundation in fact, and, poor boy, this instruction is in error. You cannot hope to help your gran. You have your own soul to save, you are written in the book, here you are on the verge of bettering yourself, and this woman sends after you, I can only imagine with what influence at work. I can appeal to the Holy Father—"

"I shall pray for my gran, sir." His mouth could scarcely shape words that might mollify this man, and he had no idea what to say. Brother Trassin had spoken to him very little except to pray over him, and now wanted to advise him not to go, and he had no idea what his father was about, unless—unless they knew of some reason Paisi hadn't gotten there.

He wanted to fling the missive down, to run, as fast as he could for better advice. But this man had already been to His Grace. Where was there, but Aewyn? And Aewyn would know nothing, not about messages that came through the Lord Commander.

"Pray for yourself, poor boy. Let me counsel you, your gran's country witchcraft may seem innocent, but it will drag you down to a deeper well of corruption, by ever so little steps, if you listen to wicked dreams. Sorcery wants you back, but you must not go. Your whole upbringing is out of wizardry and worse. Sorcery wants you. Fires, the fires you dream of at night, boy—those are the fires of hell."

His heart beat faster. "What about the fires?" His own dream from last night eluded him, increasingly, hiding details and fading from his grasp: Brother Trassin had waked him and sent it scattering and fading in the shock of being wakened. "What did I say last night?"

" 'Gran,' you cried, and 'the fire, the fire in the wood.' And when I waked you, you looked about as if you were there, not here, and you shouted aloud, 'Watch out for the beam,' as if you were seeing something not present. These dreams are devil-sent, boy, I know they are. And I told you that you should get up immediately and pray to stop them, but you said go away. So I did. I did, but I did pray for you, boy, and I had the utmost reason, in your refusal."

"It was just a dream, was all." He tried to believe that, and to argue rationally with the man. "*This* is a message from my gran. It came by horse, not devils!"

Even if my father knows something different.

"Devils, I say, devils. The gods never sent you these persistent dreams of fire and harm. The devils do. They called away the witch's grandson. He had no trouble answering. And if you fall into these visions, and go back to that benighted province, I fear for you. You have not the strength on your own to fight these influences. And think of this—think of this, boy. If the gods do take your grandmother, it may be in time to turn your soul from ruin and save her soul from worse sin. Mark me, boy: the gods in their mercy may have wished to save the young soul who lived under that roof, but you have to turn from your mother's wicked ways. The gods will not forgive a willful lapse, boy. The gods' retribution may be delayed, but not . . ."

"No," he cried a second time, and struck out, knocking the precious book of poetry to the floor. "My gran heals her neighbors. Her spells heal or find lost things!"

"Her healing is a false healing. Her knowledge is blasphemous. The gods' prerogatives are not for ignorant hands to use."

"Go away!" he cried. "Just leave, damn you! Don't come back!"

"If I do go, I take the gods' mercy with me. It may be forever, boy!"

"Get out!" He moved toward Brother Trassin, to shove him bodily out of the rooms, but Brother Trassin mistook his intent and abandoned his stance in haste, crying,

"Violence! Gods save us from devils!"

Brother Trassin fled through the arch, across the sitting room, out the door and slammed it.

Otter stood shaking beside the table, unable to prevent the man from spreading lies or offer reason to silence him. Trassin was the Patriarch's man, and bent on damning him with the priests of the Quinalt and with Prince Efanor and now with every devout Quinaltine, because this man, Efanor had warned him, was here for that very purpose. Priests had power. He had seen that, in the king's anxiousness to have him please the Quinalt and have his name written in the book, and now everything must have gone wrong. Priests in the Quinaltine might have seen the spot on the floor, and the shadows, and the lines of fire that had grown up during services; Efanor had gripped his hand: he could see them, too, though nobody else had seemed to notice . . . he had thought he had gotten away safely, escaped the harm and left it all behind.

But his dream pursued him. The letter advised him that Gran was desperate—or that his father had realized what was in the sanctuary hated him. The Five Gods surely hated him and wanted him out of their sanctuary, was it not clear? His father's gods wanted nothing to do with sorcery, or the Aswydds, or him. They were going to send him out with soldiers, in the dead of night, when dark things should be abroad.

And now that man ran down the Guelesfort halls crying out about devils and violence, and the report would get to the Quinaltine, and it would be bad. If he stayed to argue, or got into some tangle between his father and the priests and the soldiers—and who knew what had happened to delay Paisi, or if he had gotten there at all?—Gran might die alone.

Beware this man, his uncle had said, pinning great importance on it, and he had failed to mollify Brother Trassin. Trassin was his enemy, things in the Quinaltine had gone wrong, Efanor had probably told his father, and everything had collapsed in ruin. He would be lucky if he ever saw Aewyn until they both were men, and by then they might be enemies, as Guelenfolk tended to be toward Amefin.

Gods save Gran, he thought. Tears made the room swim. And he was too distraught to face Aewyn before he left, or to try to explain. His father would hear a worse report from the priests than he had already gotten. Aewyn might protest, but his father would lay down the law and run him out at night, for fear of appearances, and he just had to go, that was all. He had to.

He went straight back to the clothespress, took his second-best cloak, wrapped up all his changes of linen, all the food laid out on the table in that, and his outdoor boots, and put on his third-best cloak.

That was all he took. The Quinalt amulet, he laid on the table. It was Prince Efanor's, and it was silver, and he would not be accused of stealing it. For the rest, he tucked up the bundle under his cloak and left, only hoping to all the kindlier and more numerous Bryaltine gods that no one noticed him. He headed not toward the west, the stable side of the Guelesfort, but down the eastern servants' stairs, and out the eastern door.

Then he crossed along by the iron fence and the hedges, in what had begun to be a thick snowfall. He ignored the hulking shadow of the Quinaltine that loomed above, and when he passed the outward bow of the building, into the little courtyard, he refused to look toward the windows of the second story, either, one of which was his father's.

He had to brave the stables, all the same, so he took care not to be seen at all as he came around the western flank of the keep, and approached the stable fences. He kept his head down and his face shadowed by the hood as he slipped along the outer fence into the stable itself, where the few courier horses and the king's own horses alone had not gone down to pasture. In the near dark of the interior he lifted a plain leather halter and ordinary lead rope from its peg beside the nearest stall, ignored the inquisitive blazed nose that poked out to sniff the air around the theft, and was gone out the door again, down by the main Guelesfort gate, which was, by day, not usually shut.

Here he expected to pretend to be a serving boy on an errand; but the guards were inside the guardhouse, out of the weather, and paid no attention as he simply walked out.

In the town streets, he lengthened his stride, taking only moderate care to keep his head down and keep the wind from blowing the hood half-back. He kept the cloak clutched about him and the halter and the large bundle under it, and hoped for at least as much luck as he entered the lower city and approached the town gates.

Here, too, the thick snow obscured a mere straggle of farmerfolk and craftsmen going in and out on ordinary business. He simply walked close in the tracks of a pair of craftsmen, head bowed. With them, he passed beyond the gates, out onto the road that led through a scattered few craftsmen's dwellings, past a few fences, and then took a brisk stride along beside snowy winter orchards and fields and pasturages, leaving other traffic behind. Oxen and cattle huddled near haystacks, or in the lee of shelter walls. He saw horses in pasture, a few, but he had his mind set on one horse, the one to which he had some legitimate claim, at least, not to be called a thief.

He wished he had been able to bring Paisi's own bridle, and most of all his saddle, which were stored in the tack room up above. But that had been too great a risk, and someone would have stopped him. He hoped the halter would fit, or that he could make it fit. He was cold to the bone, and his feet were numb by the time he reached that pasture where Tammis ranged. The sky was gray and the whole world else was white, and he feared that no sensible creature would come to a call in this weather. He stepped through the rails and trudged out into the midst of the pasture. They had learned a whistle for Tammis—none worked on Feiny—and when he whistled into the blowing wind, once and three times, then he saw, indeed a dark head come out of the little copse of trees a distance away.

He had no apple for a bribe, but in his bundle he had honey sweets he had saved from the table, and when Tammis had nosed up to him, he could deliver a small offering.

He slipped the lead-line over Tammis's neck to be sure of him while he was enjoying his treat, and cold-numb fingers managed, with some little difficulty, to get the ill-fitting, cold-stiff halter over the piebald's poll and settled behind his ears.

Then he could lead Tammis toward the gate. Tammis had no notion he was being stolen. He went cheerfully enough. There was little else he could give him, he knew, but the bread, if a horse would eat it. And how they should feed him when he reached Gran's, not to mention his own horse's appetite, he had no idea. He supposed he should take both Feiny and Tammis up the hill once he got home and turn them over to Lord Crissand, praying him to send them home to his father, so he and Paisi should not be obliged any further.

The thought hurt. He wanted not to think that far ahead.

He was careful to close the gate once he had passed it. The horsemaster had lectured him and Paisi very strictly about gates, as if he and Paisi had not come to Guelessar knowing that already, regarding Gran's goats, who could manage most latches for themselves.

And there, in the snowy lane, he seized Tammis's shaggy mane, poised himself, and vaulted for his back, bundle and all, the way the stableboys did. The first attempt, encumbered by the bundle, he slid right off Tammis's rump and woolly side, but it was close enough to encourage him: the second try, in which he brought Tammis close to the fence and shifted his bundle to the hand that gripped the mane and the rein, let him make a leap, wriggle his knee across Tammis's well-padded backbone, and thence ease astride, Tammis being a fairly patient horse.

Off they went, then, Tammis ambling along in no great hurry at first, then warming into a jog that kept them both warm. They reached the high-road, and Tammis was sure at that point that they would be going north, toward town, but he reined him about in a wide circle and turned south-ward, as the merchants traveled, with no one in sight north or south, in the threatening weather.

He had gotten away clear. He was going home, the same way Paisi had gone, and he would keep faith with Gran, at least. If she wanted him to go back again, he would tell Gran that the ways of Guelessar were not for him, that he was homesick, that he might see his brother later, on his regular visit—all such excuses as he could contrive.

And maybe his father would indeed come riding past with Aewyn as they always had, and maybe after much of a year had passed, they could ex-change greetings and he could pay his respects to his father and patch things as if nothing very bad had happened.

Or maybe there would only be soldiers, to collect the horses, and bid him stay away from Guelessar forever, since he had done things so badly and made trouble with the priests. That notion, which he thought more likely, settled like a leaden weight in his chest.

He had dreamed of Guelessar in his childhood, and thoroughly enjoyed his first days in the Guelesfort, oh, so full of wonders; and with Aewyn for his friend. But they had taken a dark turn in the Quinaltine, at Festival, and he had no wish to see all the good memories go sour, or do further harm to his father's reputation or to Aewyn's. He wished no one ill—wished no harm, even to Brother Trassin, who had wanted to pray for him and save his soul, but he felt the urgent need, for this hour, to be far from here as fast as he could persuade Tammis to travel before the tangle grew deeper and darker. He just had to get home and be sure Gran was all right.

What he would do then—then, and forever afterward, he had no scrap of a notion. He had planned everything toward Guelessar, toward his father. Now he found himself not quite a man and no longer a child—even his time with Gran had become perilous, perhaps on the verge of passing. She was very old, and frail, and he and Paisi both knew she might leave them someday soon.

Then what? Then what, and where?

And what will I be, if I come home too late this time?

Gran had sent him out to find his fortune. His time with Aewyn, and among the books, had all been aimed at growing up and becoming a man who could support the family: Aewyn had been so convinced they would grow up together, and be allies, and now all that plan was gone, he began to realize it was not Otter the child who was coming home to Gran. Otter had grown up in his winter in Guelessar, grown up and gone away and looked to have very grown-up men angry with him and fearful of him.

Lord Crissand might not be as well-disposed as before, either.

Where was safety for them, then?

Tammis's hooves found packed snow in a track where carts had passed, and thumped along good-naturedly, his breath frosting on the wind. Snow turning his shaggy mane white. Tammis carried him home, not at all the Otter who had left, but another creature altogether, one he hoped had, on this last day, grown warier and become harder to catch.

iv

IT COULD NOT BE TRUE. IT COULD NOT POSSIBLY BE TRUE, WHAT THE BODY-guards whispered among themselves.

"Who said Otter should go away?" Aewyn asked, breaking into his guards' privacy in the little chamber in the hallway and standing squarely in the door.

The men—grown men, his father's men—were all caught, and there was no graceful way to dislodge him without answering his questions.

"Your Highness," Selmyn, seniormost, said, with a grave manner, "we very much regret to be the bearers of news His Majesty surely wished to deliver . . ."

"Why would my father send him away," Aewyn cried, "when my father brought him here in the first place?"

"There seems to be some trouble," Selmyn said, "Your Highness."

"What trouble? What trouble would it be?"

"We don't know," Selmyn said, red-faced, clearly embarrassed. "But word is out that he has to leave—there's a Guard contingent to ride escort tomorrow morning, Dragon Guard, Your Highness. He was to go to Amefel before the sun comes up. And watchers we know are running up and down the stairs in some haste."

"The hell!" It was not language he was permitted to use, but Aewyn said it, and stormed out of the doorway and out into the hall and across the grand stairway landing to reach Otter's rooms, his guard trailing him.

Why? he intended to ask Otter, first off and without preamble. Whatever trouble Otter had gotten into, there had to be time for cooler tempers to prevail. His father had gotten the family temper from his father and his father from his grandfather, and Aewyn had his own. They could all shout and threaten, but a quiet few words with Otter first would settle his stomach.

Then they could both go and talk to his father, and his father would listen to him. He knew it.

But when he opened Otter's door and walked in, he found the fire still burning, but no sign of Otter, not in any of the rooms, only a book on the floor and a piece of paper beside it.

He picked it up. He read it, and things came half-clear, at last. Lord Idrys. Master Crow, no less. That was not just a problem. It might be deadly.

"Where is he?" he demanded of his useless guards. For the first time he was frightened.

"We have no idea, Your Highness," Selmyn said, and Aewyn brushed right past him and headed back the way he had come, and on to his father's rooms.

More guardsmen, standing outside the doors, came to abrupt attention as he headed straight through their midst.

The last, seniormost, had the temerity to lower a hand, barring his progress.

"I'll see my father!" Aewyn said. "I'll see him now!"

His guards had overtaken him. His guards and his father's cast combative looks at each other, and the seniormost signed for silence and slipped inside properly to inquire if the king could possibly be interrupted.

Aewyn shoved the door open and walked in without leave. The guard's quick move saved the door from banging.

"Father?" he called out, and saw the far doors shut, those that barred off the royal apartments, which generally meant a conference in progress. He headed for them, jerked the first open, and found his father, indeed, in conference with the Lord Chamberlain, who had been leaning over a table full of charts.

"Aewyn?" his father asked, and rose to his feet—not startled, no. Upset.

Aewyn went at the matter in his father's own way—head-on. "Where's Otter?"

"In his rooms, one would have thought."

Aewyn shook his head. "He's not. He's heard. *I've* heard. He got a message from his gran by way of the Lord Commander. And you had already arranged the Guard to go with him in the dead of night, without seeing *me*! Why did you not tell *me*, Father?"

His father turned to the Lord Chancellor.

"My lord king," the Lord Chancellor said, excusing himself, and Aewyn clamped his lips together and said not a word until witnesses, even the guards, had passed outside the doors.

Alone, his father stared at him until it occurred to him that he would lose, in any test of wills. It was his part to bow his head, unclench his jaw, however difficult, and adopt a milder tone.

"Why was I not informed?" Aewyn asked again, trembling with outrage.

"Where is he?"

"Not in his rooms. The fire's still burning, but he's not there. Neither is Brother Fool."

"He was to leave," his father said, ignoring the epithet. "Tomorrow. I've told the stables to notify the Guard if your brother should try to leave. I was going to speak to him tonight. Or earlier, if he appeared. I was going to send him off with a proper escort, all the help he and his gran could want." His father drew a deep breath and his brows knit. "There was a message."

"I read it."

"It was a lie," his father said. "Or at least, it was intended to give him an excuse."

"*You* did it!"

"I fear I did."

"Then he's taken off to help her, and it's a lie?"

"He won't have gotten a horse. Or passed the gates. The Guard will bring him back."

"He'll have walked out. He'll have taken Paisi's horse. He's out there, in the snow."

"How do you know that?"

"Because if he couldn't get a horse at the stables, he knows where Paisi's is, and he was going to ride him to the lodge."

"What does the lodge have to do with this?"

"We were going there, and he was going to ride Paisi's horse, but I said you'd get him a better. But if he's gone home, and not asked anyone, then he's gone down and taken Paisi's horse from the pasture."

"Where will he have a saddle?"

"He couldn't get one."

"The boy can't ride!"

"If he has to, he will," Aewyn declared. He had not a doubt in the world. "He'd do it, for his gran. He loves her. And he's not here! Father, how *could* you?"

His father sank into his chair. He looked tired and downhearted. "It wasn't my best plan. Damn the luck, sit down. No, *sit,* I say! If you break into men's councils, be ready to hear things that may displease you. There was no message. No real one, at least."

"Then why is the Lord Commander—" he began to ask, but his father lifted a hand.

"Hush. Hush and listen. There is serious trouble. There is trouble in the Quinaltine, beyond the matter of the spilled incense."

"It was all cleaned up. And that wasn't his fault!"

"It was not all cleaned up. Beyond it, I say. Marks remain, which some can see. I can't. You can't—I trust you can't."

"I don't think so."

"To your uncle's eyes, and to your mother's, and to Otter's, I'm sure, the spot persists. It reappeared, on the new stone. And trouble is rising. Rumors. Accusations of sorcery that sit very ill. The Bryaltines are generally a peaceful sect, but the years since the war have brought a certain militancy to part of the sect, that which roots itself in Elwynor . . . in your mother's kingdom. Hostilities breaking out between Bryalt and Quinalt in Guelessar is not a good thing for the treaty, for you, and most especially for your mother and your baby sister in any visit this spring. Do you understand me in this?"

"I understand about the Bryaltines. But that's not Otter's doing."

"Most firmly it is not. But the manifestations are visible to your uncle—which, indeed, you are not to say, boy!"

"No, sir." He was troubled. He knew his uncle was saintly and devout, and had a voice in the Quinaltine, and moved the priests when others couldn't. He knew his mother saw things. "But what if there is a spot?"

"It's not that. It's an imperfection. A sign. There are haunts within the Quinaltine."

"Haunts!"

"Something like. Or something worse. Our Otter is not welcome there, whether by the dead or the living, whether or not the scratches on the stones were helped along by mortal hands. There is something the matter, Efanor assures me. For his own safety, he should go away for a season—only for a season!—and then, then, I promise you, he will come back when things are quieter. We need not have the heir to Ylesuin involved in any whispers of impropriety, or, gods save us, blasphemy."

"Blasphemy! He never—"

"Patience. Patience, I say, and we'll have him back in the summer, or at latest, in the fall: it's become imperative to have him back, not to have given in to this. He'll come back a little wiser, better known to the people, to the priests, to the court. And ourselves a little wiser in the meanwhile. We'll keep him out of the Quinaltine then. And things will have settled. They do, with time. Be patient."

"I can be patient! It's all very well for me to be patient! But he's out in the snow! He's had dreams about his gran, terrible dreams!"

"More than the one?"

"More than the one. And he's been terribly scared for her."

"Damnation."

"So send someone to bring him back! To tell him it was all a lie!"

"He's on his way. He should go."

"Papa!"

"But I'd not have him riding away with no saddle, taking that damned message for the truth, either. I am entirely at fault here. If he's afoot, we shall find him. And I count on you," his father said, lifting a finger, "to remain here, dutifully, attending Festival as you should, being a very model of good behavior. I'll ride after him myself, beg his pardon, and ask him to come back to us this summer, when you may go to the lodge, hunt, do what you like. May I count on you?"

He had never heard of his father apologizing. Ever. For the king to ride off and miss the last ceremonies of Festival was no small thing. He nodded solemnly. "Yes. Yes, Papa." He hadn't used that word in the last year. But this was his papa talking, now, the man who had used to carry him on his back. It was his papa, not the king, who was going after Otter, and who stood the best chance of finding him. "Tell him . . . tell him I'll see him this summer, and I'd have done something to stop him if I'd known."

"I'm sure you would have," his father said, and stood up and hugged him, and rang for the Guard. "Get my cloak, get my horse, get an escort. Now!"

"My lord king," the answer was, and things happened quickly from that point.

Aewyn could only trudge back to his room, his troubled guard shadowing him. He wanted to turn and shout at them unreasonably to go away and do something useful, but they had to be there. He was the heir, and the Prince's Guard always had to be there, for the rest of his life, no matter what he wanted.

V

STABLEBOYS SCURRIED, THE STABLEMASTER PROTESTED HE HAD AUTHORIZED no use of a horse, and sent some feckless boy to take inventory, great loving gods! *inventory* in the tack room, as if that mended matters, or as if he had time to hear it. But a halter was missing from the stall nearest, and no one could find it.

"Mind your *doors,* man, mind your gates and fences, now that the horse and the boy are missing!" Cefwyn seized Anfar's reins from the trembling stableboy and hauled himself into the saddle. He had not waited to arm. He had no helm, no lance, only a mail shirt his bodyguard had brought with them and which he had donned, waiting for his horse and his guards' horses to be saddled.

"My lord king," the stablemaster called up to ask, "shall I send to His Grace?"

"Do that," he said shortly. His brother needed to know: he was in charge in his absence. He had already ordered a message to Idrys, to get out on the search, too, and have the escort that should have taken the boy on to Henas'amef find other horses and get onto his track, too: he had just taken the horses, for his own personal guard.

With that, he turned Anfar's head and rode out into the snowy courtyard, and on toward the gates, his bodyguard scrambling to keep up with him.

It was Marhanen temper that blazed past the gate-guards and damned them for lazy dogs; it was a more patient frame of mind that rode through the feckless traffic of his city streets, taking a reasonable pace on snow-packed cobbles and in among ordinary walkers.

But he had words for the keepers of the southern gate.

"Did you note a boy go through, probably in a hooded cloak? A boy afoot?"

The confusion that greeted that question, the guilty hesitation in the men, informed him that they had not, and dared neither lie nor tell the whole of the truth. They had likely, at the moment the boy had passed the gates, been doing exactly what he had found them doing: warming themselves in the guardhouse and having jam on toast.

"There will be one man on watch outside hereafter, no matter the weather: one man at least will be out in the elements, come flood, come ice, come all the heavens falling, day or night, to the end of time, and I want a list of those that come and go, for all time to come, at this and every gate, damn you!"

He was ultimately the gate-guards' master, no less than his brother the duke of Guelessar, and if he had berated the stablemaster for his easy ways, twice caught, now he berated himself for slack, peacetime policy with the city gates here and elsewhere about the realm—it was peace: it had been peace for a decade and more: people had gotten fat and easy. And the burden his order for name-taking imposed on honest citizens might not be temperate or even wise, now that the gate was open and the horse and the boy were gone, but he had the most unwelcome feeling that the easy times were in jeopardy. He would leave it to Efanor to make sense of it, once the guards had remembered their jobs were not sinecures, even in peacetime. Efanor, once shown an error, mended it.

Efanor had attended the boy in sanctuary, and discovered his distress, and tried to protect him, when the king, under public witness, could not touch his own son. Who must have been terrified beyond anything he showed.

Would he had taken a different course. Would he had never agreed to leave the boy believing that damned message for any length of time, nothing so long as an hour, which he had hoped was only enough time to deceive Brother Trassin and see him out the door. All through the boy's visit, he had left Otter to Aewyn, thinking the world at peace. He had feared too much attention from him might frighten the boy, or, at the other extreme, encourage too much presumption of favor.

Now he had fractured the peace, high and wide.

Now, please the gods he might find the boy still at the pasture, still trying to get up on that tall beast, but he doubted it. Otter was no great fighter, but he was agile, and clearly no moss grew on that lad once he had formed an intention to move.

He only hoped the horse might simply slip the boy softly into a snowbank and take off for his home fields. He hoped, in the whiteness ahead, to see a cloaked figure afoot and coming toward them, dashed in his hopes of escape or doggedly headed toward Amefel afoot.

But when he came to the byroad that led off to the Darkbrook pastures, tracks in the snow showed a boy going in and a horse coming out onto the main road.

No need to divert off the road to the pasture lane and back. The condition of the tracks showed a passage old enough, but not buried: they had to move. The horse in question had only a boy's weight to carry, and the horse, a piebald gelding, an accidental breeding of one of his own mares, was nevertheless strong, fast, and surefooted on bad ground.

Did the boy have any food with him, for him or the horse? Had he taken more than a cloak for cover? The snow, whipped off the ground by the wind, made a disobliging veil across the road, blurring all distant sight, making too great a haste reckless indeed. He put Anfar to all the speed he dared, and his guard rattled around him.

But what had he asked himself before this, when luck had seemed to favor the boy and when he eluded searchers and found ordinarily competent men sheltered in the gatehouse, in an uncommonly strong spate of snow?

Simple bad luck?

He dared not assume it was.

They followed the track until it merged with that of local farm carts and foot traffic, and lost itself, near Pany Well. The sun sank, colored red, in the magic-ridden west.

"Your Majesty," Paras said then, the captain of his bodyguard, riding close. "There's no catching him. His horse has no weight to carry."

He didn't look at the man. Temper boiled just below the surface, the hateful Marhanen temper, which broke things and did wild things that only added fuel to anger.

He breathed once, twice, three times before he simply turned Anfar's head toward Guelemara, and his guard swung in about him.

Well, he said to himself, staring straight between Anfar's ears, *no question where he's gone, and if more than luck aims him, no question he'll get there safely.*

Follow him? Gossip enough attends him. Everything I do is marked and noticed, parsed and interpreted, and gossiped from here to Olmern.

And what can I do now? What's fit to give a boy, to pay for the hellish ride he'll have had?

Favor for the grandmother he loves? That she already has. That she would have, regardless.

A message? More cold words on paper?

I'll ride out myself before too many days, he thought, when this racket dies down. *I owe the boy far more than any letter.*

It was full dark when they met Idrys and his men coming toward them, on a road otherwise deserted, at the snow-choked bottom of a hill where their outward passage had already broken the drift.

Idrys, wrapped in a hooded cloak, saluted him, and asked no foolish questions. The boy was not with them. They were exhausted and out of sorts in their meeting.

"Two men will go on to Lord Crissand," Cefwyn said, saying nothing about the message that had started this journey. "Send a man on. This message for Lord Crissand: treat my son as a guest in your province, treat his man as mine, treat his grandmother as a woman I favor. Protect them against hostile influences by any means necessary, and supply them with whatever comforts they may lack. And the messengers will visit my son's house and say this: your father and brother send their love. You will visit us again come summer, when we hope for a quieter season. All the house regrets your leaving. Must I repeat it?"

The skills of a courier would have made it sure, word for word and with no variance, but, "Aye, my lord king," Idrys' lieutenant said, out of the dark. "I shall remember it."

Idrys' men did not promise what they could not perform, not twice. He nodded, stripped off his glove, and gave the man a lesser ring, the one he used for messages. Cold fingers transferred it: a warm bare hand closed solidly on it, across the moving gap between Anfar and the other horse.

"If you should overtake the boy on the road," Cefwyn said, "do not attempt to bring him back against his will. Tell him his part of the message, escort him safely to his grandmother's house, then deliver the message to Lord Crissand before you come back. Find out what the grandmother may need and personally see she has it."

"Yes, Your Majesty."

Two of the Dragon Guard rode off into the night. Cefwyn said not a word as Idrys and two others of his men turned about to ride with them. Silence persisted another few moments.

"A clever boy," Idrys said.

"He is that," Cefwyn muttered. "And your damned message went awry. It went greatly awry, Crow!"

"It went half an hour early. Trassin heard the gossip in the kitchen from a horse groom, and came upstairs to the Guard office, looking for the message, *before* it went the path we intended. He took it and flew right to the boy."

"So were you at all tracking him?"

"Oh, tracking every step, and always a step behind. The brother brought this missive to the boy—and cometlike, blazed to the Quinaltine in great agitation. This indeed, we attended, attempting to get a man to report from inside the Quinaltine. The watcher upstairs had gone downstairs on his track; another was summoned to go back to the room and assure the boy's safety. The boy had left. That man left to report to me. His Highness arrived and went to you."

"Would you had let Trassin go and brought the boy to *me*. Damn it all. Damn my own complaisance. *I* may have an enemy in my own son."

"You already *have* an enemy, my lord king. His mother continues alive, of all the Aswydds that were. And the boy evidently managed to leave the room in the scant few moments my men upstairs had followed Trassin downstairs. Downstairs, one of my men, realizing pursuit of the monk had drawn two men from upstairs and from the eastern door, and fearing that the monk might have done the boy violence, hurried upstairs—which left no one watching the lower hall. He found the room vacant and went to the west hall to inquire of the Prince's Guard, who had not seen him at the Prince's door or on the stairs. The Prince then heard the report—hence there, and to you, and meanwhile my men had gone down to report to me—while the boy was eluding our precautions at the stable and also at the gates, likely the Guelesfort's western gate, a miraculous single step ahead of our inquiries all the way. We did *not* hear about the horse in pasture until one of my men consulted the stablemaster. But that was after you had left, my lord king."

It was not in Master Crow to apologize. He came within a hair of it this time.

"It was not the advice I had, Crow. It was my taking it. I lied to my son. I never liked it. I should never have done it. And damn the man! What has he told the Holy Father, do you know?"

"That the boy attacked him."

"Attacked him? Our Otter? Never!"

Idrys asked darkly, "Will you tolerate this teller of tales?"

"Nothing to provoke His Holiness, Crow. Leave him to Efanor. For now. This will be silenced. Or I shall take other measures."

"My lord king."

He knew Idrys; Idrys knew his ways. The arguments between them were old, the disagreements frequent, but they did not long revisit things done and beyond recall, like the untidy chance of a horse groom in the kitchen. Or the chance of a boy choosing exactly the right moment to duck down a stairway or out a door.

It was exactly the sort of luck that had attended them for days, was it not?

For a time after that exchange, the creak of saddle leather and slight jingle of armor was all the sound about them. There was nothing left to do, Cefwyn thought, but what Idrys' very trustworthy men were now doing, going on to Amefel and being sure the horse did not throw the boy and leave him afoot. There was no hope left of his finding the boy tonight. Nor was there any hope of amends to the boy for the lie. There was only a long, cold ride home from here, and an explanation to his wife and to his son. Sometimes, trying to do justice, trying to balance one need against another, the king of Ylesuin missed the mark very badly. And this was beyond bad luck.

His hand, still bare, sought the inside of his shirt, where Tristen's medallion lay, warm against his chest, hidden from all sight.

Keep him safe, he wished, like a prayer, but not to any god. *I've tried so long to keep from doing wrong with the boy. I kept my distance this season to let the boys manage for themselves. I tried to bring him onto the rolls, into public view, where people could see he's such a well-favored boy. I tried to do well for him. And now plainly I've not done the right thing. Nothing I've done in years has gone this badly amiss.*

Keep him safe.

Keep all of us safe from whatever's afoot in this business. Something surely is.

Sometimes, when he thought of Tristen, he felt a comforting warmth, a sense someone was listening.

Tonight the warmth failed and faded, and he put the glove on quickly, numb to the bone.

CHAPTER FOUR

i

FESTIVAL ENDED, THANK THE GODS, IN SUCH AN UNPRECEDENTED GLUT OF CHAR-
itable bread and ale that the city reeled homeward in much better humor.
Street preachers found no audience in a driving snow. Bread and ale had
appeased the populace, Brother Trassin had dropped from sight and hearing, apparently withdrawn to cloistered service for his health, and the Holy
Father, miraculously recovered from his fever, approached the royal precincts
to be appeased with gold.

"The hell he will!" was Cefwyn's initial response: he had had perhaps
an hour of sleep before services, had missed breakfast in favor of that hour,
had had to confess failure to his son, and was still in no good humor; but
Efanor bent near the kingly ear, and whispered, "The stone has stayed clean
the while, and the scratches on the altar are diminished."

"Conveniently!"

"The Holy Father has declared a miracle and declared the omen por-
tended the imminent fall of a cleric the Holy Father rightly despises. It's all
gone to religious debate between the Holy Father and the street preachers,
brother. It's to the good of us all, not least the boy, who's quietly written
down in the book as blessed, for anyone to see, and the Holy Father has
declared him—Guelen."

"Give him a hundredweight for his masonwork," Cefwyn said sourly,
wishing it were within his prerogatives to hang Brother Trassin. "And his
cloistered spy. *Guelen,* for the gods' sake!"

"Guelen. But still bastard."

The old man approached. Cefwyn summoned up a smile and a gracious
word as the Patriarch came to pay his respects, in this first royal audience of
the new year.

"Your Majesty," the old man said, and bowed. Cefwyn took his hand and
kissed his cheek.

"I hate him," Aewyn said afterward, leaning near him on the other side, standing, and Cefwyn, on his throne, and facing more petitioners and a headache, leaned his head against the angry young brow.

"Don't hate those who serve you, boy. Shape them with skill or be rid of them."

"I wish you'd be rid of him," his son said. "He's to blame for this. He might even have done the scratches. I know he sent Trassin."

"And has apologized and will not transgress again against your brother. He has written him down Guelen, not Amefin. Should we appoint a new man, to make new mistakes? We shall just have to find an honor for your brother, a good Guelen title."

"It wasn't a mistake," Aewyn said glumly, "and he's not our friend."

"Good lad." Cefwyn kissed his son's convenient brow and pressed his arm. "But we know what he did and have that to hold over him when we need. Keep his sins in mind. They're as good as coin."

"Otter's not Guelen. He won't want to be Guelen. He's Amefin, and he likes being that."

"Hush," Cefwyn said, in the approach of the duke of Carys. He managed a smile, a gracious extension of his hand to one who was truly a friend.

Three days on, one of Idrys' company came back, having turned back at the river ford to deliver a report. "The lieutenant believes the boy has crossed the river dry-shod," that man reported, "and the lieutenant crossed on into Amefel to carry the message as ordered. He sent me back to advise the Lord Commander and understand the situation in the capital."

"Stay and warm yourself," Cefwyn said, "and put yourself at your commander's orders." He did not dispose Idrys' men, not ordinarily, and Idrys would have his own questions to ask the man. He was not utterly surprised that Otter had eluded them, and would, at this rate, be home or close to it. He hoped the boy had indeed had a dry crossing, and slept warm.

He had had a dream of his own last night, however. He had dreamed he rode after the boy, and that he fell farther and farther behind, until in a white gust, Otter vanished. That dream continued to haunt his day.

Aewyn picked at his meals, an unheard-of degree of distress. He had discharged two of his servants for reporting his mood, he had taken to the library and demanded maps of Amefel, and sulked through the family dinner that quietly celebrated the end of the Bryalt feast.

"Where is *his* chair?" he asked loudly, and the servants froze in confusion. In fact the table was arranged for the intimate family, and there was no place set for Otter.

"He will be back," Ninévrisë said reasonably. "Your father has made that very clear. And I believe he will come. Do not you?"

Aewyn frowned and pushed his peas about the plate, disconsolate. He only picked at his dessert, and that final display, with his surliness toward his mother, truly roused Cefwyn's temper, but he kept it under tight rein nonetheless.

The evening was full of storms. Aemaryen was fretful. Even the servants went about glum and downcast, and one dropped a dish, a crash that dented a gold-rimmed plate and brought down the majordomo's silent fury.

Your father has made that clear, Ninévrisë had said.

Sent, and by a guardsman. He had been reluctant to put that royal apology on paper. He had turned back, when he had told his son he would do better than that, and his son had hoped, had he not? A son always hoped his father could work a miracle.

Afterward, in his office, at his desk, he found a blank sheet under his hand and the pen near, and he picked up the pen, and found himself wondering again what he could write, what he dared commit to paper. Messengers had been intercepted before this, and a gods-cursed run of bad luck in the visit counseled caution.

His queen was waiting. His servants would not go to their beds until they had seen him to his.

But after all the hurry and flurry of the dinner, after all the press of petitioners and favor-seekers, there was a silence, a very lonely silence.

It became a very resentful silence.

One more, he kept thinking, one more piece chipped away by the priests. A son, this time. The half of me, before this, when Tristen had quietly slipped even out of Amefel and sent him only a letter, saying, "They hate me too much."

Too cursed much. The damned priests. Always, the damned priests. And the people he ruled. The hatred of Guelenfolk for the Sihhë who had ruled the west had not faded at all. Hatred had sent Tristen from the world of Men—though Tristen would never accuse his people or blame those who drove him out.

The anger that had slowly welled up came brimming over, rendering him furious beyond words. He more than suspected traitors among the priests, mortal men who thought they knew better than their king. The scratches and the spot were all too convenient to create a furor, not yet a sedition, but so easily could the matter have gone to riot and bloodshed, given the bloody-handed history of the Quinaltine and its priests.

Efanor claimed a manifestation, and he did not disbelieve in such powers; but on the other, and from a king's jaundiced view, it might have a common, human, seditious origin, even human conjuring of the forces Efanor warned him against. Oh, that that were the truth, and that he could find the author of it and get his hands on one priest's throat—

But he was wiser than that. Wiser than his father. He drew no absolute conclusions. He refused the answers his temper wanted—the assumption that hidden enemies in his own realm had done it, forces he already detested, the old contenders for power over the king . . .

Anger and imprudence had ruled his father Ináreddrin before him, distrust of those around him had let the very conspirators, agreeable men, into his father's deepest confidence, until ultimately those men had brought his father down. The temptation to see enemies and opposition where there was only frustration was, oh, so easy when one wore the crown. It was natural enough that the common folk feared an Aswydd bastard from across the border, it was natural there be whispers . . . it was natural they look to the gods for signs.

The gods hadn't helped *him,* had they, when the kingdom tottered on the brink of sorcerous ruin?

Magic, however, he had seen work. Sorcery and wizardry he had seen in abundance. Religion he had not seen work at all, except to watch it deny him friends and drive an innocent boy out into a snowstorm.

So damn all priests—the gods never helped him to what he wanted, never did anything that he could see but gather money from rich and poor alike, paying back a little bread and ale for the poor, and observing silence on sins for the rich.

The gods were not particularly good about silence for *his* sins, leaping gleefully onto his mistakes, not even sparing his attempts to do good. The gods deserted him whenever he relied on them in the least—and yet, in all justice, he knew he was never really faithful to them—not like Efanor, whose piety was always tinged with just a little sensible doubt—

But Efanor still prayed. Efanor saw the same things he saw and somehow managed to think the gods existed behind the false appearances, managed to find divinity hidden behind the priests, power behind the superstition and the terror, all with a doctrine that Efanor never was able to explain.

And Efanor had at least said he liked the boy, had he not?

Efanor had counted Tristen a friend, had he not?

And if there were gods, and if there was faith, Efanor had a grip on that realm and saw merit in the boy. So he was not wrong in what he had done.

Above all, he didn't deserve to have all he loved forever hedged about and threatened by priests as well as dark magic—

Dark magic. *That* was the worst of it. Magic of things Tristen hadn't created, and didn't wield—magic the Aswydds had slid into when they were kings in Amefel.

There were facts the Marhanen house would have to deal with: not only was his bastard son half-Aswydd, which entailed a strong Sihhë connection, but there actually ran a faint thread of Sihhë blood in his other son—in Aewyn, himself, through Ninévrisë.

And that was the knowledge that tainted his relations with the Quinalt priests: that, the way he knew secrets about them, they had his queen's heredity to call up anytime they wanted to declare war on him. Challenge them for their misdeeds, and they could challenge him with that.

They had been affronted, when he brought an Aswydd bastard here, installed him in the house, then held him over into Festival. He knew it. He had known it would be not be smooth going when Tristen asked him to care for the boy.

Had he misinterpreted what Tristen asked of him? Should he have cherished the boy in Amefel, near his mother's influences, after all, instead of trying to remove him from that district?

So, well, and his men had failed to find a single rider in a snowstorm . . . no miracle, that, no magic—at least not in the single event. But add up all the others. His first riders, the ones sent out to find Paisi and report back, had said not a thing. He had no idea what was going on at Henas'amef, or whether the boy's ill dreams—and his own false message—were unhappily true.

A dark presence shadowed the doorway. Master Crow was abroad at late hours.

"Crow?"

"My lord king?"

"Damned inquisitive Crow. No news?"

Idrys shook his head. "No, my lord king." A silence. Idrys didn't leave. "The storm is abating. There's a star showing."

"Oh, things are remarkably settling. The boy is arriving where Tarien desires him to be, is he not? Now all is peaceful."

"There's a thought worth a shudder."

To save a kingdom—a king worked under a different sort of law, did he not, with different constraints? Mercy was at times the wrong mercy, and a king's mistaken kindness made orphans and widows, laying the dead in heaps and windrows.

Had he possibly been selfish to refuse a murder or two, of a sorceress, even of his own son?

His personal virtue didn't reside in the gods. He found it in Tristen's mercy. The Quinalt, be it noted, had driven Tristen away from him and left him without counsel, except his brother Efanor.

And Idrys. Always Idrys, this dark advisor.

"There will be one more mission," Cefwyn said to Idrys, "and put a good man on it. This letter must not lose itself in a snowstorm, or go astray, or be read by the messenger. It will contain very damning things."

"My lord king?"

"Sit down. Be still. I have to think."

Crow sat. Cefwyn picked up the quill, uncapped the inkpot, wrote, at considerable length for a royal message. He wrote, and sanded and sealed it.

"To whom goes this?" Idrys asked, when he delivered it to Idrys' hand.

"To Crissand. Treat it with extreme caution."

"Shall I ask?"

"It states that he should be on his guard regarding your very sensible misgivings. And that he should send a message westward."

Idrys' chin came up slightly. "Indeed." Idrys did not disapprove of the notion. Clearly. "High time, indeed, my lord king."

He more than forbore to check the man in his liberties, he encouraged him, for his soul's sake—knowing one old advisor at least would never lie to him. He sent Crow out to rouse a messenger at this hour, with the conviction his Commander of the Guard would choose a man of strong loyalty, who would treat the missive as critically as a battlefield dispatch.

And if his own head weren't burdened with a crown he had never wanted, he'd take horse this hour and ride all the way to Ynefel tower himself, by way of Henas'amef, while he was about it. Devil take the Quinalt and all their works—if he had not the Crown to burden him, he'd take wife and son and daughter with him and stay at Ynefel for all his days, in the company of an honest friend, the one man who had never deceived him, never counseled him to take the expedient, darker paths.

It was not, alas, a choice he had.

BOOK TWO

CHAPTER ONE

i

A BRISK AND SUNNY DAY, AND THE PIEBALD'S FEET BROKE AN ICY CRUST AS THEY traveled. Otter looked over his shoulder now and again as the road rose. Yesterday he had met merchants coming toward him: they by no means scared him. He bade them a courteous good day and wished them well on their travels, well-wished in turn. He lied to them, knowing that if the king's men met them, too, then they would give news of anyone they had seen traveling this way, so he gave his name as Marden, which was Gran's distant neighbor's name, and said he was going to see his uncle in Trys Ceyl, which was a sleepy place on a ways south from Henas'amef.

Good day, they had bidden him, and gone on their way. Perhaps they had met his father's men by now and had told them the lie, when asked sharply about a young man on the road. He had kept his face muffled against the cold, no unusual thing, and perhaps they failed to know he was that young. He had no idea.

But he had crossed the Lenúalim on thick ice, leading Paisi's horse, afoot and spread out seeming more prudent for them both, despite cart tracks having left their marks on the snowy path. Above and below the shallows of the ford, the river had not quite frozen, and he had had enough bad luck already to make him wary—but the ice had held. He was well on his way now, and the land he saw today began to have the familiar higgledy-piggledy order of crooked fences that distinguished Amefin ways from Guelen. There were few straight lines in Amefel, nothing of the Guelen sense of order. Certainly the road observed no overall economy of direction, wending among hills and bobbing over a rise and down again.

He thought that he was near home now. He thought that he spied Diel Tor under its snow blanket, and was sure that there had been such a rock, and another, like a pig asleep, on his way to the border. He knew for certain he had seen that twisted tree by the bridge.

He kept going into night, then wrapped in his cloak and huddled up against a tilted stone with the horse near him. His feet kept going numb, and he took off his boots and rubbed the life back into his toes, then struggled to put them on again, never sure that taking his boots off did more good than harm—but Paisi had told him, one winter when he was a small boy: "Never let fingers an' toes go dead, or they'll die, an' turn black an' rot, an' if e'er ye get wet boots, boy, you run breakneck to the house straightway an' take them wet things off quick as you can. Or if ye have to, run barefoot in the snow a bit an' then rub 'em and sit on 'em a while in your cloak . . . s' far better 'n frozen boots."

He was so cold he couldn't tell if his boots had gotten wet and frozen in the night. He had tried to prevent that eventuality, and this night, shivering, he tucked up as tight as he could into the cloaks, head and all. That slowly helped, and he dared sleep just a little. But well before daylight he grew so miserable he set out again, the horse moving slowly along an ill-defined road.

Morning, however, brought the sun, which shone like a lamp through the film of clouds and occasionally broke through. He drowsed as he rode, lying on the horse's bare back, and waked, the horse pitching him slightly forward as it nipped the tops of grasses that poked through the snow and pawed up others, along the margin of a cultivated field.

It was the first graze they had found since a day ago. He had given the horse anything of his food the horse would eat, and his own stomach was as empty as he could remember. He let the horse wander down the drystone wall, eating as it went, while he had the rest of the sausage, and they were both happier for it.

A raven sat down on the wall, cocked its head, and whetted its beak against bare stone. It had a dark, glittering eye, and seemed to watch him with a certain smugness, as if it knew his venture to his father's house had brought nothing but disaster.

He didn't like it staring at him. It showed no decent fear of a boy's presence. Leaning from the horse's back, holding to the ragged mane, he scooped a handful of snow off the wall and shied a clenched fistful at the bird, which only dodged and settled again.

The grain was gone, the last stalk ripped up. He had had the last of the sausage. And he thumped the horse's sides with his heels and got the horse moving again, leaving the raven in sole possession of the wall. The sun, friendly for the moment, hid its face, and the wind picked up out of the west, chilling his face and his knees.

But toward evening they came to a brook, and it was a crossing Otter had known all his life. They broke the ice on shallow, fast-moving water, scarcely enough to wet Tammis's hooves, and climbed a shallow bank. From here on Otter knew exactly where he was, which was on Farmer Marden's land, not far from home, and he urged the horse to all the haste he could manage.

By sunset a hill stood against the northwest sky, and on that hill a walled town, which was Henas'amef, and tallest of all in the town, the faint outlines of the keep, the Zeide. A tower stood atop all, scarcely discernible except at sunset, and in that tower his mother lived, and in that keep his lord, Crissand, ruled; and, right along the highroad he traveled, was Gran's place. He kicked the horse and applied the end of the halter rope, making all possible haste before full dark could come down, and determinedly not looking toward that tower, which had watched over him all his life. He felt its presence now as he had felt it for years, familiar and uncomfortable, his mother's eyes continually watching his back, finding out all his mischief and his doings.

But here were the fields he knew. There was the old, broken berry bush, stark against a snowy land; and there was the boundary stone that was older than anybody remembered, and nobody knew what it marked, except it had Sihhë signs on it, almost weathered away. There were a pair of trees, winter-bare, whose outlines he knew, the farthest ranges of his earliest childhood wanderings, and there was Farmer Ost's old oak that stood by itself in a pig lot, with a rickety fence and the pig boy's cottage just down the lane that left the highroad.

There, there in the last of the daylight, he saw Gran's thatched roof, the wonderful twisted chimney, perfectly fine, with smoke rising out of it. It was a sight finer than Guelemara's tall houses: smoke, and someone home, and the warmth of it going out into the gathering dark like a banner on the wind.

He leaned to open the gate and rode into the yard, past a fence of stones and old, weathered logs, on which snow lay in ridges. Goats peered out of the shed as he latched the gate back, from Tammis's back. The geese scattered as he turned Tammis into the friendly warm dark of the goat shed.

A horse snorted and shifted inside, and Tammis gave a low grunt as Otter slid down off his sweaty back, right next to Feiny. The comparative warmth was wonderful, the familiar smell of their goat shed was about him, Feiny was here safely, which meant Paisi was, and aside from Feiny, it was as if he had never left. In a moment more he heard steps crunching through the snow, coming toward the shed door.

A shadow with a stick in hand demanded:

"Who goes there? Who's in our shed?"

"Paisi!" he exclaimed.

The stick lowered. "Otter? Is it our Otter?" The shadow rushed forward bearlike to embrace him, thump him about the arms and back and smother him in an embrace. "Otter, me lad!"

"How's Gran?"

"Oh, a little soup and she's fine, she's fine, lad, despite she complains. Come on, I'll see ye in."

"I have to rub your horse down."

"The hell ye do. I'll see to 'im. Just you go inside and 'splain to Gran why ye left a warm spot to come home."

"I had a message," he said. He wanted to tell all of it, the sanctuary, the bad dreams, the way the king his father had tried to advise him, then meant to send him off in the dark of night. "A priest dropped a pot and it scorched the floor and nothing was right after. Nothing was right before, for that matter." Tears welled up, as if he were a child, and he had stopped being that. "I came home, Paisi. I just came home, was all. It was time."

"Poor Otter." Paisi hugged him tight, a warm, homey-smelling refuge against the dark and the cold and the confusion of priests and royalty. Paisi tousled his hair, faced him about, and slapped him on the rump. "Go in the front. I barred the shed door. All's well. Gran'll skin ye."

He had to laugh, though his eyes still watered, half from the cold and the pungent dust of the shed. He found the door—Paisi had flanked him by coming around from the front, barring the shed-side door for Gran's protection, and he trudged through the shin-deep snow in Paisi's tracks, right around to the front door.

It opened before he got there, and Gran was on the other side of it, skinny Gran, in her ragged old robe and her layers of many-colored skirts, with her white braids done back in a tail as she wore them at night—she was set for bed, or had risen from it. She had her stick in hand and a worried frown on her face.

"Well, ye do smell different," she said, hugging him and not minding his snowy feet on the floor. "Ye don't smell like my Otter."

"I'm so tired, Gran."

She kissed him on the cheek and immediately began saying there was soup on—there was always soup on, and Gran added whatever came in, day by day, with more water. The smell of it mixed with the smells of old cloth, and moldy wood, and goats and horse. The drying herbs that hung from the dusty rafters over their heads sifted bits and fragments down onto the wooden floor, along with snowmelt.

She set him down on the bed he shared with Paisi, dipped up soup, wiped the rim of the bowl with a much-used cloth, and handed the bowl to him with a chunk of bread to sop in it.

"The young duke's men came an' ask't after us," she said. Lord Crissand was the only duke he'd ever known, but to Gran he was forever the young duke. "They give us a whole sack of flour an' another of baked bread, besides sausages an' cheese and several venison pies. An' then they come back with grain. What's this o' bad dreams, lad? Ha' ye done somethin' silly?"

He had drunk a little broth from the rim of the bowl and had the warmth flowing down into him. Her question caught him with his mouth full, and he swallowed hard, burning himself. "We both dreamed, Gran."

"Paisi said the same, the fool. Ain't no trouble 'cept the old joints."

"She's lying," came from the door, as Paisi opened it and stamped off snow on the mat. A cold gust came in with him and ceased as he shut the door behind him. Paisi's hands were all over horsehair and mud, and he wiped them on a rag that hung with the cloaks, by the door, before he splashed up water from the little washing basin to finish the job.

"Ain't," Gran said meanwhile.

"Is," Paisi said, toweling off. "I found 'er abed an' fussin'."

"Oh, well," Otter said, "if she was fussing, then she was fine."

"See?" Gran said.

"The duke's men was here," Paisi said. "Yesterday. Your da sent food an' blankets by way of the duke, so we knew you was all right with him. And here ye come, saying all's wrong. What happened?"

"I tried to see home. And spilled the water and oil, and got caught, and that was the start of it, but it only got worse." He had the soup and the bread in hand and could not let it cool. He dipped the bread and ate, explaining as he went. "The king wasn't angry, but it upset the priests. And the Quinaltine . . . the Lines . . . they were breaking."

"Was they?" Gran settled on the other end of the bed, a slight weight. "Breakin'?"

"And the spot on the stones, and the priests upset." He dipped another bite of bread and ate it, desperately, even if it tasted like ashes. "And I'd made trouble for everybody. And I kept dreaming. I kept on dreaming, and I didn't know if Paisi had made it. And then I had a message."

"A message, was it? The duke must ha' sent, before ever he brung the food out. But that were fast travelin', that message, boy."

"It must have come from Lord Crissand," he said. It seemed to him, too, that it had been fast traveling, and he had passed no courier coming back. But perhaps the duke had been beforehand with everything and already intended to help Gran.

Paisi said: "But ye can't ride, Otter. Ye was mad to take out like that, wi' no food, nor shelter, nor yet a saddle nor proper bridle, good gods! What if the horse had throwed ye?"

"Well, he did, a few times." He'd landed, fortunately, in snow, and not on his head. "But I got back on."

"Lucky he didn't run off," Paisi said, laying a hand on his shoulder. "Gods, ye're still cold. Ye shouldn't have."

"They were going to send me in the dark, with soldiers. I didn't want to go with soldiers, Paisi. I just wanted to be here." His jaw clenched without his wanting it. A muscle jumped, and his heart beat harder. "I did everything the king asked of me. But I'm sure he thought I was a fool."

"Ye ain't a fool, and he didn't think any such thing," Gran said. "I ain't feelin' he's angry, to this hour."

Gran's feelings were not to disregard. It comforted him to think that. It was as warm as the food in his belly, and brighter thoughts occurred to him, now that the adventure was over.

"Prince Aewyn has become my friend," he said. "We'll always be friends. And Her Majesty wasn't angry at my being there."

"That 'un, she wouldn't be," Gran said.

He got several more bites down, the two of them just staring at him as if they could hardly believe he was there, and Paisi got up and put a small log on the dying fire. It was late. They ought all to be going to bed, but Gran got him another bowl of soup, and he began, finally, to be warm inside.

"The horse," he said, on another mouthful.

"The horses is both fine," Paisi said, but it came from a far distance. He was home, but he wasn't. He had gotten where he had to go, but he hadn't. He had found out who he was, but he didn't know why it had failed to satisfy his questions. He was back at his starting place, and everything was to do again, all the questions to ask again, all the mistakes to make again . . . trying to find out where he should be.

"Boy?" Gran asked him, and he couldn't even look at her. He just sat, with the bowl in one hand and the bread in the other, and stared away at white, white snow and dead branches, as if the journey had never ended at all, and he wasn't finished.

He wasn't finished. He couldn't be home yet.

"Otter, lad." Paisi took the bowl and the bread from him and set it aside, then tipped him right over onto the bed and started pulling his boots off, then threw covers over him. "There's a lad. Just too tired, ain't we?"

"Not finished," he said. His teeth were chattering as he pulled his own belt off. "Not finished yet."

"Well, no, I don't suppose." Paisi was humoring him, tucking him in like a child. "We're all right, here. Don't you fret."

He shut his eyes, still seeing snow, and dead branches. It was like that, as if he couldn't finish his journey at all, nor come home until he'd done something very important, something that had only started in Guelemara, when the shadows, the horrid shadows, had started running between the stones. He was aware when Paisi came to bed, warmth and weight beside him under the covers.

"Are ye asleep, Otter?"

"I dream, Paisi. I dream of snow."

"Well, sma' wonder, that."

"You've got to take care," he said, then slipped away. If Paisi said anything or asked anything after that, he didn't know.

But when he waked, Gran was up, and stirring about breakfast, making porridge in the small pot, and Paisi was lifting his head from the mattress.

"There's breakfast about to go to waste," Gran said, as she said most mornings, if they were still abed. Paisi got up, and Otter got up and huddled near the newly fed fire, both of them to take warm bowls in hand. Otter filled his belly with warm porridge and a bit of toasted bread.

"That's better than the king's table," he said to Gran, who grinned at him, pleased, but not believing him in the least.

And the snow came back while he ate the bread. It came back into his heart and into his vision, and he never wanted it, but nothing was finished. It began to grow in him, the notion, then, for the first time, that there was one other person than Gran and Paisi and the king and queen who'd had something to do with his mother and his birth, and that he'd never seen him, nor had to do with him, and that there were things he could learn nowhere else. Ill luck had dogged him every step of his visit to Guelemara, and the source of it was not his father, not Gran, nor Paisi, nor even Brother Trassin. He had brought it there with him, in what he was, and who he was born. Those who loved him most would never tell him there was no hope. They would go on trying to make him better than he was born.

But one person had no reason to lie to him, and one person in the world might see him for what he was.

He felt at that very moment that feeling of eyes at his back, that feeling that the tower, so faint and minute on its hill, was nearer to him and more real than the walls about him, when ordinarily Gran's walls could keep that attention away from him. Now they were failing. He didn't want to think about his mother. Gran's walls were near, and strong, stone and wood and wattle, and potent with Gran's magic, and at that very moment he saw Gran look very sharply toward the north and say,

"Stop that!"

The feeling of being watched went away then, like a candle going out, so that he could breathe again. Gran hadn't troubled about the snow; but the tower she rebuked, and wove her magic about him, like warm winds.

But it was not warm enough to stop the snow. It drifted through a forest, all winter-bare, and lay trackless and unvisited in his inner vision.

"Otter?" Paisi asked.

"I'm not done," he said, and set the porridge bowl down and stood up, aches and all. "It's not finished."

Paisi laid a hand on his arm, but Gran motioned him not to, and Paisi let him go. After that, he felt as if he had been set free, even blessed. He looked at Gran and saw no forbidding, no disapproval of him.

"I have to go," he said.

"Not to her!" Paisi exclaimed.

"No. West. I have to ask him—I have questions to ask."

"Of 'Im?" Gran asked. "*What* will ye ask 'Im, lad?"

"I have no notion yet. But he was there when I was born, wasn't he? And when I went to Guelemara, where I thought all my life I was supposed to go, it wasn't where I was supposed to be. I was wrong to go there. I didn't like it, Gran. I liked Aewyn, and the king was good to me. And Prince Efanor was. And the queen. I liked them all. But Guelemara didn't fit me, and now, all the way home, I kept thinking I had to be sure you were safe; but now that you are, I don't know what to do. I can't go ask—" He made the slightest nod of his head toward Henas'amef, toward the tower, and felt a shiver, even so, as if a tiny chink were opened in Gran's spells, exposing them to a very persistent force. He tried not to pay attention to it. All his safety seemed elsewhere. Westward. "He's what's left to ask, isn't he? I have to go and ask him—whatever occurs to me to ask."

"Then ye're right. Ye should go there," Gran said. "I'd never stop ye."

"Can't it wait," Paisi asked, "at least until the snow melts?"

"No," he said. "No. I can't wait. Soldiers will be here." A shiver came over him, a terrible sense of urgency. "I'm sure they were behind me on the road. They will come, and I have to go. I have to go today."

"It ain't fair to leave Gran!" Paisi said. "She's lyin' when she says she ain't that sickly. She was sick when I come here. An' we can't go off an' leave her."

"Then don't think of leaving her alone, Paisi. I'll go."

"M'lord!"

"We're home, and I'm not 'm'lord' here, and I can do for myself. I'll take my own horse. He's had food and shelter for days. Now yours can rest. There's only one horse fit to go, anyway."

"It ain't right!" Paisi protested. "I'm not to leave ye! Himself said I wasn't to leave ye!"

He set his hand on Paisi's shoulder. A year ago, he'd not been tall enough. Now he could, and looked at Paisi almost eye to eye. "But I'm going to *him*, Paisi. That makes it different. And I can ride. I fell off often enough on the way home, I learned, didn't I? This time I'll even have a saddle."

" 'Tain't a joke, m'lord."

"No," he said, "it isn't, Paisi. Just take care of Gran."

"I'll fit Feiny out for ye," Paisi muttered. "An' ye ride slow on 'im, and ye mind your way. That's a treacherous, wicked horse, I had me fill of his manners on the way here. An' 'at's a dire, dark wood, Marna is. Sensible people don't go in there. Not even bandits go in. Or if they do, they don't last long."

He had seen the borders of Marna Wood when he was a young boy. He had gone that far, with Paisi. He had seen the dark, dead trees, and Paisi had told him then that things died, that went under those branches. The trees there never leafed, except a little straggle of branches, and never died, either. It was magical, in itself. And Ynefel lay beyond that boundary, across the river. That was where Lord Tristen lived.

So it was the way he had to go, and when he knew that, he could breathe again. It was not that he wanted to go at all. He had changed since he had last ridden out from Gran's yard. He had learned to live in the king's household. He had learned to stand straight and speak up when asked; he had learned to say m'lord this and m'lady that, and how to hold a knife and spoon—all useful things, but none useful in the world now. He knew how to tend goats and make cheese, and these were skills that would feed his body, but never his soul: not for him, to live in this little house. He suddenly knew that, and it was a lonely feeling, but it was at least a peaceful feeling. It was not that he meant to leave forever. But he had to leave, for now, for as long as he had to. And Gran had Paisi. That meant everything was as it ought to be. The world was astonishingly simple, when he removed himself from Guelemara, and from here.

So he put on his boots and his cloak, while Paisi, who had shoved his feet into work boots, had gone out to see to Feiny. Meanwhile Gran made up a packet of food for him.

"An' there's ample grain for the horse in the shed," Gran said as she tied up the bundle, "as the young duke has sent, an' gods, we've had a wicked time keepin' the goats from it, ha'n't we?"

"I'm glad His Grace has taken good care of you," he said. He was done. He took the packet, and by that time Paisi had come in, saying Feiny was saddled, and had his gear, and had a pack of grain besides a blanket Paisi had used.

"Which ain't as clean as it was," Paisi said, "but it ain't the Guelesfort, an' the washin' 'll freeze like planks in this weather, won't it? You got to watch Feiny, now, I'm tellin' ye. Don't you get too confident with 'im. He's feistier 'n Tammis, tricksy as a downriver peddlar. You got to do with him the way ye do with ol' Crook-horn, an' slap 'is jaw if he offers to bite."

"I will," Otter said, and hugged Paisi and hugged Gran last. "You take care, most of all. You take great care, Gran."

"Go on wi' ye, flit here, flit there, home again an' gone. Give 'Im our respects, hear? Say I said so. Mind—" Here Gran seized him by the arm with more strength than seemed likely in her hand. "Mind ye skirt Althalen, and leave the highroad there. Don't ye stray into the old ruin, and above all don't go so far as the ford at Lewenbrook, where the old battlefield is: that ain't the way. The old places has their ways of drawin' a body in, if a body has the Sight, as you do, and they don't let go if they lay hands on ye. The gray lady ain't no harm at all, nor's her daughter. But don't gawk about and don't poke into any old stones."

"I won't. I won't, Gran." The stinging in his eyes was not the smoky chimney's fault. It was his own, for standing there too long, with Gran pouring every warning in Amefel into his head, all in a rush. He kissed her, then ducked out the shed-side door, and found Feiny waiting for him out in the daylight, all saddled and caparisoned, ready and fretting. He had learned, however, on the road, not to dawdle about any business with horses, and after giving Feiny a rub on the nose and a pat on the neck to let him know who he was dealing with, he gave a little hop to get a grip on the saddle and get his toe in the stirrup. Then he rose, high as the shed, able to look down on the thatched eaves, Feiny dancing under him.

Paisi came out to wave good-bye. Gran came as far as the sheltered front door, and the longer they delayed with the door open, the more the chimney would smoke up Gran's mantel-stone, besides the cold getting into the house and chilling away all the effort of heating it. He waved back, and thumped Feiny with his heels and took up rein—quickly, and firmly, because Feiny started off with a jerk of his head, trying to get the bit. Feiny had his own notions, at the gate, of turning back eastward, Paisi was quite right.

West was his rider's firm choice, however. Otter used a heel to reinforce that choice, and Feiny threw his head and veered off and fussed the whole width of the road before he would turn westward.

But it was a clear enough morning. Again, just to the north, he could see the town under gray cloud, with the lowering smoke of cooking fires obscuring the heights where the Zeide sat.

The smoke obscured the tower, but he felt that reproachful gaze, the same as he had felt it every day of his life until he had left for Guelessar, and the whole last bit of his way home.

He knew it was there the same as he knew the place of the sun in the sky—more constant than the sun, it never changed. It never moved, or sank, or rose. Unlike the sun, it was sometimes warm, sometimes cold, and this morning it changed subtly from one to the other, as he went along the road. It grew colder, and more troubled, as he rode past the turn that would take him to Henas'amef.

He refused to look in that direction. He had no intention of going up there for any farewell. He gave a kick, and Feiny jumped, and launched into an outright head-down rebellion along the road, a revolt that tried his strength and courage before he could haul that stubborn head up again and get moving westward at a sane pace.

But what Feiny chose next was a heavy-footed jog of a gait he was not to encourage, Aewyn had told him that. Feiny clearly didn't respect his handling, and with trepidation, he thumped his heels in and kept a firm grip. The discussion went on, Feiny throwing his head and trying to turn around, and himself kicking every time the horse stopped, struggling with the reins, and finally, finally, getting his way, the horse having sunk into sullen obedience, in the right direction at a sensible, smooth pace. There weren't other horses to follow. They were leaving safe, warm places. It was a cold morning, and Feiny didn't want to go west. The horse's ears switched occasionally but stayed flat and angry.

But now that he and Feiny had reached a truce and settled the direction for the journey, he found his first time to think.

And thinking called up Aewyn, and Guelessar, and the meeting with Paisi and Gran, and leaving home again, when he had just reached safety.

He was a fool, he told himself. Then he doubted everything, and asked himself what he was doing riding away, and why he feared the soldiers, and why the presence in the tower scared him so this morning—as if he were caught at something wrong, when he knew he wasn't wrong.

He hadn't been wrong, in Guelessar, only out of place. Now he ran from his mother, chasing questions the answers to which he wasn't sure he wanted to know at all, and going into a place where some people had gone and never come back. Was that a reasonable thing to do?

There were bandits, some years. He didn't know if there were new ones, after Lord Crissand had hunted out the last. There were the old places, the ones Gran had warned him to avoid.

And Ynefel itself was nowhere a reasonable person ventured to go.

He didn't, in fact, know what he was looking for. All his life, Paisi and Gran alike had been sure his father would come for him—and he had, had he not?

But that had gone awry. He had come home, all dressed in finespun, and with horses Gran had no way to feed, and with soldiers following him. Paisi insisted on calling him m'lord, even yet, and that wasn't right—it would never be.

Gran's place was still home: he was grateful for that. And it smelled right, and it was warm and comfortable, but he didn't fit into it the way he had before he'd been to Guelessar; and he knew he brought troubles as well as help from outside. He didn't know what might happen next, but the moment he was happiest, when everything had been the way he wanted—everything started going askew; and the moment he trusted what was what, things changed. That alone had been dependable, ever since he had ridden off to live among Guelenfolk.

Deep in his heart he found not only pain for that fact, but anger. That dismayed him. Gran had taught him most of all not to let anger put down roots—because, she had said, those roots found things; and perhaps they already had. They had dug down into his loneliness, into boyhood lessons with the Bryalt priests, who detested him, and his living with Gran, who he had early discovered wasn't his real grandmother; and waiting for a father who wanted him to be what he was not, and finding a brother who wanted to be his friend but couldn't be simply his friend, not considering his position, and the fact that a Guelen king would find it hard to have an Amefin brother. He discovered he had lived in narrow bounds all his life, sheltered from this, ignorant of that; and now, when he'd just gotten out into the world, he'd skidded right back down into Gran's place, a burden to Gran.

The more he thought of it, the deeper those roots dug.

Add in the humiliation of going to his father in cobwebby, oil-soaked clothes, when he'd tried for the first time to use what he'd learned from Gran. Everyone assumed he had the Gift. Gran had always hinted he did. And the very moment he tried to use just the edge of what people accused him of having, everything tumbled into ruin, and all his good luck vanished.

Wasn't that a warning, for a wizard or a witch, when luck turned, when like a tool breaking, it cut the hand that held it? Gran had always talked about Luck, and how it flowed, and how there were winds of the world that didn't move the grass, but that might move a king, ever so subtly. A witch or a wizard had to feel that movement: that was part of using the Gift.

The winds were certainly blowing against his going back to Guelessar now, and had been, from the moment he had waked in that dream—that false dream, as it happened, or at least that greatly exaggerated dream of fire and ruin. He'd thrown over everything, everything good he'd had, and here he'd ridden in and found Gran up and about and Paisi taking care of everything just as he ought.

So what had he done next? He'd thrown over the safety he'd reached, again, out of restlessness he couldn't reason with, a fear of soldiers who meant him no possible harm, and probably—yes, out of embarrassment, pure embarrassment in turning up back at Gran's house, in failure. Embarrassment, too, before his mother, sitting smug in her tower, pleased at having him back again . . . oh, she had won, had she not?

He'd gotten just the least bit prideful in his fine clothes and with his fine horse that he couldn't ride; he'd sat down at table with the king and his legitimate brother, and this morning he'd found himself back at a dusty hearthside sipping soup from a cracked bowl, back on Gran's charity again, and giving her nothing to help her old age, nothing to deserve Paisi's helping him, or sharing his gran with him—Gran owed him nothing, except Lord Tristen had settled him on her house and asked her to take care of him.

Well, when a man needed things or looked for a direction to take, he went to his proper lord, did he not? And if his Lord Crissand was Gran's lord, still he wasn't the only lord, nor was he the lord who had laid down the conditions of his life and told the king of Ylesuin to take care of him and not to drown him at birth.

There was where his life had begun. There was where, if it had gone wrong, there was one who might set him right again and tell him plainly what to do.

In simplest fact, when he and Feiny had fought, and the horse had turned about, he had felt as if he were facing into a contrary and bitter wind, and the only relief was west, west and south and away from the farm. Maybe even Feiny had felt it. The horse had stopped fighting the course he set.

Prison like his mother's? Was that his fate, when he grew to be a man? Maybe it would not be so close a prison, but certain Guelenfolk would be happier to have him locked away and forgotten, if only on a farm in Amefel—but he feared that would not be enough for them.

And would they ever have remembered him if his father hadn't brought him to Guelemara, under his own roof?

Entanglements, Gran had taught him—entanglements worked a certain magic . . . for good or for ill, and he was entangled with everyone in the world he could possibly love, and those people he could love had entangled themselves with powers that reached down into those very stones Gran said to avoid.

A wind began to blow out of the north, so that he had to snug his cloak about him and tuck it under a knee.

Winter and the weather weren't obliged to agree with his choice of directions.

But he had known that before he started.

ii

IDRYS DARKENED THE DOORWAY. CEFWYN SPIED THE LORD COMMANDER FAR across the audience hall when he was at assizes. A scroll was in Idrys' hand, sealed and official, and if it weren't important, Idrys would not be in the doorway looking at him.

Cefwyn signaled with a move of his head. Idrys walked in, gave the requisite little bow, and came up the side of the room, past farmers and merchants wanting justice, past a felon caught in thievery—the second offense—and passed him the message, a parchment still cold from the weather outside.

Crissand's personal seal, the Sun with its rays, on red wax, and bound up with red ribbon. Cefwyn cracked the chilled seal and unrolled the tight-furled bit of parchment, more border than message.

> *Crissand Duke of Amefel to His Majesty the king of Ylesuin, Greetings.*
>   *Your men came to me requesting sustenance and aid to a certain woman, the caretaker of your ward, and accordingly I sent inquiry to her, with gifts of food and drink from the Bryalt fathers, and also medicines.*

Damn, Cefwyn thought. By the tenor of it, it was his first message to which this letter replied. What had the courier done, stopped for holiday?

But it went on:

> My men found the woman with her grandson, Paisi, who was caring for her. He had come by horse, which Your Majesty may know. I accordingly sent more grain, beyond that I had already sent, and prepared to send a message to Your Majesty. However other messengers arrived before this letter was sent, advising me to expect your ward, who would have arrived likewise by horse, and requesting me to ascertain his welfare.

More to the point. Thank the gods. Then:

> Accordingly I sent men with the men of the Dragon Guard to visit the house in question and was informed that your ward indeed arrived safely, but to my great distress, I must report that he has quitted the premises alone and ridden west, toward Marna Wood. He expressed to the woman and her son that he wishes to consult Lord Tristen. I have sent Earl Ameidan with a number of men to attempt to find him, but, given the delays in reporting, have little hope of doing so before he passes into Marna, where they will not follow. I have instructed my men to use no force nor lay hands on him at any meeting, not knowing whether he may travel at Your Majesty's urging, or at Lord Tristen's, and deeming it unlikely he might confide the nature of such a mission to others. I am left in confusion as to your ward's intent and instruction, and hope that I have not failed Your Majesty in energy on the one hand or in prudence on the other.
>
> My men will await your reply.
>
> I rest in hope of Your Majesty's good regard.

That was the sum of it.

To *Tristen*, Cefwyn thought, staring at the words on the paper.

It was, at least, not as bad news as might be. Gran was alive and well. The dreams had come to naught.

But Otter had left, and Paisi had not gone with him.

Had he ridden off directly? Had the grandmother told him to go there, and sent him well prepared and with Tristen's consent, or had she not?

Damn it all.

He looked up, transported from Amefel in the dead of winter to a hall full of anxious farmers and merchants, all watching their king read a letter that had—he tried to conceal it—greatly shaken his soul.

And what should he do? Roll up the letter and bolt from the hall, leaving the populace to speculate on some province in revolt, some attack on the realm?

He quietly rolled it up, tucked it in his belt, and picked up the document the Lord Chamberlain handed him, a complaint of theft and a counterclaim of conversion of goods, and two lean and angry merchants glowering at each other.

He heard the evidence, and conflicting witnesses, and heard his advisors, and their advocates, then rendered judgment against the foreign merchant, for conversion of a potter's wares. It was a popular decision in the hall. He hoped it was a just one. He tried to do justice in the several cases following. But to his relief, a number of the attending crowd proved to be attached to the potter, and five to the subsequent case, regarding an inheritance, a minor daughter, and a marriage—easy, since the will was clear. There was the matter of a tavern brawl, which the first time he had heard it had sounded like a city matter, and the mayor's problem before it even came to Efanor's hearing: a street preacher and a Quinaltine-Bryaltine dispute, in a tavern near Weavers Street. The argument had gotten to blows, broken benches, and an accusation, though thin, of attempted arson. Even the latter would not have been his province, and it probably would not have been Efanor's, if it were only a tavern fight. But it was now the Bryaltine holiday, the preacher had tried to tear down the Bryalt decorations and stir up a street mob to break up the tavern, and that had done it: add to that, the fact of an appeal from the queen's Bryalt priest. He ordered the offending street preacher remanded to the Quinaltine for punishment—the Holy Father was not at all fond of itinerant preachers. The Bryaltine tavern owner was to be recompensed by the Crown, and he issued an edict regarding attacks on religious symbols from either side, offenders to be chained two days in the city square, wherein the crowd might express their own sentiments without hindrance.

That was the last business at hand, thank the gods. The edict had been prepared in advance, and a message already dispatched to the Patriarch: the hearing was no more than a venting of his anger and a public warning; but it exhausted him. Rumblings of discontent in the clergy were slow to settle, Quinalt zealots had made the Bryalt holiday grim, his son moped about, neglected his studies, and erupted in temper with his bodyguard and threatened to dismiss Selmyn himself, not the most pleasant of displays.

Most of all, his son wanted to know any news that arrived from Amefel, and daily seemed to hint it was kept from him. That tried his own temper, and his forbearance, and made his wife unhappy.

Now news had come, and it was not quite the good news he had hoped to give to his son, nor entirely bad, either. It might be the wisest move old Gran could have made, sending Otter off in that direction—if he could get there safely.

He took himself back to the robing room, shed the trappings of kingship and took himself and his message upstairs, Idrys shadowing him the while, ahead of his bodyguard. Idrys being a mortal man, curiosity doubtless consumed him. But he asked no questions until they reached the royal apartments.

There, Cefwyn drew the message from his belt and handed it to Idrys, who read it.

"Gone to the Sihhë-lord," Idrys said then. "But on whose advice, my lord king?"

"That *is* the question, is it not?" On longer thought, he found himself somewhat relieved, but he could not settle in his heart what he felt about his own failure. "The grandmother's, perhaps. Certainly not his mother's."

"That one won't be happy."

"No," he said. "She won't." Nor would his son, who would begin to think about that territory and begin to inquire into matters his son had never asked. So there had been a war. So the Sihhë-lord, his father's good friend, had risen up, then gone away again, and never visited the capital, not since he was born. It had been no concern of Aewyn's.

Until now.

Wiser, long ago, if he had separated the grandmother's whole household from Henas'amef—settled her down in Ivanor with Lord Cevulirn, perhaps: his people understood wizards, and revered an honest hedge-witch, much as the Amefin did. Or down in Olmern, where Sovrag was lord. Nothing daunted that old river pirate. He'd made the decision where to put the boy when Tristen had been in Amefel, and he had never changed the arrangement when Tristen left the realm, deeming it wise not to disturb what seemed settled.

Well, he knew what Tristen would say about easy and natural courses . . . the thing that felt so right and natural to do . . . the situation unexamined for year upon year, as things subtly or not so subtly shifted: decisions forgotten and allowed to stand, though the safety in them had subtly eroded away.

Maybe—maybe he should have refused advice to send the boy home.

Otter had gotten through Festival and been written down; he could have taken ill for the last ceremonies, attendance at which was often taken somewhat lightly, if the privations and worship of the first days had rendered a body indisposed. They could have gotten through it.

But at least the boy had evaded his mother. He had not gone into the town: he had left, out of his mother's reach. That was to the good.

"I'll write a letter," he said. "All hospitality for the messenger." Idrys gave him back the letter, rolled up, and Cefwyn laid it on the desk. "We know what we know, and no more. It may be to the good."

Idrys left. Efanor arrived, before he had quite sat down to write the reply.

"There was a message," Efanor said, and Cefwyn told him the gist of it.

Efanor sat down unbidden, in the informality of the privy chambers, sat down and rested his arm on the side of Cefwyn's desk. "Well, better than I had feared."

"Better than frozen in a snowbank," Cefwyn said shortly. "Everything's better than what could have happened."

"And the woman is well."

"Perfectly well, as seems," Cefwyn said. "His dreams were for naught."

"*Tristen* wouldn't send a false dream."

"We know who would. Spare me. I have yet to explain to my son where his friend is. He will ask, of course, when he's coming back, and if he's gotten my letter, and I have to say no, the letter went to Crissand, but not to our fugitive, and nothing is mended."

"The spot on the stone, meanwhile—"

"The Holy Father's masonry, brother, is not my chief concern. And you said—"

"The blot is there again," Efanor said. "Not visible to everyone. But—"

"How many paving stones has the inner chapel? We are not destitute. They should last until thaw."

"Don't make light of it, I pray you, brother. Listen to me. This is not the Holy Father looking for favors. If your son has gone to Lord Tristen—"

"If he has. He most certainly has. There's nowhere else he could go, in that direction, and what in the gods' own name does it have to do with the Quinaltine floor?"

"I told you, after the war, after the battle in Elwynor, the foundation—"

"The foundation is flawed. The Lines run amiss. I know it. They wouldn't have Tristen deal with the matter, oh, no, nothing so reasonable. Now I'm to repave the whole Quinaltine, a stone at a time?"

"It's not that, brother." Efanor reached out and laid a hand on his wrist, quietly compelling him. "The foundations, yes, were mislaid from the start. The Lines are completely askew. I know you can't see them, but trust me in this, they're not what they ought to be."

"Given that, they never have been."

"Our grandfather founded the place on old ruins, and took them over, and they're flawed from that beginning. I've tried to mend them. His Holiness has blessed them, with no success. And, without tearing the holy precinct down . . ."

"Good gods, brother."

"Pavings are not the flaw here. The flaw is in the rock beneath."

"The Holy Father proposes to tear down the Quinaltine?"

"I've not broached this with the Holy Father."

He stared at his brother, not believing what he heard. "Tear it down."

"As we build a new shrine."

"Oh, good gods!"

"The manifestation—" His grip on Cefwyn's wrist tightened. "The manifestation has not gone away with Otter's departure. If anything, it's spreading."

"Well, then it wasn't his fault, was it? Tell that to the street preachers! Did Nevris mention to you there was a tavern brawl, which ordinarily isn't my concern; but this man was preaching against Bryalt observance, trying to burn down a tavern and blaming my son when he did it?"

"Otter, you mean."

"Yes, Otter, damn it."

"You think of him in those terms."

"As my son? He is my son. He *is* my son, brother, however inconvenient. I can do nothing about that. Nor can he. I thought you thought well of him."

"Well of him, indeed. But he's a doorway. Whose, remains to be seen."

"Gods, you sound like Emuin!"

"I heartily wish Emuin were still with us. He would tell you—"

"What, that I have a spot on the Quinaltine floor and we have to tear the building down? And it's all my son's fault?"

"No. He'd say that the door has already come ajar. The boy *sees* the Lines . . ."

"So do you," Cefwyn retorted.

"He more than sees the Lines, brother. Things beyond the Lines see *him*. I see the Lines. And I guard my own soul. Who guards his?"

"Well, damned well not the Quinalt Father, does he, despite writing him down in the book? And what will the old man say when you propose to tear the building down? I'm sure that will patch things."

"Listen to me: the Lines, the Lines, brother. I don't understand them, but they exist, they're confused, they're a trap for spirits, and as tangled as they've grown—I'm not sure even Tristen could untangle them . . ."

"They won't let Tristen through the doors, remember? They won't take blessings from a Sihhë. And we can't afford to build another Quinaltine."

"Brother, if we begin it, if we only begin it—"

"*Where?* Every morsel of ground atop the hill is built on. There's not room for a chapel, let alone another Quinaltine! And since when does the Holy Father believe in Bryalt Lines?"

"They're not Bryalt."

"Does he see them?"

"He can't."

"Nor believes in them, I'll warrant. It's a Bryalt belief. And you propose to explain to him how this exists in his Quinaltine, while explaining to him you want to tear down his sanctuary."

"And build one that's clean, and whole. I can lay it out. I know where, on the hill, there is a place."

"Where? Just suppose for a moment that I even entertain this notion. Where would you put it?"

"Midsquare. The square itself is clean."

The public square. The meeting place of the populace, the precinct of vendors and artisans, by kingdom-old right.

"Get the Patriarch to deal with the street preachers," Cefwyn said. "Get them in hand before I ever consider this thing. Do that!"

"It may not be possible," Efanor said. "It may get worse, as the Lines get worse. They want that place. They intend to have it."

"Who wants it? The street preachers?"

Efanor shook his head. "No. The things behind the Lines. The ghosts of our own dead, among other things less savory."

"You're mad. You're quite mad, brother."

"You were on the field. You saw, in Elwynor, when the dragon passed . . ."

"I saw a shadow! I am not favored, to see dragons."

"You saw it, I say. You've dealt with it. You've dealt with Tristen, far more than I. The Quinaltine is failing, and your son has very sensibly gone to him, but I cannot swear to what may result if Tristen should move from there. What he does we cannot predict. But give me my shrine. Give me that, brother."

"The people in the streets will be in uproar at the idea, every tavern will have its rumors, and your street preachers, your infernal street preachers, will seize on the matter like a hawk on a sparrow, brother. Give me a better proposal, and a cheaper one!"

"There is nothing cheaper," Efanor said, "but the Patriarch might foreseeably propose it himself. Or I might do it. It need not come from you.

"Too dangerous for you. And as suspect. I'll not have you embroiled in the matter. I'll not have you proposing it."

"If he proposes it—do I get my shrine?"

Cefwyn drew a long, long breath. Complications, controversies, gods knew—it would divert attention. They could dally for years, ripping up pavements, laying a new foundation, priests debating the design.

Ripping up the city square? Oh, certainly that would be a diversion, at a time when royal power was likely to come under challenge.

Trust that it would come under challenge, when something was loose among the priests in their sanctuary. He *had* seen strange things in Tristen's company. They tended to stay in the back of his mind, shut away from the ordinary tenor of his life. Workaday, he could maintain his balance and swear no such things existed. But he had seen the shadow sweep down the field. He had seen terrible things, and their grandfather—gods, their grandfather Selwyn—had burned candles all night in every hallway: he had had a conflagration of candles, until there was shortage in the city, the week he had died. He had ordered them burned day and night, as the light in his eyes dimmed, and he knew he was dying. He had seen things: the betrayer of Elfwyn Sihhë had seen things at the last and feared the dark above all things.

So where had they buried Grandfather? In the Quinaltine. That thought sent chills down his limbs.

"The people need a parade or two," he said peevishly. "Damn this snow. Enough ale in the public square, a few more comfortable visions among the priests. It could improve the temper in the city."

"Hold a feast. That will be a welcome diversion. Call in the lords."

"The roads are frozen, have you noticed?"

"Call them in for snowmelt. But send now. Let the word go out. That will start the people thinking toward a happy event. And who knows, there may well be a profound vision among the priests . . . vision of building."

Cynicism, in his pious brother? "You amaze me."

Efanor let go his wrist. "I have my uses, brother, dull as I may be."

"Never dull. Never that."

"Nor are you as blind as you try to be. Open your eyes. Emuin taught you how. Tristen surely did."

"Emuin's left the world. So has Tristen." The latter was the source of greater pain. Emuin had simply faded from his knowledge, part of the earth, part of the stones. But Tristen—Tristen's absence was a decade-long grief, half of his heart missing, a part even Ninévrisë failed to mend. "I so miss him, Efanor."

"So do we all." Efanor shrugged. "But we, meanwhile, have the world to deal with. He may hear your son. In the meantime, summon the lords. Make a feast. Cheer the people. There's been too much winter this year."

"Storm after storm." Holiday penance brought annual discontent in the Quinalt faith, and now, with snow still coming down, the year did head for spring, regardless. Another year of Tristen's absence. Nevris' annual pilgrimage, and the anticipation of the Elwynim . . . this time she would show them her new daughter, born this last summer: he had to commit her and the baby to the road in only a few months, and Guelenfolk here in the city would raise another hue and cry when the Elwynim acknowledged their Princess, the child the treaty had promised them. Aemaryen would never marry some lord of Ylesuin. She would rule in Elwynor.

The people might have forgotten that provision of the treaty between Elwynor and Ylesuin, as they had forgotten the king's bastard living in Amefel, and only now took to brawling, in their unease—so it was a year of forgotten matters coming due, for the populace, first Otter, then Aemaryen.

A new Quinaltine? Construction in the city square? That would be gossip for more than a month, perhaps enough stir, if the Holy Father backed it, to divert the people from the Elwynim question. Perhaps change would catch the popular fancy.

"If the Holy Father asks it," he said to Efanor. "If *he* deems it good: think of the old thief, with all those artisans to cheat. That will occupy him. To the greater glory of the gods. *That* should please the devout."

"Brother," Efanor said with a small, tight smile, and took his presence away.

Perhaps, Cefwyn thought, in the closing of that door, the visit of a couple of old southern friends with attendant festivities would soothe the spirits of the people and settle their uneasiness—even the eternal politicking of the dour old northern lords, some of them with sons and daughters to marry off, would be a pleasure this year. The zealots always exhausted themselves in Festival, and slowly settled, once the holidays were past. Religion would give way to the more forgiving, liberal days of spring.

A new Quinaltine? It was an idea to catch the imagination. Glory to the gods. A shining new sanctuary.

And more careful masonwork.

He touched the medallion he wore, remembering that not everything could come down to a building project and a revel. He had a glum and unhappy son on his hands . . . and now bringing all the lords in, and this crazy business of Efanor's, this building—

No, best leave that sort of thing to Efanor, who cited holy writ back at the Holy Father with a scholar's deep understanding, and had a knack for catching hold of the priests' fervor and turning it to his own purposes. To no other man in Guelessar would he have yielded, but he had utmost hope in Efanor, and hang the expense, so long as expense came slowly, year by year, layer by layer of a new foundation, and became a popular cause and a project to divert the damned priests. If Efanor wanted the square ripped up stone by stone, and gave him that, he should have his way.

CHAPTER TWO

i

SNOW LAY THICK IN MARNA WOOD, OUTSIDE THE WALLS, AND MOUSE CAME from his kitchenside hole this dawn with a message of trouble. Mouse would not stay for his morsel of bread on the floor, but ran in circles, stood up, his whiskers twitching in alarm.

Tristen tossed another crumb, nearer Mouse's safe door, but the trouble was in the wind, it was in the stones of the old fortress. By night the faces that haunted its walls had changed and moved. The stairs themselves proved unreliable, as if they hoped to catch an unwary foot. They shifted restlessly in the last several days and led places they ordinarily didn't visit.

All these things, and Owl sulked in the loft, making carnage, Tristen feared, among the pigeons.

Omens enough, if the place ever lacked them. The face at the turning of the hall toward the main door wore a worried look, unhappy, perhaps, in its memories or unhappy with present prospects. Tristen avoided that particular countenance, tempted, too tempted, to ask it questions: what slept in Ynefel's long existence, best slept on; what waked, fared well enough; and what had passed from the world ought to stay past, if the world was to get along as peacefully as it did.

Mouse's actions this morning were worrisome. Mouse was very old, even from Mauryl's days, prone to tremors and terrors, that was true, but the peace Tristen had sealed about his keep felt a little thinner this morning—he had sealed them in and sealed things out.

In Mouse's refusal to have breakfast, Tristen found himself thinking of old friends, and troubles. He pushed open the kitchen door, moving aside the snow, and went out into the safe little courtyard that contained the cottage Uwen had built—a little cottage with several sheds, and the lean-to stable, which had full tenancy this morning, as happened: they had brought all the horses in from pasture, the light horses and the heavy. Uwen was outside with Cook's nephew, Cadun, clumping about in the snow, carrying grain and hay for hungry animals.

"M'lord!" Uwen called to him. "Goin' to come a storm, ain't it? Feels it, in the air."

"It does," he said. That might be what had troubled Mouse. Uwen had good weather sense. He had been much in his own thoughts the last several days, and had paid little attention to the weather, which rarely signified to the keep, except to bring the horses in and lay in a supply of firewood.

"Cook's got porridge on," Uwen called back. "Wi' the blackberry honey, m'lord!"

He heard that invitation and gladly came down to help Uwen and the boy with the horses before breakfast. His own warhorse, Dysarys, was a handful, as Uwen put it—bow-nosed, contrary, and with a prodigious appetite for a stablemate's grain. They had put up a log barrier to curb his ambitions, so he took to kicking out. He never had hit anyone: Uwen was wary and Cadun, who was not so quick-witted or skilled with horses, was at least nimble at dodging.

But with his master, black Dys was better behaved, and liked to have his ears rubbed, the great, fierce deceiver: "You don't really want to kick Cadun," Tristen whispered into a backturned ear, tugging gently at it while the huge head was down in the grain bin. "There's a lad."

His hands were, of course, all over dirt and hair. He bent and washed them in the snow outside the stable, the rain barrel having frozen last night. His breath made puffs on the air, miracles of the day, and when he did trouble himself to reach out and know the weather, he smelled the storm coming, the way Uwen had.

But something else was there.

Some*one* else was there.

He stood for a moment listening to the world. Then, stamping the snow off, he went into Uwen and Cook's house, Cadun tagging behind, for a warm breakfast at a cozy table—not that he hadn't had a slice of bread, but warm porridge and blackberry honey was not to turn down. He sat with the little family—they had become his family as well—at a years-worn table, on a bench Uwen had cut and shaped with his axe—carpentry was not Uwen's first trade, but one he did well, as he did anything he set his hand to. Above them on the rafters hung bunches of herbs. A winter bouquet of dried flowers sat in an old jam jar on the table—the flowers themselves, out in the garden, were well buried, asleep. Cook had persisted in making a good deep, stone-rimmed bed, bringing in soil from the water-meadow and mulching and composting, and the years had rewarded her with abundant tame flowers and herbs, some of which survived the winters.

Their living here had gentled the old fortress somewhat and brought a little warmth even beyond its courtyard. Green leaves had appeared here and there in Marna Wood in the last few springs and summers. Trees that had seemed dead, right at the old bridge, had leafed out in their uppermost branches, whispering to the winds again, last summer, as they had in Tristen's earliest memory. The warmth of the house spread outward from the cottage, and from its hearth, and outside—

Outside, now, however, all was cold, in the breath of winter, and the threat of coming snow.

Outside was a life within that shadow, but not quite as fragile a life as seemed.

"M'lord?" Uwen asked him, porridge standing on his spoon.

Someone was coming, Tristen was well sure, now.

And up in the heights of Ynefel keep, in the loft where dust and old feathers blew in the winds, Owl opened his eyes and turned his head about as Owl could.

Go, Tristen told Owl silently, and Owl, that recalcitrant bird, spread blunt, broad wings and with two great flaps and a tilt of his wings, went out through the gap in the boards.

ii

THE DAY HAD BEEN HALF-KIND, HALF-CRUEL—A LITTLE WARMTH IN THE MORNING, but by afternoon a wicked wind kicked up, rattled through the bare, black branches, and suddenly, with a whirl of old snow off the limbs of Marna's trees, bit to the bone. Otter kept his hands inside his cloak as much as he could, except as now, when he had to get off Feiny's back and lead him over uncertain ground, down the slope of a little hillock and around a deadfall too big to move and too bristly to jump.

He had exhausted the grain, and Gran's provisions. He had spent two cold, cold nights in this treacherous place, but he persevered, calmly, surely. Paisi had always told him the woods had its tricky ways, and that it would mislead a traveler if he tried to turn around and get out. So he refused to change his mind and refused to be scared back, no matter the sounds in the dark, no matter the solitude of the place. He was sure he had come about in a circle once—but he was not to be caught by the old woods again: he had taken careful note of certain trees and looked at their shapes from more than one side, the way Paisi had taught him, so he could not be tricked unless the trees themselves changed shape.

But with the wind rising and the snow sifting down like a veil, he found it harder and harder to be sure what he saw, and once the dark began to come down, he had no choice but to stop and wrap himself in his cloak. He had brought himself and the horse up against an icy lump of an outcrop, with icicle-dripping rock between them and the gusts, to wait through the spate of snow. There was not a thing to eat. In that fact, he was more than worried.

Something pale sailed through the falling snow, sailed, and turned, and settled on a branch overhead. He looked up at it.

"Who?" it asked him; and he knew it was no natural bird. He got up on cold-stiff legs, and it flew off a little distance.

"Who?" it asked again.

Otter trembled, knowing the reputation of that bird, and whence it came—Paisi had said so, and Gran had nodded, confirming the story. He could see the fireside that night, when Paisi had told him how that creature had come into the Zeide and stayed with Lord Tristen. "It weren't no bird as ever was," Paisi had said. "An' it weren't friendly. It'd bite soon as look at ye. But it turned up where he did."

"My name is Otter!" he called out to the woods, the owl, and any listener. "I've come to see Lord Tristen!"

The owl spread its wings and flew to another, farther tree, veiled in snowfall.

Otter took the reins and clambered up on a rock to get to Feiny's saddle, fearful that the owl would move again and vanish into the woods. He urged Feiny onward, and the owl took wing, never minding that brush barred his way, and he had to fight past low, clawing branches.

"Owl," he called to it, "good Owl. Be patient. Stay for me."

"Who?" it asked, and perversely took flight.

The brush was too thick. He had to get down and lead the horse, tugged him along when the horse had as soon stopped altogether, finally having to take him close by the bit to keep him moving at all, and going near hip deep through a drift.

"Who?" Owl said, mocking him, and flew on through the snow, vanishing almost—but it seemed a bluish light outlined his wings and ran after him, like troubled water. Otter stared into the falling snow, his very eyes chilled, and kept going. Breath hissed between his teeth as he tried to warm it before taking it down. At times he lost Owl altogether, but then a passing shape brushed his hair and startled the horse as Owl winged ahead of him, glowing in the overcast.

His feet were already numb. That numbness crept from his feet to his legs and made him stumble in the snow as they left all semblance of a trail and followed a weaving course through a darker and darker forest. Feiny stumbled, and went down to his knees, and Otter pulled on the bridle, trying to help the horse up, all the while keeping his eyes on Owl, who vanished among the dark trunks and snowy branches.

Feiny gained his feet and followed, as numb and as miserable as he, Otter was sure, and Owl showing no mercy at all. He had sped through the darkest of the woods, where there was no light to be seen. The horse struggled and stumbled on hidden roots, and Otter feared he would go down and not get up: he had brought the heavy caparison, but even that was not enough. He took off his own cloak and flung it over the horse, saddle and all. Wind cut like a knife.

"Owl?" he called out desperately, casting about.

A pale shape sailed over his head and on through the trees, and he followed, stumbling, himself, on the uneven ground, and leading Feiny carefully, trying to keep them both on their feet. Ahead, a seam of twilight opened up between the trees, and Owl flew into it. They went after, passing under a network of bare branches, seeing that seam widen. It became a path, and, it seemed, a bridge, on the end post of which Owl sat, turning his face away.

Otter tugged at the bridle and brought Feiny along.

Owl spread his wings and flew as they passed the last screen of branches.

A fortress sat across that bridge, a place so overgrown and age-eaten it seemed a part of the rocks. The fortress gate cut off all view beyond the wall, except a little scrap of river and the top of a ruined tower.

Owl sailed up and up over that wall, and toward that ruined height, and vanished.

He had no choice now. He trusted himself to the old stones and the timbers and led Feiny across what might be a rubble pile or a bridge, on timbers with no few gaps. The ancient gates rose higher and higher, until they blotted out the sky. He stood and hammered them with his fist, which made little sound at all.

"Lord Tristen!" he called out to the heights. "Lord Tristen, can you hear me?"

Even his voice seemed lost, swallowed by the deep sound of the moving river under him, and he stood alone in the dark, beyond shivering in the cold. Twice more he shouted out and beat at the gate, waiting each time, in fading hope of an answer.

He had been a fool, he thought. He had come uninvited. He might die out here, no one knowing until spring and snowmelt.

Then a door opened and shut, somewhere beyond the wall, and he called out again, desperately: "Lord Tristen! It's Otter! Gran and Paisi's Otter! Can you hear me?"

Footsteps came, faintly in the distance beyond the gate, and then closer and closer, muffled by new snow, crunch, crunch, crunch. An inner bar grated and thumped back, and the gate swung and creaked inward, just enough to let him and the horse pass through.

He eased through the gap, seeing first a snowy courtyard, and the black bulk of the keep, and then, right by him, a grim man in a cloak and gloves.

"Sir," he said respectfully, though he knew this thickset man could not be the lord himself, and he found his teeth chattering when he did it. "I've come, I've come—"

"Ye're here," the man said. "Ye'll come in and have a warm bowl and a cup o' tea." The man took the reins from his fingers and patted Feiny's snowy neck. "A horse in a cloak, is it? My son'll see to 'im. Ye'll come along."

"You're Uwen Lewen's-son."

"That I am," the man said, and led him and the horse toward a low, ramshackle, and snowy cottage, with a long stable beside it, and other horses. That pricked Feiny's interest, and drew a soft, low grunt, and an answering restlessness from the stable.

"He kicks," Otter said, warning Master Uwen as the horsemaster had warned him, but now a young man had come out of the cottage, the open door of which shed a momentary rectangle of light onto the snow. He shut it, walked out, and that young man received his orders from Master Uwen.

"A good rub and a careful feed," Uwen said. "He's been without, summat, hain't he, lad, an' ain't ye, both?"

"There was grain yesterday," Otter said, "but not much."

"Good lad." Uwen's heavy arm landed about his shoulders and swept him on, irresistibly, into the light of the door and up the steps into the cottage.

Inside, the warmth was thick and all-enveloping, and a red-faced, grayhaired woman bent by the hearth, ladling up a bowl as Uwen shut the door. The latch dropped. The woman set the bowl on the table, with a spoon and a piece of bread.

"Sit," the woman said, no more to be questioned than Gran, and Otter eased his numb feet past the bench and sat down.

"The silly lad let the horse wear 'is cloak," Uwen said. "Which is a good lad, by me. Kick the boots off, boy. Warm those feet. Floor's warmer 'n that frozen leather."

He had a piece of bread in hand, dipped in the good thick soup, which was hot, and good, and the wonderful bread was fresh-baked. He obeyed, however, using one foot to shove off the other boot, and ate and struggled with the second boot at the same time.

"That's a boy," Uwen said, and bent down by the table and pulled the boot off himself, and rubbed his icy feet with large, warm hands. "Half-froze, is what. Best is warming from the inside. Where's that tea, wife?"

"Here," the woman said, and set a mug down by the bowl, which was just in time to wash down a bite. Otter did that, and felt his throat overheat all the way down. It made his eyes water, and Uwen tugged the hood back off his head and felt of his ears, which were cold and sore.

"Well, well," Uwen said, "he'll be well enough." As if he were a sheep they were looking over; and mannerless as a sheep, he'd devoured the bread and sat with spoon in hand to get the substance of it, the best soup he'd ever had, even better than Gran's.

"It's so good."

That pleased the woman.

"Welcome here," Uwen said. Hoodless himself, he proved crowned with grizzled stubble, and had an old scar on his cheek that ran right back into his hair, a soldier's kind of mark, and that fit with what he knew of Uwen Lewen's-son. "My wife's Mirien, but ye can call 'er Cook, which is what she likes to be. The boy, he's her nephew, truth be told, but son he is to me, and good as, ain't he?"

"A good boy, Cadun is," Cook agreed. "A hard worker. Another bowl, young lad?"

"Otter. Otter is my name. And just the tea, please, good mistress."

"Oh, courtly, 'e is," Cook said, setting her hands on her hips. "And well-spoke, and wanderin' in the woods in the dead o' winter."

"And callin' on names we know," Uwen said. "Gran an' Paisi's boy, he is. Ain't that what ye said?"

"Yes, sir. Yes, sir, I am. I came to see Lord Tristen, if you please."

"And that ye shall," Uwen said, "when m'lord calls ye, when he calls ye, but meantime ye're fed, an' your horse is fed, and ye can sleep right by the warm fire if ye like. Belike ye could do with warm sleep."

He wanted to see Lord Tristen. He had come all this way, at such hardship, and wanted what he had come for, immediately, if he possibly could. But when Uwen offered a hand to help him up, and with the warmth of the room and the weight of the food and drink in his stomach, he suddenly found it was all he could do to step over the bench end and totter to the fireside.

The boy had come in from tending the horse, meanwhile. Cook chided him to shut the door and bring the cloak over, and Uwen spread two thick blankets by the fireside. Otter sank down, and Uwen spread his cloak over him, horsey as it still was, and still chill from outside. In a moment more the fireward side of it was warm, and Otter shut his eyes.

Another blanket came atop him, heavy and pressing him down, down and down where it was safe and the storm could never reach.

iii

HE STIRRED FROM TIME TO TIME DURING THE NIGHT, CONFUSED MOMENTARILY not to be at home at Gran's, in his own bed, or asleep under the carved-wood ceiling of the Guelesfort, or freezing under snowy branches. But there was the homey fire to tell him where he was, and from time to time Uwen, in his shirt, came and put another small log on, just to keep it going through the cold of the night.

After a time the wind stopped howling, like a dog that had given up bad behavior, and the beams of the house popped and creaked in the cold, but Otter rested snug where he was, and slept, and slept, until all the aches melted out of him.

He began to be aware in the morning that the house had begun to stir, that, in fact, Cook was up. She had her hair in a long gray braid. She cleaned the table and set out bowls, then swung the pothook out and poured in cracked grain and a small kettle of water right at Otter's feet.

"Not so's ye need stir out," she said, swinging it back over the heat. "Water's set to boil. Sleep a bit more."

He did. And waked again when Uwen's son lifted the pot off with a wooden hook and carried it to the table.

"Porridge is in the pot," Cook announced. "Go get Uwen."

The boy went outside, and Otter sat up and raked his hair into something like order, still in his clothes, and finding the air warm and his bones bruised slightly from the fireplace stones, which he knew intimately, down to the one that jutted up a little, right where his shoulder wanted to be. But oh, he had slept, and he had been warm.

It was a wonderful place to be, and still felt as if he had waked inside a dream. The porridge went into bowls, there was honey for it, and he scrambled up and folded up the cloak and the blankets, to clear space around the fire.

"Yesterday's bread," Cook said. "An' today's porridge. And blackberry honey, which goes right well." Uwen came through the door, snowy-booted, with the boy coming after. "Sit down, sit down, all."

"Horses is fed," Uwen remarked, taking his place on the bench. Otter slipped onto the end of the bench, not to take up more than his share of room, and not knowing which side of the table he should use. "Ain't heard from m'lord this mornin'. He don't always stir out. He'll send when he takes a notion. Or maybe he'll drop in for breakfast, who knows?"

"Does he know I'm here, sir?"

"Likely. Likely he does." Uwen held his bowl as Cook dropped honey in. "Thank ye, wife."

Cook went about her business, feeding them all, and there was tea, and all the porridge they could possibly eat, and a great deal left over. Uwen said: "Never you mind about what's left. The horses'll be right happy to clean it up."

The cottage was tidy, though pots and horse harness and farm tools hung from the rafters, along with herbs and dried flowers, though there was not a straight beam in the place, and there no few patches in the daub—it was a lot like Gran's place, except the harness and except a rack that held a soldier's armor. A sword and shield stood in the shadows on the other side, in the corner, and his heart thumped when he saw it—a black shield with the white Sihhë Star in the center, arms still hung as a banner in the hall at Henas'amef. But here it wasn't a dusty banner. It was what Uwen Lewen's-son had carried in war. It, as nothing else, seized Otter's attention and held it, in little glances sideways, as if it, and all it stood for, would vanish from the mortal world at any moment. It couldn't be part of the world any longer. It couldn't go where ordinary people lived their lives. It was exactly as Paisi told him in stories, but the last trace of it in the world of Men was that banner in Lord Crissand's hall, that no one ever carried in the festivals and processions.

He finished his porridge. He offered, as he did at home with Gran, to wash the dishes.

"I do for Gran," he said.

"Aye, well," Cook said, "d'ye hear that, Cadun? Here's a guest offerin' to wash the dishes, an' is that right?"

"No," Cadun said, well taught, "no, it ain't, aunt."

"Well, so, get to it. An' our guest may sit, or walk about as he will."

He wasn't sure what to do with himself. "I'll go see to my horse," he said. That at least was his to do, and no one objected, so he got up, put on his cloak, and slipped out the door.

The snow had drifted deep in a curving line across the courtyard, a ridge waist high, distant. The brown tops of dead flowers stuck above the snow where it had blown thin, right along the cottage wall. A row of horses stood snug in their stalls, with a line of snow behind them where it had drifted against rolls of straw.

And above all, undeniable, the dark mass of the fortress rose up and up, towered and cracked and showing jagged edges here and there where there should have been more of a roof. He looked, and realized there was a face in the masonry of the nearer tower, a face that seemed to stare right at him. But that was a trick of his cold-stung eyes. He blinked, and when his eyes cleared, its eyes were shut.

The whole world was quiet, quiet enough that he could hear the rush of air when a shadow passed him, the wind of blunt wings brushing his hair.

Owl swept upward then, into the morning sun, up and up until he had to squint to follow him.

When he looked down again, a set of footsteps led from his own feet to a small set of steps, and a humble side door to the keep, as if he had walked that way, when he had never moved.

That little door stood open, dark inside the keep.

He caught his breath, stood doubting a moment, then walked over those tracks, and up those stairs, and entered that doorway.

It was a scullery all in disarray, pots lying on their sides, a beam fallen down right onto the grating of what had been a fireplace, long, long ago. Dust covered everything but the very center of the keep, beyond the arch, where the outside sunlight fell on an often-walked track across old stones.

He followed that track. He hadn't seen Owl. He didn't know if Owl had come into this place. But Owl leapt up from a rafter near the door and dived down and through the open doorway ahead of him.

Owl had led him this far safely. He took the guidance offered and followed, out into a wider room, where was a stairs, and at the bottom of those stairs a newel post on which Owl settled. He went that way, ignoring all else, as close to Owl as he had ever come. Above, around him, as he looked up, a webwork of stairs led to crazed balconies and ledges, up and up, again, to places where the wall was rent and sunlight came in, shafting through the dusty heights. A wayward sunbeam let in a flock of winter sparrows that circled confusedly in the tower, and that same light fell on faces in the surrounding walls, faces like those outside, some shocked, some somnolent, some seeming to cry out.

He looked down again at Owl's amber eyes and reached out for comfort, to offer Owl a perch on his arm if he wanted.

Owl struck like a serpent, and he snatched a bleeding hand to his mouth as Owl leapt up and flew off, spiraling up and up into the dizzy heights. Sparrows fled, fluttering and diving in terror, escaping every way they could find, but Owl lost himself in the heights, leaving him with the taste of blood in his mouth.

"Owl is not a grateful bird," a voice said, a young voice, a calm, still voice that resonated off every stone of the keep, as if it came from everywhere at once. "You came to see me?"

The voice settled to his right hand, and came from there, and when he looked beyond the bright light of the center of the hall, he saw a dim nook and a table, where a young man in dark colors stood by a fireside.

"To see you." This young man could not be a man present at his birth. Lord Tristen should be older than Paisi. But nothing seemed sure at the moment, and he walked aside, sucking the wounded hand to stop the blood. "Perhaps. If you are Lord Tristen."

"Come," the young man said, and he walked close, even yet seeing none of those signs of age he expected. "I am Tristen Sihhë."

"Lord Tristen," he amended himself, finding his manners, and thought he should bow—but this was not just a duke of Ylesuin: this was the High King himself, the king above even his father, if he ever cared to go out of Ynefel. He thought he should kneel, but there was no convenient place, in the little nook next to the chairs, and he was caught, snared, the while, in a gray, pale stare like his own. The Sihhë-lord's hair was as dark as his own, and his face might have been a brother's. "My lord." He hadn't intended to call him that, of all things, as if Lord Tristen were *his* lord, but there it was: it fell out of his mouth all in a rush, and it was, after all, true, from the hour of his birth. He managed to say: "Otter is my name."

"No," Tristen said casually. "Otter is not your name."

It was as if someone had stripped his cloak away and left him in the wind, not knowing where shelter was.

"You are Elfwyn," Tristen said. That was the name his mother had given him, and now the Sihhë-lord gave him, and it was his, and he had no wish at all to wrap that dark name around his soul. "Elfwyn Aswydd."

"My lord," he said again, and felt the world sliding. He had called him that twice now. What had Gran always said, about three times fixing a charm?

Breath came difficult. This was the lord who had permitted him to live. And who might as easily unsay that gift. "I came to ask," he began.

"Candles are precious this season," Tristen interrupted him. "The boat from the south won't come until snowmelt. There is breakfast, if you have slipped Cook's hands."

"My lord," he began, intending to say he had had breakfast, and there that word had slipped his lips the third time, and this time felt strangely comfortable, like long-forgotten old clothes. "I've eaten already, thank you. But I came—I came—"

"At least for tea," Tristen said. "You are shivering." He turned, this power not of the world, and sifted tea into a pot, then took the kettle from its hook, poured, and hung it back in its place. He set two cups on the table, besides, with a honey pot, a spoon, and a plate with half a dozen small cakes, the provenance of which Otter had missed in the shadows. "Sit down, Elfwyn Aswydd."

He sat, obediently. Tristen set a cup before him and sat down across the table from him. Firelight flickered on those gray eyes. Tristen took a sip of tea. He took a sip, too, using the cup to warm his hands.

"Will you have a cake?" Tristen asked.

"No, thank you very much, my lord."

"So why have you come?"

"My lord, I—" The size of the question appalled him, and he didn't know where to begin, without wasting the Sihhë-lord's patience, and losing his only chance. "I was in Guelemara. The king—my father—" He was always uncertain with that word.

"How *is* Cefwyn?"

"Oh, well." As he would have answered Gran about a neighbor. "He's well. The queen and the baby. And Aewyn. They all are well."

"Go on."

The interruption had driven all sense of order out of his mind. "I was there, with Paisi."

"Paisi and Gran. Are they well, too?"

"Yes, my lord, very well. I just left them." He attempted desperately to find his thread again, trying not to shiver, and could not look away from those eyes. "But while we were there, in Guelemara, I mean, Paisi and I, we dreamed Gran was sick, so Paisi came home. I tried to stay for Festival, and I—" He was hurrying, and wasn't sounding sensible at all. "A priest dropped the smoke-pot in the sanctuary, and the floor took a mark, and the Lines, my lord—the Lines—"

"You saw them."

"Yes, my lord. I saw them." He suddenly lost himself, trapped in the fire-changed gray of those eyes and remembering the acute fear he had felt then. "I saw them. And Prince Efanor gave me a Quinalt charm, and took away Gran's, but that didn't help. Then I had a message from Gran that she was sick and needed me, or I thought it was from Gran, but it was probably from Lord Crissand. So I left."

"So Guelemara was no good place for you," Tristen summarized, tucking in all the loose ends, and his voice was quiet, weaving its own spell of calm, and attention. "It was inevitable you should try, less inevitable you should fail, perhaps, but there, the course is set. You've chosen to leave."

"To come here," he said, hoping he understood.

Tristen shook his head. "Here is only part of it. If I changed what happened, it wouldn't altogether change what *will* happen. Cefwyn is well. You are. That's to the good. And you say you left Gran and Paisi well?"

"Very well, my lord. But my father's soldiers were after me."

"Your father's soldiers. You know they'd never harm you."

"But they'd bring me back. And I was making trouble for everyone, where I was."

"You weren't the trouble," Tristen said. "You are who you are."

"*What* am I?"

"Not what," Tristen corrected him, "*who*. You're Elfwyn Aswydd. That was always your name, but you never owned up to it. Now you have to be both Elfwyn and Aswydd, before you can be your father's son."

"I tried to be his son," he said. And added, which made sense to him, but not, he feared, otherwise: "Prince Aewyn is my friend."

Tristen nodded, as if he did indeed understand how two difficult matters tied together. "So he should be," Tristen said. "You are his brother."

"I want to be. I never want to be a trouble to him. I don't want to be a trouble to anyone."

"You are who you are," Tristen said again. "Do you understand yet how Elfwyn Aswydd can be Aewyn's brother?"

It wasn't the same as Otter being Aewyn's brother. He finally saw that, at least glimpsed the edges of what Lord Tristen was telling him.

"You should have carried your real name before you went to Guelemara," Tristen said. "The name Otter misled you. It misled all expectation around you. People were careless. Drink your tea. It's cooling."

He drank it. He tried to take in the deeper sense of what Lord Tristen was telling him. He had come for counsel. He had expected to ask sane questions about where to go next and what to do next, and have a plain answer—not to find himself led this way and that and questioned repeatedly about various people's welfare. *Should have carried your real name,* Lord Tristen said. Should he have gone there as Elfwyn Aswydd?

Should he, then, have come to Guelemara as part of Lord Crissand's household, and tried to be Lord Crissand's relative, somehow, when Crissand had two sons of his own who had every right he did not?

"What should I do now?" he asked. "I shouldn't go back to Guelemara, should I?"

Tristen sipped at his own cup. "That would be one course. But that won't happen now."

"Do you know that?" He hadn't felt magic moving, not at that instant, but now he did, the prickly sensation he got when Gran was working, and he kept his hands about his cup to keep from shivering. He daren't look aside from this young man. He feared what he might see behind him. "I'm afraid to go to Lord Crissand. It's not that I'm afraid of him. He's always been kind. But if I go to him, it means going near my mother."

Tristen didn't answer immediately. He stared past him into the fire. Then he said, looking straight at him: "You took the name of Otter. That made you someone else and kept you safe from her as long as you were Otter. Now things are different. You've chosen to come back, and you have to make your own safety."

"I can't," he said, and when Lord Tristen gave him a misgiving look: "I don't think I can, my lord."

"That's the difficulty, isn't it?"

What was the difficulty? He had known Gran to speak in riddles, but Lord Tristen didn't make clear sense to him at all.

"I don't understand, my lord."

"What do you think you ought to do? Why did you come here?"

"To find out if I've done the right things. To find out what's happening. The dream about Gran being sick wasn't really so, not as bad as seemed when Paisi and I dreamed it. And then I dreamed of fire." He'd forgotten that, until just that instant, how profoundly that dream had scared him. "And if it wasn't Gran, it was my mother that made us dream, wasn't it, my lord? She didn't want me to leave Henas'amef. She didn't want me to go away from her. But I did. What if she's making all this happen, and it's not just me? I hate her!"

"No," Tristen said sharply. "No. Cure that, above all else. Don't hate her."

Gran had given him the same advice. And he'd tried to take it, when he was Otter, when he was a boy with nightmares in the dark. Gran's arms had ceased to hold him by then. Gran only sat by his bedside and gave him advice, Paisi sitting cross-legged in a nest of blankets, likewise wakened . . .

That night. That night only last year.

"I've tried," he said. "I've tried not even to look at the tower, all my life. I think she hates that most."

"And she likes it best when you hate," Lord Tristen said quietly. "Be advised. There are two paths in front of you. One of them is what she wants."

"And the other, my lord?"

Tristen lifted a shoulder. "It may be what you want, or not. It depends on what you choose."

"Where should I go, then? Should I go to Lord Crissand?"

"Crissand has to be part of everything," Tristen said. "And it was a good choice, for you to come here. Your father is my friend. I know him, and I know your gran, and I know he'll see to her. You should trust him completely, at your next chance, though he makes his own mistakes. You say the Lines appeared. Was it only in the Quinaltine that they frightened you?"

"Yes, m'lord."

"And what happened?"

"It was like ink running, like ink running between the stones. And then the Lines. They were red. They seemed to be breaking."

"Did you tell your father about the Lines?"

"I think Prince Efanor did. And the man, the one that was spying on me for the Holy Father, Brother Trassin—gave me a message, and said the king—my father—was going to send me home in the dark of night. I didn't want to go with soldiers."

"But wasn't it, after all, his will you do so?"

"It was."

"So you ran before he could do send you home. You outran his good intentions. You caused him worry. He *has* been worried. He does feel very sorry."

"So do I." He couldn't look anywhere but at his own hands. He didn't want the questions to go on in this direction, about his welcome with his father. "I don't know. I don't know, m'lord. I was just scared."

"And angry that he was sending you home."

"Scared," he said. "And worried about Gran."

"Angry," Lord Tristen said, which happened to be true, and he had never quite realized it until now, as if something had been clenched up tight in his heart for years and years: anger, that his high hopes were dashed down; anger, that he had ruined all his chances.

"Jealous," Lord Tristen said. And that could not possibly be true.

Was he jealous of Aewyn, who had had a father, and enough to eat, and a palace to live in?

Every visit of the rich men on horses to Gran's front fence had hammered that difference home. His father had come every year, but his father had always ridden away, with Aewyn, on horses with rich caparison.

He was shocked to find that was at the heart of it. Anger. Jealousy. All the wicked thoughts he had smothered and tried to ignore in his heart were still there, stored up through the years. His discomfiture had disturbed them, and now when Lord Tristen probed into his opinions, they came floating up to the surface like rotten matter from a brook.

"I don't want to be angry with anyone," he said. "My lord, I love my father, and my brother."

"As you love Gran and Paisi. You have no cause for anger with them, do you?"

Only with his mother, he thought at once. He had just cause for anger at his mother, who lived in the tower, and at the poverty that made life hard. The lords who lived up on the hill and had books and feasts whenever they liked—he didn't hate them. But he found he was jealous. Otter had never been jealous, not humble Otter, who was grateful for everything, and was obliged to be. But if he was Elfwyn Aswydd, he was born to his mother's debts and his own hatreds . . .

Elfwyn Aswydd was his mother's son, and a dead king's namesake, the Marhanen's enemy.

"You do love them," Tristen said.

"I do love them," he said, but to his profound dismay it was no longer clean and pure, that love. "If I'm Otter, it's easy to love them."

"You have two paths," Tristen said. "And you may not have your own choice."

Two paths. And no choice. He did not understand, not at all.

"You are Elfwyn," Tristen said. "Elfwyn Aswydd is your responsibility to shape. Bring all the things Otter knows, and be Elfwyn, as you have to be. There is your best path, if you can get on it and direct it as best you can. The direction it may take yet is not in your power: but what sort of man walks that path, when you are a man, that you *can* decide."

He did grasp it, then. And suddenly he knew, if he were Aswydd, if he were to be pushed and shoved by fate, what he most wanted for himself, and where he'd set his feet if he could. There was what the Aswydds had, as Gran had, what he'd attempted to have, that morning with the oil and water. He hadn't much Gift, but he had a little. Tristen had something far, far more than any Aswydd, something that Gran wouldn't explain to him, but said Sihhë-gift was inborn, and natural for Lord Tristen, and made his very wishes powerful enough to rearrange kingdoms.

"Could I stay here with you a time, my lord? Could I learn wizardry enough to stop my mother? If I haven't Gift enough, could you possibly give it to me?"

Tristen leaned back from the table, regarding him with a troubled frown, then got up from the table altogether and walked to the fireside. As he went, Elfwyn turned on the bench, and watched him standing there, half in fire, half in shadow, staring into the flames and considering for some little time.

Then Tristen looked his way. And might have spoken, but a curious thing happened. A brown, quick movement appeared at the shadowed end of the table, beyond the glow of the fire, a scruffy little creature that advanced near the plate of cakes and sniffed at it.

"Ah," Tristen said, and a smile transfigured his face: it had been ageless and cold and terrible. Suddenly it was young, and kind. "Mouse is out. He's very old, and he's gotten very fond of Cook's cakes. Give him a bit. Owl is never grateful, but Mouse is."

Feed the mouse, Elfwyn said to himself in no little disgust, feeling anger, feeling his senses reel. Yet obediently, shaken to his very heart, and still waiting for his answer, he broke off a few crumbs, and held them out. The mouse stayed where it was, whiskers twitching, beady eyes bright, not trusting him. He pushed the crumbs toward Mouse, and pushed them farther, and the little creature darted forward, snatched one, and sat up and ate it.

"You did not insist on your own terms," Tristen said. "And you have experience of small, shy creatures."

"A little," he said. They'd had a fallen sparrow once that they had fed, he and Gran and Paisi, a quick, bright little creature, but it had flown away that summer and not come back. A silly creature, a silly act of charity, in a world in which sparrows fell daily, unrescued. As Mouse was silly, and that a Sihhë-lord took notice of Mouse *or* a stray boy suddenly seemed equally unlikely.

"I'd thought owls were fond of mice," he said, an outright challenge that drew first a frown, then a guarded smile from Lord Tristen.

"You won't see them both at the same time," Tristen said. "Mouse rules this nook. Owl has the whole keep else."

Elfwyn pushed another crumb close. Mouse took it and scurried off.

"He feels safer below," Tristen said.

"You said that my father shouldn't kill my mother," Elfwyn said, around a bite that stuck in his throat. "Or me. Why?"

"Which?"

"Why, either one?"

"If he'd killed either of you, it would have changed him," Tristen said. "And if he'd killed your mother, only, what would you have heard of him? That he'd killed your mother. And what would you have thought of your mother? That she must have been a good woman, would you not have thought, if you had never known her?"

"I'd have been very mistaken."

"Trust your father," Tristen said. "Trust him and all his house."

"I would. I shall, from now on. And Aewyn."

"You were to go hunting together."

How had he known that? "Yes," he said meekly, thinking it a demonstration of the Sihhë-lord's vision. "We were, this spring."

"Have you killed?" Tristen asked him.

The question shocked him. He had no immediate answer.

"Owl kills," Tristen said again. "Are you Owl or are you Mouse?"

He didn't know what to say. "I was Otter," he said, and attempted silly humor, to relieve the terror that Lord Tristen's disapproval evoked in him. "I suppose I could hunt fish."

Tristen looked at him still with that curious intensity. "Fish, perhaps. But no greater game. You should not kill. It's very well for your brother, but not for you. What are you thinking, now, Elfwyn Aswydd?"

"That you were a great warrior," he said, the truth startled out of him without his thinking. "They say you've killed battlefields full of men."

"Far too many," Tristen said somberly, and for a moment there was that distant and terrible look on his face. "It saved my friends at the time. Believe me—keep from blood. Your own balance is far too delicate."

"But just hunting?"

"A precious thing, your gran's teaching in you. Don't cast it away for sport."

"Aewyn isn't wicked. If he hunts—Aewyn isn't wicked, is he?"

"Nor will be made wicked for a deer or two he intends to eat. Be Otter when you must. Not Owl. That would be a terrible thing, were you to be Owl."

He all but laughed, the admonition was so strange, as if Tristen were half in jest, but he suddenly doubted that and stayed solemn—as if Tristen, giving him that advice, had echoed something as simple and true as a child's story, the kind of advice Gran had used to give, when he had been on his worst behavior, and she forgave him.

"My lord," he said, blushing hot.

Then Tristen did smile. "Are you sure about the cakes? You could take one or two."

"Mouse can have them," he said. Suddenly it seemed quite reasonable to be discussing Mouse as if he were a person, with a man the whole world feared. "Thank you, my lord. Thank you." His thoughts plunged deep, and came back up from the depths again with the pieces he had tried to gather before. "But my questions—"

"Your questions."

"Can you teach me? Can you make me a wizard?"

"You are not yet what you will be," Tristen said, "and I have been waiting for this question for longer than you know."

"Waiting, my lord?"

The fortress groaned, and in the tall room beyond, the sounds of massive movement began, a terrible squealing of wood and shifting of stones.

"Come and walk outside with me," Tristen said as if nothing at all had happened. "Let us see to your horse. Uwen says he took very little any harm of this, grace of your good care, but I shall see to him all the same. Then we can sit by Uwen's fire and warm our hands. The sky may clear this afternoon. I rather think it will. You may go fishing with Uwen if you wish—he does enjoy it. And I shall look toward Guelemara, such as I can, and see what I can see."

Look toward Guelemara . . . as if he could, so easily, look there from this isolate place. And was he to do nothing but fish all afternoon?

Magic was what he had come here to call on.

To hear the Sihhë-lord so simply propose to do something this afternoon, as if it was a troubling chore that had to be done—he had invoked a power he had only suspected in his mother before this: he was, on the one hand, glad to have come, and on the other, appalled that he might have set something in motion that he had no means to command. He was used to Gran's gentle nudges at planting weather or her recourse to the Sight, which told her sometimes when a neighbor was coming or if someone was sick.

He didn't know now what he expected from Tristen: a rumble of thunder, a flash of lightning from the greatest magic in the land—should there not be some such appearance? Or had the shifting of the stones and timbers of the keep been an illusion, a trick of his own ears?

He walked where Tristen led, back through the high hall, uneasily looking up as beams creaked. In that moment he saw Owl sitting on a high railing, three or so levels above. Owl ruffled up and turned his head away, pretending not to see him.

iv

FEINY HAD GOTTEN NICKS AND CUTS FROM THE ICE, AND HAD A COUGH. HE was not an easy creature to deal with. But, warned that Feiny kicked and bit, Tristen only said, calmly, "He knows you now, and he won't." Tristen laid his hands on the cuts, one and all, and the redness went, and Feiny gave a great sigh and lowered his head, butting gently and gratefully against the Sihhë-lord's hands.

"Now, see, we might have brought a cake, mightn't we?" Tristen asked. "The horses like them. We left them inside. But there might be an apple in the barrel yonder."

There was one apple. How it hadn't frozen and spoiled, a farmer lad couldn't imagine, but it hadn't, and Feiny took it gladly. He was the only horse in the stable at the moment. Tristen said Uwen and the boy had taken the other horses out to a pasture beyond the walls, though where a meadow might be in the depths of Marna Wood a farmer lad couldn't well imagine either.

Meanwhile the clouds had parted above the keep, and the sun shone down, suddenly blinding bright, as Uwen came back from the postern gate. Uwen and Cadun joined them at the chore of breaking ice on the stone water trough, thumping it with sticks until it broke.

"Elfwyn would like to go fishing," Tristen said.

"Well," Uwen said, "well, it's a sunny day. Fish for supper might be a good thing. We can do that. Get the gear, Cadun, me lad."

Tristen walked away, paused to wash his hands in the horse trough, then went back in by the way they had come, through the scullery door. Elfwyn— so he had to be—stood a little nonplussed, cast back into Uwen's domain for the while and not sure what might come next. Was Tristen going inside to open some grimoire and cast spells, and was that why he was banished? Or would Tristen simply look into the fire for his answers?

"Here we are," Uwen said, when young Cadun came back with poles and baskets, and a dirty pot that likely was bait. "Out to the bridge. That's the best place."

So the three of them went out the main gate, and out onto the age-worn span, where Uwen rigged poles and hooks. Indeed, it proved to be a bait pot, a very smelly bait that had to be shaped around the hook.

"The fish find it right tasty," Uwen said. "But don't neither of ye get it on your clothes. Bad enough on the hands, an' it takes a mort o' scrubbin' t' clean it off."

"Don't fall in," Cadun added. "Old Lenúalim is tricky here."

"Is it all the river there is?" Elfwyn asked. He knew the Lenúalim as a broad, great river, one that divided the realm in two and made the border.

"Oh, it's deep enough here," Uwen said, as all of them settled on the rim of the old stone bridge. "It's mortal deep. There was a battle here, in old Mauryl's day, so m'lord says, and the rocks themselves was cracked top to bottom. Not all's mended, and the crack down there's deep, deep, far deeper than I ever had a line reach, I tell you. The water's narrow here, but it's fast. And just enough room for an Olmern boat to squeak under the span, if they take their mast down. The river gets bigger and wider when the brooks in Marna flow in, but no deeper, I'll wager. And then it goes all the way to El-wynor, where the big bridge is, an' it widens considerable. An' so on, until it bends round between Amefel and Guelessar and goes south, where it spreads out shallow and lazy. Ye cross't the same river comin' here."

Elfwyn peered over into murky green water, into which he had dropped his line. Ice rimmed the rocky sides, but none stayed in the center, which roiled with the power of its moving. He sat, patiently watching his float stream outward on the current. He knew how to fish. He'd sat many an afternoon by Weir Brook, near Gran's place, with Paisi. And they used poles. Paisi wouldn't let them use traps.

On account if it rains, Paisi had said, and them traps clog up, you kill all them fish to no good. Besides, a weir can trap limbs an' end by floodin' Farmer Marden's turnips, an' him with a great temper, which ye know. Line's much the best.

He never did know how Paisi knew where it would flood if they had made a weir, as the name of the brook suggested, but he suspected Paisi had found that out himself once. He had always found it pleasant to rig a line and sit for hours, catching a few small fish, never more than they could use at a meal, and mostly watching the water move between the banks and the sunlight dancing on it.

This water moved under the old bridge with far greater power, and deeper mystery, and he feared it, thinking how fragile they all were, up here. He was startled when his twig-float bobbed. He snatched the line and pulled up.

"I have it, I have it!" he cried, hauling the line with one hand and all his fingers. It fought, a great heavy silver fish, and when he finally hauled it safely onto the stones, he had to seize it with both hands to stop its struggle.

"That's a fine fish," Uwen said. "D' ye need a knife, there?"

He held it pressed to the icy stone, his bare hand freezing from the damp as he worked the hook out of the gasping mouth. Its fins stuck him painfully, and hastily he reached for Uwen's offered knife.

But the fish's round eye rolled in its socket and stared back at him, comical, like the laughing fish in Aewyn's book, while its gills labored as it struggled for breath. He held the knife. He held the fish, pinned against the icy stone.

And he couldn't kill it.

He let it go. It flipped into the air and sailed free, down and down until it vanished in a silver splash, with a flip of its tail.

Cadun cried out. Cadun tried to catch it for him. But he sat there, seeing the blood he hadn't shed this time, but had shed, oh, so many times before, and he saw Aewyn by the fire, showing him the book with the brook and the fish. He hadn't killed this time. He hadn't been able to do it, nor wanted to watch if Uwen or Cadun did.

Uwen caught his eye. "M'lord ain't no fisher, neither," Uwen said sympathetically.

What had happened to him? He didn't know, but he couldn't have killed that fish to save his life. He shamefacedly laid down the pole, and tucked up next to the pillar at the edge of the bridge, where he could simply watch the water.

Be Mouse, Lord Tristen had said, and sent him out fishing with Uwen all the same. He sat there, with the door of the wall ajar on the bridge, and with a view of the courtyard and the lower tier of the fortress to remind him it all was real, and that he had talked to Lord Tristen today, and had breakfast with a mouse. His finger was cut, where Owl had bitten him, an oddly shaped cut, from a sharp beak.

Uwen and Cadun caught fish, which met their ordinary fate. He didn't watch. He sat staring at the water.

The place is changing me, he thought. *I can't do what I did. Clearly I can't be a cleric. I'm learning to ride, but I can't be a fighter if I can't kill anything, so it's no good my learning the sword, is it? What shall I be?*

"Enough fish," Uwen said, eventually, and they took their catch and went back to the cottage. Uwen trimmed and dressed the fish they had, sending him with Cadun to wash.

"Ain't never caught a fish?" Cadun asked him.

"I didn't want to catch this one." Elfwyn scrubbed his hands in icy water and tucked them under his arms to warm, after.

"Why not?" Cadun asked. "He was a big fish."

"Maybe that's why," Elfwyn said. He didn't want to talk about it. He wanted to go inside the cottage, and did, and sat by the fireside. Uwen brought the fish to Cook, and said something Elfwyn couldn't hear before he went out to wash.

"M'lord invites you to supper," Cook said, "as I'll cook and send over with ye, if ye will, young sir."

He wasn't ready, he thought. He remembered, with a thump of his heart, that Lord Tristen had been looking for answers, all the while he had been finding questions about himself and things he thought he could do, and would do.

"I will," he said respectfully, and watched as Cook put their dinner on to cook, apple tarts, first, that smelled of southern spice. Then plaincakes, that rose and split and baked all brown on hot iron, and last of all fish that no longer looked like fish, nor smelled like the river.

He was both troubled and relieved to find that the smell made him hungry.

<h1 style="text-align:center">V</h1>

MOUSE HAD HIS SHARE, BOTH OF PLAINCAKES AND CHEESE. AND IT TURNED OUT Tristen would eat fish, even if he lent no hand to catching them.

"I was Mouse today," Elfwyn said. "I wasn't much help catching fish. I couldn't. I don't know why."

"There has to be Owl," Tristen said. "If there weren't Mouse, Owl would starve. And if there weren't Owl, Mouse wouldn't be Mouse."

He thought about that. He wasn't sure he understood it, entirely, advice one direction and then, of equal force, from the other, like shifting winds. Were both things true?

But they dined on plaincakes and crisp fish and apple pie, a wonderful repast, in which Mouse had a share, sitting on the end of the table, his little whiskers twitching busily between bites.

"Where is Owl?" he asked, and Tristen sailed a glance up and away, toward the dark that now ruled the rafters outside the dining nook.

"Outside the walls, hunting," Tristen said. "It's his hour."

Tarts filled out the meal. Still Lord Tristen had said nothing about his business of the day.

After the tarts, the silence.

Elfwyn stared into the fire, unwilling to question his betters, or to nettle Lord Tristen with asking.

"So," Tristen said, "have you a question?"

"Have you an answer for me, my lord?"

"That your father is worried for you, and that his men have reached Lord Crissand, who is greatly distressed at your departure. That Paisi has cut a great stack of wood, and has blisters, and Gran is baking bread tomorrow."

He was not sure he believed Lord Tristen knew so much, so dear and of so little of use to him. The report of people he loved stung his eyes, all the same. He pressed his luck. "And Aewyn?"

"Aewyn is shut in his room, not coming out, and he refuses his new tutor."

He wasn't quite so sure he disbelieved anything, now. Aewyn would do exactly that.

"But nothing of my mother."

"Your mother and I have little to do with one another," Tristen said, and asked: "Has Gran shown you hedge-wizardry?"

"A little," he confessed. He corrected himself. "I've watched her."

"And did your looking show you things in Henas'amef?"

"No," he confessed, uncomfortable. "It only brought trouble."

"Has she ever taught you wards?"

"I've watched her."

"They're old, in the Guelesfort. If not renewed, they weaken. A spell reaching out the windows can weaken them further. Think of that when you reach out of a place. You make yourself visible when you look out—you open doors and windows as you do. More, they will never close with the force they might have had if you hadn't crossed Lines with your seeing, if you have not a skill the equal of the one who laid them down."

"I don't understand, my lord." He hesitated to ask, but he feared what Lord Tristen was saying. "Did I make the trouble in the place, myself?"

"Wards are a simple magic," Tristen said, and rose from the table without answering him. "Come."

He followed, out into the dark, where a few candles sprang to life without

Lord Tristen even seeming to notice them. Lord Tristen led him to the stairs, and up and up the rickety web. The steps trembled and groaned underfoot, and Elfwyn gripped the rail as he went.

They passed one of the faces. He would have sworn it turned, when he looked back, and did catch it in motion.

"Don't look at them," Tristen said. "Don't talk to them. Not all are trustworthy."

Did they speak? He heard nothing but groaning, nor wanted to hear. He gripped the rail, white-knuckled, and kept close to Lord Tristen as they arrived on an upper balcony.

"You may sleep up here tonight," Lord Tristen said. "My wards are constant about the keep, and you will not weaken them."

Tristen took a lighted candle from its sconce, pulled the latch of a door, and let him into a small, stone-walled room with a shuttered horn-pane window. A crack split that wall. It ran around the window and up and down, above the ceiling and below the floor. It was a little room, with scarcely room for the bed and table it contained.

Tristen went to that window and ran his hand across its sill, across the crack. "Follow the line of the window, not the rift: the wall is a Line that Masons drew, do you see, and the stone is a barrier. But in that protection, for us to come and go there must needs be breaches, doors and windows, and these are its weaknesses. Locking a door is a ward. So is a wish to draw a line and to keep harm out. Draw it with fire or with the warmth of a hand." This he did, and now a faint blue light showed in the shadowy places, a Line brought to life.

Elfwyn drew in his breath, alone with this power, and with magic itself, and not knowing what might happen next.

"Stones remember such things very well," Tristen said. "And doors and shutters become part of them. The Line Masons draw is potent, if renewed."

"It glows," Elfwyn said, and this caused Tristen to look sharply at him.

"Not all will see a light, but this is a magic Men can use even without Seeing, and one you can use without fear—it lies upon the earth, deeply, and has the earth's bones for strength: it will not come back on you or betray you. It can be broken, by great strength, but never turned against you. Only beware of casting outward, of looking beyond those wards if enemies are about."

"Are there enemies?" he asked, not believing they would ever come here.

"You know you have enemies," Tristen said.

"The priests," he said.

"More than that," Tristen said. "Be Mouse. Mouse did not grow as old as he is by ignoring Owl. He always looks about him."

"I don't know where to look," Elfwyn said, hoping for an answer, but Tristen walked to the door, and he made his appeal. "Show me wizardry. Teach me. I want to learn."

"So you can be Owl?"

He didn't know the right answer to that. Tristen gave him no clues. He had always been good at saying what the authority that ruled him wanted to hear, and now he found authority who gave him no clue how to please.

"I don't know, my lord. I don't know what's right."

"Be content. Be content right now."

"But will I see Aewyn again?" he asked. "And will Gran be safe from my mother?"

"Patience is one thing you lack," Tristen said quietly. "Patience is one thing you must gain. Vision is another."

Elfwyn drew a breath, and another, seeing he was losing ground, and that the very person who held all he possibly wanted had, indeed, posed him a lesson: not one he wanted, but at least Tristen posed him a challenge he could overcome.

"I shall try," he said quietly. "If I understood what you mean, I think I could do better."

"Words Unfold to me, in their time. Perhaps these words will Unfold to you."

"Unfold."

"Like a flower blooming," Tristen said. "They open."

"I wish they would," Elfwyn said in despair, and Tristen said:

"Wishing may indeed help."

He might have said, in bitter honesty—It would help me more if you explained to me, but the candle-shadow caught Tristen's face at that moment, and turned it from young man to that grim and somber visage—the Tristen Sihhë of legend, the terrible man on the black horse, the man who became a dragon.

Patience and Vision. Simpleminded advice, each syllable of which struck his heart like a hammerblow, at this dark, lonely hour, in this place.

"I shall wish, my lord. I shall wish it earnestly."

A somber look, directly at him. "Beware of the quality of your wishes, and beware, not of anger, but of selfish anger."

"Only *selfish* anger, my lord?"

"This too: love you must have, love that comes to you from outside, unbought and unasked for. Do you understand? You cannot hold it. You cannot compel it. But you must keep it when it comes."

He had had a glimmering of that sort of love. He had it from Gran. He had it from Paisi. He knew it now with particular poignancy. He had had the merest taste of it in Aewyn, before Guelen hate drove him out.

"How do I keep it, then?" Elfwyn asked.

"Deserve it," Tristen said.

The air seemed too heavy to breathe.

"Give as well as get," Tristen said. "Be honest. Be more than just. Be kind. And consider carefully what you are and what others are."

Kind. That was Gran's sort of advice. It wasn't what he hoped to hear as a beginning of wizard-work.

"Above all," Tristen said, "you mustn't stay here when I leave."

Elfwyn's heart beat faster and faster. "Are you going somewhere?"

"I believe I must," Tristen said.

"May I go with you, my lord?"

Tristen shook his head. "No. You will go ahead of me. My enemies are your enemies, and not to your good. You have a knack for opening doors. You must go with first light."

"Sir?" He was completely dismayed. He'd learned nothing, and now was he dismissed?

"You must go," Tristen said, "well supplied, and with Owl to guide you out. Otherwise, you might not find your way back to your house. Gran and Paisi are waiting for you."

"Yes, sir," he said, deeply disappointed.

"For the safety of us all," Tristen said, "remember everything I've said. Your enemies will want you to forget, and to fear, and you must do neither. Sleep now."

Elfwyn sank down with one knee on the patchwork quilt, and Tristen lit the candle on the little table beside the bed, then left, closing the door. The latch clicked, and Elfwyn found his eyes growing heavier and heavier. He didn't want to sleep. He didn't want to be shut in this room. And he most of all didn't want to leave in the morning, but he saw no choice for himself. Tristen had never answered his questions, except to warn him—you have a knack for opening doors, as if everything were his fault, the way Trassin had said; and except to explain about wards, and to strengthen one, right in front of him, a crack that, unmended, split the wall and let in the cold.

He got under the covers, having no other recourse. The bed was comfortable and not at all musty, the bedclothes well kept.

And now that Tristen had mentioned Gran and Paisi, he felt a rising anxiousness for them, a surety he truly needed to be going back, that this place, even Uwen's cottage, was not the right place for him.

He didn't know what had turned his opinion around. He suspected Tristen had, and he wished he hadn't, and that his answer had been different, but Gran—Gran did miss him, and Paisi did, and if Lord Tristen was going to ride out into the world again—then the power that had decreed he ought to live in the first place would come and see how things were in the land, and maybe set his life in order. At least there might be a hope for him.

He slept.

And waked again, with the candle out, and in darkness. For some reason he felt alarm. He heard a series of noises, like someone thumping at boards just outside the door.

He lay still, fearing to move, for a long time, and ashamed of himself. Then there came a scratching at his door, as if someone were playing a game with him, and that made him angry. He rolled out of bed, and pulled the latch, to face whatever it was in the light outside.

A rush of air and a battering of claws and broad wings drove him back in.

Owl, he realized. Owl had prevented him leaving. The terrible sight of swinging stairs and faces alive in the walls lingered in his vision, branded there by the one burst of light, before he had slammed the door to keep Owl away from him.

He reeled away, and sat down on the bedclothes, then recalled what Tristen told him about wards.

He made a pass of his hand across the door, and all about the wall, wanting, this time, not to be the one who opened windows. He did it all around three times, to be sure. Then he tucked down into the warm covers, hearing the sigh of wind outside. But everywhere he had just walked, the wards glowed palest blue.

Did I do that? he asked himself in wonder. *Did I do that?*
Or did Lord Tristen?

vi

A GOOD BOY, TRISTEN THOUGHT, SITTING BY THE FIRE. HE WISHED PAISI MIGHT have come with the boy, though if Gran was ill, there was ample reason not.

Gran being ill, now, that was a very grave business, one that might bring danger on them all prematurely, and whether it was the course of nature or not, he felt uneasy to have that news.

He had reached so seldom out of Ynefel. It was never wise to put forth magic carelessly, however potent, and he disliked breaching his own wards, for whatever purpose.

But this boy—

This boy was the very reason he had pent himself up in Ynefel in recent years: he had been reluctant to lay hands on the situation too early and often, fearing he might blind himself to what truly was moving through it. Now, clear of the quiet workings of Tarien Aswydd, he had gained a certain perspective, enough to see past others' fears. And his own.

Elfwyn's heart was clean, still clean. But he had seen him attack Owl himself, up above, and he had felt the wards, how they quivered, not quite what they had been. There was in the boy that little darkness that could well nest something else, something older and more dangerous—*that* was the thing to fear. The sins at first would be inadvertent, the opening of a window for the best of intentions. The boy was a cipher, and with threads of connection running under doors that could not safely be opened . . . not safely, because there was no sure way to close them after.

And that Elfwyn had recourse here, unasked—that was worth a question: he had battered at the gates asking help—but at whose will? Something had wanted the boy to come to him. Perhaps it was even his own will, in some obscure, inclusive circle of his wards about those he loved: Sihhë magic could work that way. He wondered if Gran herself was strong enough to do it, or if possibly—least likely—the boy's own will had found its own direction.

That was what he had indeed hoped, even wished over the infant, who had become Otter and now Elfwyn—that Hasufin, who had created that intended vessel for his own shell, would be driven so far from the world he would be ages finding his way back; or at very least—that the vessel itself would not be overcome without such a struggle that it would advise him of the danger.

There was a hollow spot in Elfwyn, as in the first Elfwyn's child. Perhaps there always would be that hollow spot in the boy—not want of a soul: he had that. Perhaps it was want of love. At least what wanted *him*—an old enemy, the oldest of enemies—had not gotten in at his birth, or thereafter.

He was still an innocent. Thank Gran for that. It was not an old soul who had gotten past his front gates, to Uwen's peril, but a young and innocent one, not quite as innocent or as vulnerable as he had been, but still clean. The power that wanted him born had not gotten in.

But this year the boy, nearly a man, came under attack. Everyone attached to the boy now came into danger. Elfwyn was Unfolding, like a word; and that Unfolding would shape him—would, at its worst, work like luck and move everything and everyone aside who opposed the Shape he was born to have—would, blind force, like a seed in the ground that pushes and shoves to reach life below and above, become stronger as it progressed. Elfwyn might yet prove a shell, a husk around an undetectable seed.

That was the danger. Elfwyn was no match, yet, for what might begin to flower in him.

Had he done wrong to preserve the child?

Preserving him, he preserved Cefwyn. He preserved a good king, and a good man, and his friend.

Preserving him, he preserved himself from a deed he could not contemplate and still be himself.

Preserving him—and knowing where he was, and trying to fill that hollow place—

Well, at least they had a watch over him.

Tristen bent, reached to the woodpile by the fireside, and put a stick in, letting the fire take it, watching the bright light that had always been wonderful to him—warmth and pain, the two first lessons of his life, close together and so finely divided. His body, after all his wounds, bore only one scar. It was on his hand, the first one.

Perhaps, he thought, he should go immediately as far as to Henas'amef and meet with Crissand . . . or send, as he could, and bring Cefwyn here. One stride through the gray space, and he could do that.

But above all, he had to be careful. His own will was potent: he could fill that hollow in Elfwyn with a Word, and if he did, and if he began to work toward a thing in the outside world, he himself might bend the world in ways that he could not predict . . . precisely because Hasufin was gone from the world. His enemies had a value to the world: they could oppose him, and most things could not. He had all but unstoppable power. But he had learned a hard lesson in Elwynor, that his own will was not necessarily wisest or best for the world.

The stick burned to a wisp of ash and fell away. He rose from his seat then and walked out into the echoing great hall, and to the door.

A face appeared there, looking inward.

"Mauryl," he said. "Mauryl, my teacher."

The face seemed to change somewhat, or maybe it was the candleflame moving.

He remembered his days with Mouse and Owl, prey and predator, how he had learned to esteem each, and how such things as a rain barrel had taught him, when Mauryl lived in Ynefel.

It had all come crashing down one day, when the beams fell, when a foolish boy had made a mistake with the wards.

"A boy has come here, Master," he said. "A boy has come to me for help. What shall I do?"

Dared he go out into the world and learn what had become of the things he knew, what mortals had come into the world, and who of his old friends had left it?

He wasn't sure, tonight, that he had the courage.

The eyes of the face moved, and looked at him.

"Let him go," the stone face said.

Let him go, echoed through the depths of the fortress. Not simple words. Mauryl's words never were. They had to be understood at every depth. Let him go.

Let go of him. Don't touch him. Let him fly free. Let him do what he will.

It was not what he wanted to hear. Mauryl's advice rarely was.

Mauryl himself had been known to be wrong, had he not? Wrong, or Mauryl would not be as he was. But Mauryl had, at the end of his life, known his enemy.

Let him go.

He waited until daylight, then, and went out to the yard by first light. Uwen was up and about, tending the boy's horse.

"Saddle him," Tristen said. "Our guest has to go this morning."

Uwen's hands stopped their work, a soldier's hands, gentle at their present task. And Uwen straightened his back and looked at the sky, which was overcast and sifting snow, before he looked back again. "Weather's hard, still. Shall I escort 'im to the edge, m'lord?"

"No," Tristen said. "Owl will guide him, such as he can. We shall be riding out ourselves, soon, to Henas'amef. But not today."

A little silence. Uwen never asked to understand what he did, but seemed to know, at times, more than most Men.

"Aye, m'lord," Uwen said, and kept at his brushing. "I'll have 'im ready just after breakfast."

After that encounter, he went inside to write a message, and to wait until Cook's boy brought cakes over, and until Elfwyn stirred forth and came down the stairs.

"Breakfast," Tristen said, and offered him cakes and tea. "Did you sleep well?"

"Mostly, my lord," Elfwyn said, which was truth with a hollow spot, too. Tristen said nothing to that, only shared breakfast with him and put him out of doors with his own good cloak, a fire kit, and a packet of cakes to go with him.

"Uwen has your horse saddled," Tristen said, "and grain for him in the bags. Owl will guide you. Don't stop or turn aside for anything."

"Yes, my lord," Elfwyn said, as they stood on the steps. "Thank you very much."

It had a wistful sound. Elfwyn had wanted ever so much more from him. But he left in possession of his right name, and he had heard the truth and had a bag full of Cook's cakes. There were less useful answers to a petition.

"Be careful," Tristen wished him, and took him by the arms and looked him close in the eyes, searching for any flaw. It was not apparent in him, except that little frown: anger, always anger. "Find Paisi, care for Gran, and take this—" He drew a little sealed paper from his belt and gave it to him. "Take it to Lord Crissand and wish him well from me."

"Yes, my lord." The boy tucked the paper into his own bosom, and took his bag and his blessing, and went down the steps to the courtyard, where Uwen and Cook and Cadun all waited outside to bid him good-bye.

In a moment more he had disposed his baggage and gotten into the saddle, settling his cloak around him. Then he waved good-bye to Uwen and his household, looked last at him, with a little respectful bow, then rode quietly out the gate Uwen opened for him. He left of his presence only tracks in the courtyard snow, tracks the sifting white would soon fill. Ynefel was almost as it had been. Almost.

"Go," Tristen whispered to Owl, and Owl flew from the height and passed the wall, swift as an arrow.

Perhaps, Tristen thought, he should have given the boy plainer warnings about his mother, but that might expose the boy to more influences once he began to wonder more persistently about her.

At very least a warning not to go near his mother would act as a grain of sand in a boot, a slow irritant that might drive that particular boy to doing the very things he ought not. Best lay wards about the young man, as he had done, and keep him safe and quiet, as untroubled by outside forces as he could make him.

For the other matter—he had written a message to Lord Crissand, bidding him not admit Elfwyn any longer to his mother's tower, no matter what, and to await his arrival.

CHAPTER THREE

i

OWL WAS NO BETTER THAN HE HAD BEEN, A TRICKY BIRD, LEADING PLAINLY AT times, and at others vanishing among the barren limbs, turning his head, and pretending to be a snow clump. Elfwyn had had hopes of better behavior, but Owl was Owl—untrustworthy in the finer points. Maybe it was a good thing to be feared, Elfwyn thought, during one of those times Owl had deserted him, and it was certainly very humbling to be Mouse. But he could see why Owl wasn't a pleasant creature, or the sort anyone would want for a friend. Owl did what he had to do, and what he wanted to do, but he repaid a kindly hand with a bite—which was going to scar his hand for good—and he scared people he was helping.

It was not a sort of creature he wanted to be, he decided. He remembered the fish, which was swimming the river now, alive, and he was glad of it, although he had eaten what Uwen had caught. He remembered Mouse, sitting up and eating the crumbs he gave, so wary and wise a creature, and so fragile Owl could carry him off in an instant. But he was clever, and quick, and hard to catch. Perhaps it was not such a bad thing to be Mouse.

Owl flitted ahead of him and was lost again.

Owl appeared, usually when he had stranded himself and had to retrace his steps in the maze of branches at some little difficulty. Apparent trails turned out to be mere bare spots in the woods. Trails such as Owl led him were oftenest as choked with brush as places that were not trails, and there was no sign at all that the way they went now was the same way he had come in.

He slept the night, with enough to eat and with enough for Feiny, and waked with snow sifting down on him, a white dusting that grew worse as he rose and rode. Within an hour the downfall grew so thick it obscured everything but the nearer branches.

Owl had left him, of course. He was of a mind to stop until Owl came back, but it was a cold and inconvenient place, where he had realized he had lost his guide. He was on a ridge, and he decided to ride to the bottom of it, where there was shelter from the wind, before he stopped. He weaved his way down between clumps of sapling trees and down onto a flat place. But Feiny lurched, there was a crack of ice, and all at once Feiny fell through an icy shelf into water and spilled him onto cracking ice, going down sideways.

He flailed out amid cutting slabs of ice, Feiny struggling beside him, breasting cracked sheets of ice. The water was no deeper than his waist—Feiny was able to climb out, once he had righted himself, and he did, too, holding to Feiny's tail, but he was soaked nearly through, and instantly shaking, teeth chattering. Feiny, in his heavy caparison, was soaked. He knew not many things about finding his way in the world, but he knew that he had to find shelter, and he had to warm himself and dry out or die. He let Feiny stand, left the wet wool felt on him for warmth against the wind, and got to the fire kit he carried attached to his belt. The red fiber beneath willow bark, willows growing all about, here, was the least damp fuel he would have at hand: he was trembling so he could hardly keep from curling into a ball, but he persevered. He peeled bark on the underside of a dying limb and collected his little knot of dry fiber. He broke off dry twigs from limbs, and swept a spot clear in the snow, where he sat to work with a pile of dry kindling on a bed of wet, slick leaves, warming himself with furious effort with the fire kit.

He drew sparks. Over and over they failed, or only livened for an instant, and died in the wind. He hunched over his little pile and kept trying, his hands cut, but cold beyond feeling. His feet were numb. He felt nothing from his knees down. And if there was any virtue in this flint and steel being given by Lord Tristen himself, he hoped it would take.

One spark lived, and spread to two strands of the red fiber, and three. He sheltered it with his hand, and made a window between his fingers for a little wind to reach it, until heat burned his palm. Then he added twigs ever so gingerly. He fed it and fed it, while the feeling left his upper limbs. He stumbled about on half-dead legs, broke dry branches he yanked from off the oaks on the higher bank. They smoked, their upper surfaces being soaked, but they burned, and he dragged back larger ones and put them in, building a blaze in a spot clear overhead.

Ice had formed in his hair, and it dripped water, now, down his face when he faced the fire he had made. It sent up smoke in plenty: he hoped Lord Tristen himself might see it, and know he was in trouble; but he began to be warmer.

He drew Feiny closer to the fire. He limped over under an oak limb he had seen, still clinging to its tree, a big dead limb from which the bark had fallen. He seized it, wrenched it back and forth and dragged it back, posing the arch of it over his fire, ramming it down so it would take.

His feet had suffered all he dared allow. He sat down by a considerable fire, worked off his boots and stockings down to bare feet, and rubbed life back in until it tingled and hurt. Feiny, having sense, had stayed close by the warmth, and showed no disposition to leave him and go running off. He fed Feiny a little: the grain had not gotten wet, and Feiny's barding was not wet through, particularly on the side that had not gone into the stream. It was, he was glad to know, quite warm inside. He got down a good blanket, which had stayed dry, and, shivering, took off his cloak and his other garments, wrung them out with all the strength he could command, spreading them on the arch of the large log, then, within his blanket, huddled close to the fire, searching with his eyes into the thicket for more such limbs.

Fool, he said to himself. He should have had better sense than to ride Feiny across. Nothing else had been that flat. The spot had been too sheltered, and too inviting, and if not the fire kit and the stand of willows, he would be freezing to death. As it was, he set his boots and stockings nearest the fire but could not get them dry again before he had to go out, barefoot in the snow, and crack off more dead limbs and pile them on. The cold hurt his skin. His limbs jerked uncontrollably as he worked, but he hauled back whole branches, unwieldy as they were, and made a larger and larger fire, until it melted back the snow, and melted the cover off a rock overhang, and melted the very edge of the icy stream.

Lord Tristen, he wished, in Owl's absence, *Lord Tristen, help us. Help us, or we freeze to death in your woods.*

But Owl stayed gone, and he piled on the wood hour after hour, until he had a good bed of coals under the burning wood. Whenever the bigger logs burned through, he heaved both their burnt ends closer in on the coals, and kept the blaze high and strong, fire that melted all the snow that fell, and only whipped about in the driving wind, too strong and hot to fail. He sat in the smoke stream, where the greatest warmth was, and finally had strength enough to set his cloak and other clothing up on a frame of dead willow branches, likewise in the smoke, where they would dry faster. The dark came down around him, and by a firelit dawn, he had gotten his clothes and boots dry enough to put on, but not dry enough to risk leaving his fire yet. He unsaddled and fed Feiny, who had kept warm near his fire through the night, and having warmed himself again, he decided he finally dared sleep, his head on his forearms, and all of him tucked in a fire-warmed, smoky blanket, in smoky air.

His nose and his eyes ran. He waked whenever the fire needed feeding, but slept, and finding himself, and now the blanket, damp from the air about him, he dared not leave the fire for long. He stayed all the next miserable day, ranging farther and farther about to find dry, deadwood still on the trees, chilling through in the process, then warming himself again. He was dirty and smoky, but at least not starving, thanks to Cook's cakes, which he ate sparingly, the while, and which he would have sworn were not so numerous. He began to be quite pleased with himself now that he had recovered from his folly and saved himself and the horse, alone as he was. Paisi, he thought, would be proud of him. Uwen would nod, in that way he had, and approve. He had done as much as anyone could do, on his own, and with no help at all.

In the morning the snow had stopped, and he got up, saddled the horse, and used the end of a log to break up his bonfire and shove the coals and burning wood out onto the ice of the brook, where it fell through. Then he mounted up and rode along his side of the brook, which at least offered him a road through the trees.

Something brushed his shoulder, and shot along in front of him. Owl had turned up, after two nights and a day, and continued remarkably well behaved until the sun was high, after which he disappeared again, faithless bird.

Elfwyn decided he could be as obstinate as that. He stopped, got off the horse, and waited, sitting, wrapped in his cloak, on a relatively warm fallen log until Owl decided to show up again. He was feeling quite pleased with his management of calamity, sure that Owl would come back, and having slept well enough and eaten a bit of a breakfast. Paisi, he thought, again, would be proud of him; and he was more and more anxious to get home again and tell Gran what he had seen and have her word on things—she and Paisi both had known Lord Tristen, and would want to know everything, every tiniest thing.

After he had gone to Lord Crissand, that was, and—

He had a terrible thought, and looked in his purse, which was empty of everything but his fire kit and a little willow bark; and felt about his person— he remembered putting it into his shirt—but he had had every stitch of his clothing off in that terrible hour, and he had been shaking all over, numb, and the wind had been blowing, so he would never have felt a little thing like a letter fly away from him.

It was a day behind him, that place, and he had no idea now how to find the fire site, or how he would find a scrap of paper in a snowfall. The snow had covered everything. He had been so pleased with himself for staying warm, and never once thought of the message he was carrying, never once put it in a safer place after he had tucked it inside his shirt that morning he had left.

Fool! he said to himself, distraught. *Fool! So smug, so sure . . . and it's gone.*

He sat there, however, having no other answer and no rescue for his folly. Owl came back, perched smugly on a branch nearby, waiting for him.

"I've lost it," he said aloud to Owl. "What shall I do? Can you tell him?"

Owl paid no attention at all, but took wing before he had quite gotten back into the saddle.

He had to get back to Gran and Paisi and get their advice about the message he had lost.

But what would Lord Tristen's message have said? It surely advised Lord Crissand of what Tristen had already said to him, that he intended to ride out and probably pay Lord Crissand a visit—that, at least, he knew, and he could at least advise Lord Crissand that there would be a visit.

And then he had a reason to ask Gran if she could See what Lord Tristen was up to—because he ached to know when Tristen would ride out, and whether that riding out had to do with him. He had had a kindly welcome at Ynefel, no question—but Lord Tristen had looked into matters, as he had said, then decided to send him out first in some degree of haste.

That haste, he had denied to himself for the last several days, but haste it was—urgency was certainly what he had felt in his dismissal.

Well, Guelenfolk had certainly wanted him gone from their premises, which, now that he was gone, probably made things easier for his father.

He would never expect that a place like Ynefel and a Sihhë-lord should have any fear of him at all—but why, then, had Lord Tristen decided there was so much hurry about dismissing him?

That was what it had seemed to him, that at first Lord Tristen had been preparing to have him stay in Ynefel keep a few days, and then something had changed, and Tristen had flung him out onto the road into a coming storm.

Surely Lord Tristen, who could look out into Amefel and Guelessar, could have watched over him, right on his doorstep. Instead, Owl had run off at the very worst moment and left him, as if the bad luck that attended him was too much even for Owl to overcome, because he was a wicked boy, bent on ducking himself in a brook and losing a message Lord Tristen had meant to send . . .

Maybe he was truly cursed from birth, the way the Guelenfolk thought. Tristen had told his father not to kill him—but Tristen had told his father not to kill his mother, either, and everybody agreed his mother was the wickedest woman that ever lived, so that was no recommendation.

So what was he? And why were people everywhere he went so much better off without him?

He felt cold despite the cloak and the horse's warmth, chilled right to the heart.

Tristen hadn't been willing to teach him wizardry. Maybe he had been too dangerous, too evil to teach—though Tristen had seemed to consider it moderately, and had shown him wards, and when he had done them—which was wizardry, was it not?—they had clearly worked.

So maybe he wasn't irredeemably wicked. Lord Tristen might be testing him, whether he could overcome his birth.

He hadn't done well so far, losing the message . . . but he knew it now, and it was no time to sit on his hands and mope, as Gran would say.

Telling the truth to Lord Crissand was the most urgent thing, and when Tristen did come to Henas'amef he would go to him at the first chance and confess outright that he had lost the message. Tristen had dealt with him kindly, even if he had stripped his comfortable name away from him and told him to carry the one he was born with: it didn't mean that he was damned. It meant that he was no longer a child, and he had to be a man, and deal with that name.

Be Mouse, Tristen had advised him, and not Owl.

Timid and brave, like Mouse. Wise, like Mouse. Not fierce and faithless, like Owl. He would not have understood that about those two creatures if he hadn't visited Ynefel and seen how they were. He wouldn't have thought twice about them if Tristen hadn't made him stop and think about their natures, and his—and he'd not been able to kill the fish, had he?

That had been a test. He knew that now. He'd doubted it when they'd had fish for dinner, all the same, but Tristen had said something about its being all right to be Owl, but not at all right for him . . .

Which meant Tristen had seen some virtue in him, had he not? And Lord Tristen had, after all, taught him wards, and given him the fire kit, last of all. Tristen had given him exactly what he needed and left him to rescue himself.

What were his two words, that Tristen had given him, that he had to gain for himself?

Vision was one. Clearly, if he'd been looking at what he was doing, he wouldn't have ridden his horse onto thin ice. If he'd Seen himself, stripping all his clothes off, or paid any attention to what fell on the ground, he wouldn't have lost the letter, would he? Vision was something he'd needed to have, and hadn't.

The other word was—

He could see Tristen telling him, but the image faded when he tried to think of that second word—it faded, like a dream by daylight, a simple word, an obvious word, the sort of word that anyone ought to possess. It was something he had, quite indignantly, thought he already possessed, but Tristen hinted he did not . . .

Love, might it be? He had wondered often enough in his life whether he had been loved enough, or by the right people. He had wondered whether he had enough of it, on his way to Ynefel.

Love was important, love from mother, or father, or brother—and the one he knew he had won, but one of the three he knew he never would, and the middle of the three, he doubted he had deserved. Love, but not yet from his father and certainly never from his mother. Tristen said whatever it was, that it was all-important for him . . . but was it love? Love was what he had been hoping for, lately.

Tristen had said . . .

He became convinced there was something he had forgotten entirely, something that rested just outside his reach.

Worse, more things began to escape him, faster and faster. The snow had whited out the world, and now it whited out the very memories he had hoped to carry away with him—since his struggle against the cold and the weather, he had more than lost the message, he had let other details begin to escape him. He wanted to write them down, but found nothing on which to write and nothing with which to write. He scratched it with a piece of sharp twig on his own bare hand, until it bled: *Vision,* he wrote.

Owl was gone. In the very moment when he had broken off a twig and written it, he had misplaced Owl again, or Owl had misplaced himself.

But in the next little space of riding, the woods thinned before him, and he saw snowy meadowland, and when he had ridden a time across fenceless meadow, he came on the snow-covered and untracked ridge of the east–west road. In a time going east, he found a milestone, capped with ice, half-buried, and hard to read.

Thirteen, it said. Thirteen snowdrifted miles from Henas'amef, and it was only noon. There was hope of making it by sundown, if only Feiny had it in him.

CHAPTER FOUR

i

FEINY COULD NOT, AFTER ALL, DO IT BY SUNDOWN. AND THE CHOICE HE HAD was to camp by the wayside, in a ditch, with the grain all gone, and all Cook's cakes eaten yesterday, or keep going into the dark at as steady a pace as Feiny could manage.

It was long, long after dark before he rode within view of Gran's first fence, and Gran's house sitting quiet and dark. He rode up to the gate that kept the goats in, and led Feiny on around to the goat shed, up against the house. He opened the door ever so quietly, and led Feiny in, but Tammis, safe and warm inside, saluted Feiny in a reasonably quiet voice, and he suspected he was heard inside the house. He was cold, too cold for clear thought, but Feiny had carried him long and hard, and he was of no mind to leave him comfortless. He unsaddled the horse and rubbed his sweaty back down with grain sacking that hung—he knew it by habit, rather than sight—by the outside door, while Feiny tried to force his head into Tammis's bin, hoping for grain. The goats bleated into the dark.

There was far too much commotion to get past Paisi's hearing. He heard the front door open, as Paisi had done before.

"It's me!" he called out, to forestall any caution. "Paisi?"

"M'lord," Paisi cried, coming into the shed, and shoving two sleepy goats out of his path. "Ye silly lad—ye could ha' rapped at the front door an' had help."

"I was trying not to wake Gran."

"Who's wide-awake, an' who knew you were comin', as was! We waited supper a while, an' then so as not to waste lights, we went on to bed." Paisi flung arms about him, slapped him on the back, and hugged him hard. "Gods, ye silly boy, ye're safe. Did ye even get there?"

"I saw him," he said, in his own defense.

"Gran thought so," Paisi said. He found the grain bin and the bowl they used to dip it up, and poured a measure into the trough, to Feiny's immediate preoccupation. "He's fine, he's fine. You just come inside, lad. Get yourself warm and fed, an' I'll come back an' tend the horse."

Warmth and food came very welcome. He went in by the back door, out of the shed, blinking in the dim light of the banked fire. Gran was indeed out of her bed, using the pothook to swing the pot over the coals, but it had become too heavy for her in recent years. He gave it a shove, his hands still gloved, and hugged Gran gently, wanting to stand there a good long while, just in that comfort.

"I saw him," he said. "He was very kind. He was younger than Paisi," he added. That never ceased to amaze him.

"His years ain't ours," Gran said, as Paisi came in and shut the door behind them. "Nor ever shall be." She made him stand back and took his cold face in her two warm, age-smooth hands, making him look into her eyes. "Aye, ye seen him, hain't ye, lad?"

"He said I was Elfwyn. He said that was my name."

"Then it has to be, now, don't it? Come, sit on the bench. Paisi'll dip ye up a bowl."

He did. He took what he was given, ever so grateful to be home, and safe. There was fine bread and butter, good potato-and-cabbage soup with a bit of pork besides.

"His Grace sent it," Gran said.

"The King's Guard came by," Paisi said, having a bit of soup himself, as Gran had some of the broth. "An' then His Grace of Amefel's men, wi' a right sensible Bryaltine father, wi' some good aromatics for Gran."

If Paisi thought a Bryalt father was sensible, that was a wonder in itself.

"So we ain't wanted for a thing," Paisi said. "How was it, wi' Lord Tristen?"

"He remembered you and Gran very kindly," Elfwyn said. "He invited me to dinner, and to sleep the night in Ynefel."

Gran nodded solemnly. "Ain't surprised," Gran said.

"And he said the king was worried about me, and he showed me wards, Gran. And mine glowed!"

"Ain't surprised for that, neither," Gran said.

"And then he said he would come to Henas'amef. I don't know whether only to Amefel, but he gave me a letter for Lord Crissand. And I lost it, Gran! I fell in the brook, and I lost it!"

There was a small silence. "Did ye, then?"

"Well, what shall I do?"

"What do ye incline to do?" Gran asked him.

"Go to Lord Crissand first thing tomorrow and tell him as much as I know."

Gran nodded. "That ye must do, then. Paisi told the king's men you'd gone an' where you'd gone, and they didn't follow. An' Lord Crissand knows where ye were, o' consequence, so he'll be wonderin'."

"First thing in the morning," he said. He was melting a puddle onto the floor, off his boots, and it had become muddy from dirt in the shed. He put the bowl down, having eaten as much as he could, and the bowl clattered against the stones as he set it down, his hand was shaking so. "I think I'm a little tired, Gran."

"That ye be," Gran said. "Paisi, get 'im to bed. Is that horse settled?"

"They're settled."

"Great hungry horses—thank the gods 'Is Grace is feedin' 'em. The goats is gettin' fat off just the grain an' hay they spill. Go to bed, Elfwyn, lad."

Gran called him that name, as if that name was his own even here, but in spite of everything, welcome had settled all around him, warm and good as Gran's house always was. He gathered himself up, and sat down again on the bed he shared with Paisi, and managed to get his boots off, and his stockings, which had holes in them, and had worn bloody blisters. There was mending and washing to do, when there was light enough. He took off his belt and fell into bed, which still seemed to move with Feiny's weary gait, and that was that—he managed to lift his head only when Paisi came to bed.

"Good to have you back," Paisi said.

"Good to be back," he murmured into the crook of his arm, head down again, nose buried. Gran's amulets were all about the bedstead and under the mattress, which was goose feathers, and ever so comfortable, especially with Paisi's warmth by him. The snow could fall tonight. He was warm and back to his beginnings, as if his soaring rise to princedom and his passage through Ynefel had never happened. He was only Gran's boy again, more than a little lonely, but protected.

Vision, Tristen had said. He had that scored onto his hand. And now he saw Gran's place as safety in a cold, dangerous world, and the humble beginnings he had longed to escape. Gran's love, and Paisi's—those were, he thought, his first and greatest treasures, those he never had valued enough. He lay with Paisi's warmth next to him, and the cottage snug against the wind, no matter how hard it blew.

That was the way Paisi kept things. He hoped to be as clever with his hands. It was a Gift, potent unto itself.

Vision. Seeing things for what they were and what they could be.

What was that other word?
It still eluded him.

ii

OWL WAS BACK IN THE KEEP, DISAGREEABLE AND PEEVISH. HE HAD LOST A FEW feathers, and sat puffed and mad-eyed on the newel post upstairs.

It had not gone well. Luck had not run the boy's way, and a good deal of his path had become obscure, deeply shadowed.

Perhaps, Tristen thought, he should have ridden out with him and conveyed him home. He had foreseen trouble. But the world had been shadowed these last few days, and it would have meant, had he gone out from Ynefel and devoted himself to one boy, on one solitary track through the woods, that he would lose track of other things, to the peril of all.

More, his presence risked drawing more attention than the boy already had on him. The boy had fallen into a dark place, one of those shadows Marna had within it, where even Owl had had trouble finding him. Likely the boy had not known that old stones lay near, likely had never even felt the gap in the earth, but he had gotten out of the trap and away, and come out of shadow unscathed, at least.

Leaving the keep now, abandoning his vantage at Ynefel, meant he would suffer a degree of blindness during the boy's passage, which would have brought the boy into greater danger. He would suffer a degree of blindness to movements in the land when he did ride to Henas'amef—the balances there had already shifted, tipped, trembled on the edge, and if he moved, he sensed, he would tip them right over.

None of what had happened in Henas'amef of late was what he wanted. If he went there, when he went there, it would shake the world and the world beyond it. But what had been gnawing away at the peace all these years had its own intentions, and undermined, and shifted, and would have its way, sooner or later. The boy was the lever that moved things. He had been born for that.

The boy, however, had gotten safely as far as Gran's house, and slept inside her wards tonight. It was Cefwyn and Crissand who had their troubles at this hour. Those did not grow quieter. Peace might last a little longer.

Perhaps he should still delay going, and only see whether things settled now that the boy himself had settled to rest for a time. The intervention of a Sihhë-lord in the affairs of Men had rippled the calm surface of ordinary years, and he had seen how his withdrawing to Ynefel had smoothed things out for a time: things that ought to sleep slept more deeply, the longer he kept his distance. The whole world drew an easier breath.

And should he go now, hastening everything, to divert this boy? He was a good lad. Gran had made him that.

Uwen came and went among Men much more frequently, usually with Cook: the two of them had gone, generally as plain travelers, into villages, and now and again as far Henas'amef itself to consult with Lord Crissand, or to exchange messages—oh, with far less fuss than the lord of Ynefel would generate, and very little ripple in the peace. They were quiet, and clever, and came back full of news and gossip—news he would not have thought to ask, names that quickened fond memory—servants he had known, and minor lords, and sometimes they brought news from Guelessar, or down the river: familiar names, like Sovrag, and Cevulirn, that conjured warm evenings and happy moments as well as dreadful. The two of them had ridden out, and came back bringing him the oddest trinkets, a curious tin box, a fine pair of gloves, packets of spices from the southern trade . . . all these things he valued, but the things he most longed for no one could bring him in a bag of trinkets. A quiet supper with Lord Crissand was what he wanted, or rarest and dearest desire, with the friend of his heart, with Cefwyn himself.

Oh, he had made ventures, but never since the boy had grown old enough to ask questions.

He had met with Paisi, oh, at least half a dozen times, at the edge of Marna Wood: if not for Gran and the boy, Paisi would have gladly ridden into Marna and begged to stay.

He remembered a dirty-faced boy, who had also been Paisi, in the streets of Henas'amef, the day he was lost. Paisi running errands for Master Emuin. Or holding a baby who could not go back to its mother.

Time ran back and forward for him when he let his mind wander. He had visions at times . . . he had been a dragon once—he had felt his own power increase beyond all bounds, had felt the earth shake, seen men cast to ruin in a breath. He had drawn apart, to keep his influence out of the world, but, oh, he was so tempted to go into Guelessar, and to turn up in his old friend's path, and just to say, as Cefwyn had used to say to him, "Shall we go riding?"

Those had been the best times of all.

And when, since that day, he did go out into the world, when the poor or the desperate begged for health, for fortune, for justice—he had been the Dragon, and the power was always there. Oh, indeed, the touch of a Sihhë hand could work such magic . . . the people knew it. Some, if they knew the price, would pay it . . .

And whenever he worked, he knew. The smallest magic could just as easily, and not by his intent, bind an unwarded soul to his own life, as Paisi was bound, as Gran was. Healing could just as easily make some desperate man an open gateway to things that man would never expect to meet. Men prayed to their gods. They prayed by their own understanding, reckless of what they invoked, and wanted things, wanted so very much—and sometimes with such complete justice and need—

Some things he granted. But some things he never would. He would not, for instance, raise the dead. Mauryl had done that, had clothed a soul long in the dark.

Had good ever come of that?

Mauryl had never said—but then, the final word was not written, and Mauryl himself had never known the outcome of his Shaping. That was all he dared say of himself, that he tried to do the best he could, which was as little as possible.

He would not, for instance, deal with children, or try to bend them one way or the other. Childhood baffled him. He hadn't grown that way. He had simply stepped into the world as he was and learned it as he could. He understood that, in Elfwyn, he dealt with a creature not yet a Man, but something nearly a Man, a creature with a Man's passions, but not quite a Man's desires; a Man's yearning, but not a Man's self-restraint. That would come. And when it came, there would be another new creature, one which had not existed in the world until Cefwyn had engendered that life in Tarien Aswydd's womb. Elfwyn Aswydd was *not* Tarien's remote kin, long dead, or Cefwyn's grandfather, also dead. He was something of both, and neither. He was a wild force, a power unto himself, and most unpredictable of all, he was still in that stage of things Unfolding within himself—not as things had to *him,* out of a mature knowledge and the distant past, but taking shape out of bits and scraps of what other people showed him and what his intellect could make of it. There was, in fact, no knowing which way Elfwyn Aswydd would turn.

His mother had her own plans for him; but worse, she had made herself a window through which other things could look, and her plans, set into motion, had never been all her own. Her time had run, irrevocable in the world of Men. Threads had come together in a design that wove through and through this boy's existence. Hasufin Heltain was one thread. Heryn Aswydd was one. Orien was. And Tarien Aswydd.

Stubborn he was—and what else? He was Cefwyn's son, equally.

He sat thinking until the sun rose, trying to ponder what this boy was.

And in the morning he walked into Uwen's cottage. There he found that Uwen was sharpening his sword, tending his own weapons for the first time in a long time.

He sat down by Uwen on the bench and took a cup of tea from Cook.

"Ye're thinkin' about the outside, are ye, m'lord?" Uwen asked him.

"That I am," he said quietly, aware that Cook was listening with one ear, while putting bread to bake.

"Is it the old enemy, m'lord?" Uwen asked.

"I don't know," he said. "How could you suspect?"

Uwen shrugged while the whetstone kept moving. "The boy. The Aswydd woman. An' the king. Things is come together lately."

"That they have," Tristen admitted.

"An' last night ye had the whole hall lit."

The candles came and went. He rarely thought about them. "I suppose I did."

"So," Uwen said. "Ye ain't slept much since the boy went out."

"I often don't."

"Ye ain't, 'cept Owl is back, so the boy's got where he's goin'. An' Dys, he come in on 'is own from pasture this mornin'. Ye called him."

"Did I?" He was amazed. He'd wanted the horse. He'd wanted Uwen. Both knew that without his saying so.

"So," Uwen said, looking up and down the gray-sheened edge of the metal. "So, well, the bones is some older, but these hands ain't forgot."

He'd worked his little magics to keep Uwen hale and strong, and Cook and Cook's son, too, since Cook made Uwen happy . . . it was his little secret, a furtive and quiet magic, worked within the walls, and this without polite asking. Dys didn't age, nor Petelly, nor any of the horses. Cadun grew up, but never older, and if there was wrong in that, he only hoped Uwen forgave him, if Cook and Cadun did not. This morning was as close as Uwen had ever come to remarking on his own long good health.

But he needed Uwen. This was the truth inside the truth: he knew that time ran too fast for his liking, and that Men faded. With them, with this one comfort, he was content; and without them, he was alone.

Since the day he became a Dragon, he held in his heart a vision of a place frozen in ice, remote from all Men—a place before Men, and before love, and before everything. He couldn't quite remember a time he had been there, but he feared it more than anything. It was that place where the Enemy had been, and yet it seemed to him that he had been there before he knew Mauryl, that he had watched Mauryl arrive at those gates, oh, long before many other things had happened, and long before there was Uwen, to tie him to *this* place and *this* time. Tristen had lived his first year in the world of Men less than two decades ago; lived that year, and the next, and many after it. But the cold place was there, always, in the back of his fears, an icy fastness where nothing he loved had yet existed. It had been so easy to spread anger out onto the winds, like the Dragon, and be there again; but once he was there, he might not remember how to get back.

Uwen was his strength, but also his weakness. His Enemy would ever so quickly exploit that weakness if he entered the world again; and his need for Uwen would bring Uwen grief if ever his care had a lapse. He knew it. So did Uwen know it, wise man that he was. He became sure this morning that Uwen knew his somewhat guilty secret, counted the years he had spent here, and did forgive him.

"So," Uwen said, "do I go, or do we go together this time, m'lord? Ye've waited for the boy. Now he's gone where he's goin', or Owl ain't a prophet."

"Brave Uwen. We shall both go, and go soon, I think we must. But something is moving, and if I leave the tower, I shall not have the vantage to see where it goes. The wind is up this morning. Do you hear it?"

Uwen looked up, on blue sky and a clear day. "Is it that, m'lord? Is it woke again?"

"I don't know. Put our packs together. We shan't take a great deal with us when we go, and we may go at any hour, day or night."

"Aye, m'lord. Just my gear, an' yours. As used t' be."

iii

THE GOOD CLOAK FROM GUELESSAR HAD FARED THE WORST—IT WOULD NEED mending as well as washing, and there was no time for either. Elfwyn put on Paisi's best—Paisi insisted; and the two of them kissed Gran and took the horses the king had given them, and rode out to the highway, himself on Feiny, with his saddle, and Paisi on Tammis, with nothing but his halter.

It was a brisk, snowy ride to the gates of Henas'amef, under a blue bright sky at first, then under the frowning shadow of the battlement. They rode cautiously, climbing an icy street they had never before traversed on horseback. And the people of the town, who would never have looked twice at two walkers, looked up at them curiously and suspiciously as they passed like lord and man. Some might know Paisi, who came and went in the town, and if they did, they knew who they might be, though they might wonder greatly that they now came in on horseback. One or two such made the sign against evil, but only one or two, likely more piously Bryalt than the rest—in the main, the townsfolk hung charms about their houses and had no fear of witches or their cures: oh, no, it was the taint of sorcery that drew the ward signs, and the looks askance.

Overall, the town was in a fading holiday mood—the last vestiges of tattered dead evergreen festooned housefronts and shops, the Bryalt holiday having come and gone and lingered during his venture west, and people were likely in the very last throes of too much drink and leftover holiday cakes. The shops were still mostly shut, this early in the morning. The evergreen dripped with icicles here and there, shed needles, or hung haphazardly tattered, ruined by days of wind and weather.

Paisi had not come into town for holiday, so he said. He had been just off a long ride, had been too busy mending leaks and repairing the goat-shed fence for Gran, and besides, as Paisi had said, he had been too worried about a certain fool for a number of days after.

"I was never in danger," Elfwyn said, and knew that he lied, and wasn't sure why, except he had no desire yet to tell Paisi what Paisi was so curious to learn—what Tristen had said, or what he had said to Lord Tristen.

He wanted to have the visit to Lord Crissand behind him, that, before anything else, and he didn't want to think about where he had been, or about Lord Tristen at all until he had to. There was, besides Paisi's completely reasonable desire to know, that presence that loomed above the town, less so, ironically, as they were nearest to it: the houses cut off all view of the Zeide and its tower, and seemed to cut off all sense of it as well. Elfwyn had ridden out from Gran's place refusing to look toward the town, and refusing to look up when they drew close to it: he chattered with Paisi or minded the frozen mud, or anything at all he could contrive to keep his mind off that place—he so dreaded coming into town.

But here, in that strange absence of notice from the tower, they rode calmly up the street, and quietly up to the Zeide gates, where gatekeepers, respecting anyone who came on horseback, made haste to open them.

Things came suddenly uncommonly clear, details of the iron gates, of the stones themselves—of that tower, when they had come through the gates and into the broad courtyard of the keep. He wanted to look up. He had the most dire urge to look up. And didn't.

Vision, Lord Tristen had said. Vision was what he needed, but his Vision of that high window was not with his eyes. He knew what it looked like. He knew every detail of that window, its stone ledge that ran all the way about the tower, the dark birds that sometimes congregated there. He knew the window was vacant at the moment. She didn't need to look. Her Vision existed whether or not she looked—was that possibly what Lord Tristen meant, that he needed that kind of wizardry, his mother's Gift, that was always aware? He wanted nothing of his mother, not a whisper of her talent. When he had approached Lord Tristen about wizardry, he had been thinking of himself and Gran, and the things she had shown him, not—not his mother's sort. Not sorcery.

Gods, had the Sihhë-lord seen something else hiding in him?

He felt an unease at the very pit of his stomach when he thought that. He had not been ambitious. He had not even thought of *that* Gift. He had wanted something he didn't think he owned, not really. Wizard-gift. Not sorcery.

He almost did look up.

But Paisi rode toward the stables, where strange horses had to stay, and Feiny turned that way, too, away from the tower, and a wall curtained the sight of it. Elfwyn got down where Paisi had and turned Feiny over to the stableboy, too, while Paisi informed the boy the horses should have water but needed no grain.

"As we ain't stayin' long, that we know," Paisi said.

Elfwyn flung his cloak off his arm as they approached the side of the keep, so as to show the door guards he carried no weapon, only the knife he used for meals, and Paisi flung his all the way back. The guards did challenge them at the side door, atop the stairs, but only for a moment, and one of the men walked with them down the hall inside, as far as his captain, in a little office.

"The boy's come in," Elfwyn heard that man say, as if it were evident to all the world which boy, and the answer he didn't hear, but the same man came out again and led them down the lower corridor to the great audience hall, beyond the central stairs.

He had hoped for something quieter than a public audience. It was early in the morning. Was it court day, with all the town coming in? That was the very last thing he wanted.

The man ushered him through, stopping Paisi at the door with a gesture, and at that Elfwyn looked back.

"It's proper, m'lord," Paisi said. M'lord again. The king's son, again.

There had been a time Gran's foster grandson would never have found his way into an audience, and he wished now he were bidden, like any ordinary countryman, wait until and if summoned.

As it was, he was bidden straight inside, his father's son, into an echoing great hall, and he had to find a place for himself along the wall and stay quiet, while the guard went and added him, he supposed, to the official list a man kept at a table.

As if he were a man. A lord. At least of a rank with the angry merchant who was pressing his case with Duke Crissand at the moment. Crissand questioned the man patiently and quietly, from his chair at the head of the hall, being advised by various persons concerned in some way—Elfwyn understood, at least, that it involved the recent holidays, and a drunken brawl, and broken tables. The man was a tavern keeper, perhaps, not so high-flown as the list of people who came in with petitions for his father, over boundaries and marriages and blood feuds.

His was, it might be, the highest business, after all. He had to report to the duke that he visited Tristen with no leave to do so. He had to report that he had left the king's palace, too, without leave—the soldiers had been here, telling as much as *they* knew, and maybe making demands he be brought back again, for all *he* knew. And here he stood, a subject of Amefel again, wanting grain for two horses. He had no idea whether it was good or bad, from Lord Crissand's view, that Lord Tristen was arriving soon: fool that he was, he had come here to confess the lost letter—it was not the happiest of appearances before this man, who generally had done very well for Gran and deserved better than a boy's lame excuses.

He didn't know what ground was under his feet, if he wondered about such matters: he didn't know, he didn't understand the business that had always flown over his head, or why bad dreams, which had turned out false, had drawn him back here, and sent him to Lord Tristen, where he had outright failed to ask clearly whose were the dreams, or why had he dreamed, or were they possibly a warning?

Fool, he said to himself, not to have asked, not to have put the letter where it wouldn't drop away from him, not to have thought of it when he had taken his shirt off. He had probably flung it right into the brook, to boot.

Dreams. His mother's work, he became more and more convinced. He'd believed what he'd seen and hadn't looked past his initial fear.

Vision, Lord Tristen had said. Looking at things. Seeing what was. Seeing through things. Seeing through his mother's wiles and the web of fear she flung up. Here he stood, terrified of her, while thinking she was the likely source of trouble that had separated him from his father and brought him here.

So who had gotten exactly what she wanted, after all?

And he still trembled at the thought that she was just upstairs. She was probably laughing, right now, probably delighted with her work, and no one challenged her. If he had the least smidge of Gift, himself, he would use it to face her and make her know the day was coming when she wouldn't be so pleased with her son.

Children had come in, while the merchants were arguing, two curly-headed children and a third, in the arms of a lady, who sat down by Crissand's side—his wife, his children, two boys and a little girl, happy children. The men fought, and the children sat and played quietly on the steps, the model of a family, such as he had almost had, in his father's household—his father had bent every law to try to give him that.

While his mother—

He hadn't Seen, had he? He hadn't even thought about her, except to know he was escaping and going to Guelessar, and he had thought, when the tower set behind the hills, that her gaze was off him, for the first time in his life.

He had a sudden notion that even losing the letter might be his mother's doing, his mother, wanting to prevent whatever Lord Tristen wanted, wanting to make all the trouble she could, and striking just as soon as he was far enough from Ynefel.

She had a habit of making the most trouble she could. He was here, within easy cast of her tower, and all of a sudden a great many things came clear to him, that it *hadn't* been Gran's worry, and it hadn't been simple bad luck in the woods, and it was his mother's great pleasure that he'd had to come here to take the blame for everything. That was the love she showed him.

Crissand served judgment on the tavern dispute, in a loud voice.

The baby began to cry at that, and the duke softened his face and his voice, and took the baby from his lady, kissing her and holding her in his arms until she quieted. "Clear the hall," he said, which Elfwyn took for a general dismissal.

"Not you, lad."

He turned. He saw Crissand beckon, one crooked finger beside the baby's arm.

"Come here."

He came down the long aisle. He presented himself and bowed deeply. "My lord duke."

"Cakes and cream for the children," Crissand said, with a snap of his fingers, and gave the baby back to his wife. "Otter, lad, I'm very glad to see you back."

"I'm ever so sorry, m'lord. I came and I went, and I had a letter for you . . ."

"Your father sent letters," Crissand said, "in great concern."

"I—" He didn't know what to say. "I'm very sorry. Lord Tristen sent, and I lost the letter."

"Lost it?"

"In a brook," he said, to have it done with. "But he says he's coming here. Or at least, that he's coming to Henas'amef."

"Indeed," Duke Crissand said, and got up and came down the steps to set a hand on his shoulder. He was a young man, for his office, and had a gentle face, a kindly manner. "Why, did he say?"

"I think—I think—I don't know," he finished in a rush, uncomfortable to have the duke treat him kindly, after all the trouble. "I wouldn't venture to say. I told him what had happened—" No, that wasn't quite true. "I asked him—I asked him to tell me what to do, because things hadn't worked in Guelemara, and the Guelen priests were upset, m'lord, and I had your message about Gran being sick—"

"I sent no message."

He was confused, confused, and a little dismayed, then limped on with his news. "I left, then. I came home. But I thought with all that's wrong—I thought I should go to Lord Tristen. And Lord Tristen said he'd take a look at things, and after that, he wrote you a letter for me to carry, and said he'd come soon. But I lost it. I'm very sorry."

"His messages are not easily lost."

"I don't know, m'lord. I don't know. I fell in the brook, and I was freezing. And when I thought again, it was gone."

"Well, well . . . you've no idea what it said."

"It was under seal, my lord."

"So. And what matters did you discuss with him, if you can say?"

"Myself," he said. "My troubles." His face went hot. "It was time I left, m'lord. There was all kinds of trouble. I kept dreaming about Gran. I'd sent Paisi back. I tried to See home, a maid saw me, and the priests were all upset."

"Ah," Crissand said, as if this time he'd reached the sense of it. "Well, well, the Quinalt is upset often enough. Your father sent his love, that first."

"Did he?" He was ever so desirous to hear that.

"In no uncertain terms. When I should be able to lay hands on you, he asked I give you my protection as before—this, mind you, has never been a burden; and he wishes you very well, very well indeed."

That news relieved him so that he found no power of speech at all for a moment. He had come a long, hard ride, from Guelemara to Ynefel and back, he had come here to be blamed, even punished. Now he just felt worn thin, as frayed as the old cloak he wore, and shaking in the knees.

"I am very glad he forgives me, my lord. And I wish him all my love."

"As you should. As you well should. Letters have flown about you, let me say, his to me, by his guard looking for Paisi, mine to him, his to me again by a second lot, come chasing after you. Now Tristen's letter lost, gods save us, the gist of which we can only guess. I've no doubt Lord Tristen wishes me to take care of you, which I do, nevertheless, and to take care of your gran, which I have always done. If it there's more, I'm sure he'll be here soon to set it straight. If it was lost, he probably knows it. If it wasn't regarding your welcome here—he'd probably have sent one of his birds."

"In the storm and all, m'lord,—"

"Rough weather for them, no question, but they do get through, quite amazingly. He doesn't need a rider to reach me. Or to reach your father, at greatest need. He can travel in ways that don't regard the weather. Don't fret about it. You simply stay at home for a bit, take care of your gran, let the priestly storms blow over in Guelessar—the Guelenfolk are always contentious at Festival. They're forever seeing omens in the sky and portents in their ale. Their opinion comes and goes by spring. You don't have any urge to do anything foolish, like ride off in another direction, do you?"

A canny question, Gran's sort of question. Lord Crissand himself had the Sight, at least that, so Paisi had told him. A little of the Gift ran all through the Aswydd line.

"No, sir, I don't want to ride anywhere, except to go back home and take care of Gran. Though after all that's happened—I think I want to visit my mother."

"An idle whim, or a burning need?"

"To tell her I'm back," he said, hedging the truth: he couldn't help it—it was old habit. He amended that. "To tell her that if everything that's gone wrong lately is her doing, people see through her. And to tell her face-to-face who I am. I'm not Otter any longer, m'lord. I'm Elfwyn. That was what Lord Tristen said to me. My mother named me to spite everyone, particularly my father and the Guelenfolk. She meant to make trouble. But it's my name, all the same, and Lord Tristen said I should carry it, so I will. I don't have to be trouble to my father or to you, m'lord. I intend not to be. Once Lord Tristen's heard what she's been up to, I don't think she'll get her way any longer. I'm not sure after that, that I'll ever be able to talk to her again. I don't know, but I think she's why things went wrong in Guelessar. And before I can never see her again—" He felt a tremor even thinking of so momentous a change in his life. "I want to see her once."

"I wouldn't upset her with threats, young sir. You see her once a year. That's likely far more than you really want to visit her. Isn't it?"

"I do want to see her. I want to remember what she looks like. She keeps fading, in my thoughts. And I want to see her this time, really see her. I need to."

A frown, a thinking frown. "She's our prisoner. Lord Tristen's prisoner. And your father's. You certainly aren't hers. And I advise you to think of her as I do, as little as possible. But my guards will admit you there, whenever you wish." Crissand passed him a small finger ring. "I lend you this. See your gran has all her needs. This has every power I would entrust to a son, and the guards all know it. See your mother if and when you choose."

"Your Grace," he murmured.

"This ring is more than a ring. It comes from him. It will guard you as well as supply you. Do not let it leave your finger."

"I shall take great care of it, Your Grace, and bring it back as soon as—"

"Wear it for your gran's sake, until Lord Tristen comes, to be sure you want for nothing, nor meet any need or obstacle this small thing can clear. This I lend you, since we do not have his letter, or know his intent: this will keep you safe until he gives me better advice. But know that if you do any mischief, this ring will not be good to you. Dare you wear it?"

"I," he began, the ring clenched in his fist and that fist held against his heart. "Bringing this near my mother—if she took it from me—"

Crissand smiled. "Let her try. Challenge Ynefel? That is what it would be. I think it will rest very safely on your hand in such circumstances. She will be of no mind to touch it, or you, while you wear it."

He put it on with trepidation. His whole hand tingled. "My lord duke," he said, still perturbed, and Duke Crissand patted his arm and held it close for a moment.

"Your father's son," Crissand said, "far more than hers. Head-on and headlong, reckless in all things. I love him, but I do advise him, and you, as much as I can—be careful."

"I shall be, m'lord."

Crissand let him go then, and he bowed, and walked away, and bowed again, as respectful in this grand hall as people would be in leaving his father's presence. He went all the way out the double doors, where the guard was, and Paisi was waiting for him.

"He gave me a ring," he said, and showed it to Paisi, a silver band worked in vines and grapes. The guard saw it at the same time, he was sure of that, and he was extraordinarily proud to be back in his father's good graces, and to have a thing from the duke of Amefel that the priests in Guelessar would never, ever countenance his wearing. It was a vindication, the very power he had hoped for to defend himself and Gran and Paisi, and he by no means intended to misuse it or to let any accident befall it. "So I can see my mother, he says. So he'll know where I am. With this I can bring Gran anything she needs."

"Will ye really see your mum?" Paisi asked, who must have been listening.

That settled him to earth. Not yet, he decided, although the thought had taken root in him that he should do it before Lord Tristen came, and before she thought she'd scared him into lasting fear of her, and before he lost all chance to see her.

He just didn't want to face her yet, while he was still so tired he wasn't thinking clearly. Tomorrow, perhaps. Tomorrow, he might come back into town.

iv

YOUR SON HAS RETURNED SAFELY, CRISSAND WROTE THAT SAME MORNING. WHEN *your ward reached his house, he indeed went west, and reports he has seen Lord Tristen, who he says has informed him he should carry the name Elfwyn. He reports that the lord of Ynefel will come as far as Henas'amef, how soon and in what intent, unfortunately, I do not know. He says that Ynefel gave him a message for me, but that he lost it on the way, in bad weather. This alarms me, as I am sure it will trouble us all.*

In the loss of Ynefel's message, I have lent your ward the ring which Ynefel gave me, the nature of which I have made clear to your ward, and which he did not fear to take, except that he feared its presence might incite his mother. He has indeed asked to visit her. He is convinced her ill will may have caused certain misfortunes, and he seems to believe that Ynefel's arrival may deal with her. I am uneasy in his intention, but mindful of your request to allow him all former privileges, and considering that, indeed,

things might be afoot in which my forbidding him might have consequences
I cannot foresee, I provided Ynefel's ring as a protection against her influence
and trust that his power will not permit harm to your son. Priests inform
me that she has remained quiet, though your son's insistence that she bears
responsibility for his difficulties continues to trouble me as I write. I hope
that I have done wisely in granting this request, and I shall continue vigilant
in her case.

In all matters Amefel remains staunch and earnest in service of Your
Majesty and Ylesuin. Likewise we remain confident our brother lords round
about will be ready, as before, to support Your Majesty by all efforts, in-
cluding our attendance in court in Guelemara, no matter the season, if re-
quested. In this our brother lords surely concur.

Amefel salutes you and the Bryaltine fathers hold you in their prayers,
against all harm, in constant intercession . . .

So it went, the usual formula at the end, with unusual force, considering.
If he himself had leaned to any sect, it had been to the Teranthines, the sect
of wizards, which had few rites, nineteen gods, a great deal of study, and not
a single other adherent within all Amefel, that he knew. His hand felt naked
without the ring he had lent the boy, and he felt less aware of the world than
he had been. He had been long on the edge of wizardry and sorcery, he had
the latter hanging quite literally over his head, and the absence of that trinket and its perceptions ought to be a relief, but it was not.

And the boy—the boy, another Aswydd, and now claiming that name—

He cared nothing for his own title. He had had no ambitions to be duke
of Amefel, or aetheling, that peculiar honor that was, in history and in le-
gality, a kingship in its own right. Amefel had wished to be like Elwynor,
which was independent under Ninévrisë; but Amefel had become, by bloody
murder, more closely bound; the aethelings, the Aswydd house, however,
had continued to rule . . . payment for a bit of treachery.

No, he hadn't wanted the title. But he had a wife, and the children, and
his boys, other Aswydds, might remotely be in danger, if Otter—now Elfwyn Aswydd—found adherents to put forth a claim to set him in that office.
He had faith in Cefwyn Marhanen—to say that any Aswydd had faith in a
Marhanen king was unprecedented; but he did, in the man, if not in the lineage. He had faith that this Marhanen king was very unlike the last two, the
first of whom had slaughtered the last remnant of the Sihhë-lords in Amefel,
namely Elfwyn Sihhë . . .

Cefwyn Marhanen had taken a most uncommon friend, and, after all
but wiping out the Aswydd lineage, had set him in power, and saved Lady

Tarien, and kept his own Aswydd bastard alive—at Tristen's behest, true, but also because Cefwyn was a new thing in that bloody line—a Marhanen king who stuck at murder . . .

An Aswydd duke with a family to protect ought rightly to take precautions now, establish ties to Bryalt priests, who always had been uneasy under Cefwyn's rule . . . find others who chafed under what were essentially fair laws and fair taxes: but what would that make him if he followed his own father's course?

He found no course for himself but to stay loyal, and care for the king's son, and hope to the gods he so frequently offended that events would not come sliding down on his head, or worse, on his wife's and his children's heads. He trusted Cefwyn. He trusted Tristen. And the young Marhanen prince—Aewyn—himself half-Syrillas, which was to say, of the house of the Regents of Elwynor—with a sister, now, who would someday sit on the Regent's throne . . . Aewyn seemed apt to be a good boy.

Another tangle, Cefwyn having the current Regent as his queen, gathering the Aswydds into his house on the one side, and the Elwynim Regents on the other, the Marhanen king now bringing into his own bloodline even a little Sihhë lineage—

It might be frightening, for those who had learned to hate the bloody Marhanen as a matter of local faith. Frightening, too for the Quinaltines, who had learned to think of their faith as the king's only faith—and also for the Bryaltines, who had gotten most of their wealth from Amefin and Elwynim folk greatly opposed to the Quinalt and the Marhanen.

Now a living Sihhë sat in Ynefel, the Regent slept with the Marhanen king, and the duke of Amefel had a half-Marhanen, half-Aswydd boy in his care who might one day overthrow him and dispossess his children.

But Crissand stayed faithful, all the same, knowing that when everything came together, when powers that slept moved again, the world would shake.

Gods, he had had misgivings when Cefwyn chose Festival as the time to bring his firstborn son out of rural obscurity. It had been bravely done, thoroughly in character for Cefwyn, who had all the best traits of the bloody Marhanen, courage and will, and a less favorable one—a tendency to do the very thing that would annoy his detractors the most, simply because it *would* vex them, and give him, perhaps, a chance to bring those forces into the open . . .

Well, the tactic might work in the field, and even work in politics with the Guelenfolk and the northern provinces, but it was damned dangerous where it regarded Aswydd blood, and forces that couldn't be seen so readily, forces another Aswydd did recognize, right over his very head.

Dared he think the boy might be right, that that decision of the king to bring the boy to Guelessar had been Worked, and nudged, and moved, very quietly?

Dared he write an honest Aswydd opinion to the Marhanen king? *You were bespelled once, into begetting the boy. Don't do the things you find yourself tempted to do. Don't corner an Aswydd in hot blood and Marhanen temper . . . we don't go at things head-on. We never have. That woman is a prisoner, but she is still aware of her son.*

He did add a postscriptum, but not that. He wrote: *If you should decide to come to Amefel for any purpose, pray wait for Lord Tristen's arrival here. Then questions can be asked and answers given.*

Tristen, when he did stir forth, tended to a harbinger of troubles. But having Tristen here, whatever the attendant perils of his company, would make him feel ever so much safer.

V

IT WAS A DAMNED GREAT MESS, IN CEFWYN'S OPINION—THE WEATHER DELAYED the messages he hoped for, the Quinaltine fuss simmered on, and he had no word at all from Tristen by any means. He hoped his son had found a quiet place to winter over.

The secret business at the Quinaltine was at least proceeding under Efanor's direction, the notion of building a new Quinaltine being still closely held in a very small circle, the Holy Father tending toward the pronouncement that the Quinaltine as a physical structure was not unalterable, that it was, with priestly blessing, able to be enlarged—that was the Holy Father's current position: that they might enlarge the sanctuary forward and move the altar to what was now the front steps, which would make it larger than the Guelesfort itself, and, no, that would not happen . . . Cefwyn had decided *that* matter before ever it became a whisper on the wind. Efanor had informed the Holy Father, who was balking at utter abandonment of the sacred precinct, and on and on it went.

And he had a hearing to attend on the morrow, a most distasteful hearing, a rural squire dead under unprovable circumstances, six young girls being his sole issue. The eldest, aged twelve, and not particularly outspoken, was betrothed, since his death, to a neighbor and second cousin, Leismond, while the grieving widow had drowned in the same sinking boat, so the report was. The servants had allegedly made off with the household silver, neither servants nor silver being yet found. The fishermen on the estate, meanwhile, had no one seeing to their rights. The marriage document only wanted a royal seal, perfunctorily granted, ordinarily, but he liked nothing about it. Marriage with the girl sent the land to Leismond, who coveted a river access, and the fishery—Squire Widin's death was in that case suspiciously ironic—and he suspected it just possible the twelve-year-old bride might likewise come to grief within a fortnight of her marriage. He could delay a royal permission until the girl reached majority: that was easy—but the estate was failing fast. He could take temporary lordship of the land, which bordered the royal hunting preserve, cast a number of peasants out of their homes, set up a pliable and seemingly foolish child as a royal ward, denying Leismond or putting him off indefinitely. But that meant the Crown paying out six attractive dowries, or the children forever on the eldest sister's husband's charity—and where was he to find a husband besides Leismond who wanted to take in five underage and penniless sisters-in-law? The girl, questioned, denied she had been coerced. Oh, no, no, Leismond had been kind and helped them. It all reeked to the heavens.

Gods, he hated cases like this one.

He found himself at that window again, where on a happier day he had looked down on his two sons at practice. The yard was deep in snow, now, and desolate. Aewyn moped about, attending his studies, and having pinned a large map of Amefel above his study desk. Aewyn had stopped his rebellion, finally, and admitted his new tutor was a decent fellow, and that learning history was a good thing. Aewyn had even, by way of apology, he supposed, given him a very nice copy of the Rules of Courtly Order, written in a young hand that had begun to have clerkly flourishes perhaps unbecoming in a future king.

It was such a sad compliance, where there had been such joyous skirting of the rules . . .

He looked down at snow-covered stones, and measured the depth by the degree to which the rosebush in the corner was buried: only its pruned top and heap of mulch was above the snow, which seemed at its thinnest, there. A great icicle hung down from the eave, and several predecessors had crashed below, in the cyclic warming and chill of previous days.

His breath made a fog on the window, a veil between him and the courtyard. And suddenly his vision centered on a disturbance in that fogged glass. A word appeared.

Come, it said. Just that. *Come.*

Chilling as the first warning, to caution . . . and what dared he do?

He wanted to rush downstairs on the next breath, call for his horse, and ride, unprepared and unheralded, but a king had obligations . . . his person to protect, for the kingdom's sake; documents to sign, matters which had been most carefully negotiated; the fate of two children to decide, that case on which important things rested . . . not least Efanor's question of the Quinaltine . . .

He looked twice more at the window glass, to be absolutely sure, before he wiped it out with his sleeve and left no record.

Tristen had his other son in hand. Tristen wanted him to come to Ynefel. That was what. But it wouldn't be a matter of his son's life and death, not with Tristen protecting him. So the urgency was a little less.

He labored through the next few hours, wishing he knew exactly what to do with the Quinaltine, knowing that a priestly fuss was bound to break out in all its fury, with Ninévrisë here with Efanor, and Ninévrisë the higher authority, a Bryaltine, an Elwynim, and the target of all discontent: that worried him most. She was due, when snowmelt came, to take Aemaryen to Elwynor, the baby to be presented to the Elwynim as their heir to the Regency, their Princess, the fulfillment of the Marhanen promise to that kingdom; and she could not delay that journey for her own people, even if she became embroiled in priestly politics on this side of the Lenúalim.

Best she go, now, ahead of time, rather than late: best Efanor sit in power over the priests without the controversy of an Elwynim queen. Efanor knew how to argue with the Holy Father: gifted with the power of the king's commission, and his alliances as duke of Guelessar, he could make progress with the Holy Father, if the Holy Father had no one else with whom to politic.

He had to get Ninévrisë and her ladies on the road early, that was what.

Then he could go to Amefel and from there on to Ynefel, where he ached to be, at least for the season. The prospect was beyond attractive.

"A little snow never can daunt me," was Ninévrisë's answer when he told her his intent. "But why so sudden?"

"Tristen Sent," he said. To her, he could tell the entire truth. "He has Otter in keeping. He wants me. And I have to go."

"Aewyn will go into mourning if you don't take him with you," Ninévrisë said, and that was the truth. He had thought of sending Aewyn with her, but it was very much the truth . . . and very much better politics among Guelenfolk not to have his son and heir in Elwynor while his wife, the Regent of Elwynor, was presenting his sister to the Elwynim as their own treaty-promised possession.

"He could meet Tristen," Ninévrisë said. "I should ever so much wish to go, myself . . . but the treaty—they expect us this spring."

"I know." They stood at the same window, which now had one smeared pane, and he took her in his arms and kissed her. He loved this woman. He loved her for her steady calm and her lightning wit; and now for finding a clear, smooth way to do in an organized way what had seemed so impossibly difficult before he broke the news to her. Of course she would go. Of course a winter trip would be a strenuous adventure, but this was a woman who'd ridden to war, managed a soldiers' camp, and could wield a weapon without a qualm. A little snow didn't daunt her, indeed, not even with an infant in arms.

"I love you," he said.

"Flattery, flattery. You'll leave Efanor to manage things?"

"He can do everything I would do. More, with the priests: he knows all their secrets. Only you stay safe."

"You keep an eye on our son," Ninévrisë said, straight to the heart of the matter, a warning with a mother's understanding of their son's habits and the possibilities in the venture.

"He is growing up," he said, to reassure her. "He made me a copy of the Courtly Order, do you know? It looked like a clerk's hand. He mopes, grievously. He reads, this winter. He hasn't stolen a horse or run off to Amefel. It's the other boy who did that."

"What he did *when* Otter was here—No, no, I don't blame Otter at all. He's a wild creature. He always will be, I fear, and no ill against him. Our son, on the other hand, *needs* to read and mope a bit. Kings have to do that."

He rested his head against hers. It was a comfortable place to be. "Perhaps this one needs to do a little less of it. His penmanship is too good. I ache to be out there, Nevris. I ache to be in Ynefel."

"And I, to tell the truth. I ache to be on the road, snow and all. We'll have to conspire, and appoint a tryst."

"Where?"

"In Henas'amef, at first bloom?"

His head came up. He looked at her. "That's a long time for us to be away from court."

"Time enough for Efanor to be thoroughly weary of petitions. Time enough for the Holy Father to know he can't bluff Efanor." Her fingers ran, warm and soft, over his brow, and a smile quirked her lips. "You've gotten a little worry line, love. Shed it before it sets. It doesn't become you."

He kissed the fingers in question. "In Henas'amef," he said. "We'll ride home together from there, at first bloom."

"Crocuses in the muddy fields," she said, "and standing puddles to drown a pony in. I love Amefel in the springtime."

He laughed. Iron bands let go from about his heart, when he thought of those muddy roads, and Tristen, and a ride or two together with him, the way it had used to be. He would never convince Tristen to go hunting. They would just ride, and visit odd places, and let the boys tag along.

And Nevris would come. And they would ride where they liked and meet old friends.

His people would be jealous, him conspiring with the Elwynim Regent down in Amefel, all the lords' politicking therefore obliged to be done in the Amefin court, which meant a long, long ride for the northern ones—that might, in fact, mean far fewer of the northern, more quarrelsome lords at court this season. They might not think their petitions quite that desperate.

The south, now: it would be more convenient for them. He might manage a meeting with Cevulirn and Sovrag as well as Crissand. It would be old times again, the way they had begun.

He went and broke the news to Idrys, who lifted a brow, and said, "Indeed, my lord king," and shook his head before he went off to disarrange the Guard from its winter quarters.

He broke the news to Efanor at dinner, and Efanor gave a long, thoughtful sigh, and shook his head, and said, "I'll send the thorny cases on to you, dear brother. A muddy ride will damp the petitioners' ardor. But before you go riding off, write a decree to possess the tract I have in mind. I have a large space on the hill—one that could give us the building space we need."

"Where, for the gods' sake? Who's died?"

"Grenden. The only burgher so situated, elderly, and rattling in that house of his."

"You'll have the authority."

"Best this come from you. I have in mind to settle Lord Grenden on a portion of the royal lands, a new estate at Mynford. It's terrible hunting there. New management and enforcement of the boundaries might improve it. But with it goes an elevation, to the honor of a new place at court, new arms. He's lusted after nobility all his life. And at his age, a little sanctity might come welcome."

Grenden. Grenden, was it, a rich man who had bought a vacant property on the hill, abode of a house perished in the war, a partisan of Ryssand's, and in no favor. Old Grenden was always at court, in outdated finery, an object of gossip. "You know our grandfather would have found the man guilty of something and outright seized the old house."

"Oh, aye, but Grenden's old, he doesn't hunt, and he has no issue. The estate will revert in a decade, or he'll take my very kind advice and adopt Squire Widin's six girls."

"Oh, I do like that," Cefwyn said. "The cousin goes begging. And the new lord Mynford gets Widin's holdings, with the fisheries and the farms across the river, no need to clear the deep woods. An ample dowry . . . safety for the girls. A posterity for poor old Grenden."

"See? So simply solved. The old trees at Mynford stand, the deer increase, we have the hilltop grounds for the Holy Father—he doesn't think it can be done—and we get Widin's orphans out of the hands of Leismond."

"Brother, you have my utmost confidence."

Efanor smiled, his shy, true smile, not the one he showed ordinarily. "I win my case?"

"You win it. I'll sign your decree. You have the spring court, all your own. I'm for Amefel."

"I do miss him," Efanor said. "Give him my regards. And Crissand, too. Tell Crissand I shall be riding by, when you come back. I'll be due a rest of my own, by then."

"Done," he said. "And you'll have every right."

Packing went apace, then. He requested Ninévrisë entrust Aemaryen to the nurse for the night. They spent the early evening dining alone by the fire, and the later evening as lovers. They still were, after bringing two children in the world: missing Nevris was the only sorrowful part of the trip.

In the morning, having summoned Aewyn for breakfast, he broke the not-unwelcome news.

"I take it," he said, "that you would gladly miss your history lessons in favor of a small trip outdoors."

"I've done my lessons," Aewyn said, frowning, his defenses up. "My tutor can't say I haven't."

"So you might like to ride to Amefel."

"To Amefel!" The sluggard who had shared their table so glumly for days vanished, transformed and bright-eyed—though warily asking, "Might I? Truly?"

"Your brother has slipped off again, in directions not prudent. I think I may ride that way. You might stay with Gran for a few days, if he isn't there, while I go looking for your brother."

"I can find him," Aewyn said, all too pertly. "I have no doubt I can find him."

He let that pass for the moment. "Go pack," he said to his son. "Take clothes, no trinkets, and nothing heavy. Do it yourself. Think of it as a hunting trip and a court visit."

And when his son had left a half-eaten breakfast and walked from the room, half-running, he got up and set his hand on his wife's.

"Dared you think he would be reluctant, my lord?" Ninévrisë asked him.

"Take care of our daughter," he asked her, "and of yourself."

"Take care of our son," Ninévrisë said. Her hand closed on his. "How will you explain this venture to the court? Have you thought of that?"

"Why, there's a letter from Crissand. A pressing matter. Letters have flown back and forth like snowflakes. Everyone knows it." He kissed her cheek. "And I leave Idrys to support Efanor."

"Dare you?"

"He will obey Efanor," he said, devoutly hoping that was the case. His departure did remove a certain restraint he imposed on his Commander of the Guard—but Idrys would indeed support Efanor and protect him from his charitable impulses, if not meticulously obey him. He need not fear for Efanor's life, at very least.

And, uncommon for royal processions, by midmorning he was already on horseback, with his son, a fair company of the Dragon Guard, and a smallish pack train, mostly carrying clothes and three tents. They would sleep under canvas—he wished to give Aewyn the experience of a winter camp—and delay as little as possible along the route. Ninévrisë, with far more baggage and a train of ladies, purposed to depart the capital in two days, and cross northerly into Elwynor. As for the weather, it blew hard for an hour, then spat snow into their faces the moment they passed the city gates.

It was a gray day, windy and biting cold, but his son's face was bright. So, he suspected, was his own.

CHAPTER FIVE

i

THE RING TINGLED AT TIMES. SIHHË-WORK, GRAN HAD CALLED IT, BUT WHETHER she meant the ring itself or the spell on it, she declined to say. She refused to touch it, herself, saying it would burn the hand that tried to take it, until it went back to its master. Paisi, whose eyes were better, said it looked like a pledge ring from the town market, with its little design of vines and grapes, not outstandingly well made, but silver. Sihhë-work in silver, Paisi said, was much better made.

The ring gave him one night's sound sleep, at least. But he waked in the memory of freezing in the woods, and of losing Owl, and then of coming home to Gran's and finding the place all burned.

He waked with such a start he thought surely he must have waked Paisi, but Paisi snored on, and he lay in the dark, sweating and seeing horrors in the common shadows of the room. The fire in the fireplace seemed like a beast caged and trying to break free, and the ring on his finger was cold as ice.

The horror stayed with him. He hardly dared shut his eyes, and when he did, he had to drag himself out of the same horrid dream, in which he wandered among burned timbers and fallen beams. "Gran," he cried, and no one answered him.

He escaped it, back into the terrible dark of a familiar room, and lay there, not daring to move for a very, very long time. He turned the ring with his thumb, and tried to think of Lord Tristen, or Lord Crissand, but all he found was dark.

"M'lord?" Paisi asked him, at midmorning the next day, when he cut his hand trying to bend a damaged hinge, where the wind last night had caught the shed door. He just stared into the dark of the shed and lost himself for the moment, sucking at the wound.

"Did you sleep well?" he asked Paisi, that noon.

"Oh, aye," Paisi said, matter of course. And then asked, more carefully: "Did you, m'lord?"

His mother had slipped her dreams past Gran's wards, past the protections of a ring Lord Tristen had blessed. She fretted. She threatened.

"I think I'll visit my mother," he said. "There's day enough left. I won't stay but a moment. But I have to. I don't want any more dreams."

Paisi frowned, utterly sober. "Well, ye won't go alone, m'lord, not there."

He didn't refuse Paisi's offer. Gran was at her knitting—that, she could still do, though stitching taxed her eyesight and had for years.

"Paisi and I will be going into town," he said, and Gran said, "Well, well, take care," and let him kiss her cheek. "We'll be back well in time for supper," he said. "We might stop at the smith's and get him to bend that hinge. Our hammer can't do it. We're taking it along."

"Ye can bring a few apples," Gran said, "an' there might be tarts."

"Apples, indeed," he said, feeling better about the venture, and went outside. Paisi was finishing up saddling Feiny, in the kind of light, blowing snow that might come from the heavens or off the thatch, and he helped, and mounted up. Paisi and he rode out the gate, as before, and down the road. Carts had passed, yesterday, market bound, and come back again.

"Ol' Semmy's sold 'is 'ides," Paisi remarked, reading the tracks and the habits of their neighbor.

"Good profit, in a scant market," he said. He had his wits about him. Everything seemed easier, now that he had taken the decision to go, and he and Paisi talked about the road, the weather, and Ynefel—which Paisi had tried to get out of him for days. It all became easier to tell.

In his inmost thoughts, he wanted to have the visit with his mother before Lord Tristen came. It was what he had told Lord Crissand, that afterward, things might be confused, and he wanted to do it now, before the rules changed. He wanted, once, to stand up to her and not be afraid, before Lord Tristen came to put fear into her, or to put some new barrier between him and her. He didn't want to lose that chance, and the dreams she sent told him now with cruel clarity who had drawn him back from Guelemara, and who was at fault, between him and his father.

He and Paisi rode through the town gates and up the hill. "You might go to the smith's while I'm about this," Elfwyn said. "Get the hinge fixed. And we can get the apples on the way back to the gate."

"I ain't goin' anywheres but where you are," Paisi said doggedly. And that was the way things would be.

The ring won admittance for both of them, at least as far as inside the Zeide, and to the bottom of the tower steps, where his mother's guards stood, day and night.

Paisi would have climbed those stairs with him: Paisi was greatly afraid, and still would have done it, but he stopped Paisi down where the guards stood. "Wait for me. She would raise a fuss about your coming, if only to worry me. I won't be long. She won't like what I have to tell her. Not this time."

"You don't take to heart anything she says," Paisi said in a low voice, but he did stay with the one guard when Elfwyn started up the stairs with the other.

He wanted to know what she had been doing, why she had been doing it, and if one actually wanted bad news in the world, his mother was as good a source of it as he knew . . . she had a habit of telling the truth, on many occasions, especially if it was a truth he didn't want to hear.

Bony child, she'd been in the habit of calling him, and again she'd said: Your hands are as rough as any peasant's. Your father's son, and with such beautiful hands. It's shameful.

He reached the door—the door was barred, but not guarded above: he suspected the guards didn't want to stand that near, but the one had come up the steps with him and lifted the large, protected bar—it was necessary to free the bar, first, from a central restraint which no prying from within the room could reach. "You knock loud," the man said, before he opened it. "You give it three good hard raps when you want out. I'll stand right out here."

"Thank you," he said, and as the door opened, stepped inside.

It was a modest place, a room with figured carpets, a bed surrounded with draperies, and an alcove with windows that had shutters, though his mother rarely drew them. She stood by one of those five windows, the sunlight falling on a face that still was beautiful. She had red hair, and it flowed down her back, loose as a maiden's—or a witch's locks.

"Mother," he said. "I take it you want to see me."

"Ah, my dear boy." She came toward him, grandly offering to take his hands, and, mindful of what his right hand had, he gave only his left. "What," she exclaimed, pressing the offered hand in both of hers and leaning forward. "No kiss for your mother?"

He hadn't the fortitude. He didn't recoil, but he did step back. "A kiss when you've won it. And you haven't. You've tried your best to make me miserable."

"Oh?" she asked, and turned her shoulder, walked a space into the shadow. "How *is* your father?"

"Fair-minded and honest." He found himself launched in a battle of cold words, an art he had learned from her. He had had as much as a year to think how he would meet her questions next time, yet always she confounded him in her own game. He gave up subtlety this time, his newest mode of attack, which took all the courage he had. "You sent the dreams, Mother. I know you did, so don't lie to me. I've been to Lord Tristen. He advises me carry the name you gave me, so I will, from now on. Does that satisfy you?"

"I'm sure it's no great matter to me," she said, "since you're an ungrateful boy. You always were. And how *is* the Sihhë-lord?"

"He'll speak for himself when he comes here," he said, "and he will, soon. He didn't like what he heard."

"Oh, did you bear tales? And have *you* come to threaten *me*?"

"I came to warn you. He will come here. He's not pleased. Neither am I, Mother. So if you want one soul in all the world to be sorry for you—"

"To be sorry for *me*?" Her laughter was silver, and her hand flew to her breast, delicate and eloquent. "Dear boy, I don't need your charity. You may need mine. Your sojourn in Guelemara was far from happy and fortunate, lad! The priests cursed you, didn't they? Quinalt priests will never love you. Quinalt priests dug up our dead when your dear father hanged your young uncle: at your dear father's orders, our graves were emptied, and the moldering dead went into exile, all, all bundled into a common cart and hauled off across the border, for the sanctity of Amefel, you understand—to satisfy the Bloody Marhanen's spite. Not enough to kill us and exile us. He set up that traitor downstairs, that smiling, perfidious man, who doles out his charity to you—does it taste that sweet?"

He forgot, annually, how he lost arguments with his mother. She changed subjects, switched arguments, and never stopped for breath. "I came to tell you those two things, and to be sure I was right about you. I've done both. Good day, Mother."

"Your father lied to you. Lied, boy. Where was his concern for you, hiding you away, herding goats, peddling penny cures? And now he brings you to Guelemara and humiliates you, dragging you right under the noses of the Quinalt priests, knowing how they hate you, provoking them to act—oh, he's not innocent of harm, boy. He wants to blunt any success you might have by setting the priests against you. He wants you frightened, and grateful, lapping pity and protection from his hand. Isn't that the way it was, there? They chase you out, and you're grateful to your father, who gave you pretty clothes and sweets? Fool, boy, *fool*!"

"You named me Elfwyn."

"Elfwyn you should be, and are not! Elfwyn! The Sihhë blood runs in your veins as it runs in mine, and, twice fool, you go riding off to Tristen Sihhë, as if he has any reason to protect you and see you rise in the world."

"He protected me once."

"From your own father! From the Bloody Marhanen! And Tristen kept you and me alive because he himself wanted a hold on your father."

"I don't think he needed that one."

"Little you know."

"I know my father. I know black from white. And I now know you."

"Oh, there was a great deal of gray in that decision, indeed there was. You really should learn to live in that territory. It's safer, for the likes of you, neither fish nor fowl, neither Man nor Sihhë. A royal goatherd—what a life for you! You'll inherit the goats. You'll deliver cheese and milk to the duke's table like a good fellow. Oh, damn your soft heart, boy, don't be blind to those who have everything to gain if you bow the head and tend your goats . . . and that includes Crissand and his whelps. Now you bear his ring, don't you? What a day!"

He felt the ring burn on his finger. He should have left, but he knew she would at least give him her arguments, dark as they were: they were often the dark side of truth, and curiosity and dread alike pinned him fast where he stood.

"Tell me," she said next, "how did you like your legitimate brother?"

"Well enough," he said, defiant, and knew instantly that staying to enter her next argument was an utter mistake. His mother regarded him at the moment like a morsel on a plate—and said nothing more. He ached to defend Aewyn, and she didn't even attack.

"And Tristen," she said. "Sweet, dear Tristen. Did he teach you magic?"

"He *is* magical." His heart beat at his ribs like a creature trapped. "You know that."

"And did he give you advice?"

Wilder and wilder, that heartbeat. Vision and a word he had utterly forgotten. Did she know how he had failed? "Perhaps he did. Or not."

"Dear, dear. My son has learned to lie."

"I'm not sorry for coming here," he said. "I came to pay my respects and to tell you I'm here, and under what name. Since you gave it to me, I thought in all courtesy you should know. I'll be going now."

"You live at their pleasure. You have a right to all of Amefel, and they house you in a hovel with goats."

"It's my choice."

"Fool, it never was your choice. You have the blood to rule, and no priests should dare drive you out like a whipped dog. Was it pleasant, the ride home from Guelessar? Was it pleasant to have the people in town look at you and know the bastard was banished again? Damn them! Damn them all! Why aren't you angry? You bow, you respect that upstart lord downstairs. This is your province, and you have no knowledge what's inside these walls and under these stones! Open your eyes, boy, and see what you could have, if you only claimed what's within these stones!"

Vision, Tristen had said. And now his mother challenged him with riddles, and a dreadful presentiment flitted past the back of his mind. *Stones,* the word echoed, and his mind saw the masonry downstairs. But he daren't look, daren't look at what vision his mother could give him if he let her. He stepped back, felt after the wall, and the door.

"That's right, that's right," his mother mocked him. "Turn your back on your power. Even the old granny's held you prisoner, so, so easily. You're so biddable. But I tell you I will see my son sit on the throne of the Aswydds! I will see him raise whom he will raise and throw down whom he will throw down, and more than that, far more than that, Elfwyn Aswydd! No one will whisper behind your back in that day!"

That last lanced through like a knife, right to a sore spot. He wanted not to have people whispering ill about him, he wanted that very much, and in that moment something in him moved very unpleasantly, touching those depths of anger he had never believed he had.

Anger, Lord Tristen had said. Anger moved him and made his choices. He had thought he was humble and willing to stay what he was.

Vision, he said to himself, and clenched his hand on Crissand's ring, turning about again. He saw his mother suddenly not through a son's eyes: he saw her not as beautiful, but as someone who had been beautiful, and now faded, a blowsy autumn beauty around a dark and potent heart—he could see it, a dark glow that touched a power he had no wish to use.

"Damn you!" she cried, furious with him, as if she saw something as terrible in him. She strode two steps across the carpet, struck him, and abruptly jerked her hand away, with a cry of pain. "Him!" she cried, cradling a wounded hand. *"Him!"*

He had no idea what she meant, if not Lord Tristen himself. He found the door and he battered on it, as when he had been a child she could chase him from this room in tears.

The door opened. The guard was there. He exited the room . . . soon to forget the detail of everything she said, he knew: he always did; but the rawness of upheaval she engendered in his heart would linger for days.

"You will not be his!" Tarien screamed after him. And the door shut, and the bar thumped down.

He avoided the guard's eyes, nor did the guard ask questions, only brought him downstairs again, where Paisi sat on the stone base of a column, waiting for him.

Paisi usually asked him how it had gone. This time Paisi asked nothing at all, only got up and walked with him down the hall, toward the daylight. Faster and faster he walked, and Paisi with him.

When he was out in the cold and the daylight again it was no better.

"I shouldn't have gone," he said.

"Come on, then," Paisi said. "We'll get the horses, an' we'll go home."

Paisi didn't say a thing about the smith or the apples. Nor did he want to delay to run those errands. He knew how most of the things his mother said could fly right out of his head before the sun set, and he wanted to go to Gran and tell her what he had heard, while he could still remember enough of it to get her advice about it, or just to have her hear him, and salve the sore spots with her voice and her touch and her own spells.

Most of all he wanted to be as far from his mother as possible, as quickly as he could. He would not have believed she could possibly breach the protection he wore. He had thought because it came from Lord Tristen it would keep him safe even in her presence: it had stung her when she tried to harm *him*, but now he wasn't sure of its power, and doubt itself was a weakness.

Perhaps, he thought, it hadn't gotten *through*. Perhaps it had stirred something already within its protection. Perhaps what disturbed him sat in *him*.

He put Feiny to a trot as they cleared the town, and Paisi kept beside him, all the way to the turning point, where the road to Henas'amef forked east and west. Their way lay a little east, and just as they turned, he saw a smear of dark smoke on the eastward sky.

"I don't like that," Paisi said, but Elfwyn didn't even stop that long: he laid his heels to Feiny, and sent him flying on that homeward track, Paisi coming up hard behind.

It wasn't weather for burning brush. Snow persisted in sifting down from an ill-disposed heaven. It wasn't such a day; yet by the time they had passed the second hill, the smoke rooted itself exactly where Gran's house was.

Elfwyn's heart sank, utterly. He was no rider, but he put Feiny to his utmost speed and risked both their necks, and the nearer he came, the worse it was. Gran's whole roof thatch was ablaze, and as he came skidding to a stop in front of the gate, he didn't stop to open it: he jumped down and climbed the fence and jumped, landing and slipping in the firelit snow. Heat melted the snow in the yard, heat billowed out at him, and when he reached the door and yanked it open, fire rushed out at him, driving him stumbling back.

Paisi seized hold of him, held him fast, and he fought to get free.

"No, no, lad, ye can't, ye can't, ain't no one can go in there. Come on. She might ha' gone out th' shed."

He ran with Paisi around the back, to the yard where the goats stood, firelight reflecting off their slit eyes, and the geese ran this way and that to escape them, all confused. He went as far as inside the shed: the house door was shut, and fire showed in the seams of the logs that made the shed wall.

"Gran?" he cried, searching that darkness. "Gran?"

"Lad," Paisi said, close by him. Paisi had an armful of Feiny's tack and shoved it at him. "Get it out. Get out."

"You get out!" he shouted—the roar of the fire made it necessary to shout, and he carried the gear out and dumped it on the snow, as Paisi rescued a load of tools—that was all they saved.

"As Gran'll skin us if we let all burn," Paisi gasped, his face all smeared with soot. "Get another load. Get the grain out."

"Where's Gran?" he asked, shaking Paisi by the arms. It was as if Paisi had an overwhelming conviction Gran wasn't there, couldn't be there, as if Paisi, who had always been his rock of safety, was as confused as the goats and geese. "Paisi, she's not out here!"

Paisi turned a shocked face toward the fire, toward the house, as if it had only then come through to him.

"She ain't," he said, then Elfwyn took a firm grip on Paisi's arm, to be sure he didn't rush back in. They stood there, they and the goats and the geese, and the horses beyond the fence, while the fire roared up, coming out the door, rushing past the shutters and licking up the thatch.

"She did it," Elfwyn said, finding a thread of a voice, when breath itself was hard. "She did it. The ring protected me. It didn't protect Gran. And it doesn't protect you."

"The hell," Paisi said, and Elfwyn held him harder, and they hugged each other, there being nothing else they could do. They stood there, burned on one side, frozen on the other, and shook like rabbits, until a terrible crash sent sparks flying out at them, scared the goats and geese and the horses, and stung them all into backing up. The whole center of the house had fallen inward, and the open roof shot flames to the twilight sky.

There was nothing to do but stand and watch it, arm in arm, holding on to each other.

"She didn't See it," Paisi mourned. "Sure, she didn't See it comin'. It's a terrible end, a terrible way to go."

"They burned the Aswydds," Elfwyn said. He hadn't been alive then, but his mother had told him that. "She did it. No question she did it. *Him,* she said . . . she hates *him,* and she couldn't hit me, so she burned the house down. I dreamed she would. I just didn't know what I dreamed."

Paisi's grip held his arm hard, now. "Was it fire ye dreamed?"

"The second dream was. And the third. And after." It was hard to speak. Smoke had made his throat raw. "I hate her, Paisi, I hate her beyond anything in the world."

"No." Paisi shook his head fiercely. "Ain't good. Ain't good. Gran'd say it ain't good."

"Well, she's not able to say, is she?" He said that because he hurt, but he was sorry in the next moment because he upset Paisi, and he pressed Paisi's head close to his. "I loved her. I loved her so much, Paisi. I didn't know I did, but I do. She's my gran, no matter. And when Lord Tristen comes, he'll deal with my mother. I can't, damn it, I can't!"

"Can't help Gran," Paisi said, and wiped his arm across his face. "House was hers anyways. No good to me, was it? We just got to tidy things up an' get the fire out. She'd hate it burnin' on like this."

"Have we got the bucket?" Elfwyn asked, trying for practicality.

They had, and they took turns working the windlass for the well and hauling water up, and the other would take the bucket and fling it on the fire, bucket after bucket, starting with the herb garden that ran along the wall, and working up to the door and the windows. They worked on and on into the dark, when the interior of the house glowed and lit the pall of smoke that hung over them. They worked, and finally the fire began to sink. It was all blackened timbers by first light, black sticks thrusting up out of a heap of ash and smoking embers. That was all there was.

Paisi had burns on his hands, when gotten, neither of them was sure. And by the time the sun was rim up on the horizon, Farmer Ost arrived, with his ox hitch and his cart.

"Who's there?" the farmer called out as he came. "Is ever'body all right?" And Paisi said no, Gran wasn't, which was the first time they had said that truth to someone else.

"Gods a-mercy," Ost said, heaving down from his cart. "I saw the fire in the night. I should ha' come straightway."

"Weren't nothin' ye could do, by then," Paisi said, and clapped the old man on the arm with a hand hanging shreds of blistered skin.

"Gods, ye're burnt."

"Both of us," Paisi said, and laid his other hand on Elfwyn's back. "We done all we could. Ain't no farm left, just the goats an' the geese, and us and our horses. Gran'd want ye to take the goats an' geese. Ye been a good neighbor, and ye're first come. Far as I'm concerned, ye can farm the land, though ye must go to the duke an' say so, which I'll agree to. I ain't no farmer. Never was."

"What shall we do?" Elfwyn asked. There was no living in the goats and the geese: there never had been. It was all in Gran's trade in simples.

"I'd say we wait," Paisi said, "we go to town an' we wait for him who's comin', an' that's the best thing. How else are we to feed the horses, 'cept we go to the duke an' tell him what's what."

He wasn't saying, before Farmer Ost, that there was anything but bad luck to blame, nor did he invoke Tristen by name, but Lord Tristen was, Elfwyn thought, the only choice they had. They caught the goats and geese for Farmer Ost, they told him their names—all but the youngest geese had names, at which Farmer Ost nodded and agreed—though Ost said he would come back for the geese with a proper crate: the goats would go in the cart, tied in place. Paisi threw in the tools, which were more valuable than the goats, and then, with an oddly forlorn look, tossed the bucket into the cart with the rest.

"Just fixed that damn thing," Paisi muttered, and they went to gather up their rescued horse gear, which was mostly Feiny's, and had to be fitted on with burned and bleeding fingers.

Osten was off down the road with the goats and the tools.

"I hope he gets back after those geese," Paisi said, as if it were a matter of ordinary business. He tried to talk in an ordinary way, but Elfwyn was in no sort of spirits to talk at all, now that they faced the ride back to Henas'amef.

I did it, he kept thinking. *I did it. I made her angry. She'd already told me what she would do, and I was a fool. I brought it on.*

The town guards questioned them as they came in. "What's happened with you?" one asked, and Paisi answered, "Candle burned the house down, I guess. We're to see the duke."

There was a frown at that. There was, on the one hand, the evidence of wealth, in the horses, and of disaster and bad luck, in the soot that blackened both of them. But Elfwyn showed the ring on his grimy hand, and the guards immediately let them pass.

"Ye want one of us should come up wi' ye?" the senior asked.

"No," Elfwyn said. "Thank you." Nothing seemed real or right. His whole hand tingled, and yet he didn't feel the sense of threat he was accustomed to feel: it was a furtive presence watching him.

She knew, he thought. Maybe, hurting him, she'd hurt herself—maybe gotten the pain of his burns. He didn't know, nor wanted to go close to her, but he had no choice but go to Lord Crissand as their immediate lord, and the source of all help. He knew Paisi was right.

They rode halfway up the hill, to the Bryalt shrine, where there was a house of healing, and a fountain for washing on the public side street. They washed there, letting the soot stain the water, and the lay brother who attended the place came out to provide his services.

"We have no money," Elfwyn informed the old man first of all. "It went in the fire. But you can ask the duke."

The old man looked at them, and looked at the two fine horses, which told a different story, then shook his head and waved his hand. "You wait," he said, "you wait," and he went into his little shrine. He came out with unguents and bandages, and would have tended Elfwyn's burns first, but Elfwyn insisted the man deal with Paisi's hands, which were much worse.

He was only getting to Elfwyn's hurts when a panting handful of the duke's own servants showed up from the street, bringing more unguents, and two cloaks, which they refused to put on, being so dirty—"I can't," Elfwyn said, and by then the pain and the exhaustion all but overwhelmed Paisi, who simply sat down against the fountain rim and had his head in his hands. He felt like doing the same.

"His Grace had a report," the foremost servant said, "and wishes you may come up to the hall as soon as you can."

It was what they had to hope for, on a day in which they had lost every material possession except two horses they couldn't feed, and Elfwyn bent down, the one to make the decisions now, as Paisi had done, down at Gran's farm.

"We have to get up and go," he said, his head close to Paisi's, his bandaged hand on Paisi's shoulder. "I'll help you get up. When we get up there, there'll be a place to stay, a roof over our heads, and whatever we need. The duke has sent his own servants down. I think the gate-guards or the priest must have sent word up the hill. Paisi, can you stand up?"

Paisi managed it, and with the servants' help, and the priest's, they got onto the horses and rode up the hill and through the gate to the stables.

There they turned the horses over to His Grace's stablemaster and limped on into the scullery, where His Grace's own physician came down to see to them, and the chief of his servants came to see they had drink enough, and a little watered wine, and warm water to wash in, besides new clothing.

Servants led the way to rooms upstairs, in an arrangement not unlike the Guelesfort, though much older. It was all carved, dark wood, and there was, again, a small servants' quarters where the staff wanted to bed Paisi down.

"No," Elfwyn said. "He's not my servant. He's my brother."

"I ain't," Paisi said quietly. "Cousins, at best, by adoption, as is, an' I'm his man, an' shall be. But I'll stay close by m'lord tonight, if ye will—he'll rest best if I do."

It was quiet, after the servants left. It was deathly quiet.

And, clothes and all, lying atop the coverlet, they went to bed.

"We're back where we was," Paisi said, lying on his side by him. " 'Cept it ain't the Guelesfort."

"It's my fault!" Elfwyn cried, tears welling up, and Paisi put his hand on his shoulder, gently so.

"Ain't. Gran'd have a fit to hear ye say it, so don't. If it was her, lad, that was an old, old war, your ma wi' Gran an' Lord Tristen. Ye ain't nothin' t' that fight, yet. Ye may be. But ye can't be yet, so no such talk. If ye was a wizard, say, I'd ask why ye didn't See it, ye know—"

"I did See it. I Saw it in my dreams."

"Oh, aye, an' maybe I saw fire, too, which could mean Gran might burn the soup: it's one thing to See, it's another to know what ye Seen, an' still another t' stand up an' fight the likes of her."

"I tried, and I shouldn't have gone up there. I thought I could do it, and I was an utter fool. I thought the ring would keep me safe, and I didn't think about Gran and you not being protected, the same."

"Aye, but Gran were a witch, an' Saw clear as can be if it was in her to See it. You was there, lad, right enough, but there was Lord Tristen himself could ha' stepped right in—he can do that. He can arrive like lightnin'. I know't him to do it. An' he didn't come, nor know ye was steppin' into trouble, so ye can't blame yourself for not knowin, nor'd Gran ever blame her Otter for what a witch herself couldn't stop."

He wept for Gran, quietly. It was all he had left to do. Sleep came down on him in the middle of the day. He slept into dark, and waked when servants brought supper in, but neither he nor Paisi ate much.

He lay awake after that, dry-eyed, and thought black thoughts about his mother, just upstairs, unscathed, a hateful and dangerous proximity that he would have to ignore just to share this roof, which he *would* have to share, perhaps for the rest of his days, thanks to his mother's ruining his chances in Guelessar. Gran was dead, part of that heap of ashes, not even a grave to mark her place in the world, while his mother lived on, smug and happy, he could imagine it, in having destroyed a woman so much her better—

He grew angry, terribly angry, and anger unleashed the hate Gran had always advised him to avoid—hatred of his mother and his circumstances, alike, as if his soul had burned as raw as his hands last night. He didn't sleep. He couldn't, now. It seemed forever before daylight crept into the unfamiliar windows of an elegant room, a clear sky with a slight pall of chimney smoke rising into it.

Town smoke. More burning, tame burning, by people who thought fire was their servant.

Paisi waked, stretched, knocked his hand into the bedpost inadvertently, and winced. He blinked, perhaps taking a moment to realize where he was, and to remember their circumstances.

"I'd better get breakfast for us," Paisi said, as if they were back in the Guelesfort.

"Let servants wait on us," Elfwyn said. "They will."

"Not on me," Paisi said. "I'd rather be stirring about, m'lord, I had, and I know me way about this place like the back o' me hand." Paisi had served in the Zeide before, when he was Lord Tristen's servant, and Master Emuin's before he left. "Servin' here was no shame, m'lord," Paisi informed him. "It was somethin' I was proud of."

"Then do that," Elfwyn told him, surrendering the whole matter, and watched Paisi leave. He lay abed for a few moments after Paisi had left, wishing he could pull the covers over his head and spend the next several days asleep, but the pain of his burns and the memories behind his eyelids gave him no rest at all, and he had never even taken off his boots last night, no more than Paisi had. He got up in defeat, washed the finer marks of the soot off his face, now that clear daylight was coming through the windows.

But before he had finished, a flow of servants started through the doors, bringing buckets of water, and trooping through into the bath. Others brought a wealth of clothes—far more than a plea of Paisi's would have arranged. He let the servants bathe him: the water hurt his burned hands; he dressed in his own choice of the abundance the servants provided him, plain brown, but very fine. A gray-bearded man of serious mien—he remembered him as Lord Crissand's physician—came in and renewed the salve and bandages.

"Paisi was burned worse than I," he informed that man, who reported Paisi was bathing and changing down in the scullery, where he likewise would be treated. "My apprentice," the physician said, "is very skilled, young sir."

He was glad at least that Paisi hadn't had to wait for such comforts. Breakfast arrived, a choice of breads, on fine pewter plates, with jams, a pile of what looked to be boiled and peeled eggs, with a plate of smoked fish and another of cheese. It was more than he could possibly eat . . . but he knew from Paisi that nothing he sent back went to waste in the kitchen.

He sat down to eat, alone, and had finished by the time Paisi came back, all shaven and combed and bandaged. Paisi walked in, gave a little bow.

"There's blackberry jam," Elfwyn said. The servants had all left. "If you like."

"A smidgen," Paisi said, and took a sliver of bread with jam, standing up. " 'At's good, m'lord."

The division was between them again. But Paisi said he had been proud of his service here—he always had been: Paisi had served Lord Tristen, and Master Emuin, and perhaps, Elfwyn thought, it was only his present lord who suffered in the comparison.

"I've been thinking," Elfwyn said, "we should get a proper stone to mark the place. If Farmer Ost gets the land, at least there should be some marker where the house was. We can find one in the fields and move it there."

Paisi sat down across from him, now that he had finished his bread and jam. "Ost himself has that hitch of oxen," Paisi said, "and considerin' the land, an' all, he'd do Gran a favor." So they began to lay their plans.

"We can put a bird on it," Elfwyn said. "A sparrow. Gran would like that. Maybe we can get a carver to work it proper. We do it now while the ground's hard, or wait till summer."

"Snow's going to lie deep another month," Paisi said. "Ain't no great hurry. She'll sleep a bit to herself. She ached so much, m'lord. 'Tis at least a warm bed she got."

Paisi wept then, and he began to as well. But then he thought of his mother, smug and satisfied in their pain, and went dry-eyed. Paisi wept, while Elfwyn sat and stared out the windows, wishing death and ruin on his mother's head.

"I think I'll go upstairs," he said, purposing to get up, and Paisi took a heartbeat to understand that. Then Paisi shot his hand across the table, dislodging dishes, and seized Elfwyn's arm, bandages and all.

"No," Paisi said fiercely. "No! Ye can't. Ye're angry. And Gran always said that wasn't good. You quieten down, m'lord. Ye wait, ye wait to see her. Lord Tristen's comin' here, ain't he? It can't be that much longer, and he'll settle wi' your mother. You can't. Ye daren't."

He settled back into his chair, knowing that Paisi was right, that he would only fail again, and perhaps put others in danger—Paisi himself, or Lord Crissand, this time, to much greater ruin. He looked down at the ring he wore and wished he had taken it off before he visited his mother. He meant to do so when next he did.

But not today. Not, at least, today. He and Paisi stayed in the rooms, doing very little but nibble at the food—more arrived at noon, with Lord Crissand's regards and an inquiry whether they had other needs. They had none. They ate, and, drawing the drapes, they tried to sleep, but dreams intervened, terrible dreams, from which Elfwyn waked with a cry.

"There, it's all right, lad." Paisi put an arm about him.

"It's her!" he cried in indignation, and swung his feet over the side of the bed. "It's her doing it! She gives me no peace, Paisi!"

"Could be. Could be the Zeide itself. It's full of haunts."

He was quiet, then. He sat there in bed, forearms on his knees, and finally curled back over and went to sleep again.

He dreamed of birds, scores of birds, in a rift in the wall. He thought of Gran's marker, and the bird of peace he'd intended, but these were raptors, all, with cruel beaks and mad, murderous eyes.

"Birds," he told Paisi, when, again, he waked with an outcry. "There were birds in the wall . . ."

"Was it?" Paisi asked him, the two of them in the dark, the seam of sun long since gone from the draped windows. It was utterly dark, except the banked fire in the other room. "Was it, now?"

"It's a silly, stupid dream. I don't know why birds should be in a wall."

"Not so silly as that," Paisi said. "There's a haunt like that in the Zeide, in the lower hall, right down the way, an' I don't like you dreamin' of it. Ye don't ever go into that place, if ye see it. Ye go the other way, right fast. All the servants know about it. It's right down from where your ma's guards stand. It's them Lines again, is what Lord Tristen said."

"He didn't settle it, when he was here?"

"Oh, haunts has their ways of breakin' out again, an' this is one Lord Tristen himself has used, so I guess it ain't easy to block up—ain't never done any harm, that I know: it's more scary than harmful. There's cold spots upstairs, there's one in the pantry, but this one's noisy."

"Noisy."

"Like wings beating. Servants skip right fast past that spot, an' the old stairs beside it. Your ma's guards ha' prob'ly seen it more'n once."

"Lord Tristen showed me about Lines," he said, and for the first time it occurred to him that he could draw a protection around them, in this room, the sort that Gran had used to do, and which, in going out of Gran's house, they had lacked. So while Paisi watched, he got out of bed and walked about the room, drawing the Line with his hand, especially across the gaps, like the tall windows, like the fireplace, and the doors. He drew them once, twice, all about, and a third time; and then, to his own amazement, he saw a little blue glow attend the passage of his hand.

"Do you see it?" he asked, but Paisi shook his head and asked what he meant.

"The wards," he said. "They're working. If I'd done them at Gran's, if I'd done them the way Lord Tristen said, maybe Gran would have—"

"No," Paisi said sharply. "Don't ye think such a thing. If Gran's own wards didn't work, an' her a witch, how's yours to? Lord Tristen hisself might ha' set 'em and kept your ma's spite out, but ye ain't Lord Tristen, m'lord, for all love. Some things is just too strong for a lad."

"Like the birds."

"Like the birds in the wall, aye, like that. Ye c'n hold 'em back, or, well, someone like Master Emuin or Lord Tristen hisself can stop 'em for a while, but the wards tend to fade if ye don't keep at it, so I understand, even for the things they done."

"I'll do it, every night, before we sleep. Maybe they'll get strong enough to keep her out. Maybe we'll get some honest sleep, and I shan't be waking you up every hour."

"Maybe," Paisi said. "An' when Lord Tristen comes, he'll set 'em so's they'll hold fast. He'll settle the haunts, too. All of 'em. Too many folks 's died in this place, too many of 'em angry, not least of 'em Lord Crissand's own da, who was murdered down the hall, an' Lord Heryn, that your da hanged off the walls. Come to bed."

He gave a sigh and came back to bed. And in truth, he did burrow his head into his pillow and sleep, deeply.

But before morning he waked again in a sweat, and heard a furious scratching at the glass and leadings of the window.

"Paisi," he said. "Paisi! Do you hear that?"

Paisi snored.

It was a bird, he decided. A determined, even frantic, scratching at the glass, something trying to get through. But it had stopped when he sat up.

Maybe—the thought occurred to him. Maybe it had been Owl. Maybe Tristen had sent Owl to them.

That thought he found encouraging.

But he dared not open the drapes to try to catch a sight of the creature.

He dared not stir from bed, not until the sun sent a shaft of daylight through the curtain slit.

ii

LORD CRISSAND BADE HIM ATTEND A QUIET DINNER THE NEXT EVENING, ONLY Lord Crissand himself, and his lady, a plain woman with a beautiful voice—not in looks, but in manner, she put him in mind of Queen Ninévrisë, and he was glad she had come to grace her husband's table. She could chatter on lightly about the keep, about the birth of a servant girl's infant, about the need for spices and the hope the thaw came soon, and somehow wove a calm about her that did not make it necessary for him to talk about Gran, or their fortunes, or what they were to do with themselves.

That was Lord Crissand's part, when the lady had left, and they shared a late cup, stronger than Elfwyn's wont, and perhaps intended to send him to his bed for the night. It tasted strong on his tongue and tingled on its way down, but he drank it, all the same.

"Will Paisi farm the place?" Crissand ended up asking. "It's poor soil for anything but goats."

"He wanted Farmer Ost to take it over," Elfwyn said, which he hadn't intended to say, until Ost could make his own petition. He hoped he hadn't done wrong. "Ost was good to our gran, and came to help her that morning, so we hoped to give the land to him. We were going to put up a stone."

"Well, you wear that ring," Crissand said, "so the gift will stand, won't it? And that ring will get certainly get a stone set."

He had forgotten. He began to pull it from his finger in some confusion. "I should give this back."

"No. Not yet. You keep it until Lord Tristen comes. A stone, you say. I'll have a proper one set up, right on the roadside, where travelers can see it. A stone for an honest, good woman. A brave woman, who sheltered kin of mine—you are my cousin: I take you for such, with all good will. And you should know, I would have taken you in much before now. You went to Paisi's gran on Lord Tristen's advice, which I hope was a happy place for you. I hope you bear no thought that I failed in kinsmanship."

"I'm a bastard cousin, m'lord, and I hope I was never a burden." The kindness Crissand showed him opened wounds and brought him unexpectedly close to tears, and to truth. "My mother—my mother likely killed Gran, to spite me, because I visited her. I made her angry. She couldn't come at me, so she killed Gran, the same hour as I left her."

Crissand's face, ordinarily clear-eyed and kindly, darkened. "If she did that, then she may find terms changed. If you're to be here, perhaps it's time we found a new place to lodge this woman . . . I do not call her your mother: she has never merited that good name. If her sorcery did start the fire, then she's a murderess after being pardoned once from a death sentence, and she will not stay under this roof to trouble you, not by my will, and likely not by Lord Tristen's."

That was the best news he had had. But conscience made him say: "She would try to strike at you or yours, then, my lord. You should take the ring back for your own protection. And send your lady and your children far off while you deal with her . . . her Sight doesn't reach the river. Or it didn't seem to: I dreamed, even in Guelessar. And I'd no notion she'd come at Gran when she couldn't hurt me. I never once thought of it. Now I'm afraid to stay here, my lord, for your sake."

"Keep the ring," Crissand said. "Keep it on you day and night. Between her and my household, Lord Tristen set other protections. They hold. They hold, thus far."

"Gran's protection didn't hold her out."

"Tristen will have no trouble dealing with her. I've sent a letter to your father and told him your news, that Tristen is coming to Amefel, and I would by no means be surprised if your father came south himself. I have also sent to Lord Cevulirn, and would by no means be surprised to see him come out of Ivanor: he would scarcely forgive me if he hears Lord Tristen is abroad, and I failed to tell him. And Sovrag of Olmern, and even old Pelumer of Lanfarnesse. We dealt with Hasufin Heltain, who was a hundred times the threat that woman is, and I assure you we will find a way to deal with Tarien Aswydd. Go to bed, cousin. Trust this house has protections much beyond that ring: it travels with you. That is its particular virtue."

"I am greatly honored, m'lord."

"Cousin." Crissand shook him gently. "Go rest. Sleep."

"I shall, sir." He gathered himself up, made a little bow, and left, a little unsteady from the unaccustomed drink and warmed by the touch, and feeling a little disconnected from the world, with all the changes in his fortunes. He walked out of the little dining hall, and down the late-night darkness of the broad corridor, in which the servants had extinguished all but a few candles. All he had to do from there was go to his left and immediately up the main stairs.

Perhaps it was the wine—the lights seemed to dim as he turned in that direction, as if someone had extinguished the candles one by one, while past the great stairs, farther down the corridor, near the place his mother's guards stood, he saw a blue light and perceived the sound of wings.

It was the haunt, he thought. Or his dream. But he was sure he was awake.

He knew its threat. He knew he should run right up the stairs, but up above looked dark, and light only down here, and he stood looking down that rightward hall until he could see that blue light stronger and stronger, like the light of healthy wards. It began to cast the shadow of wings on the other wall.

That way lay his mother's tower. Her guards would be there. They must see it, too. And what if it *was* his mother, testing the strength of those wards?

He could reinforce them. If her guards were in danger, he might make a difference and prevent any harm. His mother might strike him, but he could engage her and keep her occupied: in that regard he had no fear for his own safety.

He went in that direction, and with every step the pulse quickened in his veins and the dread and, indeed, the resolution increased.

And his curiosity. That, too. To his alarm, he didn't see the guards. The light of the haunt overwhelmed the hall and blotted out the sight of them. This, he thought, was where he should stop, and having what Lord Tristen had taught him, he should reinforce the wards. He saw, along the floor, faded, near white old Lines, where the stonework was mismatched. Over them lay new, stronger blue lines, like that blazing blue of the haunt itself, shadowed with beating wings, a sound that became like thunder in his ears. He looked, and a wind out of it began to stir his hair. There was in fact a gap there, and when he even thought of mending it, the Line belled outward and swept him into a place of long perches, beating wings, and slashing beaks.

Now in mortal fear, he cast about to escape the haunt, and stepped out, across the Lines, but found himself not where he had been, but at the blank face of a wall, behind which he sensed an even greater horror—he had no notion what should be that terrible in the blank wall he could see, but without even thinking clearly, he spun about to escape, rushing in among the birds, as the lesser danger.

The birds vanished around him. He stumbled against an upward step, a short stairs in utter dark. He banged his shin on further steps, and staggered up through the clinging, dusty folds of a curtain to . . .

To the hall where he had started. The place the haunt had been was now just as ordinary as a wall could be. Night candles gleamed placidly in the sconces, untroubled by any wind, and the guards, his mother's guards, down the way, stood at their posts as if they had never noticed the haunt at all.

He had just come up a stairway from a level he had no idea existed, behind a tapestry. And if he had more courage, he might go back down the steps behind that tapestry and confront what he was sure now was simply too much strong wine, or an overwrought mind, or too many dreams.

He had not the courage to go down into that shadowed place. The memory was too strong. He simply turned, trying not to look like an utter fool for having blundered through a curtain, and walked back toward the grand stairs and up.

Paisi was awake, sharpening his dagger by the fire, bandages and all, as Elfwyn slammed the door of their chambers shut at his back.

"M'lord?" Paisi asked him.

"It was the haunt, Paisi." He came breathlessly down the short entry hall to the fireside, to light that still could not overcome the memory he had of that cold blue light, the sound of wings that still buzzed in his ears. "It was the haunt. I was just *in* it."

"*In* it?"

"It was the wings, and I was somewhere else, then, back in the hall and nobody else even noticed. The candles didn't blow out. The guards didn't leave their places."

"That haunt leads places, is what," Paisi said. "An' once't Lord Tristen and Lord Crissand went all the way to Elwynor by that haunt."

"To Elwynor!"

"Or elsewhere. No knowin' where ye was. Ye stay away from that place. Ye don't above all go in there."

"I didn't! Or I didn't mean to. I don't want to again!"

"Ye sit down, lad. Ye ain't used t' drink, an' ye had some, didn't ye? Ye pour your own water in, if someone serves ye strong wine. Specially if it's more 'n one. Damn, I knew I should ha' come down t' serve ye."

His head spun and felt stuffed with wool. And he hadn't wanted Paisi acting as his servant, standing behind his chair. But he'd wished at the time he had dared pour water into what the duke offered him, which was clearly costly wine. Next time, he said to himself, he would do it, and never mind the embarrassment. Crissand had called him cousin, treated him like a grown man. Crissand, however, would forgive his manners.

"Maybe it *was* just the wine," he said. "Maybe I've had too many dreams."

"There's a good lad. Or maybe ye did see the haunt. I ain't sayin' ye didn't."

"I'd swear I did." He didn't speak for a while, only sat and watched the fire. "It scared me. It scared me more than anything, and I can't even say why it did. It was only birds, after all."

"Dead 'uns," Paisi said, and kept sharpening the blade. "An' how's 'Is Grace?"

"The duke," he said, remembering. "His Grace said it's not just Lord Tristen who's coming. He wrote to my father and maybe *he'll* ride down when Lord Tristen does. And the lords of the provinces southward. Do you think my father will come?"

"Oh, aye, he's bosom friends wi' Lord Tristen. He always has come, if *he* rides out."

"You already knew that?"

"I wasn't goin' t' promise it in case of something different happenin', but it's likely enough."

That good news tingled all the way down his limbs, and he let himself ever so slightly believe that it could be true. If Tristen was here in person to keep his mother at bay, things might work out with his father, too. That scratching at his window might indeed have been Owl. And curse the fear he'd had: he'd been too scared to let Owl in.

"His Grace said he might," he said to Paisi, "and he said, too, that he'd raise the stone for Gran, a marker right on the roadside where everybody can read it."

Only the king or the duke could put something on the public right of way. Even a goatherd knew that.

"That's grand," Paisi said, not too enthusiastically, and shrugged, looking into the fire. After a moment he said, with a sigh: "She'd say it was too grand for her, wouldn't she?"

He thought about that. "She would."

"I tell you, I think she'd like it if we got the oxen and moved her in a country stone wi' no writin' nor fancy carvin' at all. She'd complain she couldn't read any writin', nor ever could learn. It was just a frustration to her, an' her eyes were too poor when I tried to teach her. But she'd like a good stone."

The manners of the fortress, its fine clothes and its ambitions had settled into him so quickly he'd fallen right into the duke's grand notion, had he not? Paisi was who could make him know what Gran would say, so plain, so matter-of-fact in her speaking. Gran wasn't someone, he thought, who could be honored by the duke. She was someone who might honor a duke or even a king with her blessing, from such a stone. Calm and peaceful as the earth, she was . . . always had been.

And it was strange, that when Paisi had said that, just in her words, he heaved a deep sigh, just like Paisi. He could think of her again, not the fire, not the ashes, but Gran as she was, smiling at them, or poking about her stove, all the fire in the house tame again and under Gran's dominion . . .

As ought to be, he thought. As forever ought to be. A pang of grief still touched him when he remembered now, but for a moment he was convinced that Gran was all right, despite his mother, despite him and his mistakes, despite everything.

His mother might have power—might have blackest sorcery—might have broken loose the Lines and let loose the haunt in the night . . . but he'd gotten out of it, hadn't he, all on his own? Despite anything she did to try to scare him or get him up those stairs, he could live under this roof, growing wiser, and stronger, and never, ever visit her again, despite all her tantrums and threats.

Lord Tristen would see to her. And then there would be justice for Gran.

iii

THE WINGS, HE DREAMED. THE WINGS. THE WINGS WERE IN THE WALL. AND ELF-wyn knew even amid the dream that he was only dreaming, and he turned over and slammed the pillow with his burned fist, which hurt, and dragged him halfway out of sleep.

But when he fell back into the pillow he fell into the hallway again, and something pursued him, down the hall, around the turn to the library. He knew the library door: he had visited it with the duke when he was still small. He knew every detail of that amazing room, the eagles on the doors, carved shapes that screamed out of the wood, and he worked feverishly to get the latch open in time, as the pursuit of the hunter birds beat and thundered behind him, rattling the very stones of the keep. In there was safety, in there was what he had to have, and the birds behind him threatened that . . .

The door came open. He was in the library, with its tall windows, its many tables, its tall stacks and shelves of books; and he was so sure that the answer to the hallway behind the tapestry was somewhere in this room, behind something, hidden, and if he could get it, and if he could solve that puzzle, then he would be safe, and Paisi would be safe, and nothing would ever threaten them like this again.

But the blue light and the wings had reached the library door, and beat to get in.

Lord Tristen needed to know. He had to have what was in this room, and if it went elsewhere, even he was helpless. Tristen grew weaker and his mother more powerful, high up in her tower, so long as this thing stayed hidden . . . she struggled, sending the haunt, to get it into her own hands. If she got it, she would be unstoppable. She was on the track, with the birds, and he couldn't find it.

Elfwyn waked, bolt upright in bed, and sweating. Paisi slept, snoring in his sleep, common and welcome sound.

When sunlight came through the windows again, he was too ashamed to tell Paisi. It was just one of his dreams, fading, now, in import and in detail. He couldn't even remember why he had been so afraid of birds, of all silly things, and what he had been after, and why he had waked screaming.

His mother's work.

Or a warning. There were other haunts here. There were other ghosts besides a gathering of birds, hadn't Paisi said so.

iv

THEY WENT DOWN TO SEE THE HORSES IN THE MORNING, TAKING A TREAT FROM their breakfast, and finding them in excellent care and glad to see their masters. They lingered there, talked a time with the stableboys, and Paisi and the stablemaster fell to discussing people they'd known in the war years, before Elfwyn was even born.

Elfwyn knew none of the names, and the wind was cold. His coat was thin, suited only to indoors, and he grew rapidly chill. So while Paisi talked, he simply slipped off quietly, waved, so Paisi would know he was going, and went on inside the fortress, intending to go up to the room and get his warmer cloak before he went outside again.

He didn't know why he walked as far as the center stairs of the lower west wing, when he passed a perfectly fine stairs he could have used to go above; or why he walked farther than that, down close to the haunt; but he could see, down in the east wing, and with the lower hall lights all lit, where the guards stood watch, and the blank wall where the haunt had appeared.

Yes, there was indeed a tapestry there, or some sort of hanging, short of that place: it was not the only one in the hallway: there was no sign it concealed any mystery. And on from that, beyond the guards, but before the end of the hall, was the intersection of the east–west hall with the north hall.

That way led to the library, and a view of a small garden—he remembered it from his childhood, when he had visited here; and suddenly the dream came back in particular detail. He walked that far, and did see, indeed, a difference in the stones, both in the style of stonework and in the pattern where something had been walled up, a change even in the quarry from which the floor pavings came: something had been walled up and changed, and the Lines here might not be what they ought to be . . . Tristen himself had repaired it, and in great temerity Elfwyn ran his hand along that wall, not looking at his mother's guards, who must think him a very peculiar sort.

Stay inside, he told the haunt. *Mind your place.*

The tapestry however, gave under his fingers, hiding a short stair just as in his dream. He moved it back, and cautiously, mindful that the guards were out there watching this trespass, went down those steps into a dark lit only by a seam of light from under the curtain. He felt his way down, and came up against a blank masonry wall.

Something else was walled up here. These stairs had surely led somewhere, once. But the little light that came in under the tapestry gave little definition to the stones, and his own shadow covered all possible detail. Nothing here seemed so imminently frightening, but he began to think it was not a good place to be. He decided to ask Paisi what had used to be here.

He went up again, into the hall, and past the place of the haunt then, trailing his fingers along the wall, and past the guards, who stood facing one another, leaning on the columns near them and talking with one another, so absorbed in their conversation they seemed not to have seen his odd behavior. They never looked his way. Or perhaps he had entered again into the dream. The feeling of that dream began to overlay the hall as it was, but the shape of the hall, exactly as his dream had believed he remembered it . . . was exactly like this, when he was sure he would never have recalled such detail as the moldings and the shape of the arch at the intersection.

Now he burned to know if the library doors themselves were exactly as what he had dreamed, or he remembered from so long ago, and he walked that hall, and found the doors open, not shut. He peered into the shadows behind one, and saw the eagle with its beak open, indeed, carved in the upper panel, and when he walked into the doorway, he saw the tables as he had dreamed, and the windows, and the shelves . . . and there was something here. He had dreamed there was something here, of such importance, such dire importance . . .

An old man in dusty robes intercepted him. "Sir?" that man asked. "Are you looking for a particular book?"

It was what one did in the library. "A history," he said, trying to seem like a lad bent on business. History was his favorite kind of book. He feared to be caught by a stranger, like this man, and questioned on matters he could ill explain. "A history of Amefel."

"Well, now, there is that. There are several. Might I ask your name, young gentleman? Are you a guest?"

"My name is Elfwyn Aswydd," he said, and saw the old man's jaw drop. "I'm Lord Crissand's guest," he said, trying to erase that dismay. "My name used to be Otter. His Grace always has lent me books, for years and years."

"The boy in the cottage," the old man said.

"In Gran's cottage," he said, with an uncomfortable lump in his throat. Clearly the news had not gotten to this place. And all the while, his dream nagged at him with the most dire sense of something, some secret, some hidden thing within this room that he had to find, that could reach out and kill everything he loved. "Might I just look around, sir?" He showed the duke's ring, and the old man peered at it somewhat more closely than the guards ever had, and straightened and bowed, and bowed again.

"His Grace's permission. Do be careful," the old man whispered, meaning of the books, of course, but the caution stirred the hairs on his nape, all the same. There was more and more in this room that seemed oddly familiar to him, as if he'd seen it all before, down to that very stack of books on the first table, or the exact clutter on the old man's desk, which he could never have expected to see.

His heart beat faster and faster. The old man directed him to a table, and brought him books. The *Chronicle of the Eagle* was one. He opened it very carefully, handled the stiff parchment pages exactly as this man's predecessor had instructed him. The old man hovered a little less near, told him where other histories were kept, and drifted off about his duties.

He leafed through, standing, finding nothing in particular that caught his eye, except a grand illumination of the Battle of Lewen Field, with soldiers dying and the Eagle banner flying conspicuously. The Sihhë Star was there, black and stark. That he had ever seen that emblem in its proper place still seemed incredible to him, and the ring tingled on his hand as he thought about it.

The fear, however, dogged him, like something standing just at his shoulder, something that darted from one side of his vision to the other, taunting him. He strayed from the table to the shelf the old man had pointed out.

He saw, on the shelves, a large, ancient volume: *The Art of War,* translated by . . . but the name had worn off the spine. There was *The Red Chronicle.* That book drew him, as one he had long heard mentioned, and he reached toward it, thinking to take it from the shelf.

Steps came up behind him. He turned, empty-handed, and the librarian passed over a heavy volume. He felt, for some reason he couldn't understand, an unaccustomed guilt and distress at the interruption in his reach, as if he had lied to the old man and could not even remember the lie he had told.

The codex the old man gave him was, indeed, *A History of Amefel.*

"You may read it at this table," the librarian said, and drew back a chair for him. He sat down, and opened it very carefully, and read at length. It was not the best copyist who had produced this volume, in an overblown script. It was a labor to read it, and he found it a dry, scholarly style, nothing that informed him, nothing so perilous or exciting as he had hoped to find in *The Red Chronicle.* This one began with very old records, back in the reign of the High Kings, and named every single lord of every single holding, with all the begetting and descending and disputing.

Still, in courtesy to the old librarian who had particularly offered this to him, he stayed at it, laboring over the obscure script, and curious, stiff illuminations of people who stood like pillars, with exactly the same faces and differing gestures. Paisi finally surprised him, having tracked him down.

"I wondered where ye'd gone, m'lord," Paisi said.

"I wanted to read," he lied. He suddenly realized everything he'd done since leaving Paisi outside was one long lie, and he didn't know why he wanted to be here now, but he did and was afraid to be. The book at least gave him respite from dreams and uncertainties: its dry difficulties drew all his faculties into one effort, and left no time for extraneous thoughts, or remembering Gran, or wondering what he would do with himself hereafter. It was only time he had to fill to get from waking to dark, and reading filled it well enough.

Paisi was all over dust and smelled of the stables, not books. "So shall ye be up to supper?"

"In a bit. Go up to the room and rest if you like."

"More like down to the kitchens to get a bite," Paisi said. "I'm half-starved. D' ye want anything, m'lord? Shall I have your supper sent upstairs?"

"In an hour or so," he said. "Thank you, Paisi." He didn't feel hungry. He turned a page carefully, wishing only not to be distracted from where he was, as if he were walking a rail and mustn't fall off, mustn't distract himself.

Paisi, probably annoyed with him, or at least not understanding what he was about, left on his own business.

This book was not the thing he wanted. But the library was the place he wanted. He didn't want to leave it. He didn't want to look away from his pages. He just wanted to stay where he was, where his heart didn't hurt and his memories and his dreams didn't keep slipping into his head.

"Might I stay longer?" he asked when the librarian said that he had to go to supper, and went about to turn out the few old men who had occupied other tables.

The old man looked at him carefully and gave him a key. "These are very, very few," the old man said. "You may come in and read, lad, as pleases you. I can see you read like a scholar. Admirable. Admirable in a lad. But have extreme care of candles, bank the fire, and lock the door when you leave. These books are the kingdom's treasures, and irreplaceable."

"I shall be careful, sir," he said, taking the key, which tingled in his fingers, the longed-for prize. "I shall be ever so careful."

He stayed a little while after. Once he was sure the old man was gone, he got up and took *The Red Chronicle* from its shelf. He read by close candlelight—the windows were dimming—how the Sihhë-lords' reign had extended over Amefel, Elwynor, and most that was now Ylesuin. In those days magic had been ordinary, and the Sihhë lived long lives, spanning generations of Men, doing as they pleased. Guelemara had not been the capital in those days: it was a place called Althalen, in Amefel. And a great wizard, Mauryl Gestaurien, had served the Sihhë-lords, from the fortress of Ynefel. So had Selwyn Marhanen, a warlord under the Sihhë King.

Nothing was then as it was now. Gran had never told him these things. Paisi hadn't.

And this Selwyn Marhanen, this warlord out of Guelessar, had defended the borders of the Sihhë from attacks from the south, while making secret alliances with a priest of a militant sect, the Quinalt—in that day when most Men were Bryalt, or, always in the case of wizards, Teranthine . . .

Was the Quinaltine not yet built, then? Or all the great city of Guelemara? He tried to imagine the world as it had been, and leafed carefully ahead to see that Selwyn Marhanen had killed several of his brother lords among the districts of Men, and entered into agreements with others. The Sihhë King in those days was Elfwyn, Elfwyn Sihhë, who relied on the Marhanen and trusted him.

The guttering candle wavered, making the letters crawl and move. He looked up, realized that the windows were now completely dark, the fire in the little fireplace was out, and his whole body was stiffened from long sitting.

He shivered, held his chilling fingers above the candleflame to warm them, and simultaneously realized, with a little touch of dismay, that Paisi might not realize he was still here, now that the door shut.

There was tomorrow. There were any number of tomorrows for books. He shut the *History of Amefel* on the table, to protect its pages from drafts, before returning *The Red Chronicle* to the shelf. He would, he told himself, be back when he was not cold and hungry and getting to the end of a candle stub. He lifted the candleholder to light his way to the door, careful not to spill the brimming wax, and as it tipped, a little did spill into the catchbasin, and the flame leapt up on a clear wick, showing him the way, indeed, but making all the room a threatening place, the tall cases and the looming stacks full of secrets, tales that had shaped his present existence, laws and rights of rule—so, so many things he didn't understand and needed to know, if only to defend himself from forces he did not comprehend.

But for now he took his single candle to the door and let himself out, blew out the candle stub, and left it on the ledge outside the door, to be renewed by servants who saw that such things appeared in due order. The halls were mostly deserted, and he remembered that horrid apparition—he hadn't realized he'd trapped himself on the other side of it, after dark, and he didn't want to go near that place, not even with his mother's guards on watch down there.

There was, however, the way the servants used.

He went down to the end of the short hall, and found, indeed, the servants' stairs, and climbed up those short, dark stairs to a dimly lighted hall above—one bend and another, which took him above the haunt. He hurried along, breathless, trying not to break into a fearful run. Servants were going up and down the halls at this hour, collecting the washing and used dishes of other residents, the minor lords of the town and the province, lords who lived here, or visited here, where now a witch's son found refuge from calamity.

He didn't feel he belonged in this place. He wanted not to be here, under his mother's witness. He wanted to be back in Guelessar if he had to live in a palace. He wasn't sure he wanted to read more of the book, and to know how his namesake had died, and, in detail, how Aewyn's family had turned on the Sihhë King.

He reached his own door, pushed the latch and whipped inside, breathlessly glad to meet light and warmth and, indeed, the smell of supper.

"Well, now," Paisi said. "Thank the gods. Where *was* you? With 'is Grace?"

"In the library, still," he said.

"I came by, an' the door shut. I hoped ye was with 'is Grace, but I couldn't get no sense out of the servants. There's supper, if ye wish 't."

"In a bit. A little wine, maybe."

"That we can do." Paisi went to the table and poured a cup, and from a second pitcher, water. "What was you readin' so late and so urgent?"

"A history. A history of Elfwyn King."

"Oh, well," Paisi said, worried-looking. The same boding dark was outside the windows, firelight glittering on the glass, as he gave him the cup. "That ain't too cheery, is it?"

"No. It wasn't." He didn't want to explain the tightness in his chest or the unrest in his heart. He drank, and sat down by the fire, ignoring supper. It was only the drink he wanted, to take the dust of the place out of his mouth and the attraction of it out of his mind. "It wasn't."

Paisi stretched his feet out in front him, warming his boots. "Well, I got a far simpler question for ye. I was talkin' to the stablemaster, an' they were talkin' o' takin' the horses down to the pastures as they do, to the winter stables. But the four paddocks left free down there is way on the end, an' they're askin' if we're apt to be needin' the horses too often. I said I'd ask you."

"I don't know," he said, which was foolish, because he did know, and there wasn't much chance they'd be riding about the countryside anytime soon.

Unless Aewyn came with his father. There was that.

"Maybe they could stay up here just a little longer," he said.

"It's fair cramped here, m'lord. They'd be happier."

"I don't want my horse down the hill!" he said, more curtly than he meant. But he couldn't think of a reason. He took another sip and swallowed half the cup after. "He's mine. I want him here, is all."

"I'll tell 'em so," Paisi said. "Ain't ye goin' t' eat, m'lord?"

"I'm not that hungry," he said glumly, but he came and sat at the table and picked at the food, and had another cup of watered wine. Paisi had his own wine plain, not in the brightest of moods.

They sat for a while. "If Aewyn should come," Elfwyn said, to mend his earlier tone, and because what had sat for hours at the bottom of his thoughts had finally bobbed up to the surface, the conviction that nothing they would do here was permanent—"and with Lord Tristen here, too—I might want my horse—I'd hope to go riding with Aewyn. I don't know when they will come. I don't know what might happen."

"Aye," Paisi said then, seeming happier having a reason. "That might be. An' then I'd have mine, too, because ye ain't t' go nowhere wi'out me, hear? Ain't got Gran to look after, and if you go ridin' off wi' Lord Tristen or 'Is young Highness, I'm goin', no question. So I'll tell 'em that."

Paisi didn't ask about the books. Elfwyn didn't mention the detail of things he'd learned. The forced good humor of yesterday, dealing with Gran's death, had grown weary on them both. Gran was a matter they neither one mentioned this evening. There was nothing they could plan for themselves: all they could plan remained at the king's pleasure, and the duke's, and Lord Tristen's, when he might arrive. The rooms they shared were only lent, nothing their own, and they had no duty except to each other. Even that needed very little: house servants did all the work and all the carrying, and arrived more often than they needed, so Paisi was at loose ends, and Elfwyn even more so.

They waited uneasily and without speaking about their unease—waited for Lord Tristen, waited, possibly, for the king, and for Aewyn to come. They waited for what might change the whole course of their lives, and finally sighed and decided on bed, to face another day of much the same.

CHAPTER SIX

THE WIND TURNED FOUL TOWARD DARK, CARRYING BLOWN SNOW INTO THEIR faces, stinging eyes and noses. It was a hard day's ride for a boy, and Cefwyn rode between his son and the wind while the Dragon Guard rode around them, and ahead, trampling the snow into a broader path.

Aewyn's flow of questions had stopped even before the sun went down.

If they did not come to the way shelter before too long, Cefwyn thought, he would order tents broken out of their small pack train. In this weather, and with a boy in the company, they traveled at least with canvas, and firepots, and a certain amount of food already prepared.

A guardsman rode near to say they had smelled smoke, and the waft of it came with the messenger, borne on the same wind. "The shelter, Your Majesty," that man said, pointing ahead, and so it must be—one of the little three-sided stone waystops he had ordered built along the King's Road south and north, where there were wells or nearby water: he ordered his foresters to provide each its small store of firewood.

That was their destination tonight, the last such shelter before they would cross the river—the bridge had gone down in the fall rains: old Lenúalim was notoriously hard to bridge, all along this shore: not that it ran deep here, but wide. It took down bridges with ice, or scouring, and most recently lightning, which was so strange a circumstance that no few had named it as a sign there ought not to be a bridge over the river at all. So they would ford it at the old place, by the last shelter before the monastery, which was said to be frozen over, and Cefwyn had no desire to risk doing it in the dark. They had pressed hard today, bypassing one shelter at midafternoon, determined to reach this one, and to make time so that they could cross by fair daylight tomorrow. He had thought he might have overreached, and doomed them all to the labor of making a roadside camp, and now the news that they were coming into a shelter occupied, and with a fire already going was cheerful news.

The smoke was more definite on the wind as they rode, so that all the company knew it. The pace picked up a little. Aewyn said not a thing, only clenched his cloak about him and stayed beside him, brave lad, at a faster clip.

Two guardsmen broke ahead of the party, to be sure who was there; and it was a little space before they came atop the rise and whistled a signal back to their comrades that all was well.

It was a rush, after that, weary horses encouraged to move, with the smell of smoke and shelter in their nostrils and the prospect of grain before them. It was, Cefwyn thought, a small merchant party they would meet, with a fire already built, possibly with useful wares or commodities to offer fellow travelers. Winter merchants, traveling to the villages and back, were usually the younger traders, and the hungrier, especially to be out on the road in a bad streak like this.

There was no such party camped around. Guardsmen dismounted, and Cefwyn did, neglecting to help his son down at the moment, his attention all for the single man at a small scrap of a fire, a huge pile of ash, but only a little fire; and a man wrapped in his cloak and a single blanket.

"Here's your king," a guardsman said. "Can you stand, fellow?"

"Leg's broken," the man said, and scanned the lot of them, looking for authority, as it seemed. Cefwyn came to stand in front of him, and, as the man flung back his cloak and the blanket, he saw the red and black Amefin colors and, indeed, a roughly splinted leg. "Lord Crissand's courier," the man said through cracked lips. "Your Majesty."

Cefwyn squatted at eye level and saw a man, indeed, in dire straits.

"A message," the man said, and felt within his coat. He came out with a crushed and bloody letter, in a hand itself black with scabs and dirt. "My lord—my lord—said it was urgent. An' me horse went down on the ice."

"Care for this man," Cefwyn said. "More wood." It must have cost this man agony to get back and forth between the diminished woodpile and the fire pit. "Cut more, if you need." Any cutting on the king's right of way had to have royal permission. It had that, tonight.

"What is it?" came a young voice. Aewyn had gotten down from his horse, and finally found a question, squatting down beside him as he broke the seal and held the letter, fairly written, in good black ink, so that the fire lit it from behind.

Your son has returned safely, Crissand had written, himself: he knew that strong, clear hand. *When your ward reached his house, he indeed went west, and reports he has seen Lord Tristen, who he says has informed him he should carry the name Elfwyn. He reports that the lord of Ynefel will come as far as Henas'amef, how soon and in what intent, unfortunately, I do not know. He says that Ynefel gave him a message for me, but that he lost it on the way, in bad weather. This alarms me, as I am sure it will trouble us all.*

In the loss of Ynefel's message, I have lent your ward the ring which Ynefel gave me . . .

Lost it on the way, for the gods' sake. That was uncommon bad luck, for one of Tristen's messages.

Surely Tristen *knew* it was lost. Didn't he? Had Crissand gotten another message from him by now, since the dispatch of the letter?

And Otter—Elfwyn—was safe. Safe, and going under his given name, by Tristen's instruction.

And carrying Crissand's ring, as potent as Cefwyn's own amulet. That was welcome news, but it indicated Crissand was very worried, and wanted to be sure where the boy was.

Tristen, gods be praised, was coming to Amefel.

"What does it say?" his son asked, trying to see.

"That your brother has made it back safely."

"Then I shall see him!" Aewyn cried.

Should he see him? Cefwyn wondered. Tristen was involved. The boy had come back under some instruction from him, and there the matter of Ynefel's ring, and Otter—Elfwyn—electing to visit his mother, of all damned things. *He is convinced her ill will may have caused certain misfortunes, and he seems to believe that Ynefel's arrival may deal with her. I am uneasy in his intention . . .*

Not the half of it, Cefwyn thought. Crissand wrote: *my forbidding him might have consequences I cannot foresee,* and *I hope that I have done wisely in granting this request, and I shall continue vigilant . . .*

Bloody hell, he thought. *Small wonder Crissand had granted Otter the ring, in that case.* Tristen was involved. Crissand hadn't felt he had the authority to stop Otter, but he hadn't liked that request to visit the woman, which might not have come from Tristen.

He wanted to be back on the road, never mind the hour. He wanted a fresh horse and a clear road, and he wanted to send Aewyn back home, to be safe in Guelemara under Efanor's not inconsiderable protection.

But—but if magic was in question, separating off his son and sending him back alone was not a safe course, either. Aewyn, with a little of the old blood from his Syrillas mother, had only the disadvantage of that magical heritage at his age, none of the protection it might give him if it ever flowered. *He* himself was blind to magic, but Tristen said things magical outright glowed in the daylight to certain eyes. And if his son glowed like that to certain eyes, then he was a damned sight safer with Tristen in the neighborhood than he would be going off into the dark with a covey of equally blind Dragon Guard.

"What else?" Aewyn wanted to know, tugging ever so slightly at his sleeve.

"That your brother is no longer Otter. He's now saying his name is Elfwyn. And he seems to have visited Lord Tristen, who told him that was his name. Here, you can read it. What questions you find in it, I fear I can't answer. Just keep the letter safe." He stood up and gained the attention of the Guard captain. "Make a litter. Two men to take Lord Crissand's messenger to the monks at Aelford at a gentle pace, his care at Crown expense: his message is delivered and his duty discharged. He may go where he pleases when he is able to ride, and the monks are to provide him a good horse. The rest of you will go on with me. No canvas spread. Better the clean wind than seal us in with the smoke." The sound of an axe resounded through the shelter, a tree going down. It would be green wood and, indeed, a great deal of smoke when it burned. It would be well, too, to leave more wood curing for the next occupant of the shelter, who might come in likewise in dire need. The messenger had lain here, burning what he must to keep himself from freezing, and had had the bad luck to have no merchants come along for days.

"Did his mother cause all his trouble?" Aewyn wanted to know, regarding Otter, now Elfwyn, while the Guard started breaking out their supper supplies. "Could she?"

"It's a good question," he said. It was not a matter he wanted to discuss in front of the guardsmen. "I don't know what she can do nowadays. I don't know the answers, I warned you that. And let's not discuss it here."

"Is it a magical ring?"

He touched his own amulet beneath his coat where it rested, against his bare skin. It often lent a warmth to him, if only the comfort of friendship. "I suppose in a sense it's magical. But a prince of Ylesuin doesn't talk about magic. It's not something we bruit about recklessly in front of honest Guelenfolk, even if our good friends use it."

"But I'll see Lord Tristen?"

"I very much hope you will," he said. The flow of questions had started again, unanswerable, but it was the surest sign of happiness in his son. He reached out, knocking back Aewyn's hood, and tousled his hair, which

Aewyn hated. "Questions, questions, questions. Will the sun rise tomorrow? Generally, but I can't promise it. I'm not in charge of the sun."

"You're the king."

"I'm not in charge of the sun, however. And I'm certainly not in charge of Tristen. He's not our subject, you know: he's the High King, and it could be argued we're his. He's our friend, is all."

"He was duke of Amefel, once."

"He became free of that. I let go the oath. You can't keep a creature like him bound, you know. You never should, or you have to take what comes of it."

"What would come of it?"

"I'm not in charge of that, either, piglet. I don't know what might happen, but getting in Tristen's way isn't a wise thing to do."

"Why? What would he do?"

"He wouldn't do a thing," Cefwyn said, with his own memories of ice and fire, and far more inexplicable sights. "He wouldn't do a thing. But when he needs something, all nature bends. Sometimes it even breaks its own rules, and, no, don't ask me what those rules are. If I knew, I'd be a wizard, and I'm certainly not."

"You learned from one."

"I did. And I do wish I could provide the same for you, son of mine. But there's not a one I can find."

"Except Lord Tristen."

"Who's—" Cefwyn began to say.

"Not a wizard. I know. He's Sihhë. Which is different. But I don't understand how it's different."

"You have a bit of it, through your mother, you know. And, son, if you ever do see odd things or find things glowing when you look at them—you can tell her about it. Or tell me very secretly. And quickly. I'd never say it was a bad thing, but His Holiness would have an apoplexy."

"What's an—"

"Never mind. But I wouldn't be sorry if you did have a small touch of your mother's Sight."

"And the Aswydds have it, too."

"They do."

"Lord Crissand is Aswydd like Otter, and the duke of Amefel." A small recitation as Aewyn made sure of his facts, counting them on his gloved fingers. "Aswydd like Otter, and his father was Edwyll, who was murdered—"

"Who said such a thing?"

"Uncle."

Efanor, was it? And what other sordid tales was his brother giving the lad. "He was."

"And the duke of Amefel has a peculiar grant of power, because they were kings before us, and opened their gates to my great-grandfather. Amefin dukes are earls, except Crissand, who is a duke the way Guelenfolk think of it, and he's His Grace to us, and aetheling to his own people, who have earls and thanes and other sorts of nobles. But my brother is more directly Aswydd than Crissand is." A plaintive question. "Is it because he's illegitimate that he's not duke?"

"Yes, in plain words, yes."

"But he would be the rightful duke, would he not?"

"Wishes don't overcome his illegitimacy. He is not, nor ever can be. There are other Aswydds. But they rebelled against us and conspired to kill your grandfather; and I exiled the lot of them." The rest of it wasn't a pretty story. It was one, perhaps, that he should inform his son, considering they were going there; but the story still stuck in his throat, like the grief and anger of that night.

"How did you meet Otter's mother?"

"She was the younger sister of the duke. And I lived a wild life before I met your mother. Well, truth to tell, I was a fool when I was younger. I know all the trouble a young man can get into, which is why I say you're not to do that sort of thing. Sins come back to you."

"Otter isn't a sin!"

"No." Cefwyn managed a little smile. "My sin, but not his. I find no fault in him. But so you should know—his mother hates me."

"She's a prisoner there."

"She is."

"Because she's a sorceress."

"Because she's a sorceress, yes."

"But you made love with her!"

Innocence looked back at him, a gulf of life and years..

"Hear what I said," Cefwyn said, in Emuin's best manner. "Think about it at your leisure, and deeply. I made love. I didn't love her. She didn't love me. I'd not met your mother yet."

"You love Mother."

"Deeply."

"You didn't love Otter's mother, ever, did you?"

"I didn't. Never, never, my boy, link yourself to a woman who cares nothing for you, or that you care nothing for, either. It's a bad mistake. Your brother was conceived the one night I spent with her. The very night I met Lord Tristen. Think of that, too. Sorcery was in it."

"Because of Lord Tristen?" Aewyn asked.

"Tristen is—"

"Not a sorcerer. I know. There is a difference."

"There was a sorceress in it, all the same, Tarien's sister. She didn't get *herself* with child, but Tarien did."

"You slept with her sister, too?"

Both in the same bed, but he spared his son that particular news, and simply nodded. "Being a young fool, in one year, I got myself a son with a woman who was my mortal enemy, worse, the enemy of my own house, and my people—then became king. And that, my son, made life no easier for our young Otter—beginning with the fact that Tarien named him Elfwyn to spite us all."

"To spite the Marhanens. You said so."

"So I did. And time you know this, son of mine: your great-grandfather would have killed her and her unborn child because the mother and the aunt plotted against us, and because the babe to be born would—all other difficulties aside—mix two very troublesome bloodlines. If she had lived long enough to name him as she did, that defiance alone would have assured your great-grandfather would have killed them both. That was the sort of king he was. Your grandfather would just have beheaded her sister, married Tarien off to some hairy Chomaggari, and had Elfwyn living in a tent down in the south . . . until, of course, sorcery took a hand in it and brought the boy back to be our lifelong enemy. Perhaps I was wrong to try to make his life comfortable. Sometimes I have had that fear. But I did it on Tristen's advice. And for my own inclinations, it seemed to me a good thing—not to have my other son for my enemy, or yours. So I took the risk. I've done all I could to make him turn out well. And when you asked, I brought him to live with us. I did hope it would work out."

"I *like* my brother."

"So do I," he said, and the dark felt a little less cold, when he recalled that earnest, gray-eyed face. "I like him very well. Paisi's gran did a good job, bringing him up and defending him from his mother."

"Elfwyn calls her his gran, too. But he knows she's not really his."

"An excellent woman, let me tell you. And plain and wise, and capable of a fairly potent charm or two, by all Tristen told me. Thank the gods for her and for Paisi, too, who's been a brother to him, or no knowing how

he might have turned out. So perhaps Tristen's advice was right after all."
It cheered him to think how Gran had turned to good the evil Tarien had planned.

"What was the name of that other woman?"

"Which woman?"

"The sorceress. The other one."

"One shouldn't—"

"—speak their names," Aewyn said. "I know. But isn't it good I know that?"

"No need for you to know it. She's dead. But her name was Orien. Orien Aswydd."

A moment of silence. Aewyn tucked his coat the more tightly about him, the bitter wind skirling up a skein of sparks. "She'd be Elfwyn's aunt, wouldn't she? Does Elfwyn know about her?"

"I don't know," he said. "Paisi's gran certainly does. So does Paisi. So does everyone in Henas'amef and half of Ylesuin, for that matter, who were alive in those years. One just doesn't speak of sorcerers. It's bad luck. So, no, I don't know if your brother does know at all. Maybe you're right. Maybe it's time I did tell him, as I'm telling you."

"He doesn't like his mother at all," Aewyn said. "I thought it was odd he didn't. But I understand, now."

"What did he say about her?"

"He said she lived in a tower in Henas'amef, that she was a prisoner. That Gran was his real mother."

"Well, then, that is the truth of his heart," Cefwyn said, "and the word that counts."

They might have been any father, any son, about a campfire, against the winter storm and wind, and in the way of such conversations, apart from court and hall, and at a time when his dear wife was, by now, likely similarly cold and snowbound in the north—necessary things finally could be said, tales told, things passed on between generations, links forged.

He felt a bond that night that he had never had with his son, a meeting of man with man this night. For the first time in that firelit, sober countenance, he saw the fine outlines of the good man he would become.

He was rich, in Aewyn. He longed to have such a conversation with his other son, wanted to have it soon, before any other misunderstanding could drive a wedge between them. It seemed the year for it.

Something burned him, however, a pang like ice and fire at once. He stood up, facing into the bitter wind, and the pain centered just above his heart.

"Papa?" his son said, breaking the spell of maturity. It was the child asking, plaintively, worriedly: "Papa?"

Tristen was there, and it was no gentle touch. Cefwyn clenched the amulet under the layers of cloth, and his heart beat high, like a commitment to battle.

Tristen was suddenly on his way out of Ynefel—he had not made the motion, until now, but Tristen was coming, he was as certain of it as if Tristen had suddenly glanced at him within the same room. Tristen had looked toward him, and perhaps just now guided those last things he had told his son.

He suddenly had the notion Tristen had delayed his departure—delayed, first to guide Elfwyn to Henas'amef and last, to bring him and Ninévrisë both safely out of Guelessar, with their respective children.

Now Tristen sent him a warning, an acute warning, and moved eastward in haste.

"Why?" he asked, gazing into the dark, the other side of the fire.

But he had no answer.

"Papa?"

"We shall ride before daylight," Cefwyn said, clenching his hand on his son's arm. "The horses have to rest. Get to your blankets and sleep while you can."

ii

THE BED WAS WARM AND SOFT, AND THE BEDCLOTHES, RENEWED TODAY AS every day, smelled of lavender, an herb Gran had grown in her garden. It should have been a pleasant smell. It touched painful memory, of herbs that had hung from the rafters above a soft feather bed, their own bed, beside which Gran had died. It was a short, dark tumble from that scent to horrid memory and the pain of burns far from healed.

Sleet hit the windows, a winter that never seemed to give up. It had sounded like that in Guelessar, when he had never in his life heard the sound of ice striking glass. Happiness had been all in front of him then, spread out like a banquet. He'd had no idea that it would all go so wrong.

Elfwyn buried his head deep in the crook of his arm and hauled the bedclothes over his ears, but that arrangement rapidly grew too warm.

He kept seeing the shelves and shelves of books, and with them *The Red Chronicle,* and its dreadful story. He wondered if Aewyn knew it, if Aewyn knew about this kinsman of his and kept it secret from him, fearing, perhaps, for their friendship—

Silly, he said to himself. He was Aswydd, no kin at all to the dead Sihhë King. The first Elfwyn had been no relation whatsoever to the Aswydds.

Had he?

He outright didn't know. He could ask Lord Crissand, he supposed. But if that information was here, it was surely in that book, for him to find if he kept at it. The tale of the Marhanen warlord might lead down to his own father's generation and give him all the connections.

He remembered the shadows in the library, and his decision to go home. He had been so tired, and he could no longer remember what had finally made him leave. He had set the candle down, then realized he had to pass the haunt, but he had gotten home safely, anyway.

Had he locked the door?

Had he locked the door? He remembered blowing the candle out and setting the stub on the ledge. But he had promised the old man, in return for the privilege of the library, that he would lock the door.

Surely no one would get in there, only to steal a book, in just the few hours until morning. It was cold, and it was quiet in the halls, and he would have to get out of a warm bed and wake Paisi, all to go down there.

But the old man would get back in the morning and find that door unlocked, and he would know who had done it.

Surely he had locked it.

But he could not remember even taking the key from his purse.

He stuck a foot out, and another, and slipped from the bed. He hadn't undressed, more than to take off his coat and belt and boots—the country habit, though lords did differently. He hadn't waked Paisi, getting up. He quietly located his coat in the dim light of the banked fire in the other room, found his boots in the shadow of the bed, his belt, with the purse and the key, hanging from the chair at the table, and dressed.

Then he as quietly left, taking the same route he had used coming home, and this time he did run, on tiptoe, and lightly. No one was about the upper hall—no guards or even servants visible at this hour. He ran upstairs at the end of his hall, the circuitous route, and along the servants' hall, where not even the servants were stirring. He ran down the dark little stairway to the library hall without ever passing the haunt or his mother's guards.

The servants had renewed the candles: only one burned, in this area, and a new one, white and unburned, stood on the ledge. He tried the door latch, and it did open: he had not, indeed, locked it, and he began to reach for the key to lock it safely, then take himself back upstairs to his warm bed as quickly as he could.

But he hadn't proved that the library was still safe. He didn't know if anyone had gotten inside, did he?

He took the new candle and went to the midpoint of the short hall, lit it from the single burning candle in its sconce, and brought it back again. He opened one eagle door carefully, wide-awake now, and held the candle aloft to see if there might be any disturbance of things as he had left them.

A sudden draft blew his candle out. His heart skipped a beat. Only a draft, he said to himself. It was only the door being so narrowly open.

Something glowed red, in the deep dark near where he had sat—a glow like a windblown coal where it ought not to be, but not well-defined, either. The light was diffuse, like a ward, with a solid center. It was a color he had only seen in the tangled Lines in the Quinaltine, where horrid things had warred to get out.

He waited in the doorway, with his dead candle. He was afraid even to breathe, and tried to tell himself the light was his imagination but it persisted, cold red fire, when the Lines of the room itself failed to appear, or were so dim, beside that glow, that his eyes failed to see them.

It wasn't right. Something in that area wasn't at all right, and it came from underneath the bookshelves, from underneath a table, the counter on which that small bookcase rested. He could see wards. Not everyone could. If something was wrong, he had to know where it was, to report it.

He took a few steps forward, gently letting the door shut, in the draft that blew. He walked a few paces to the side to find the source of the light.

Right underneath the shelf that held the book he had been reading, and right beside the table where the *History of Amefel* still rested—something was there, something that, for no conscious reason, terrified him. It glowed like one baleful eye, of something which, if it were a beast, was too large to be in the room.

His ring tingled. But it protected him. He kept an eye on the glow and saw it neither grow nor shrink as he edged around two tables away, with those barriers between him and it, and looked under all, to see nothing but a glowing spot on the plaster.

It was something that wanted to be found, there was no other way to think of it: he had felt a need today to be at that table, that shelf, and he had sat there reading, searching, had he not? But he had never found what satisfied him, not even reading on into the dark.

He squatted, below the level of the tables and watched it, and moved forward one table, on his knees.

What glowed was not in the room. It was behind the plaster, as if a fire burned there. It was everything he wanted. It made no sense, but he knew it was. He crept all the way to that wall, and touched the plaster, feeling nothing but the tingle of the ring on his finger, and an answering tingle from what was behind the wall.

He had no tool to use, could think of none in the library that he had seen. He took off his belt and tried the only metal he had about him, the capped end of his belt, against the plaster, which was soft, but it was not nearly soft enough, and it would take time. He had marked the place—he could find it, even if the glow vanished with light, and now he sought to find a sharper tool somewhere in the room.

He crawled out, went to the fireside, and took a sharp bit of kindling from the little pile of wood that fed the library fireplace, but that would not be sharp or stout enough. He cast it into the coals in frustration, then, indeed, the fireplace poker offered itself. He took it, and brought it back to the counter, and knelt and dug into the plaster.

Powder fell onto the stones, damning evidence. He knew—he knew in the back of his mind that if he didn't get this thing now, before the librarian came in, he could never get at it. He could pile books there. If he got whatever it was and got out, he could pile books where the plaster had fallen and conceal the hole. Hadn't Paisi had taught him how to go quietly, how to cover his traces? Paisi had said he was teaching him hunting and woodcraft, but Paisi had confessed that he had been a thief, when there had been only Paisi to support Gran, and Paisi had said he could be a thief, for a good reason—

He had to be, now. It was his *need* to have what was buried here; it was his *right* to have it, when fate and his mother's spite had taken every other thing away from him. If he and Paisi were to find their way in the world, he had to know all the truths people kept from him, and he had to protect them both, the way Paisi had protected Gran as long as he could. Now it was his mother's sorcery that threatened their lives, and he had to have this thing to protect them all, before his mother's spite could do worse to them than it had already done . . .

He reached stone, and where mortar should have been, found only more soft plaster binding the stones together. He dug out one ill-set stone, and opened a hole where light failed to reach, and a small glow within. It died like a fading coal. He extended the poker into the darkness, and disturbed something hard and light, that lifted a little and slipped back in. The poker felt only cold to the touch when he drew it out.

He reached into the gap blindly, fearing to touch he knew not what noxious thing, but feeling he must. His fingers found a little flat and very dusty packet.

Carefully he worked it about and drew it and his hand out of the narrow gap undamaged.

He turned around, sat angling his prize toward the starlight from tall, uncurtained windows. It was a codex, scarcely bigger than his palm.

He clambered back to his feet and opened the little book in the middle, but there was not enough light on this side of the room to read what was in it. He took it to the fireside, where the stick he had thrown in had taken light.

The letters crawled in front of his eyes, refusing to take shape, as if tears blinded him, or as if his eyes had grown as dim as Gran's.

He felt the burning of his mother's attention, felt it bearing down his back, as if she were standing there right at his back.

Get it! she seemed to say to him, as fiercely as she had ever spoken. You've gone this far. Now bring it to me.

"Boy," another voice seemed to say to him—a faint, far voice, that for all the world was Gran's.

He looked up. He saw Gran, standing right there, like a figure in smoke. "Boy, don't dare let her have it."

He felt as if he were smothering, as if he could not get his next breath. The fire crackled and snapped, and part of the stick fell, flaring bright flame as it did.

Fear became horrid and acute, choking him. He shut the little book in fear, and at his next blink, Gran wasn't there. She never had been there, he thought. It was his mother who had put this shameful theft into his head, this fever like the grip of a nightmare, that he now knew wasn't right—it was his mother that had come whispering into his ear, encouraging his fears, telling him the truth could be had, and that the truth would save him and all he loved . . . it was a lie. It was all a lie, and he had looked at the book, and the letters wouldn't take shape for him.

Vision was the word; had not Tristen said that? Vision.

Knowledge. Answers held from him all his life. Dark places. The more he tried to see, frantic with fear, the more he couldn't remember the other word, and couldn't think what he ought to do with this thing he had brought into the light, except something that looked and sounded like Gran had said not to obey his mother.

A book, a book, for the gods' sweet sake, exactly what one would expect in a library, a little codex that could be hidden so easily among all these books and stacks, but for some reason, and by some one, it had been hidden in a wall instead. And for all the years of his life, his mother had made no requests for any material thing, but she wanted this—this, after a decade and more without a request.

Just holding it now made his hand tingle, and made the ring on his finger glow soft, safe blue, not the baleful red of the glow he had followed. It seemed safer, by that, in his hand, than it had been where he had found it. When he had touched Tristen's wards, it had felt like that, the tingling, and his heart had raced, had it not? It was only fear.

He felt a prickling at his nape. His mother still watched him. His mother *wanted* him, suddenly raged at him, like a silent shriek . . . but Gran had said, still quietly, as she did all things—no.

His mother should not have it. There was nothing good his mother wanted in the world, and if her desire had driven him to such behavior—and if she wanted this little book now, then he had to prevent it getting to her. He could put it back where he had found it. But shoving it back into the wall would never serve, not after all the damage he had done, and the plaster tracked about. The librarian would go to Lord Crissand, and Lord Crissand would want to see the object of his mad search, and once it was in the open, it was apt to theft by anybody else his mother might move, like a precious jewel left lying undefended in the street.

Footsteps sounded in the hall, in such great stillness, more than one footfall. His pounding heart leapt with a second fright, and he froze where he stood, then realized that the firelight he had roused might show through the seam of the doors and in those tall, uncurtained windows. Someone might wonder. Someone might open that door.

He had the key. He fumbled after it, and moved stealthily to the door and locked it from the inside. The lock clicked like the crack of doom, and he froze, scarcely daring breathe.

But what was he doing? He had the key. The librarian had allowed him to be here. He could face Lord Crissand's guards and tell them—tell them he had come down to borrow a book.

And say what, about the plaster?

The footsteps reached the door. He heard muffled voices, and his heartbeat thumped in his ears, so that he hadn't good sense. The latch moved.

And stopped, against the lock.

"We better get the captain," someone said outside.

And the footsteps went away.

He had been a complete fool. He had dug this thing out, and now there was no concealing it, no time to hide his work, or the white plaster tracked across the floor. He wanted only to get this thing away and hide it until Lord Tristen arrived, or, failing that, he wanted to think it through before he confessed to Duke Crissand.

And things could go wrong. His mother could make things go wrong. He felt her attention, and her anger on him, burning and furious, and seeking some way to set everything on end and get her hands on what he had. She might have gotten him here—with the guards out and about on a search he might even get to her stairs. She could arrange that.

But she could not make him bring it to her. No.

The footsteps were gone. She could make them turn back. She'd already reached out of the wards to harm Gran, and he might be the only soul in the Zeide keep aware enough to defy her . . .

He unlocked the door, ducked out into the dim hallway, and had the presence of mind to lock it back to delay pursuit. His heart pounded against his ribs. At any moment the guards could come back, and lies and misdirection were his only cover if they did catch him. With a trembling hand he extracted the key from the grip of the lock, then turned and ran down the hall, up the dark servants' stairs, breathless. His mother wanted him, wanted *the book,* all the while his mother knew exactly where he was—knew, and directed things awry.

He raced down the upper hall as stealthily as he could. He reached his own door, dashed in, closed the door, and shot the bar.

"What ha' ye done?" Paisi asked, from out of the shadows, and he spun against the door.

"I don't know," he said in despair, pressing the tiny book to his chest. "I don't know."

"What ha' ye got there?"

"I don't know that, either."

"Lad, lad—ha' ye completely lost your senses?"

"I may have," he said, overwhelmed. "The guards are in the library by now, and my mother—my mother—wants this. She'll get it, Paisi. And she mustn't have it. I don't know anything else, but she mustn't have it."

"Well, shall ye go rouse up 'Is Grace an' gi' it to *him?*"

"No," he said, suddenly sure, as if he were toeing the edge of a precipice, and this book the only thing that kept his balance on it. "No. To Lord Tristen. We have to get it to him."

"Well, 'e's comin' *here*, ain't he? So's we can just wait."

"We can't wait." He left the door, brushed his way past Paisi, and snatched up his cloak. "Paisi. Help me. We have to get out of here, and they'll be here, they'll be here any moment."

"Aye," Paisi said, stung into action. "Who'll be here?"

"Lord Crissand's guards."

"Do we run for it, then, m'lord?"

"We have to." He pinned his cloak on. He snatched up his gloves and his dagger while Paisi was putting on his own cloak. He remembered the key, then, and took the time to turn it out of his purse, and leave it on the dining table, his one gesture toward honesty. The ring should go with it. But the ring, Lord Crissand's pass, was their way out. "I have His Grace's ring. I can get our horses from the stable if we just hurry."

"I take it we ain't findin' Lord Tristen too easy," Paisi said.

"We do as we can."

"Then we better have food," Paisi said. "Food's what ye think of when ye're deep into things and don't know how long."

"Don't go asking," he begged Paisi, and Paisi shot back:

"Who said askin'? I'll get it, m'lord. Gettin' away is one thing, but apples an' turnips ain't in season out there in the woods. Ye get on to the stables, an' ye act the lord and get the night boy to get them horses out, an' gods help us, is all—hurry, is it? Was they chasin' ye when ye run?"

"They don't know who was there," he said. That, at least, was true, he was sure of it. No one had seen him. "But the librarian knows where the key is, and they won't be long figuring out I did it."

"I don't understan' ye a bit," Paisi said, "but that ain't no matter: I never understood Lord Tristen, neither, when 'is notions took 'im, an' if we got to find 'im in the mid of the night, I'll wager there's 'is doin' in it somewheres. Come on, lad."

He wished it were so simple. He wished it were Lord Tristen who had driven him, sweating and crazed, to steal what he had just stolen. Or that he had time to explain his fears and his choice to Paisi. But Paisi was right: every moment made it more likely his mother would get her way, and he couldn't explain: when his mother wanted something, they'd had the cruel proof just how far she could reach. She had grown stronger, or hidden her strength. And it wasn't distance that would save them. It was speed, before she could work her spells and draw someone else to help her. It was a stronger shelter, a protection Lord Crissand couldn't offer this book, or them.

They left the room, and Paisi reached past him to shut the door, normal as could be: he understood Paisi's signal to be calm, to do things at a reasonable pace. It seemed forever, the little distance to the servants' stairs at this end of the hall, but then Paisi hurried, down and down to the main floor—while all the other end of the hall, down toward the library, with light flaring off the walls, rang with voices and the shadowed movement of guards.

"Stay with me!" he begged Paisi. "Never mind the food!"

"Kitchens," Paisi hissed, and dived off down the stairs in that direction, where the kitchen hall diverged from the outbound door. He had no way to stop Paisi, only his own part to do.

He shoved the heavy door open and went out into snowfall, a white haze that haloed the single torch that burned in the kitchen yard. Remembering how Paisi proceeded, he made a careful descent of the icy steps, down to the yard, where he couldn't but leave tracks. So he strode boldly across the yard to the stables.

A single guarded light burned inside the warm, horse-smelling dark. He went down the aisle until he found the stall the stableboy used for his cot, and there he gathered up his courage, took a deep breath, and roused the boy out.

"My horse and my servant's," he said to the boy, lordlike, trying to keep a steady voice, and showed the duke's ring on his ungloved hand. "I'm Elfwyn Aswydd. This is His Grace's ring."

The boy might never have seen the duke's ring, or know what it permitted, but it was silver, it was bright in the shadow, and Aswydds ruled in Amefel. The boy looked doubtful, and afraid, then rubbed his eyes and moved, not sluggardly, despite being roused out of bed and with his shirt hanging.

He couldn't seem a lord and saddle his own horse. That was the difficulty in his plan, that he had to stand and wait, all the while dreading the approach of the guards, who might already have caught Paisi in the kitchens. Sorcery bent things. It moved a breeze to move a leaf to attract attention or sent a wayward thought to turn a guard's head, and his mother had stopped raging, now and gotten down to other means, the subtler, distant ways he was sure she had used to damn him in Guelessar . . . she was down to sorcery, now. And how did he even hope he could outride her intent to have this thing, or steal this little book out of her grasp?

Why had she wanted him back in Amefel? It wasn't love.

Why had she killed Gran and given him no other place to be?

Why had the librarian trusted him, a newcomer, to give him a key he hadn't even known to ask for?

He stood while the boy saddled Feiny, then led him into the aisle.

Swift, single footsteps approached, outside, and the door opened. It was Paisi, Elfwyn saw to his profoundest relief, Paisi carrying a heavy white bag, and passing the laboring stableboy as if what was going on in the middle of the night was absolutely as it ought to be.

"I got it, m'lord," Paisi said, handing him the bag. "You hang on to this, an' I'll help the boy."

It speeded matters. Paisi led up Tammis for him to hold the halter rope, and helped the boy finish up with Feiny's complex harness, then ordered the boy to open the stable doors.

The boy opened one door. It was enough. Paisi took the flour sack, slung it over Tammis's withers, and they mounted up, Elfwyn struggling for the stirrup—he had learned how to reach it and pull himself up; and Paisi gave a hop and was up, bareback. They rode out of the stable yard and onto the snow-buried courtyard.

At the iron gates that barred their way to the town, Paisi rang the little bell, a small, terrifying sound that brought the night watch out into the falling snow.

"Aswydd business," Paisi said, and Elfwyn boldly showed the ring toward the lamplight.

There might at any moment be a search of their room, a search leading eventually down to the stables, out into the same courtyard. But the night guards had to get on their working gloves and move the heavy iron latch, which shrieked aloud in the quiet, and heave one frozen gate open, cracking ice off the hinges.

They rode out into the upper town, took the road to the town gate, and struck a quick pace.

"There's bells they can ring," Paisi said anxiously. "There's the thief bell can stop the town gate from openin' until they ask up the hill. We got to hurry, lad."

The fine snow obscured all but the nearer buildings, and wrapped them in white as they put the horses beyond safe speed on the downhill course, but there was no traffic at all, only a shutter or two flung open in curiosity at the noise, and most shut with a thump soon after.

They reached the gate, and the gate-guards had heard them coming.

"Aswydd business," Paisi said crisply, and the guards saw the ring Elfwyn showed and gave way to it, shoving hard to open the little sally port against the new snow.

The sally port was enough for two riders. They ducked through singly and picked up the pace, quitting the vicinity of the gate as fast as they could. Snow wrapped them about, and still no bell sounded.

Paisi might indeed ask him, now that they were away, why they ran. He was less and less sure he knew the answer, except he had gone mad for the moment, and panicked, and the terror of his mother's sorcery grew less with every stride the horses took.

Fear had driven him. Fear had taken away Guelemara, and now it had taken his own town, and with Gran gone, fear behind him was all he had left for a guide.

iii

THERE WAS A DISTURBANCE OF SOME KIND, SOME RACKET FAR AWAY IN THE apartment, which roused Crissand from his wife's side. She slept, but he leaned on one arm, sure he had heard something, and grew surer still, when he heard the sounds of quiet debate, far off in his chambers . . . debate, then very quiet footsteps and a mouselike knock at the door.

Crissand got out of bed, reached for his dressing robe: Cenas, his valet, had already let himself in, and soft-footed it over to him.

"My lord, a difficulty with your guest," Cenas whispered. "He's gone."

His heart sank. "Gone where?" he whispered back.

"The gates, as seems," Cenas said, then hastened to stay with him as Crissand strode out the door and down the hall, wrapping his dressing robe about him and still barefoot.

The night duty captain was there, with another guardsman, grim-faced and still a little diffident.

"What's the matter?" he asked them sharply. "What's this, gone?"

"Your Grace, the boy, the boy who carries your ring—"

"My cousin," Crissand said sharply. "What of him?"

"He's taken to horseback," the captain said. "He and his man. He was in the library—"

"The library?"

"A fire was burning there, late, and when the guard roused out the librarian and investigated, for the safety of the premises, Your Grace—"

"What has this to do with my cousin?"

"He had one of the keys. Your Grace, there was plaster, loose plaster, and a hole dug under a counter, right through the wall. And the fire was burning."

On the surface, it was ridiculous. The whole story was ridiculous. But there had been a dark deed in the library, the murder of an elderly librarian, the flight of a thief, the burning of certain wizardly manuscripts—Mauryl Gestaurien's, no less. They had thought they had recovered the remainder, those that had been carried off. He rubbed his face, asking himself if he had slipped in time, in a dream that had subtly changed the shape of things.

"And the librarian said he didn't know, that there were four keys, and he had one, and you another, my lord, Master Rue the third, and your cousin— your cousin the fourth. So we went upstairs. No one was there, and the fire was left burning in the hearth . . ."

"Plague take the fire! Where is my cousin?"

"We looked to the kitchens, where boys do go, Your Grace—"

"Go on."

"And found tracks in the snow, from the side entry and from the kitchens, both to the stables, and the night watch had saddled their horses. The boy showed your ring."

"Clever lad," Crissand said, with a sinking heart.

"And they went out the town gate, the same way. It's come on a blizzard, Your Grace. It's snowing to beat all."

"It would," he said. "Double the watch on the tower. Search Lady Tarien's room for any book or scroll or scrap of parchment. Whatever you find, take charge of, keep, and throw her in irons if you find any such thing. Tell her nothing. Nothing! Meanwhile, get my horse and get the guard out to ride with me. Good gods, why didn't you rouse me before this? Which direction did he go? Has anyone looked out to find the tracks?"

"The gate-guard didn't say, Your Grace."

"Damn!"

"Your Grace," the captain protested, but Crissand stalked back to his bedchamber, the servant chasing him and calling on others to wake.

Clever, clever boy, he said to himself. *Snowing heavily, no report on where he'd gone, and no tracks left by now.* Elfwyn had searched for something lost before he was born, something no one expected ever to find, and, if the recovered books were any guide, he had looked for something that any witch or wizard would give his soul to obtain.

Then he'd run, whether or not he had found what he was looking for.

But there was the ring. There was that, once he wondered about it, and once he simply wanted to know. Tristen had bound it to him in that way, so that his idlest wondering would find it, if he wished.

The boy had gone west. No question.

iv

SNOW, SNOW SO THICK IN THE DRIVING WIND THAT IT WHITED OUT ALL THE world, and it was only themselves, and the horses. They moved, and seemed to go nowhere at all, like a dream of pursuit in which one could not gain, only lose. The only measure of distance was the anger that came at them from behind, sorcerous anger, sorcerous desire, so dark and hot a passion it burned through the cold, and snarled even conscious thought into a tangle of guilt and uncertainty.

Elfwyn glanced back from time to time to be sure at least of Paisi, riding near him; but the cold and the wind discouraged any attempt he made to speak, or explain. Paisi had never questioned him, beyond knowing that the guards were after him for theft, and he didn't know how he would explain to Paisi what had driven him to this extremity, or why he was so sure this thing, this horrid thing, would reach to his mother if it stayed where it was. She might have lied and murdered and prodded and tormented him into laying hands on it for her, but she could not get up him those stairs.

But someone else could bring it into her reach. And Crissand would blame him. His mother's spite would whisper into Crissand's dreams at night, reminding him that his guest had lied, and stolen, and deserved only his contempt. Things would happen, until Crissand believed it, and worse and worse happened.

He should take off the ring Crissand had given him, the thing Crissand had said would betray him if he betrayed Crissand's trust. He should take it off and fling it into a snowbank, but it was a precious thing, and in his keeping; most of all it was Tristen's magic, not his mother's sorcery, and he was not sure but what it was the protection that had let him, however belatedly, recover his wits and run away. It might even be leading him to Tristen.

And if it had any power, he should try to use it. Shivering and blasted by the wind, he tried to marshal his thoughts, and to tell the friendly powers of the world, as best he could, that he was no thief: he muttered into the wind, "Lord Tristen, can you hear me? Can you find us? We can't see, we can't find our way, and my mother wants this thing I have. I think it belongs to you. Maybe I should never have taken it, but now it has to come to you. Please answer me."

But no answer came.

Maybe, he thought, he should just have left a note in his room, explaining all he could. But he had thought only of running. He had left the key, of all things, but never a word to explain himself. It was too late for all second choices. And it was wizard writing in the book. And hadn't Gran always said that such things had a mind of their own, a way of getting where they wanted to be, when they wanted to go? There was his mother's will, and there might be the book's own inclination, this *thing* that rode against his heart, urgently needing to be somewhere else, perhaps back with Tristen.

Are we so sure? a voice said to him. Is this thing leading us to him, or wide astray in this storm? Has it urged us to honesty? Has it led us to any good act?

Maybe he could have stayed where he was and sent Paisi with the book. He could lie to Crissand. He could even tell the truth. But the book would be away from his mother.

No. He would not have sent Paisi alone with this thing. Paisi had always taken care of him, but now, all of a sudden, he found himself trying to protect Paisi, and taking care of him, and he could never ask Paisi to take on his mother, which was what it would amount to. His mother might try to stop him, might try to kill him, for all he knew, but she would not come at Paisi—he would not let her come at Paisi, come what might.

A blast of sleet-edged wind came right in their faces. It made Feiny veer. He fought the horse full circle, then reined back the way he thought they had been going, and kicked him into motion in the direction he felt was west. Then he looked back to be sure he and Paisi kept the same course.

With a chill straight to his heart, he saw nothing but snowy murk, not even the ground he was riding over.

"Paisi?" he called out into the night. And shouted, over the blast of the wind, "Paisi!"

The wind howled, and skirled sharp-edged sleet around them. There was neither up nor down in the murk, and no answer came to him, none at all.

V

HOURS ON THE SEARCH, AND NO TRACES IN THE WIND-DRIVEN SNOW. THE STORM had blown past, but covered all tracks. Crissand was chilled through, his men likewise. A flask went the rounds, but it lent only false warmth, a comfort for the moment, and a cure for raw throats.

There had been three choices, the ruins of the farm; the highroad back to Guelessar, toward Cefwyn, which seemed unlikely for a boy running from theft; or the way west, the way that Tristen would come, and Crissand's every impulse, every wondering about the ring, the boy, and his reasons, had laid his wager firmly on the latter, not even stopping to investigate the ruin.

Now, however, the surety he had felt in his choice of directions abruptly faded, leaving, like most magical touches, only a vague conviction that one's reason had been unreasonably overset, and that choices previously made were all folly and unproven. Before, the fact that there had been no tracks could be blamed on the wind; afterward, Crissand could only wish he had in fact investigated the farm before leading four good men out into a driving snow.

But he knew the tendencies of things magical, and since they had come this far, he told his men they should press on as far at least as Wye Crossing—this to encourage them that there was a sure limit to his madness, and that they would get back to warm quarters before they froze.

But when the snow turned out to have made drifts across the road short of their mark, and chilled and weary men, however brave, hesitated and reined about in dismay, it seemed time to reconsider even that. Nothing had broken those drifts, not since they had begun to form.

Folly, Crissand thought now. He had made the wrong choice. The ring had misled him. It meant the boy to escape. It might even be Tristen's doing. He hoped that it was. He refused to think any magic could overwhelm what had been his own guide and talisman all these years.

But he felt a little less safe in his long-held assumptions, where he sat, on a cold and unwilling horse.

Then from across the snowy flat of the surrounding meadows, out of a little spit and flurry of snow in the dark, a rider appeared and advanced steadily toward them.

"It could be a haunt," one of his guard said, and his captain: "Hush, man. Don't be a fool. We're out here searchin' for riders, aren't we?"

A figure muffled in a cloak and atop a winter-coated, snow-caked, and piebald horse, as if he had ridden straight out of the blizzard of several hours ago. There was reason his guard viewed this arrival in alarm. It wasn't ordinary, that rider. It looked white in patches, itself, in the ambient snow light.

And it kept coming toward them, not down the road, as they believed the road to lie, but from across the fields.

"Halt there!" his captain called out. "This is His Grace the duke of Amefel! Who are you?"

"Paisi, Elfwyn Aswydd's man," the answer came strongly enough, then, distressedly: "Your Grace, Your Grace, gods save me, I've lost 'im. An' all the food is with me!"

CHAPTER SEVEN

i

THEY HAD HASTENED ALL THE WAY, HAD PRESSED THE HORSES HARD. THEY HAD looked to stop at Gran's for the night—but the closer they rode, the more stranger and more ominous things seemed. Gran's chimney did not appear at the turning where it ought.

And when Cefwyn rode past that turning, with his son and his guard, the house was all ashes and timbers, its yard gate open to the road.

Aewyn rode ahead, plunged off his horse, and had gotten to a dangerous place among the timbers before the guards overtook him, and Cefwyn had.

"His dreams!" Aewyn cried. "Papa, his dreams!"

"Hush," Cefwyn said, laying a hand on his son's back. "Hush. They may have escaped."

"Here's horse tracks, Your Majesty," a man said, back by the shed, which had survived half-burned. The ashes, the burned beams, cool now, supported a load of new snow. But Cefwyn went out, taking Aewyn with him, and sure enough, where the remnant of a roof had partially sheltered the ground, tracks showed. At least one man had walked here. So had a horse. And there were no remains—there was evidence of horses in the shed, but no remains.

"They may well have gotten out," Cefwyn said. And, squeezing Aewyn's shoulder: "They would have gone to the town for help. Let us go."

Aewyn ran back to his horse and climbed into the saddle, impatient until they were under way, jaw clenched, trying to hold his distress like a man. He spoke hardly a word—no one did, until they came within sight of the town.

The day's sun was sinking fast and the horses were hard-used before the walls of Henas'amef rose distinct above the snowy fields—only one gate was open, and men were out with shovels, digging clear a path for the gates to swing. The odd, west-sweeping storm that had made yesterday's travel a trial had unloaded about walls and gates, reason enough for a crew to be out shoveling.

The gate-guards had joined the work party, and at first stood stiff with alarm as they spied a determined party of riders flattening a broader track through the snow, but Cefwyn had ordered the banners out, and the gate-guards no more than stood to attention, and laborers swept off their hats and cowls, Amefin folk, but never in these years hostile to their king. Cefwyn had no hesitation in riding close by these men with his son. A bell started to toll, the gate bell, advising the town and the hill above of arrivals worth attention.

"We shall have a hot drink with my brother," Aewyn said doggedly. His son was white about the lips and cold-stung, ruddy above—a weary, desperate boy who nevertheless had endured a ride hard even for well-exercised guardsmen, with bad news at the end of it. Cefwyn found he had been far too long in chairs instead of the saddle, and far too long eating too much fine food, and he was glad enough to think of shelter over their heads tonight, where he hoped to find at least some good news. But there was that tall, ghostly tower, which vanished behind brick and stone as they rode through the gates. It loomed above them, like a living presence.

An unannounced royal visit had a certain bitter history in this province—people who stopped their late business on the street stared not only with astonishment, but in stark dismay. It was a very different feeling than they had had coming here in summer, well heralded and with Lord Crissand to meet them at the gates in festivity, with Gran's place safe and welcoming. This was a suspicious town, an Amefin, Bryalt town, where loyalty to the Marhanen ran only so deep, and once Guelen riders passed the walls, they were scrutinized . . . particularly if things had gone wrong here.

He didn't think his son had ever encountered that sort of examination from anyone, let alone found it meeting them up and down the street. Aewyn had fallen grimly silent, and looked anxiously to left and right of them as they rode up the hill, past shuttered windows and occasional spying from the narrowest crack.

The gate-guards above, however, those at the Zeide gate, were instant to open and clear their way in complete compliance, and the ringing of a bell at that gate brought not only servants, but Lord Crissand himself, running out cloakless, despite the snow.

"Your Majesty," Crissand said, starting to kneel below Cefwyn's stirrup, but Cefwyn dropped down to his feet and snatched him up by the arms before he could do it. "Your Majesty," Crissand said, out of breath, "your son was here. He has left."

"Gran's farm was burned."

"Burned, yes. And Gran is dead. But your son, and his man, they came here for shelter. They *were* here. Then your son left, in the middle of the storm."

"Yesterday."

"Yesterday, Your Majesty."

"Where did he go?" Aewyn asked, entirely out of turn, and Cefwyn drew a deep, carefully patient breath and asked the same question, in more courtesy.

"Do you know, my friend?"

"West," Crissand said with conviction. "His man Paisi came back. They were parted in the storm. Your son carried my ring. I gave him that . . . I wrote to Your Majesty . . ."

"Best discuss it inside," Cefwyn said. Crissand was freezing, shivering in the cold wind, clearly full of news they needed, and much as his heart wanted to go chasing off after the boy, the horses were done. He was done. Certainly Aewyn must be. And even if they were to leave on a further search tonight, they would have to supply themselves off Crissand's resources, saddle new horses, and perhaps go out with Paisi to guide them. If the boy had been gone a day, there was no chasing him. Tracks would be covered.

"Your Majesty," Crissand said, and led them up into the fortress itself by the side entry, up steps made both foul and passable by ash and sand, a black area that had frozen into ice all about the steps. It had the feeling of times past, of another winter when the snow had kept coming, and things had gone vastly awry.

Tristen was coming. He believed it. He cast Otter's welfare on it . . . perhaps more than one Otter's welfare, counting the boy's connections to that tower above them. He did not want Aewyn exposed to risk, and the more calmly they dealt with this, the more he could settle his son to calm and reason.

They entered the lower hall, right beneath his old rooms, when he had been viceroy here, and walked down the hall to the little audience chamber, an intimate room with a good fireplace. Heat inside met them like a wall after so long in the cold.

"Find Paisi," Crissand said to one of his guards. "He's up in the boy's rooms. And get mulled wine up here. Tea, with it."

The man hastened, all but running back down the hall, shouting indecorously for servants and for a man to go find the witch's grandson; but before they had even shed their cloaks, Paisi himself showed up at the door.

"Come in, man," Crissand said. "Come in. You're wanted."

"M'lord," Paisi said, in a quiet, miserable voice.

"Your Majesty," Crissand said, and offered Cefwyn the seat from which Crissand himself would hold audiences in this room.

Cefwyn sat. He pointed Aewyn to the chair nearest, Crissand to a lordly seat opposite, and said to Crissand, "No ceremony, man, just the news, from the start. What happened here? Where did he go? Have you still got his mother?"

"Her, I have, Your Majesty," Crissand said, settling into a plain chair, and proceeded to tell him that Paisi's gran was dead in the fire, that Otter had violated the library and destroyed a wall, finding a book, to which Paisi could attest. Then Otter had taken off ahead of all inquiry, with Crissand's ring to ease the way, convinced that this newfound treasure should go to Lord Tristen.

"We met Paisi, coming back," Crissand said. "Paisi had lost him in the blizzard, and all my sense of where the ring was, had faded at what must have been the same time. I had no more indication where he might be, nor have, to this hour. I fear he might have traveled some distance, but I have no more sense where he is."

"Paisi," Cefwyn said. Paisi waited, standing, hands clasped, gripped on each other until the knuckles were white. "Have you anything to contribute?"

"Nothin', Your Majesty, only I'd ha' died before I'd ha' left 'im. He were goin' t' find Lord Tristen, was all he said. He said what he had, had to go to him."

"Not the worst notion," Cefwyn said, as much to comfort Aewyn as because he needed to say it to Crissand or to Paisi. "How did he find this thing?"

"One hardly knows," Crissand said, and Paisi, when Cefwyn looked at him:

"He was uneasy wi' his ma," Paisi said. "He was thinkin' because he'd told her Lord Tristen was comin', she'd took it out on Gran an' burned the house down, an' he said 't was his fault, which I said not, but he weren't easy in his mind. They was goin' to send the horses down t' winter pasture," Paisi added, apparently extraneously, "an' I ask't him, an' he said no, right sharp, then again, no, you was comin' an' Lord Tristen was comin' and there might be cause to need 'em, so I told the stablemaster to keep 'em here."

"When was this?"

"The day before. The day before that night."

"That night," Cefwyn said.

"He had a key to the library," Crissand said, "which the librarian gave

FORTRESS OF ICE

him, because he identified himself as Elfwyn Aswydd and had my ring for
authority. He read the *History of Amefel*. He was there all that day and
stayed after the librarian left."

"An' he come home, he drank wine, he didn't eat more 'n a bird, an' woke
out of bed," Paisi said, "whilst I was sleepin'. He went down there, and they
say he made a hole in the wall under a counter, and there was plaster all
over. All I know is, he come back wi' a book an' sayin' the guards was after
him. An' I should ha' done better, I know I should, Your Majesty, but 'e were
scairt, and sayin' that book had to get away from 'is ma, fast as it could."

"From his mother," Cefwyn said. "Was this what he said?"

"Aye, Your Majesty. An' bein' as I served Lord Tristen an' Master Emuin,
meself, I weren't inclined to ask too deep where it was any wizard writing—
if his ma wanted that thing and he wanted to go to Lord Tristen with it, says
I, better run for Lord Tristen. So we did. But we didn't never get there." Paisi
was, in his way, a hard man, from a hard life, and it was something that his
chin trembled when he said it. "The wind come between us, an' the snow
blew, and then he weren't there. I searched and searched, and I couldn't find
'im, an' I suppose he couldn't find me, neither, Your Majesty, because I know
he'd ha' tried."

"I've sent men to Marna today," Lord Crissand said, "attempting to get
through. As yet there's been no report, but there's not been time for it."

"You've done the best anyone could," Cefwyn said. A slow chill ran
through him when he contemplated the several branches of the facts at hand.
He sat in a room he well knew, in a seat he had occupied when he first laid
eyes on Tristen. In that hour he had looked into eyes that knew absolutely
nothing of the world of Men, the innocence, the absolute innocence he had
never met in man or child since. That gaze had challenged the validity of
everything he believed, made him question what he knew for real and just,
all those things, in the very hour he was warm and guilty from the Aswydd
women's bed—because Mauryl Gestaurien had called up a soul from out of
the dark, and clothed it in flesh, and sent Tristen into the world to confront
his enemy.

Mauryl's enemy, certainly. Mankind's enemy, by complete inconsequence,
he feared, to that entity—individual Men, that force swept aside as casually
as sweeping dust off the step. It was beyond dangerous, Tristen's enemy. It
was absolutely inimical to everything he loved, and he, and his, had been
in the way of it—it had tried to lay hands on the stolen books, he much
suspected—and the Aswydd woman, Elfwyn's mother, was only its hands
remaining in the world.

313

He'd never been as afraid as he had been in those days. He'd stared it down, on a battlefield in Elwynor. He'd risked everything on that field, and the next, and he'd won, instead, against all expectation, thanks to Tristen.

He had a lifelong friend in Tristen, a friend who'd been unable to stay in the world of Men simply because, in some ways, Tristen was still that innocent, that bewildered by petty wickedness, although he had been reborn to face something very, very dangerously wicked, supposing wickedness was even a word it understood.

Gran was dead, her protections evidently inadequate. And a book had gone missing, from a hiding place they had supposed empty, the books in question either destroyed or in Tristen's possession, at Ynefel. The boy was right: if, all protections fallen, he had found something of the sort, that was exactly where it belonged.

Breath in the room seemed very close at the moment. He looked into Paisi's eyes, and into Crissand's, no king in that moment, but a Man with other Men who'd seen the same improbable things he'd seen and carried the scars of it.

The amulet he wore gave no clue, no hint of a clue what was happening in the world, or where Tristen was.

Find him, he wished his old friend. *Find my son. Keep him safe. A book is loose in the world.*

And nothing answered that plea, not a whisper or a sensation.

"Your men will not arrest Otter, will they?" Aewyn asked, breaking the spell.

"By no means," Crissand said earnestly. "But persuade him to come back, that, if they can."

"I could persuade him," Aewyn said. "He would believe me."

"No," Cefwyn said, more sharply than he intended. He softened it immediately, seeing the shock on his son's face. "No. For his sake and yours." The thought of what they might be dealing with turned him cold as ice, and he reached a hand to his son's arm, wondering what he might do to occupy his son and keep him safe and busy, this close to Tarien Aswydd and without Tristen or Elfwyn to protect him. "Best you go to Captain Awen and get down to the kitchens: there's a good warm spot, and you can do as I used to do, nip a late meal from the cooks. See the men are fed. That's the job you can do for me."

"I don't want to be down in the kitchen! I want them to find my brother!"

"Well, they can't do it on empty stomachs and no rest, young sir, and don't dispute me in front of another lord, even if he is an old friend."

"Father," Aewyn said, looking quite undone, and having just let fly, when very good behavior had been the rule for two whole days, even when they had come on the ruin of Gran's farm. "Forgive me, sir." This last to Lord Crissand.

"Your Highness," Crissand said, with a sober nod of his head, and a very weary prince got up from a hard chair and limped on out the door, collecting his cloak as he left.

"The boys got on well," Cefwyn said, an understatement, in the boy's departure. "He's had a long, hard ride, he's seen unpleasant sights, and he's chilled through."

"Understandable in a grown man," Crissand said, formality gone.

"Paisi, sit down."

"Your Majesty." Paisi made that diffident little protest, but he sat down on the raised hearth of the fireside, without fuss or ceremony.

There were matters to discuss: old murders, old wars, in which they all three had had their part. An absent friend, who should have arrived much before this, if things were ordinary. Magic had that way about it: ordinary Men might be diverted by a stray breeze or a whim, but when the real storms of magic raged, determined Men, being blind to it, could sometimes blunder on by sheer will through forces that would stop a wizard cold.

Had he blundered through such opposition, he and his ungifted son, in getting here at all? Gran was dead. Crissand had had to turn back. Paisi, trying to track Elfwyn, had simply blinked and lost him into the night. And after, Crissand had lost all awareness where Elfwyn was. Crissand knew that situation, when magic moved things where they had never intended to be.

A Man fell right on through the sieve of magic and stood staring and wondering what was happening, when the shadow-ways were at issue. And gods knew where Elfwyn was now, or who had moved him. He only hoped it was Tristen himself; but Tristen, years ago, had not found the book his sorcerous-born son had found, despite his searching, and Tristen had greatly desired to find anything left of that cache, which no one had ever explained being there in the first place—not to mention the murder of one elderly librarian by another.

A book had been left, after all the murder and connivance. A book had been overlooked, forgotten, missed, even by Tristen himself.

That was not a good thing, either, not at all.

ii

CAST OUT, AFTER A REASONABLE OBJECTION, WAS AEWYN'S VIEW. OF COURSE HE knew the men were tired and his father was tired—and cross. He was tired and disappointed and vastly upset, and he had been a little forward, but he would go on and look for his brother, if anybody listened to him, and all that his father and Crissand were doing up there they could do on horseback, out looking in the meanwhile. This was a town. There were other horses. He was tired, but he could keep going. He hadn't meant to be disrespectful to his father, who often talked to Lord Crissand as if he were family . . . but he was right, and they weren't finding his brother, and he certainly didn't deserve to be sent down to the kitchens and shut out of any news they might get.

But his father being king, everyone had to obey him even if they didn't like it, and if his father said he was to see the men were fed, nobody else was going to do it if he didn't, and they would all suffer for it. So he walked on to the guard station where all the soldiers gathered—there were enough inside that they were spilling out into the hall and hanging in the doorway, exchanging rumors. They stood up straighter when he walked up.

"I'm to go with you to the kitchen and be sure you have your suppers," Aewyn said.

"Your Highness." There was complete attention from his father's guard.

"And sometimes staff knows things the lords don't," Aewyn added, "so we may learn something while we're there." He had learned that wisdom from Paisi, who despite his scruffy appearance and his southern speech, was a very wise and clever man. He had been a thief, and knew all sorts of ways to get past precautions and locks, and to go unseen.

And that thought put an idea in his head, a wicked and desperate idea, and one he knew would upset his father, but things were more desperate than anyone seemed willing to say. Paisi's gran was not just sick, as Otter—Elfwyn—had thought; she turned out to be dead in a fire, and Elfwyn had run off from Paisi, or Paisi hadn't been able to keep up with him, which was the same, so things couldn't wait until morning. Elfwyn never would part from Paisi, especially if something had happened to Gran . . . Elfwyn hadn't stolen any book because he was naturally a thief, or because Paisi was; he'd stolen it either because it was his, or because it was important for him to do that, and maybe even Lord Crissand wasn't supposed to have it in his possession.

Otter had gone to Lord Tristen and come back again, and maybe it was

Lord Tristen who had wanted him to do what he'd done and sent him here to do it. Wizards . . . and Lord Tristen was something more than a wizard . . . did things for reasons nobody could understand at the time, but it was for the good, if it was a good wizard doing it. The things Lord Tristen did were good things, white magic, hadn't his father told him that, and told him never to say that to the Quinalt brothers?

That was because Amefin folk and Elwynim did things differently from the start: they respected witches like Gran, they hung charms in their windows, which no Guelen dared do, and they danced at festival—altogether a wilder, freer folk than Guelens, in his estimation, and maybe one reason why he had always liked his brother, who was ever so ready to enter into a bit of mischief and never really feared any rebuke but Gran's. Who was dead. And it was very sure that whatever had caused that fire was not Lord Tristen, and was not friendly to his brother, who was alone out there.

He walked down the kitchen steps at the head of his father's towering, armored guard, and presented himself to the kitchen staff. "My father's guard wants supper, if you please, and hot tea and mulled ale." It was what they had ordered upstairs, and he knew the guardsmen would gladly agree to that. "And who is the chief cook?"

A white-bearded man came forward and bowed. "Prince Aewyn? May I serve?"

"That I am," he said. "And you may. My father and the duke are in conference upstairs, and my father wishes his men fed and comfortable."

"Your Highness." A gratifying bow, and a wave of his hand sent the staff into motion.

"And I personally wish to ask, sir, if you know why there would be a book in the wall of the library?"

The cook looked confused, entirely, and guiltily distressed. "Perhaps you could ask the librarian, Your Highness."

"I may. I wonder if you've heard anything about it. What *are* the rumors?"

"The rumors, now." The man wiped flour onto his apron, looking worried. "The rumors, Your Highness." He lowered his voice considerably, and took on a secretive look. "As there was a murder there, back in the last duke's time. One librarian killed the other, both old men, and books was missing, which never was found . . . except . . ."

"Except, sir?"

The man hesitated, and hesitated twice. "They was found last night, or at least . . . the boy, the Aswydd boy . . ."

"My half brother," Aewyn said, to help the narrative along.

"Yes, Your Highness. Rumor is he took 'em, and fled the town. His Grace went after, but only him an' the man came back, the witch's grandson."

"Paisi."

"Aye, Your Highness, Paisi. And neither hide nor hair of the Aswydd—your half brother, begging your pardon, Your Highness."

"No, no. I'm very anxious to hear every bit you know. Which way did he ride off?"

"West, as seems. Thinkin' is, with *her* up there—" The cook gave an uneasy glance over his shoulder and up, as if the tower threatened above him. "Whatever it was, he went west, and maybe south, too, maybe to Marna, as nobody can guess. Things finds their way to Marna, if they have to. That's the rumor, that."

"Very good," he said, as if he were his uncle hearing a case: he was disappointed that it was no more than his father had found out upstairs. "Very well." He nodded, to send the man off, then, seeing that the men were entirely interested in the pouring of ale and the heating of an iron, over at the side of the little kitchen, he simply went back up the stairs, put on his cloak, and took his gloves from his belt.

The kitchen stairs led up right near the western door of the fortress, the little, informal door that led to the sooted steps that led down to the stable, and many people might come and go by it. He put the hood up as he left the bottom of the steps and crossed the yard, taking advantage of the weather, and he moved as Elfwyn had shown him how to move, not like a hunter, darting and stopping, but like a person on perfectly ordinary and lawful business. Paisi had taught Elfwyn, and Elfwyn had taught him, and now it became useful.

He slipped into the stable yard, where the stablemaster and his boys were tending the Guard horses, and on inside, where his and his father's fine horses were afforded stalls and special care.

The horses they had come on were much too tired to go on, and only great good luck would get him through the Zeide gate and through the gate below on horseback at all, so it was no good taking one of the others. He simply took one of the guardsmen's bridles, as an inconspicuous and average sort of bridle, with enough adjustment for whatever he might catch down in the fields. He took bait, a little worn sacking from a peg, with several dippers full of grain, and stuffed it into his coat, then simply slipped out the lesser front door of the stable and walked to the gate, where he had to have his best lie ready. He was carrying a message to a cobbler, to arrange mending for the visitors' boots . . . none of the guards might recognize him, if he kept his hood on, covering fair Guelen hair.

But a handbarrow was coming in, it seemed, and the guards were engaged with the man bringing it. So he took his luck as a good sign and slipped past and down, unremarked, just a servant from the hill on late business headed down to the lower town.

He had no food for himself, except to eat a little of the raw grain, if it came to that. That was a difficulty. But it would not, he was sure, take him that long to find his half brother, the same as it hadn't in the Guelesfort, after no less than the Dragon Guard had searched for hours. He knew his routes. He had had the map of Amefel in his room, and he had studied it and knew the highways and the byways and every farm and field that had ever been taxed in the history of Amefel.

More, he knew where Marna began, and he knew the shortest way, and if his brother had gone that way, he would at least spur his father and the duke into tracking *him*, since they wouldn't listen to him or even admit him to their councils. He would lead them the right way, and if he had to go all the way to Lord Tristen's keep, he had the map's best notion where that was, too. If Gran was dead, if Otter's sorceress-mother had cast a spell of blindness over the duke and everyone in the keep, then maybe he was the only one in the whole keep who hadn't fallen under that spell and who didn't think they could find his brother by sitting and talking about things from before he and Otter were even born.

Elfwyn. Otter didn't like that name, but he'd taken it for his. Why? Because it *was* hostile to his family?

What was his brother thinking of, except that he was outcast from Guelemara and now had stolen from Duke Crissand. So Otter was running from him, and had lost Gran and now Paisi, in weather like this? He must be afraid, by now, and cold and desperate, and probably lost, not having committed a map to memory.

So Aewyn couldn't sit there and talk and drink and discuss old crimes in the kitchen. His mother and his father hadn't brought up a boy who could be patient when one of his own was threatened, and if the family's other son didn't merit a search out into the night, if his father thought the Guard was too tired to go on, Aewyn would see to it.

iii

IT WAS A METICULOUS BUSINESS, GETTING DOWN TO THE TRUTH—TRUTH FROM Paisi, who begged nothing more than for them to be out searching for the boy as soon as possible, and from Crissand, who had talked with Elfwyn at some length, with the librarian who had given him the key, the guard, who had reported the matter, and the officer of the special guard who watched over Tarien: no, the boy had not visited his mother since the day Gran's house burned, nor had he passed that guard station the night he had gotten into the library and vanished: clearly, then, Cefwyn said to himself, regarding a place where he had lived and ruled for a year, clearly, then, the boy had used the servants' passages—Paisi said he had had nothing to do with it, nor had guided the boy, who, it turned out, was as slippery as his namesake.

A knock came at the door, and an Amefin guardsman put his head in to beg pardon, but there was the Dragon Guard captain wanting to speak with His Majesty, urgently.

No deference to their host: Cefwyn gave a peremptory wave, beckoning the man in, and the captain slipped in, looking decidedly worried. "Begging Your Majesty's pardon," he said, and came close for a confidence as private as might be, in so small a chamber. "The Prince isn't downstairs or up."

"Where is he?" Cefwyn asked, with a sudden chill.

"We don't know, Your Majesty. He was in the kitchens with us, questioning the cooks, about the theft in the library, as was, and we looked around, and he wasn't there."

"Good loving gods!" He flung himself out of his chair.

"The Guard is searching, Your Majesty. The Amefin, too."

"He's gone," Paisi said, and immediately put a hand over his mouth, having talked out of turn; but it drew Cefwyn's attention:

"What do *you* know about it?"

"Majesty, forgive me, but if 'e's gone, he's followed my lord, is all."

"More sense than the whole damned passel of you," Cefwyn said to the mortified captain, the Marhanen temper getting well to the fore—which was not good. He drew a deep breath and reined it back. "There are a thousand nooks a boy could get into. Ask the Amefin. But assume he went to the gate."

"Yes, Your Majesty."

He snatched his cloak off the peg, marking how his son had taken his own with him—ordinary in a boy being sent off for good, but likewise sensible in a boy who firmly intended to go outdoors.

"May I assist, Your Majesty?" Crissand asked.

"Not *your* fault," Cefwyn said shortly. "But come along to the stables. I want to know from the gate-guards up and down if any boy went out, for the gods' sake. He's been gone long enough to be out and away."

He left, walked down the hall—a king could not run—and walked down the sooty and well-trafficked steps and out to the stables in the dark. The sun had set.

No, there was no horse missing. That was good news.

"There's the horses down to pasture," Paisi said, unasked. "He'd ha' had to have a bridle or halter."

"Count them," Cefwyn said.

The report came flying back that there was one fewer bridle than horses that had come in.

Clever lad, Cefwyn thought distressedly.

"He might have gone back to the witch's farm," Crissand said.

"Follow his tracks at the town gate and at the pastures. And my guess is to search west. West. He knows where Marna is."

Fear could close in about even a sensible boy, magnifying his doubts and moving him wherever a damned witch wanted. Fear—or overweening determination—could magnify itself, if a boy was particularly vulnerable to magic. And the boy was half-Syrillas.

"I'll go," Paisi said to Crissand. "If I could borrow me horse again, m'lord."

"No!" Cefwyn said, and stormed back across the yard and up the torchlit steps, Crissand struggling to stay beside him, with an accompanying straggle of guards, and Paisi.

"We can bring horses up," Crissand said, "and supplies for the road." Every horse they had in stable but three were road-weary and incapable of a chase. "What shall I do?"

"Do it," he said. It would take well over an hour to send down the hill, get horses from pasture, and get them up here and saddled and a search underway. But Crissand gave those orders.

He gave others, to the Dragon Guard captain. "Find out exactly what the kitchen staff told him," he said to that man, reaching the inner hall, while resisting the notion to let his temper fly: it never had done him good, and would not now, to strike out at the inept, to race off on impulse into the dark and miss some clue as to what precise impulse might have sent his son out looking for his brother. He went down the hall, past the grand stairs, with the far hall and the tower guard in his view, and wanted, oh, so much, to walk up those stairs and ask the one person who might have an answer—but she would not be inclined to tell him the truth, not for threats, not for pain. She would gloat to see him come up her stairs.

Worse than that—Tristen wasn't here, she was, and if she had gotten strong enough to cause this—dared he meddle with the wards on that tower, which were Tristen's, and which might be failing?

Not tonight, not in the dark, and not with his sons at issue. If she was nudging this and that, outside her tower, let her think she was safe in her mischief—so long as Tristen was on his way here to deal with her.

He went instead into the greater audience hall, servants scurrying about him to bring candles, small frantic lights that flared past gilt columns and figures and ledges. He settled onto the ducal throne of Amefel, once the throne of Amefin kings. He had used it before. It was his right, and no discourtesy to Crissand, who arrived with his own guard, bringing a white-aproned, white-bearded man, the cook.

The old man was terrified, and could only wring his hands and say he had talked to the Prince about what everybody knew, the old murder, and the books gone missing . . .

"Book," Cefwyn said curtly. "Book. One book." The legend had already multiplied the theft. And the cook had apparently said nothing to give Aewyn any notion he hadn't had before.

"Did he take food with him?" Cefwyn asked.

"No, Your Majesty. Not that I saw."

"His cloak and a bridle," Cefwyn muttered. "So he doesn't think he's going far."

"Perhaps he won't try to go far," Crissand said, standing near him.

"I can't say." He was at a loss, and the sun was going down outside, setting on a road that had taken his sons away from him—the one by a road that might not even lie in the world of Men and the other trying, the young fool, to follow him . . . all with the highest and best intentions, to be sure.

"Have you any sense at all from the ring?"

"None," Crissand said miserably. "None at all. As if he'd vanished from the land."

He laid a hand on his chest, where Tristen's amulet rested, and it—it tingled, like something alive against his skin. For one blessed moment it seemed he did feel something of direction. It tingled. It burned.

And there was a commotion in the hall, an expostulation from the guards, and a loud and impatient voice that tugged hard at memory. The chamber door burst open, banged back, and of all things, a bearded old man in voluminous gray robes stalked into the audience hall and walked straight up the center of the room.

Emuin. Who had been dead for ten years. Cefwyn sat stock-still, watching this apparition of his old tutor, the master wizard who had been at his side through all the wars and the troubles.

He had snow on his cloak, snow in his hair and beard, and clenched a staff in a hand quite blue with cold. He stamped that staff three times on the pavings.

"Well," he said. "Well! And in trouble again, are you?"

"Emuin?" Cefwyn asked, far from certain of what he saw. The place was given to haunts and apparitions, but of all of them, this one was welcome, more than welcome at the moment. And he was dripping water onto the pavings. "My son is in trouble."

"Which son? You have two."

"That I do. And both. Both are in trouble."

"Not surprising, given their heritage." Emuin leaned on his staff with both hands. "A long trek, a damned long trek, this. I am quite undone."

"Bring a chair," Cefwyn said, with a wave to the servants, who stood gawking.

"No time for sitting," Emuin said, and turned and waved his arm and his staff aloft. "Get that damned woman out of my workshop, that for a beginning."

His tower. His place, before they had imprisoned Tarien Aswydd in it.

It was so exactly what Emuin would say.

"Not so easy," Cefwyn said. "Not so easy a matter to dislodge her, my old friend. Tristen put her there."

"Well, then where is *he*?"

"That's very much in question," Cefwyn said, and had his own inquiry to make in the general madness of the moment. "Where have you been, the last ten years, Master Grayrobe?"

"Where have I been?" Emuin repeated, blinking and looking a little confused for the moment. He looked about the hall, as if he might find an answer there, or somewhere about the cornices. "I suppose I've been busy," he said, and swung about to look squarely at him. "Busy. Busy, until it became clear there was no peace to be had." He stalked forward, to the disquiet of the guards, and flung the staff rattling onto the floor right at the dais steps. "I'll have that chair. I'll have it here right now, if you please."

CHAPTER EIGHT

i

SNOW HAD GIVEN WAY TO NIGHTBOUND MIST, ALL-ENVELOPING MIST, SO THICK Elfwyn could not even see the ground under Feiny's hooves. He had searched and called until he was hoarse, looking for Paisi, and now that it was this ghostly mist, he decided that Paisi, having better sense, and if he had lost him, would either wait for the fog to clear and track him by his trail through the snow, or he would have gone back to town, giving up altogether, and perhaps concluding that he wasn't meant to go to Ynefel with him this time, either.

"Please," he asked the gathering dark, in hope that he would cross Lord Tristen's path. "I have something I must give you. Please find me. Please keep Paisi safe."

The ring that he had hoped would inform him of Lord Tristen told him nothing. At this point, he only hoped he was headed aright, that Owl would come sweeping out of the fog and guide him . . . Owl had seen him safely both ways, and this time his journey was for Lord Tristen's benefit, and for Paisi's, none of his own, that he knew . . . because the very last person his mother would destroy would be him, if only because a fool might still be useful to her. He had no wish to be a fool, but he began to think he was not clever enough to do otherwise where his mother was concerned.

Speed, tonight—speed. As much as he could manage and keep Feiny from going down under him.

The wind picked up. He thought it might sweep away the fog and give him and Paisi a means to find each other, but the wind became a stinging gale and the fog was no less at all. It sighed, it moaned—

And then he thought he heard a voice within it, faint and far, something trying to get his attention.

It might be Tristen—but there was no reason for Tristen's voice to be so soft, that he knew. He began to think it came from his left, then from his right and again, behind him, as if it sported like the wind, and mocked him, as he was sure Lord Tristen never would. It wanted his attention, and now he began to believe it was his mother. He reached a sheltered place, beside a tree-capped and cup-shaped ridge, and for the first time he could see the snow underfoot.

Now the one voice began to be many voices, and streaks appeared in the snow, deep gouges, one and four and six and more in the bank beside him, then underfoot, as the horse jumped forward as if something had touched him with a whip.

He patted Feiny's neck with a gloved hand, trying to keep both of them from panic, and he began to wonder distractedly if he had heard Paisi hunting him, and mistaken his voice for a haunt. He grew so fearful that he kept Feiny still, still as he could, cold, now, so very cold.

Here, however, seemed safer than going on with the voices in the wind, and he turned the horse full about, walking a line, a circle, and doing it three times, and wishing his little Line to hold fast, such as it was.

Streaks ran across the snow as far as his Line, and stopped. Then he knew what he heard was no trick of the wind. He got down from the saddle and held the reins close under Feiny's jaw, where he could get good leverage. He wished them safe, wishes such as Gran would make when they slept at night, and wished the same for Paisi, wherever he was.

Nothing was going right. He was exhausted, and wanted just to sit down, but he feared doing that—he saw the streaks scarring the snow all about his Line, like some ravening beast trying to get in, and he dared not relax a moment.

"Lord Tristen," he whispered, carrying the ring to his lips. "Lord Tristen, help us."

But it was as if, as the haunt battered the Line he had drawn, he himself grew wearier and wearier. Feiny, too, drooped, and his head sank, tail tucked for warmth. He opened his cloak and pressed it across the horse and his body against it, and stood there, growing more confused by the moment and no longer certain of the world beyond. He'd lost Gran, lost Paisi, lost everything—

Everything but one. For some reason he began to think of Aewyn with a vividness that overwhelmed the snow—there was one warm presence in the world, one point of warmth in all this storm. He began to believe there was, and that they could reach each other no matter the distance.

The laughter of children came down the wind. He blinked, his lashes frozen half-shut, and he saw a strange, sober little girl peering at him from among the rocks.

The girl faded suddenly, gasping in alarm, and the wind blew a blinding gust into his eyes, making him blink.

But his brother wanted him. That, above all things.

His brother needed him.

Knew everything he had done, and still loved him.

He thought about that, as his knees went, and pitched him down into the snow. He didn't stay there. He found purchase on the rock, then on the horse's stirrup, and levered himself back up.

"Aewyn!" he shouted against the wind. "Aewyn! Do you hear me?"

ii

"AEWYN!" THE SHOUT CAME DOWN THE WIND, AND AEWYN KEPT ON, KEPT ON, though the borrowed horse fought to turn and take them away from the blasts, and, riding bareback and with just a halter, he fought to keep the horse going. It might be the wind itself that made that sound. It might be a trick of his ears. In the blowing snow and the dark he had lost all referents. He had no notion at all where the town was, or where he was. He had been foolish—when was that a novelty?—and now he had lost himself so thoroughly in the dark that if he did turn back, he could only hope the honest Amefin horse could find his way home and let some horseboy know there was trouble. He had studied his map. He knew every detail of the land. He had had every confidence in his knowledge; but the dark and the snow took all that away from him, and there had been a fog, of all things, a fog with a blasting wind. He had no recourse now but to go as near west as he could imagine, to keep on the horse's back, and keep the horse moving, by little increments, until the dawn could warm them.

Then came that voice, not on the course he chose, but over to the right, and far away. And did he then take himself off what he thought was the right direction, and go aside for a ghost of a voice on the wind? He would be a fool.

"Aewyn!" it said, and he was all but certain he heard it.

There were haunts in these places. It was far from safe to listen to voices. But hadn't his father said to him that his deafness to magic was a defense?

He turned the horse off toward that sound, and called out, "I'm here! Do you hear me?"

He didn't know if he heard an answer. He thought he did. The blowing snow completely obscured what, by the horse's lurching and stumbling, was rough ground, and he and the horse together could as likely drop off an edge into a snowbank without warning.

But a shadow appeared in the white, the shadow of a horse, and the shadow of a rock, and a strange border of snow, streaked and gashed as if a whole herd of cattle had tramped it. He was uncertain of that ground, but his horse headed for the shadow-one willingly enough, and having reached that horse, Aewyn slid down beside an object mostly plastered over with snow. It was a body. It was a smallish body. He tugged and heaved, and saw it was his brother.

"Get up," he cried, hoarse from his shouting. "Get up, damn it!"

His brother flung his arms about him and struggled to get up, holding to him as if he were a rock or a tree, and managed to stand. The horses on either side of them cut off the wind, blessed relief, but his brother seemed to drink the warmth away from him; Aewyn began to shiver, and tried to get his brother to his horse, and held the stirrup, but his brother had no strength to hold on and help himself.

"Damn," he said, shaking at him. "Otter, you have to. You have to, is all. Hold on to the cursed saddle."

"I lost Paisi."

"Paisi's safe. He's with our father. Just get up!"

His brother took a grip and tried to lift himself by the saddle straps, and the horse stood still, at least. Aewyn bent and shoved and lifted from below for all he was worth, and Otter hauled himself the last bit into the saddle, belly-down and exhausted. Aewyn got to the other side of the horse and hauled at his arm, then his knee to pull him across, while Otter struggled to help. Aewyn pulled hard, despite the horse starting off, and between his efforts and Otter's, the leg came across, stiff and cold as it was, while the beast tried to turn a circle.

"Father's waiting for you," he shouted at Otter, to make him hear, and hanging on to the bridle to stop the animal. "We came all the way here to find you. You have to stay on the horse! I'll guide us! I can find our way!"

He feared Otter would fall off at the first jolt. He was that weak. But he took Otter's reins, and got on his own horse, who, in the company of another horse, had not wandered off, and began to lead them back toward what his sense of direction told him would be the highroad.

After a time of riding, he was no longer sure where that was, and he had not found the landmark of a market road he thought he would find. He was fiercely proud of his skill with maps, and he was utterly confounded. Luck had brought him to his brother, luck that had nothing to do with his skill; he had—the priests would never approve—hoped for that kind of luck, on his mother's side of his heritage, and gotten it, or at least he had linked up with his brother's own sort of luck. If they weren't guiding themselves, now, then happenstance was, and happenstance, where magic was concerned—so his father had always told him—had a mind and an intent of its own. Sometimes—his father had told him—its intent was not quite what one would like.

But Lord Tristen was involved. If Otter—his father had said he wanted to be Elfwyn now—had gotten to him once, all he had to do was attach himself, and they would both come through this together. Was that not the way magic worked?

And sure enough, when they were the most desperate, a wall appeared before them, a shelter from the wind, and when they came up against it, much more than that: their wall had a door, and windows. It was a little fieldstone cottage, its walls so plastered with snow, and it all shuttered, it looked a great deal like the hill against which it was built.

"Otter!" Aewyn cried, getting down, his voice shredding in the cold and the wind. "We've reached somewhere, I don't know where. But it's a place!"

He knocked at the door, and, getting no answer, tried it, whether it was latched or not. The latch gave. The door opened outward a little, and when he kicked the snow away, he gained enough to get the door open halfway. That was enough for them, but not for the horses: he kept digging and shoving and heaving at the door until he had deep snow rammed up beside the door track. It was utterly dark inside the cottage, darker than the night, and he envisioned some previous owner dead inside, gone to horrid bones.

But whatever was in there, it offered walls and a roof. He ventured inside, and scuffed the floor, and he was glad to find it was earth, nothing of rotten boards that might entrap the horses: it would be cold, but not as cold as the howling wind outside. He went out again and led his brother's horse in, heard the crash of something as the beast swung his hindquarters about in the dark: the horse shied, and he hauled down on the reins and used all his strength to stop the stupid beast from bolting out the door.

His brother moaned and tried to get down before disaster happened. But Aewyn steadfastly held the horse, soothed him with a gloved hand, and Otter—Elfwyn—got down to him, clinging to the horse. His own borrowed horse had put her head into the dark, snuffing the air of this strange stable, then balked.

"I can manage him," Elfwyn said in a thread of a voice, holding to the bridle, and he let his brother go to grab the Amefin mare and get her in, all the while prepared to block his brother's horse in any rush for the door.

Something else crashed, and wood broke, Elfwyn's cursed horse finding, evidently, some remnant of furniture to back into, but the Amefin horse came in meekly enough. They had no light. The horses were both unhappy with the place, and both apt to bolt for the door and the far hills if Elfwyn's horse went. He shut it, made sure of the latch, and stood in the utter dark with his heart thumping. There was a little more shifting about, but the horses slowly grew quieter, deprived of all light, and deprived of a way out.

"Elfwyn?" he asked into the dark.

"I hear," Elfwyn said.

"I don't know where we are," Aewyn said, overwhelmed by shivers, not least from the hard battle with Elfwyn's horse, and the prospect of being left afoot. "I'm afraid to open the door. I'm afraid the horses will bolt for home. I'm going to move around a little and see what's here." The thought of bones made it far, far worse. "I'm following the wall. There's the window, the shutters, but they must open right out into the wind out there."

"I'm by a wall," Elfwyn said. "There's stone walls. Some pots. Did you bring any food?"

"No," Aewyn admitted. He had been in the kitchens and had taken not a thing when he ran. "I didn't. I'm sorry."

"I did," Elfwyn said, "but Paisi had it. And I lost him in the fog, like a complete fool. You say he's with our father—where is he?"

"Back in Henas'amef. I came after you. They were still talking." Aewyn kept moving, cautiously. He found a table, and a fireplace, and he felt into it, finding only soft, old ash, which told him nothing of how long ago this place had been occupied. Beyond that, however, was a woodpile. The bark of the logs crumbled under his grip, but the logs were solid, and the better for age.

"There's wood," he said. "There's a fireplace. I don't suppose you can enchant us up a fire if I pile up the logs."

"Conjure," Elfwyn said hoarsely. "I don't know the first thing about it. I saw Gran try once. She couldn't. I don't think I can."

"Well, try, all the same." He dragged small wood loose, working utterly blind, and shoved the pieces into the fireplace, in as orderly a structure as he could make, blind. "There's kindling. It's in the fireplace. The flue has to be open. I feel the draft. Just do it."

"I'll do my best," Elfwyn said, and came over near him, edging over on the ground. He sat there a moment, making no sound.

"Nothing?" Aewyn asked after a moment, and put his own hand into the wood. There was no warmth to it, none at all. "It's still ice-cold."

"I'm not Gran," Elfwyn said faintly. "And she couldn't do it. Gran's dead. Just like in my dream."

"I know that. We passed there. I'm sorry. I'm ever so sorry, Otter."

"Well, she couldn't conjure. And I—I'm just not a wizard. I'm not, at all. And I'm afraid to conjure fire. The only fire I'm apt to get is *sorcerous,* like my mother, isn't it? I don't know what it might do . . . burn us all, like as not!"

Elfwyn's voice grew ragged, near to tears. Aewyn closed a hand on his shoulder and shook at him gently.

"Well, but we still have the horses, don't we? They'll warm the place just with their heat. We have to rub them down and be sure they don't chill. Then we can sit on your saddle and wrap in the horse gear. That will warm us."

They managed that, utterly in the dark, and piled the horse blanket and tack near the dead fireside, and snuggled down with that and their cloaks to provide the warmth it could against the drafts that were constant in the room, from little seams that equally well let in the storm light from outside. For a time their arrangement seemed warm and snug enough to sleep a little, leaning on each other.

But warmth slowly faded from their bodies.

"There's a draft on my arm," Aewyn complained, shivering, once when they both waked, "no matter how I turn."

"At least we're all out of the wind," Elfwyn said. "And it's only a draft."

They were at least partly warm, close together. The horses shifted about and bickered, occasionally treading on something broken in that end of the single room, and the wind raged outside, a wind that pried at edges and whipped to this side and that of the little cottage looking for ways inside. Something thumped. A shingle might have just flown off: a new draft started, right above them.

"It's wicked out there," Aewyn said.

"It's bad. But morning will be warmer. We can look around for a flint or something when it gets light enough."

"I hope it doesn't snow us in," Aewyn said. "The door opens out, remember."

"There is the window," his brother said. "We can get out that way if it comes to that: we wouldn't be the first. And I'm sure there's a roof trap if that gets covered, or we can just knock some shingles off: there's one gone already, I'm quite sure."

His brother wasn't afraid of the storm. Otter—Elfwyn—had spent all his winters in a cottage like this, where the door could be snowed shut. Probably it happened every winter, and the wind howled and rattled shutters, beyond windows with goatskin panes, and all his winter nights must have been this long and dark.

Elfwyn had grown up with no servants, no guards, nobody but Gran and Paisi to see him fed and keep him out of trouble, and for protection against things that might threaten a remote cottage, only Paisi's dagger and a stick from the woodpile. He had sounded weak and foolish, he decided. His father's son should not be either weak or a fool. He had found Elfwyn, had he not, and Elfwyn had been in dire trouble until he had found this place, so he had saved both of them, had he not? He had not lost his way, even when the fog had closed in around him and he had been utterly without landmarks: a sense had guided him. He had not lost the horses, when that kind of accident might have doomed them both.

So when his father found them, his father might even say he hadn't done too badly, except not bringing food and blankets along; and neither, really, had Elfwyn done badly, for a boy who had never ridden a horse until this winter. His father would be so glad to see them, he would gloss over the part about stealing the mare, and the mare would come back sound: he was absolutely determined on that.

In all their other troubles, he hadn't even asked about the book Elfwyn was supposed to have stolen from the library. He didn't truly care about that. He supposed Elfwyn had it, and had a good reason to have gotten it, and they would settle that: Elfwyn probably thought he was going to get into dire trouble—Elfwyn was always convinced trouble would fall on him—and once they settled things with Lord Crissand (and he knew his father could), then his brother would be back in Henas'amef, and the book would be put wherever it needed to be, and Lord Tristen would come, and they would both have days to spend without worrying about anything. When he had had his few annual hours to spend with Otter—who was Elfwyn, now—Elfwyn had led him to all sorts of wonderful places to investigate. If they were going about on horseback, they could range much farther in their adventures.

When his father forgave them both, they could figure out how to get Elfwyn safely back to Guelemara, since he had no Gran to go to any longer. Paisi would come, too, and maybe be a man-at-arms, or an almost-prince's bodyguard, in which case he would wear fine clothes and carry a sword, which would get Paisi out and about the country on horseback, wherever Elfwyn went: he was a much more inventive companion than his own bodyguards, and he could think of nobody better for Elfwyn's protection.

They would be safe forever after, he and his brother, coming back to holds and keeps and well-fortified places after their rides, to safe, warm places, where the wind didn't ever sound like that.

iii

"WHERE HAVE YOU BEEN THE LAST FIFTEEN YEARS, MASTER EMUIN?" CEFWYN asked, and the old man, strengthened by ale and two rapidly vanishing seed cakes, wiped a few crumbs from his mustache and blinked, looking very real, indeed, and a little confused by the question.

"That long, has it been?"

"The boys are mostly grown, old master. They're in dire danger out in the storm." Fear and desperation made him ever so anxious to trust this apparition; experience with mysterious appearances—and he had seen them—warned him to be very cautious. "How can you have arrived here out of the dark in our hour of trouble and have no inkling what's gone on?"

"That, yes," Emuin said. "Didn't I come for that? I think I did."

"Then do it!" Cefwyn said. In every particular this old man was the man Cefwyn remembered, the man that Crissand, too, would remember, down to the freckles on Emuin's high brow and the length of his snowy beard. The ring on his hand was the same—Cefwyn remembered that well, too, a plain silver ring with a black stone; and given the character of the jewelry wizards and the like had passed around, Cefwyn no longer looked on it as personal adornment. He reached a hand to the amulet he himself wore, took it off and held it out, risking he knew not what. "This is Tristen's. Can *you* get his attention, pray?"

Emuin held up his hand, preventing him, refusing quite to touch the amulet. "One of his, it certainly is. But may we not just trust to his intentions, and not be shouting to each other all we know through chancy passages? I think waiting is far the wiser course."

"Shouting down chancy passages, is it?" He didn't like what he heard—but he did understand that reference to wizardly ways of getting one another's attention. "My sons are out there freezing to death in a storm at this moment, Master Grayfrock. Risks, I am willing to take, I assure you, and let Tristen handle whatever comes galloping through after such a message."

"Your son has carried something perilous, carries it right through the shadow." Emuin gave a wave of his hand, and it trembled. "For that, I would be ever glad to reach for him and drag him here by the hair of the head—but so would she reach after him! Have a care, and put that damned thing back about your neck, boy! For the gods' sake bring it not so near me! It could happen without our willing it!"

Boy, it was, and him having boys of his own, both older than he had been when Emuin had taken a sullen, wayward young prince in hand and taught him to dread that voice raised in reprimand. He dropped the chain back about his neck and wore his amulet openly, not caring to conceal it in this hall where wizardry and magic had honor. "Is it his mother who's done this?"

"Certainly she has her fingers well into it," Emuin said, and took a drink of ale that left beads standing on his mustaches. He wiped his mouth. "She is dangerous."

"My sons," Cefwyn said, vexed and worried. "And Tristen, for that matter. Where is he?"

"A serious matter," Emuin said, and shut his eyes, and went thin-lipped for the moment. "The boys . . . the boys have the book . . . they are alive. They're together."

"Together!" He knew not whether to be angry with his wayward heir or overjoyed to hear that he had succeeded against all odds. "Aewyn *found* him!"

"It was inevitable," Emuin said, "or close to it. Both your sons have the Gift, but not the same gift, have you discovered it?"

"Aewyn? He's as blind as I am!"

Emuin shook his head. "No. He is not blind, nor helpless. Nor are you quite as blind as you wish to think. The younger of your sons—has the Syrillas Gift."

Aewyn? "Has he? He has the Sight?"

"He has it in a peculiar way. I'd judge that he Sees, and has no idea that he does. Finding things is an untaught skill with him."

"His damned maps . . ."

"The whole world is a map to him. He Sees, I say, but will never quite know when he does, and his scope may widen with age."

"I've gotten *two* wizards?" It was not completely good news, except as related to his boys' safety, out in a driving blizzard. "Then help them wizard their way back here, for the gods' sake. If they have the Gift, then"—he made a vague, descriptive gesture—"slip them through the passages you use and get them here!"

"Hush. Hush." A look aloft. "If your older boy hadn't found what he found, the other would have come on it with *his* Gift, and the worse for him if he had: the one is at least cognizant of wizardry and wary of his mother's influence. Listen to me. The Gift is not the same in them, nor ever was, but they may link hands."

"You're riddling again, Master Grayfrock."

"The one is no wizard."

"You said they both—"

"The one is no wizard. The elder of your boys—is no wizard."

"*Elfwyn?* What is he, if not—" A most horrid notion came to him, things at which Tristen had only hinted. "He *is* my son, isn't he?"

"In the flesh, yes, I have no doubt that he is. But there is a hollow spot in him, right about the heart. There always was, from birth."

"No." He got up from his chair, to distance himself from such a claim. "A hollow spot? He's a Summoning, like Tristen? Is that what you're saying to me?"

"Tristen is not a Summoning. He's a Shaping, quite a different—"

"Damn it, Master Grayfrock, don't mince words. Is my son my son?"

"Oh, very much your son. But he's gone straight where his mother bade him go, and done everything she wanted him to do—up to a point. He has self-will. Hard-won, and hard-held, he has your self-will and your stubborn nature."

"He has a heart!" Cefwyn declared, outraged. "He has a good heart, not any hollow spot, and if you had been here where you were needed, Master Grayrobe, when you were needed, then you would have had the teaching of him as I asked you from the start, and we wouldn't be at this pass!"

"Gran did quite well. Admirably well, as happened. So has Paisi."

Paisi had stood, silent and stricken, at the side of the room the while. But now he took a step forward. "Ye're sayin' he ain't what he seems," Paisi said angrily, "but I can say there ain't a bad bone in that lad's body. He's a good, proper boy, as ever was."

"Oh, his bones are quite sound." Emuin gathered his staff to him, slanted between his knees, and the knob of it against his chest, amid his beard, locked in gnarled hands. "So is his wit and his will. It's just a hollow spot. It might never even do him harm . . . unless someone tried to fill it. Unless he allowed it, more to the point, and that is a lad with a very strong will."

"What do you know of him? You weren't here."

"I wasn't unaware."

"Damn it," Cefwyn said. "Damn it, old master, I wish you'd stayed to teach them. At least one of them."

"There was too much damage I could do, bringing wizardry of greater sort into it. Elfwyn was not ready for a contest. And Aewyn was not ready to believe his own eyes."

"What was I?" Cefwyn cried. "Was it that needful, old master, to keep me and his mother in the dark?"

"I take it you mean your dear lady."

"Ninévrisë. Aewyn's mother, damn it."

"Well, you were never in the dark," Emuin said. "You were always in my keeping, and Tristen's."

"Tristen knew you were out and about?"

"Oh, I suspect he knew, though 'tis by no means certain, I suppose. Our paths diverged. I visited Gran from time to time, indeed I did. And crossed the edges of Guelessar, and of Elwynor. I visited Cevulirn once, when his wife had the fever, but there was no great need: the lady mended on her own. I have never deserted you, Cefwyn lad, nor forgotten your boys, nor has Tristen, whose delay tonight troubles me exceedingly. I suspect he will come the ordinary way, by horse, that is, not risking the other passage."

"If *he* can't get through, good gods, how am I to believe the boys are safe? I wish you would speak to him. Or tell me more where the boys are. I would ride after them."

"To their peril and ours," Emuin said. "Looking for them lowers our wards. Trying to guide them now diminishes theirs, if they had the wit to set them, and I have the most dire feeling they forgot—they are not safe where they are, not safe at all, and where they are shifts . . ."

"Then *go* to him. You're the wizard. You can do that!"

"I can't do that! That's the very point! If I were to venture those paths your reckless sons traveled, there's no knowing in what province I might land. They're lucky still to be in Amefel!"

"What do you mean?"

"It's that book, I suspect—that book, I surmise, takes its own direction in the world, and your lad is hanging on to it, and wrenching it free of his mother, but when he moves, he, she, and it are in grievous dispute about direction."

"That woman!" Cefwyn said, and absolute loathing welled up in him, the very sort of hatred Tristen had advised him never to countenance toward Tarien Aswydd; but now, in the peril of his sons, it brimmed over. "Tarien Aswydd knows how Paisi's gran died, and why my son got out of bed at midnight to go dig a hole in the library wall! Master Graybeard, let us get your study back! Let us have answers from that woman, tonight, once for all."

"Confront Tarien Aswydd?" Emuin asked. "Perhaps."

"More than perhaps," Cefwyn said. "You worry about the wards. Assure the strength of what holds her contained. Find out whether or not she truly can reach out of the tower. You can deal with her, I've no doubt you can, and we can put that woman somewhere with fewer windows and less luxury. Crissand, are you willing?"

"More than willing," Crissand said, "whenever it regards getting the truth from my cousin. I shall be glad to know how well she's held."

"Not well!" Emuin exclaimed in sudden alarm. "Not well at all! Oh, damn it to *hell*!" Emuin leapt to his feet, leaning shakily on his staff, and headed for the door of the audience hall. Cefwyn overtook him, and Crissand came close behind as they left the hall and turned toward the tower access.

Two men lay in the hall, both down, as if they had died in their tracks, eyes wide open.

"Guards!" Cefwyn yelled, his battlefield voice, that waked echoes upstairs and down. Emuin ascended the tower steps, Cefwyn fretting behind him, hand on his dagger, and Crissand close after that, round after round of the spiral, into utter dark, except a glow that began to surround Emuin himself and spread about them.

The door above was still barred. Emuin waved at it, and Cefwyn pulled the pin and used fair force to lift the bar. It thumped back, and suddenly the door banged open in their faces, with a howling gust of ice-edged wind. All the windows stood open, and fabrics flew in the wind, the abandoned clothing, the hangings, everything flying at them out of the nightbound tower room.

"Tarien!" Cefwyn shouted into the night.

A crash shook the tower, as if a part of the keep itself had fallen. They were shaken where they stood, thinking the floor might give way, then Crissand, lowermost on the steps, turned and ran downstairs again, Cefwyn behind him and Emuin bringing up the rear.

Guards had gathered in the corridor below, in dark, the gale having blown the lights out, and in that dark the guards pointed to the curtain, which blew in tatters, beside the dark, ordinary wall that was the source of the haunt.

"Bear a light!" Crissand shouted, and Emuin, arriving breathlessly, gasped, "This is not good. Not good."

Someone had already gone for a light, one of the pine-tar torches they used outside, a light that came in at the stairs and jogged and flickered toward them, fire whipping in the gale, but more difficult for wind to extinguish. Cefwyn waited for it, hand outheld, his heart beating in foreboding as to what he might find in that room at the bottom of the stairs. But Emuin lit his own way, before the torch could arrive, and descended past the flapping curtain. Cefwyn abandoned his request for the torch and came down to protect him with drawn dagger, steps breaking little bits of masonry.

Massive blocks lay scattered outward, the stone walls chipped with the awful force with which those blocks had flown apart, and inside the room beyond, which still held the dry mustiness of a tomb despite the air that blasted in from above, there was only shadow.

Light glowed brighter from Emuin's hand, blue as day, and showed no bones, nothing but overset chairs, a ledge, and a moldering, dusty cloak.

"She's gone," Crissand breathed, from behind them.

Orien Aswydd. The other twin. The dead one, walled alive into her tomb.

"I have to find them," Emuin said. "I have no choice."

But who it was he meant to find, he didn't say. He shoved rudely past them and climbed the steps, struggling with his robes and the staff. They followed him up into the hall above, where the pine torch gave a fitful, wind-blown light; and suddenly the haunt beside them broke wide open in spectral light, a dark and angry blue, moving with the shadow of wings.

"Find Tristen!" Emuin shouted at them, and stepped off into that place as if it were a doorway.

He vanished. The light from the haunt died, instantly, and left them only the torchlight, and the lingering command.

"Find Tristen," Cefwyn said, and struck the ordinary stone of the wall with his fist, then looked at Crissand. "Bloody hell, where do we start?"

"The library," Crissand said. "The library, for a beginning."

CHAPTER NINE

TRISTEN WAS SURE THAT HE RODE NO LONGER WITHIN MARNA. IT HAD BEEN AN unguessable time since they had slept, waked, and found themselves wrapped in mist, and now Tristen rode far more slowly than he wished, courting no mishaps. This place was not friendly to Uwen, or to their horses, and he kept Uwen close, continually aware of the ice that grew about them.

They changed, these shards of ice. They were sharp enough to pierce flesh and cold enough to stop the heart. They threatened, sometimes rising up suddenly, with a sound like steel sliding on steel.

"They ain't right natural," Uwen had remarked, early on, in his calm way. "M'lord, I don't like the look at all."

Neither did he, to this hour, to this day—however long they had been caught here. And the icy realm was one kind of a trap for Uwen, but another for himself, a slippage, slow and continual, so that at first he had no memory of entering the place, and now suspected he had no memory of other things more important.

"How long do you think we have ridden today?" he asked Uwen.

"Seems to me it ought to be summat over an hour," Uwen said. "But I don't trust my reckonin' in this place, t' tell the truth." They rode in silence a moment, a silence marked by the crash and destruction of a shard, which spawned others. "Is it more than an hour, m'lord?"

"I fear it is," Tristen said. "I fear—"

But he forgot. He forgot what he had been about to say, and forgot that he had forgotten.

"M'lord," Uwen said insistently. "M'lord, ye're driftin' a wee bit. Ye've done that today, time to time."

He blinked, lost for the moment, then with a chill found he had lost the name of the man beside him, someone who was vitally important to him, someone who was warmth and love itself, and he felt something beyond fear—a loss of hope itself.

The wind blew clear, unveiling a fortress on a snowy hill, and that fortress was built of the ice, a fortress with battlements that glittered like a rusty stain under a wan and fleeting sun.

Here was the first place. Here was the first of all places in his life. It lay far back, far, far in memory. He could only come here when he had forgotten all else. It waited for him.

"M'lord," the man beside him said.

A wayward gust of mist took the vision away. They were back in the mist again, and the man had leaned from the saddle and seized his horse's rein near the jaw.

"Ye're driftin', m'lord. Come back t' me. There's me good lad."

"Uwen." He gathered up bits and pieces and drew in a deep, freezing breath. His wards had failed. He had set them about their sleeping place, but their wards had gone down, and let in powers from before Uwen's time, things long pent, that wanted free. The wards needed straight lines, or circles, even, reasonable structures, but the ice was all an illusion of shining planes. In its very essence, it flowed—was irrational, without Lines, in its depth. Given time, it warped, it bent, it stretched any Line he set on it, and just as readily—it broke, and fractured, making edges sharp enough to draw blood . . .

"M'lord!" he heard, and struggled to get back to that voice, that Man he had to protect. He knew they were going nowhere. Of a sudden he knew they had gone quite the opposite of where they ought to go, that they had been taken far from where they wanted to be . . . he could not remember that place, but he knew it was not this place.

Then another voice came, faint and far.

"Tristen," it called, desperate. "Tristen, hear me. Emuin's gone. My sons are gone. Tristen, wherever you are, I need you."

Warmth came with it, warmth that touched him, and reached inside, like the breath of summer.

"Cefwyn?" he said, and reined full about. "Cefwyn, call again. Call louder." And when it came, faint and torn on the wind: "Uwen, stay close!"

ii

"HE'S COMING!" CEFWYN CRIED. HE HAD NO NOTION HOW HE KNEW IT, BUT HE did. Kingship to the winds, he went running for the library door, knocking over a stack of heavy books and disarranging a table. Crissand was on his heels, the two of them rounding the corner of the short hall into the main corridor like two madmen.

The whole hall resounded to the confusion of two sets of guards attempting to stay with them—then, crazily, echoed to the racket of hooves within the hall itself, a thunderous clatter on the stones. Blue light flared, and wings beat in alarm as the haunt broke wide open, sending two riders and their trailing packhorses into the dead middle of the hall—not just any horses, the lead two, but heavy horses, one of them black as sin itself and the other a blue roan with a wicked eye.

A rider in silver armor swung down off the black and lit in the hall, looking toward him, a rider whose curiously crafted armor frosted in the air and gave off fog, and the other man, an ordinary Man in black leather, and thickly coated, stepped down from the roan, his armor and helm likewise frosted.

Cefwyn met his old friend Tristen with an embrace, never minding the burning chill of his touch, and stood him back again and looked into gray, wide eyes, a gaze that could drink a man's common sense and draw him into whatever mad courage.

"My friend," Cefwyn said, "my old friend. Thank the gods you heard me. The boys are lost out there. Orien's cell is empty. Tarien's fled her prison, gods know how. Emuin came here . . . did you know Emuin is alive?"

"That I did," Tristen said. "But not where he was. Did Tarien take the boys with her?"

Tristen knew nothing that they had been trying to tell him, only that they were in distress. The stamp and heavy breathing of unsettled horses was all around him, and the steam went up about their bodies. The cold of Tristen's armor seared his hands like fire.

"Elfwyn found a lost book in the library. I think it must be Mauryl's book, from the time the books were burned. He left with it, and lost Paisi along the way."

"Paisi," Tristen said, glancing aside, and Paisi said, "m'lord," almost inaudible in the echoing racket, and held his hands in his belt. "It was one o' them fogs, m'lord, was what it was. He rode right into it."

"And Aewyn left here without us knowing," Cefwyn said, "tracking his brother. Then Emuin arrived. Then the stones blew apart, the windows blew open, and Tarien went—Emuin went after her, for all I know. What can you tell me? Can you find my boys?"

Tristen gazed afar off for a moment, and Cefwyn, having poured out that ill-assorted chronicle like flotsam in a millrace, caught his breath.

Tristen looked down the hall toward the haunt, or toward the library: it was uncertain which. "The book," he said, out of that choice of calamities. "That's what it is. The spell on it avoided my finding it years ago—it hid from one thief. It avoids me now. It was Mauryl's, but not the last spell on it, I fear. And Emuin has been here. He tried to strengthen the wards in my absence. And he could not."

When had the gray-eyed innocence given way to this look that gazed through distances, and that childlike wonder become such confidence? Cefwyn backed away a pace, chilled by more than the cold that attended them.

But Uwen intruded between them and caught Tristen's arm sharply. "M'lord! This is Cefwyn, an' Uwen with 'im. Paisi, too, an' Lord Crissand. Ye hear? Hear us!"

A shudder went through Tristen's frame, and that gaze swung to Uwen, then to Cefwyn.

"Elfwyn," Tristen said. "Elfwyn came to me. And Emuin came to you."

"Not a half an hour ago," Cefwyn said. "He left, and I don't know where."

Tristen shook his head. "The ways are cut off. They've become mazes. I've not seen Owl for days. And Elfwyn, and his brother . . . I can't find them, though I know they're out there. Magic is undermined. Wizardry may have a better chance."

"Brandywine," Crissand said to someone, and a servant raced off. "We should get the horses down to the stable."

Exactly how they were to get two great destriers and the loaded pack-horses down the central stairs without calamity was another matter, but Tristen said quietly, "No. We'll be going as we came. The Line that prevents it no longer holds. You should give this place its own way, Lord Crissand. Let it be a mews, since that's what it wants to be. It might be safer."

"M'lord," Uwen said in concern.

"I cannot mend this place," Tristen said distractedly. "I even cannot hold my own course over large distances, Uwen. Little I could repair, of things that may now be broken. I sent him aside once, and my wards stood until now, until *that* reached the light. *His* must be the spell on the book, that hid it from me from the beginning, that would not go into the hands of a thief, nor be destroyed. I took it for Mauryl's spell. But sometimes there is very little difference."

Tristen's enemy was the *he* Tristen did not name, the one who had been Mauryl's student, and ultimately his murderer: Cefwyn suspected that much. Hasufin Heltain—servant of the Sihhë-lords, and the one who, even dead, had insinuated himself in Elfwyn Sihhë's stillborn son, to do murder within the house and bring the Sihhë down . . . so much he knew, too. His family, the Marhanens, had come into power in that upheaval. The reigning Marhanen knew certain details of that downfall, none of which gave him great pride or comfort. And he did not like to hear that Heltain's black workings and Mauryl's in any wise looked alike to Tristen's eye.

Tristen, in the same heartbeat, had reached for the warhorse's bridle and looked at Uwen Lewen's-son, who gathered his own reins from the hands of a frightened house servant.

"Where are you going?" Cefwyn asked in dismay.

"There were keys left in the world," Tristen said, looking straight at him. "I suspect Tarien was to get to the book. Orien was to bring it to him."

"Orien was surely dead." The image of the sorceress living this long in utter darkness, walled within her tomb, was horrid beyond any he could conjure. But there had only been the cloak left, not a bone nor a single leaving else.

"Hasufin died ages ago," Tristen said, argument enough.

"Our wards are down," Cefwyn said. "They're utterly destroyed. Will he come here?"

"No," Tristen said, when he had in no wise been above stairs, or walked the perimeter as a wizard would. But he was not the young wanderer in the world that he had been, either, whatever he had become, or might be about to become. Cefwyn felt a pang of loss, not unmixed with a fear of what his sons faced if Tristen was to retreat from the world, and as if Tristen had heard his thoughts, Tristen seized his hand. "My friend," he said, with that gray-eyed gaze. "My oldest friend in the world. I tried to get here, and every accident held me. Now I know the trouble, I shall not leave this place undefended. We shall go to the stables, Uwen and I, and put the horses up. We shall come back straightway, afoot."

Tristen let go, then.

And was not there, neither he, nor Uwen, nor two destriers and two packhorses. They left only that sort of evidence iron-shod horses left in the hall, puddles of snowmelt, a scarred floor, and a lingering smell of horse.

The stables, Tristen had said. Tristen had wanted to be there. And was.

Why, then, damn it all, had he not *wanted* to be in Henas'amef in time to prevent Orien Aswydd's rising from the grave, or Tarien's breaking out of her tower?

Every accident, Tristen had said.

The simple answer was that Tristen had indeed wanted to be here, and that a very, very potent sorcery had sent him aside—not destroyed him: it would have, if it were easy; it was not; but that was in fact its aim—even a Man deaf to magic could figure that they were under attack, and that it would not get better with daylight.

A potent sorcery had raised the dead and broken Tristen's wards. And how had it gotten past those wards, and what had made Tristen himself vulnerable . . . Cefwyn feared to guess its name, but he thought he had.

One of his two sons was blood kin to the sorceress—one of his sons had gone visiting Ynefel and drawn Tristen into this fight. The other of his sons, tied to that line by loyalty and paternity, had gone chasing after his brother. All of that was a tangle of wizardry and magic that chilled his heart. Nor was his daughter safe, with Ninévrisë in Elwynor, where magic had an ancient foothold. His whole family was tangled in this scheme of a dead sorcerer, and Tristen was the one power another dead wizard had appointed, more than that, *Summoned, Shaped,* whatever Emuin insisted, to stand on the bridge and keep the dead from taking Ylesuin back from the Marhanen's hands. Ordinary folk couldn't challenge Tristen. Not these days. But the powers that he was appointed to prevent—those could.

Those already had, in delaying him.

Back in the wars, he and Emuin and Tristen had managed to isolate the several elements of Hasufin's power and bring one down, confine another, and another, and hang one chief culprit, peeling Hasufin's power apart bit by bit, breaking it in this place and that, until Tristen had a chance.

Three pieces of that power, counting that book, had just broken loose again, thanks to Tarien Aswydd and his own eldest son, indicating that even apparent death might be a diversion.

And what did he say?

"Let us go back to the hall and wait," he said to Crissand. "If he can, he'll be back in a moment, and use the west door, this time. If I know anything about it, he'll be searching that place he goes to, trying to find any trace of the boys."

"That he will," Crissand said, who had the Sight, himself. "I have no notion where he is. But the ring Elfwyn carries is his: nothing opposing him, he may well be able to see it."

iii

THEY BOTH SLEPT AND WAKED AMID THE PILED HORSE GEAR, AND THE COLD grew more and more bitter, while exposed flesh grew numb despite the warmth of the horses sharing their shelter, and the thickness of the saddle, which gave up warmth slowly. The horses slept, it might be, but the wind howled and worked at the shingles, finding new places to get in, and made their own rest uneasy. "I think we should stay awake," Elfwyn said finally, shaking at Aewyn. "We can sleep in the day. If we had food we shouldn't be so cold, but we don't, and we should move about a little. Rub your hands. Make them warm."

"If there were light, we could see if there was a flint or anything in the place," Aewyn said, his teeth chattering from cold. Aewyn was being very brave, he thought. Aewyn had grown up in a palace, and looked to want of food as their greatest danger, but *he* recalled the chimney blocking up with snow, and their fire going out, and Gran trying to conjure. They had survived because Paisi had gotten up on the roof with a stick and nearly frozen to death getting the chimney clear.

Safe fire. That was what they needed. For his brother's safety, he needed it.

"I wish it would light!" Elfwyn cried in bitter frustration, and tried, as Gran had, to see the fire. That was how he imagined it would succeed if it did, that he had to see the fire behind his eyelids, then it would be there.

But nothing happened. He huddled under the horse blanket and cloaks he shared with Aewyn and tried, once, twice, three times, to see, not destroying fire, nor sorcery, but life-giving fire, fire safe in a hearth, imagining how astonished Aewyn would be, imagining how wonderful it would feel to have succeeded, and how he would have something to recommend him to their father, having saved Aewyn. Then he could go to Tristen, deliver the book, and say, "Teach me," in the confidence he could learn at least a little wizardry. All these things he could foresee.

But the fire would not come. The little spark of fire, the simplest, the most basic thing a real wizard could do, eluded him.

He ever so regretted that Aewyn had not been practical enough to have stolen a loaf of bread when he had come out. Or that he had not had the sense to have divided loads with Paisi. He was more than hungry, now; he was dry and thirsty, and had no wish to battle the door open and shut, just to have cold snow in his mouth.

The wind gave a particularly violent burst, battering at the planks of the door.

Then the door bumped, and rattled, and scraped laboriously outward, someone kicking the snow out of the way.

"Someone's out there," Elfwyn whispered, holding Aewyn by the shoulder.

"Maybe it's the householder come back," Aewyn whispered back.

"Who'd come home at this hour, in this storm?" Elfwyn said. The horses were growing disturbed, and stirred and made sounds in the dark, treading on something they'd already broken. "If we have to, run out the door."

"But we'll freeze out there!"

"Never mind that! Just get out! Bandits live out in the borderlands. They may have gotten desperate for shelter."

The door came open, and a shadow entered.

And stopped.

"Well," the shadow said, an old man's voice. "Well! Who's in here?"

"More than one of us," Elfwyn said aloud, as boldly as he could manage. He stood up, plotting his way to the door; but the old man's voice gave him a little reassurance. "We needed shelter from the cold."

"Oh, well." The old man pulled the door shut, making it utter dark, and Elfwyn squeezed Aewyn's hand. It still wasn't hopeless. The man had worked the snow away from the door. It would give, now, if they ran for it. The horses would bolt. They might catch them, if they were lucky.

A spark showed in the dark, midway of the old man's height. A wisp of tinder caught, and floated, held, doubtless, in a tinder pick, and flared into flame, showing the hint of a pale wax candle near it. It died. Once again, the old man tried the light, showing gray hair and the hint of an old man's bearded face near that candle.

"There's wood in the fireplace, sir," Elfwyn said. Candles, especially old ones, were exceptionally difficult to light from a tinderbox. "We laid a fire."

"Oh, indeed, did you?" The old man stumped over in the direction of the fireplace, a noise in utter darkness.

"We're sorry about bringing the horses inside," Aewyn said. "Whatever they broke, my father will gladly recompense. He'll be very grateful for our return."

Again the little light, lower, this time. The man might be running out of tinder, and they all would be in the dark. Elfwyn wished he might succeed. A little wish, given the makings and the right conditions, might help, so Gran always said.

The fire took, and blossomed, and the old man added more tinder, coming clear, with his white hair, his white beard, which came midway of his chest, and a ragged brown cloak. He fed the fire for a moment, and Elfwyn felt somewhat less afraid, seeing the man was quite elderly and frail. The voice had not entirely indicated that. But he still kept hold of Aewyn's arm.

The horses were well awake now, and restless. The light showed they had backed into a set of shelves last night, and ruined a copper pot, which suffered worse damage now. The whole place was thickly coated in dust, and wind-torn cobwebs veiled the rafters.

"Horses and all, is it?" the old man said. "There'll be grain in the bin, there." He indicated the dusty bin by the door.

"That's nice, but they mustn't eat what's moldy," Aewyn said under his breath, leaning next to Elfwyn and speaking so only he could hear, but when Elfwyn opened it, the grain was as fresh as if it had just come in at harvest, and there was a good wooden bucket in the grain for hauling it out. He brought it to the horses and strewed it in a thick line along the floor, gaining the animals' instant attention.

"Water in the barrel," the old man said then. Aewyn lifted the lid, and Elfwyn looked, expecting ice. But it was water, for sure, and he filled the bucket and took a deep drink himself, and so did Aewyn, before they brought the bucket to the horses.

"We're ever so grateful, sir," Aewyn said, while his horse was drinking.

"Oh, well," the old man said, and now there was a pot on the fire. "Use the other pail there, boy, and bring me water."

"Yes, sir," Elfwyn said, and indeed there was a second wooden bucket, in the corner. He brought water and poured it in the iron pot, which had already begun to heat on its pothook. The fireside gave off a fierce warmth, and the old man added more wood.

"Sack," the old man said, and indeed, there was a sack by the door, where he might have dropped it coming in. Aewyn brought it, and the old man delved into it, drawing out a large loaf of bread, a half a sausage, and a round of cheese, which he laid out on the sacking on the fireside. And meanwhile, though Elfwyn had seen nothing but water go into the pot, a savory smell began to go up from it, and steam to rise.

"Bowls on the shelf," the old man said, and there were three rust-brown glazed bowls, as clean as if they had come from the royal kitchens.

They had not been there a moment ago. Elfwyn would swear they had not. And despite his hunger, he conceived a reluctance to have any of that food in his belly.

"Food can be a bargain," he said so Aewyn would hear him. "And I'm not sure it's a bargain we should be making with a stranger."

"Ah," the old man said. "Be free of it, be quite free. That makes it safe, does it not?"

It ought to, unless there was something of more substantive harm in it. He had no enemy but the priests in Guelemara and his own mother, but he had something of value, something of wizardous value, next to his skin, and he began thinking that *that* might have drawn attention to them—attention far more dangerous than bandits.

"Sit, sit," the old man said. "Bring the bowls, don't gawk about, and sit down. You're a scruffy pair, you are. And two fine horses. Might you be horse thieves?"

"I am no thief, sir," Aewyn said in round, elegant, Guelen tones, and Elfwyn caught him by the arm and pulled him down by him at the fireside. In the other hand he had the three bowls, and set them down on the hearthside. The old man dipped up savory stew, and served it—could they, he wondered, possibly just have lost track of time, and dreamed the beginning, and forgotten how the old man had come here? But the wind blew, if anything, more furiously outside, and thumped away at the shutters. And he was aware of no gaps in his memory.

The old man had done them and their horses nothing but kindness. Elfwyn tasted the food very gingerly, and decided he took no harm of it. Aewyn supped it right down, with bits of bread, and Elfwyn found it so filling he had no need of cheese or sausage to go with it. Aewyn, beside him, had propped himself against the stonework of the fireplace, and nodded, but Elfwyn kept staring at the bowls, which he would swear had not been there before the old man wanted it, and the remnant of the broth, which could not have come from anything he had seen go into the pot.

The old man had worn a tattered brown cloak; but when he looked up, it was gray, and the old man wore a silver medallion, a design he had never seen before, a twisting thing, like a snake, or a dragon, and what had been grizzled gray hair streaked with black had become snowy white.

Worse and worse.

He would have run out into the night if he'd had a choice, but Aewyn snored away, beside him, and one of the horses had been indiscreet, right in the corner—it lent a touch of rural strangeness to the night.

"Excuse me, sir," he said, and got up and went to clean up the problem with a ratty broom and some straw from a pile in the corner: he swept it out the door, not without traces, and a lingering barn smell. He could run, he thought. But he could not leave Aewyn helpless. It was impossible to run.

He set the broom aside, and went to sit at the hearth, arms about his knees, looking steadily at the old man, wishing desperately for the sun to come up.

"You push at the world itself," the old man said, "but cannot budge it."

"No, sir," he said, more and more disturbed, distracted by dread. How had the old man known what he was thinking?

"The sun will come in its own time," the old man said, and wove a little pattern with his fingers. The gusts of cold air, the drafts . . . all stopped, and the room was breathless.

"My name is Emuin," the old man said, "and yours is Elfwyn."

Emuin. The Emuin of Gran's stories was dead. Surely he was dead. That Emuin had been an old, old man, even his whole lifetime ago.

"You doubt my claim?" the old man asked, with the arch of a brow.

"I'd heard you were dead."

A chuckle now, gentle and distant, as the old man gazed into the fire and grew somber. "I had heard you had gone to Guelemara. And then you came home to Amefel. Or did you? Didn't you run from Guelemara? I think you're given to running before the fact."

Straight to the heart, which beat hard, like a trapped thing. "How did you hear, sir?"

"Oh, a wayward bird." A light and careless answer, to a question carefully guarded. "And directly from your father, who arranged a message you weren't in any wise supposed to act on."

"He didn't."

"Oh, but he did. He wanted to get the Quinalt fellow out of your way and get you home to Gran before there was more trouble of a magical sort. And he ever so greatly regrets that letter."

"*Where* did you meet my father?"

"Oh, here and there, through the years, on the stairs, in the hall, in the scullery and the courtyard . . ."

"Just last. *Where did you meet him, sir?*"

A slow smile moved amid the mustaches, a darting look of very thoughtful eyes.

"Cautious lad."

"I must be, sir. I have to be. People I would believe have lied to me."

"Elfwyn. Elfwyn. Elfwyn," the old man said, and Elfwyn felt a band close about his chest, and loose again. "A fey name. The name of an ancient king, a dead and betrayed ancient king. But you, who bear that name, play at stableboy in a cottage."

"I'm not meant to be a king," he said. "I'm illegitimate." That wasn't the word he'd used all his life. He'd learned *illegitimate* in Guelemara. "I don't want to be a king."

"Do you say so?" The old man reached a straw into the fire and let it burn, delicately. A draft wafted the little flame toward the fire as it consumed the straw. It burned right to the old man's fingers.

And died with a little curl of smoke that flowed away as the flame had bent away from his hand.

"Do you say so?" the old man asked again.

"Where did you meet my father recently?"

A little frown knit white brows. The old man said, faintly, a wisp of a sound: "In the Zeide, in the Zeide just now. But I didn't stay for Tristen—the fool boy. The whole world is astir, and he's lost himself somewhere, and here you go trudging off through the snow. For what purpose?"

"To find Lord Tristen."

"To find Tristen, is it? Why?"

He had not thought of the reason of his quest in hours. He had struggled so to live he had not thought until that exact instant of the book he carried next to his skin, and now it seemed the most dangerous thing in the world to have in this man's close presence. He felt it tingle, like the ring. And he wanted to take Aewyn, ride to Ynefel, and put that terrible thing somewhere safe and never touch it again.

"Why should a boy search for Tristen, at peril of his life?"

He looked away. He had no wish to meet the old man's eyes: guilt for theft and folly overwhelmed him. He looked into the fire, and saw the ruin of old wood: he saw castles and fortifications of fire, crumbling in the heat.

"He will be by now where you were," the old man said. "Where I had rather be, this chilly night, instead of this place. Dash off into the dark, indeed. Dash off into storms the like of which your little wisp of a life has never seen. Have you ever seen the like of this weather?"

"No, sir," he said, bewildered into a glance toward the old man, which caught him, snared him, held him. "I never have."

"I have seen worse. Do you think it natural, this storm, the storms of this whole winter?"

"I think it very bitter cold."

"And yet you risked it. You fled. For what?"

He could not but think of the thing against his ribs. He didn't want to think about it.

"I know," the old man said. "Do you think I do not? What would your gran say? Why didn't you take it home?"

He was shaken. And angry. "If you're Master Emuin, you know my gran is dead. I have no home."

"Otter," the old man said, surprising him. "Slippery as an otter. Diving into dark places. Being the fool only for others' amusement."

That drew a frown. "I may be. But I look for advice from people I trust, not from strangers who may not be who they say they are."

"And you have very sharp teeth."

"Only if someone comes at me."

"Otter . . . or Spider? Which had you rather be?"

"Otter, thank you. Spiders live in nasty holes."

"Fastidious, then. You have a prince's tastes."

"No prince. A bastard, is all."

"His brother." This, the old man said with a gesture at Aewyn, whose fair hair curled in grimy ringlets about his unconscious face.

It was not a notice he wished to bring on Aewyn. If he could humor the old man until his bones warmed, until the horses were recovered, until the sun rose and dispelled this wizardous haunt, he would do that, and hope to keep Aewyn out of the old man's thoughts entirely until he waked. This man could conjure: he had seen that, and it was beyond him to deal with such a man, a wizard, who might have been drawn to them by what he had stolen and what he carried . . .

"A true prince of Ylesuin," the old man said. "*The* prince of Ylesuin. His father fears for him. And fears for you."

The first saying he easily accepted, that his father feared for Aewyn, though he by no means took for granted that this old man was his father's old tutor, or even his father's friend. The second thing stung. If his situation had risen to any care of his father's, it could never match his father's love for Aewyn, and he knew his brother's danger was all of his making. He was being led, and if he made a mistake in judgment of this old man and grew softheaded in his desire to hear what he wanted to hear, it could be his last mistake.

"You doubt your father loves you?"

"He has no particular reason to love me," Elfwyn said, every word like broken glass. "I've stolen. I've run away. As you say—I'm good at it. Slippery. The rest, you know nothing about."

"I know your begetting and your birth, your upbringing—and your talents."

"I have no talents except for getting in trouble."

"You are Aswydd."

"Not on the right side of the blanket."

"Born to a sorceress and a king and nurtured by a witch. But none of these is the source of your Gift."

"I've no Gift at all," he said, wanting to veer away from this topic. He shivered, cold despite the fire. "Nor wish to have. What times I've tried to do wizardry, I've failed. Do you think this storm will be done by morning?"

"Shoving at the world again. Tristen, now, *Tristen* could budge the weather."

"Can *you* stop the wind?"

The ancient fingers stirred, a ripple of a dismissive gesture. "I'm a wizard. That means a wise man. I never try."

It answered his secret question, the one he feared to ask: did you raise this storm? But he grew bold enough to challenge what he saw. "There weren't any bowls, before," he said. "I'd have seen them."

"Did you expect to find any?" the old man asked.

"No," he said.

"I did." A shrug, the ghost of a smile. "Best expect, if you spend the effort of looking. But do it sparingly. I assure you, the joy of some surprises isn't worth the risk of others."

Riddles with Gran's kind of sense at the core. Wizard, indeed, and by that advice, what answers did he reasonably expect to find in this old man?

Vision, Lord Tristen had said. Vision was one of his two words, and what did he see with a close look at this suddenly immaculate stranger?

Danger.

Power beyond what Gran had had. Even, perhaps, more power than his mother's.

Emuin, he claimed to be. And if he was that famous wizard, he might indeed raise a storm if he really wanted to. And there were not that many wizards, ever, more powerful than his mother. Emuin was indeed one possible answer to the riddle, if he was not a haunt.

Haunts, however, were not in the habit of coming up with bowls and grain.

"Maybe you could conjure us some cakes to finish with," he said, and the old man tilted back his head.

"Cakes, is it?"

"Well, if you looked for them . . . and expected them . . ."

"Impertinent boy!"

"Well, but you can do that, can't you?"

"Wishing for more than one needs is wasteful."

"Wasteful of what?"

A forefinger lifted. "Now *there* is a wise question. Of what? Of what indeed? Of effort, of soul, of spirit, of thought and life itself. Needing what one wants—now there's a wicked trap. Wanting what one needs, that can be a trap, too. Poverty can lead a lad from despair to envy, from envy to bad behavior. Knowing exactly what one needs, and *working* to get it, there's the wisdom. Your gran taught you that."

Gran would use plainer words. "Wishes won't draw flies. Sweat will." It had made him laugh, then. Now it reminded him of her, and of her old eyes, far kinder than these. *This man,* he thought, *if living man he is, has seen hard things. He is harder. And far more dangerous.*

"I'm still cold," he said.

"Then move nearer the fire, fool," the old man said. "Don't be afraid."

It set him nearer the old man, who had the best spot, but he did, easing up onto the hearthstones, which had grown warm. The heat comforted his ankles and his feet.

"There," the old man said. "Is that better?"

"Better, yes." But he had a greater tremor in his limbs. It was fear, and he liked that less than the cold.

"Let me see the book."

His heart gave a thump. For the first time he was sure they were trapped here, that he was outmatched by far, and that this man knew exactly what he was looking for.

"Book?" he asked blankly, and the old man sadly shook his head.

"Oh, I had so hoped for more cleverness."

He had a knife. He knew how to lay wards, too, but had he done that? He had not, despite the night and the storm and them sleeping in a place not his own. He felt the fool. "Maybe I left it somewhere."

"Maybe you didn't."

"I mean to give it to Lord Tristen, and sooner or later he will know about it, if he doesn't right now. And if *he* wants it, he could take it whenever he wants. So I suppose it really doesn't matter if you should take it. It's his, and you ought to be very careful."

"It's certainly not yours, fool. And if he could have taken it, he would have done so, long since. Whence came it, and who gave it to you?"

From underneath a table, in a wall in the library, he recalled, as vividly as if he were in that place, under the very fear and the suffocating compulsion he had had in that moment. It was dreams, again, dreams, that had made him find it . . .

"*Where* did you find it?"

"Why should it matter?" he asked, and the old man looked at him from under his eyebrows in a way that made his hands sweat despite the cold.

"Who gave it to you?" the old man asked again.

"I don't know. I found it."

"Found it! Are you a fool?"

"No, sir." His jaw set. "I hope I am not."

"Lady Tarien. Does that name touch you?"

"My mother."

"She's no longer a prisoner. Do you know that?"

He didn't. He didn't truly believe it. He didn't know what to believe tonight.

"I'll give you another name. Orien Aswydd. Does that mean anything to you?"

An Aswydd name he had heard a handful of times, but it told him nothing in particular. He shook his head.

"Your mother's twin sister," the old man said. "Entombed below the lower hall, near the haunt, right beneath her prison."

Now the fire could not help the cold. He thought about the bad feeling in that little stairway that went nowhere, the place the haunt had flung him.

"She's gone, too, right along with your mother. Her tomb burst open and there was nothing inside, not even bones. They're both fled to the winds."

"Why should I believe you?" he cried, moving away and scrambling to his feet, and Emuin unwound like a serpent, rising like a much younger man and towering over him like a shadow before the fire, between him and his sleeping brother.

"Because I am your friend, boy, and that book in your hands is deadly dangerous."

Breath seemed short.

"Would it be better in yours?" he asked, and saw, for the first time, the least doubt—the same doubt he felt about having the book. That alone made him think this terrible man might be telling him the truth, and that shook him as deeply as any threat to their lives.

"If I have such a thing," he said, "don't take it. Help me give it to Lord Tristen myself. Then I'll know you *are* Master Emuin."

"A dire thing, for a boy's hands."

"Almost a man."

"A very young man, then, who forgets to lay his wards."

That stung. "I forgot. But I'm no wizard."

"No," the old man said—Emuin, if it was Emuin. "You are not. You're something else."

"I don't want my mother's Gift." It blurted out of him, without his willing it. "I don't want it at all!"

"No," the old man said sharply, cutting him off. "You don't want your mother's Gift, your mother's foolishness, or your mother's greed. But the Gift you already have, you might manage better—far better than you have. Can you read the book?"

"No."

"Not surprising. You won't, until you want to, though doing so lies within your Gift."

"It makes no sense to me! I tried. The letters move."

"They evade you. But not for long. You have very little time to be innocent, boy, because what you guard is not innocent. It's a handbook, Mauryl Gestaurien's darkest work, Mauryl, who Shaped Tristen himself, and whose magic keeps him here, for all I can tell. The secret of it may lie in that book. Do you guess how very many forces in this world would like to lay hands on it?"

"Then help me! If it's so dangerous, then maybe you shouldn't take it either. I won't let you have it. I'll fight you, if I have to."

"Oh, lad." The forbidding shadow shifted, and became an old man leaning on his staff and looking down pensively at the floor. "Lad. Ninévrisë Syrillas held you in her arms sixteen years ago, and wished you your father's grace."

"Her Majesty."

"The same woman. While she carried Aewyn within her, she wished you well. Lord Tristen himself laid hands on you and wished you well. These are strong bonds, perhaps the stronger now that you know them." Emuin settled to the floor with a sigh, leaning heavily on the staff. "Ignorance is never safe."

"The queen. And Lord Tristen."

"And Gran, an excellent woman. She has not faded. Believe me, she is in good company."

Elfwyn sat down again, refusing belief, refusing anything that touched what he so wanted to believe . . . but unwilling to lose that thread, either.

"She wouldn't become a haunt."

"No, no." The old man sank down and leaned his staff against the fireside. "Not the sort of haunt that's within the Zeide, that much is certain. She was never discontent; but protective of her boys, oh, that she is."

"She's dead."

"Indisputably."

"I don't believe you even knew her! I never saw you there."

"I never came under Gran's roof," the old man said. "But meet her, yes, more often than any other in these years. I came to consult with her, oh, many times at the fence, when she was weeding the herb garden, or out in the meadow, when she was herding goats. I came until you started to grow inquisitive. You don't remember that, do you?"

He did remember a ragged old man at the fence, an old man with a staff—a customer, like many others who wanted Gran's cures. But if his mother could conjure dreams, this old man, this wizard—what could he do with memories?

"Then why, like any honest visitor, didn't you come inside?"

"You were not of an age to keep secrets well."

"Why did it matter?"

"How often did you see your mother?"

"Once a year." He didn't see how that answered his question, and then did. "Once a year, on my birthday. I'd see her, and the duke would give me a present. I didn't know other boys didn't get presents from the duke. But I thought it was peculiar that my mother lived in a tower and hated everyone."

A smile turned the old man's face gentle. He reached out a long, thin arm and put a small log on the fire.

"I suppose you could keep that one burning all night, if you wanted," Elfwyn said.

"Oh, perhaps I could, but why want what you already have? The wood is there. I use it, much more easily than that, I assure you. Do you think wizard-work is easy?"

"If you wanted to, you could have kept Gran from going hungry."

"If Gran wanted to, I'm sure she could do the same, but she didn't. She wanted as little of your mother's attention as she could have, and she never would have allowed your visits to the tower, except it was the agreement with your mother, and to breach that, breached other things."

"Like wards."

"Like that," the old man agreed.

"But she escaped, you said. She and Orien Aswydd. If she had a twin, why didn't I know?"

"Because that name doesn't enter pleasant conversation in Amefel. I'm surprised your mother didn't mention it. Though—*we* should have been surprised she did not. Now it seems indeed we should have taken note."

"Riddles! It's my life! It cost Gran's! My mother killed her!"

"Contain your anger. Anger will be your particular struggle." He nodded to something behind him, toward, he saw with a glance, no more than Aewyn, sound asleep, deaf to all they said. "You love him. That was Tristen's wish, and Ninévrisë's, and your father's. He is your chance for redemption and your inclination toward utter fall. Do you understand me?"

"If I betray him," Elfwyn said.

"If you betray him," the old man concluded, "or if you fail in the promises Ninévrisë laid upon you. If you betray him, it will be fatal to us all."

"I never would."

"You ought to know: Orien Aswydd wished you born. The only spark of motherhood in that house was in the woman that bore you. *Tarien* would do anything in those days to preserve your life, which she thought threatened."

"She never loved me!"

"As near as she can come to love, she loves you—loves you as her possession, as much as she hates your father for casting her aside. She wanted you. *We* took you from her, Tristen, I, the queen, and your father: *we* took you from her, and promised her she might see you once a year, or when you wished. I'll warrant you generally saw her better side."

He didn't want to hear any good about his mother. He shook his head. "She gave me sweets. She gave me things she'd made. Gran said they were charms, and wouldn't let them in the house."

"I've no doubt," the old man said. "But she tried, poor creature. You're certainly the best thing she ever created. And there is her other side. She and Orien both slept with your father. Orien saw to it that Tarien was the one who got with child, I strongly suspect. *There* was a woman ill suited to motherhood."

He blushed at hearing such details about his begetting. He couldn't look the old man in the eyes. But the old man reached out, startling him, and lifted his face with a hand beneath his chin.

"Orien wanted you born, I say. She was Tristen's enemy. And she's loose."

He drew back and still stared at the old man. "I never met her."

"No. But I have a notion just how she left her prison, and where she resides tonight. What was sundered is rejoined. They were always half of one. Now, I fear, they *are* one."

"Orien's haunting my mother?"

"Possession," the old man said. "Possessing is much different, and much more serious. I doubt your mother has much to say about it. Your mother is a skilled sorceress. Orien, now, Orien is something else. And Orien has, in the past, had an ally. He's the one to fear. He is very much to fear. He wants that book. He failed, in the past, to get it. But try as I might and try as Tristen might, neither of us could find it. I know where it is now: I have no trouble knowing, which argues that someone warded it into that place for the long years we failed to find it, and we assumed it burned along with other manuscripts, since we didn't recover it with the others. So it never left the library at all. Where *did* you find it? Which wall of the library?"

His mind rebounded from one mad proposal to the other, from a horrid fate for his mother, which he never would wish on her—to some third person he didn't understand, and back to his own theft.

"The south wall," he admitted.

"We searched there," Emuin said. "We should have taken the whole damned wall down. But again—the one who warded it didn't want Tristen's hands on it. That could be two wizards: one would be Mauryl himself. The other would be Hasufin Heltain."

"Is he that other person?"

"Orien's ally? Yes. He's Tristen's enemy. And Mauryl's."

"And mine?"

Emuin turned his face away and poked into the fire with another stick. "That is a question, isn't it?"

"Well, I don't forgive my mother. I'm sure I don't love her sister, and I never heard of Hasufin Heltain. I don't intend any of them should have the book. I want to go and live at Ynefel, and study there."

"So did he."

"Who? This Hasufin Heltain?"

"He lived there. He studied there. He ripped the place apart and killed his teacher, ultimately."

"I'm not him!" Elfwyn said. "I'm King Cefwyn's son, I'm Gran's, I'm Paisi's, and I'm Aewyn's brother, all these things! And I don't want to be my mother's! Help us get to Ynefel!"

"And would that lead, I wonder, in the direction you truly want? You have an enemy. You have more than one, I suspect. He will come at you when you are most desperate, and his ways may look like escape."

"Or like friendly old men who come offering help in the middle of the night?"

That rash outburst won a sidelong look, a terrible look. The old man dropped the stick he was using, lifting his hand, and that hand glowed with blue fire. Elfwyn scrambled backward, came up against his sleeping brother, and shook at him, holding him in his arms; but Aewyn hung entirely limp in his embrace, like the dead.

"You might be in a predicament," the old man said, "if I weren't who I say I am. But I am. And you and your brother are as safe as I can make you." The blue fire died. "He oughtn't to hear certain things. He'll sleep. He's quite safe. Let him lie."

"Emuin." He had to try to believe it. They both might have been dead, and the book taken, if he were not who he claimed. "Master Emuin, then."

"Good." The old man nodded, placid again.

He still trembled. "You taught my father."

"Indeed I did."

"You might—" He knew he had just been reprimanded, might be tested again, and that the circumstance was dire. He hardly dared voice his ambition again: ambition did not become him, in his circumstances, but his father had encouraged him. "You might teach me. If all the things you say could happen could come to be, you could show me how to avoid them. If I've made mistakes, then you could teach me how to protect myself, and my brother, *and* the little princess."

"Teach you wizardry? Useless. Teach you magic? I cannot. No more can I teach any Sihhë what resides in his blood and bone."

"Sihhë!" He laughed bitterly, refused this time with nonsense.

"Sihhë, I say. A spirit the like of which I could never conjure, nor could Tarien. Such a conjuring weakened Mauryl Gestaurien to his death, and he was ten times the wizard I am, not to mention a hundredweight the worth of Tarien Aswydd. Born or called—you are half his brother, at least have trust that *that* side of the blanket is not in doubt. Doubt your mother's half of the proposition instead. Neither she nor your aunt could have done this unaided."

"Riddles, again! Don't trust her, you mean? I never trusted her, and I never knew I had an aunt."

"Riddles I hardly know how to say—except you are the living Gift. Otter. Elfwyn. Elfwyn. Elfwyn. Say a thing three times and it binds. I suspect you were bound to that name long, long ago, and your mother had no choice in naming you."

"Tell me what you mean!"

"I mean," Emuin said, "that you have already gone to the proper source to learn certain things, and left it, one supposes, uninformed. Perhaps even *he* failed to know you."

"Lord Tristen? I asked him to teach me, and he wouldn't. He told me I was Elfwyn, not Otter."

"He wouldn't teach you, or he couldn't," Emuin said, and frowned darkly. "And he named you. Then I suspect he did see what I see."

"What? Give me the truth, Master Emuin! What did he see? What do you?"

"A conjuring," Emuin said. "A Summoning that opens a door."

"What door? Make sense, please, sir!"

"*You* govern what door, if you have the will. *Do* you have the will, Spider Prince?"

He drew a deep breath and balked, growing angry, angrier than he had been since the day Gran died. "I have the will for anything, sir, if I'm informed. I'm Otter, if you like. Lord Tristen said I should be Mouse, not Owl. And he said nothing at all about spiders."

"Good," Emuin said, looking squarely into his eyes. "Very good, Spider Prince. Otter. Mouse. And Elfwyn. But never Owl? Probably a good idea."

"Damn you!"

"Oh, that would *not* be easy," Emuin said, laying a hand on the emblem at his breast. "And many have tried. But gratitude . . . that, I would think, I am due, at least a little, for coming out here in the cold."

The anger fell away from him. Embarrassment took its place, for ever asking what was beyond his station in life and for ever cursing this man, no matter how desperate. "A great deal, Master Emuin, a very great deal, only—"

"Guard yourself from such words and such thoughts as damning folk. When you were a child you could let words fly. Now, when a man's mind stirs in you, such things become dangerous. As for the Gift, you could easily make that recalcitrant candle burst in flame."

"If I could have done it, sir, I certainly would have. I tried. I did try."

"While you believe you cannot, you will not. Will is all of it. You have decided to be King Cefwyn's son. You wish to become his acknowledged son, with all the people changing their minds about you. While that wish governs you, so you will become—with all the good or ill for your father or brother that that one choice may bring. But to become the other thing that you are, you must stop wishing to be Cefwyn's son or Aewyn's brother."

"I never can!"

"So you say now," Emuin said gently. "But the years roll on, and time changes us. You may need to renounce Aewyn to protect him from your enemies. Think of that, Elfwyn Prince."

A bitter laugh rose up in him. "I'm no prince. And I'll never renounce my brother or my father."

"Every person has will, and while wizards have more force than most, the collective populace can be gathered, and swayed, without magic—indeed they, being blind to it, can be swayed that much more easily. They are deaf to magic, but their will, my boy, can be as potent as a wizard's conjuring—more so than some. So know what you defy, when you send your wishes toward the people. Passion can do a great deal to awaken that giant. Beware of stirring it. And beware, too, of ordinary men: thwart our wishes, that they can, and open doors, or simply leave them unlatched—that they will do with amazing fecklessness, or spite. They can be the hands and feet of a wizard's wish, individually. They can open any door at all. Never, never discount them. Never trifle with them. And beware of using them. They have their own interests. They fear magic greatly, and will hate you for it if they detect it. They will often turn contrary, when they know they're meddled with."

"They already hate me."

"They scarcely know you exist," Emuin said. "And they have not decided what you are. That is why I counsel you, beware of waking that giant. Be the spider. Or be Mouse. Use the edges of the walls. Find crevices from which to watch and live quietly, if you can manage it, while you learn."

"If anyone harms Aewyn," he began.

"Let no enemy find out how much that would move you, or I assure you that will be their first recourse. Let no enemy know your weaknesses. Strive to be your own master. That is my advice. Know whence come the motions of your heart, Spider Prince, whether they are light or dark, fair or foul, whether they be what you will or what you would not: know them for what they are, and shape yourself as you would wish to become. That will be magic enough, for a start at it. Go to sleep. I shall watch."

He didn't want to. But his eyes grew heavy on the instant. He snapped them right open.

"Strong-willed," Emuin said. "But if you can't trust me in this, you can trust me in nothing. Trust me, I say!"

Something thumped, outside, in the wind. A good many things had flapped and bumped in the wind, but this came at the door. And Emuin looked that way, sharply, and set his staff against the floor to rise, not with the alacrity of a young man.

"Master Emuin?" Elfwyn asked, and leapt up and took his arm.

"Hold your brother," Emuin snapped. *"Hold on to him!"*

The door burst open. Bitter wind rushed inside, scattering coals, bringing dark as the fire blew up the chimney. Elfwyn flung himself to Aewyn's side, seized up his brother in his arms as Emuin reached them.

FORTRESS OF ICE

"Hold on!" Emuin shouted at them. "Hold my hand! We are going to your father!"

He reached. He grasped Emuin's fingers, and the wind caught them, whirled them away through gray mist, a spinning confusion of themselves, and the horses, and their gear, and all the straps loose and confused.

"Otter!" Aewyn cried, and began to slip out of his encircling arm, and to slide away from him, as if they were sliding on ice. He held tight to Aewyn's coat, and that grip began to fail, as if the wind that moved them excluded Aewyn. He had his choice, hold Emuin, or hold his brother, and he wrapped both arms about Aewyn and held on.

They plummeted, he had no idea how far, or how long a fall. He only held on, eyes tight shut.

"Otter," Aewyn said against his ear. "Otter, what's happening?"

But he had no answer.

In the next moment they landed, hard, side by side, in thick snow.

iv

IT WAS A BITTERSWEET GATHERING OF OLD FRIENDS IN CALAMITY, IN THE LITTLE hall. Past the worry and the fear that gnawed at him, Cefwyn saw the weariness that marked Tristen and Uwen, both, and Crissand ordered mulled wine and a platter of food—food Tristen neglected, though he had two sips of the wine.

What can you see? Cefwyn longed to ask, seeing Tristen's head bowed and his hands clasped before his lips, his elbows braced on the arms of the massive chair. Tristen had not divested himself of his armor, nor had Uwen, though that was the first thing a man just off a long, cold road would long to do. He simply sat, and stared into nothing, but not in futility, Cefwyn was sure. He was earnestly trying to find pieces—scattered pieces. Emuin. Orien. Tarien. And two lost boys.

And he had said nothing for the last candle measure, nor stirred, nothing more than a wisp of his dark hair blowing a bit in the draft from an opened door.

They had been up to the tower room, wherein a whirlwind had wrought utmost havoc, and left the shutters hanging askew. They had been into the cell below, and in front of the blank wall into which Master Emuin had vanished.

They waited in this small room, and the candles in the sconces dripped drop by drop into their pans. Outside, servants removed bits of stone that littered the hall, where the force of the stones blowing out had shredded the tapestry and landed clear against the opposing wall, scarring the stone there. Others, surely with trepidation, had climbed up those stairs into the tower, to clear away the debris of Tarien's life there. Comrades had taken the bodies of the guards for burial, two decent men with widows and children: Crissand had passed word he would talk with the women as soon as he could. The deaths sat on the king's conscience: it was the king's prisoner they had guarded, two brave men, completely defenseless against sorcery, all amulets and protections inadequate to save their lives.

Hate had killed them, spite directed against him. He determined, sitting there, waiting for some breath of an answer, that he would take the women and children under his own protection, the men having died in defense of him and his.

But justice for it—justice was very much in doubt.

Tristen drew a visible breath. The hands didn't move. The eyes didn't blink. Everyone hung on that slight motion.

Then Tristen lowered his hands down onto the arm of the chair and leapt up, turning for the door. Uwen jumped to his feet, and Cefwyn, hardly slower, followed, with Crissand right at his heels, and all the bodyguards caught completely off their guard, broke aside from the door, getting out of their path.

The haunt came alive down the hall, beyond the stairs. Servants ran in terror, and the thunder of wings raised a wind that blew down from the tower's ruined windows and up from the depths of the cell. Tristen reached the midst of it, the rest of them right with him, and the wind blasted them with cold and a spate of snow. Uwen drew his sword, and Cefwyn reached for the dagger he wore, as the sound of swords drawn echoed behind them all.

It was a disheveled figure that came out, a figure all swirling white hair and gray robes, turning back, his hand held out to someone invisible still within, and the winds screaming about them all.

The haunt stopped, stopped cold, leaving the area dark, and snow melting on the floor, and Master Emuin standing baffled and distraught in the middle of it.

"I couldn't hold them!" Emuin cried in dismay, and Cefwyn's heart sank. Tristen was there with him, and if anything magical was going on between the two of them, if they had said anything to each other down those corridors wizards used, Cefwyn was deaf to it, and cursed his deafness. It was Crissand to whom Tristen turned next, and said, "A cloak. He is chilled to the bone. A cloak, and the warm wine—Master Emuin." Tristen seized the old man by the arms and held him upright, the staff trailing from Emuin's hand and his eyes all but shut. "Stand. Stand fast, Master Emuin. Help is here."

"The boys." Emuin's eyes rolled open, his head sank, and it was all Cefwyn could do to keep his own hands from seizing the old man and shaking him.

"I am here, Master Emuin," he said. "Where did you lose them?"

"In between," Tristen answered for Emuin. "Take him, take him, Cefwyn. Uwen, you must stay with him!"

"As I shan't do, m'lord!" Uwen cried in protest. "No!" But without a breath or a flare from the haunt, Tristen ceased to be there—just—was not there, and Master Emuin was on his way to falling as Cefwyn seized the old man about the body and held him on his feet. Crissand helped him, and Uwen took Emuin's staff. The lot of them, guards and all, were left there, in a hall in which the snow was melting and the old man they held in their arms was colder than the grave itself.

Servants came running with a cloak, and with a cup of wine. Both were useless.

"The little hall," Cefwyn said, remembering the warm fireside they had left, its fire stoked to its fullest to warm Tristen and Uwen. They carried the old man, who weighed very little at all, up the hall to this room. Servants hovered as they disposed Master Emuin on the warm stones in front of the fire. Cefwyn knelt, holding the old man, and Crissand disposed his cloak about him and chafed his pale hand, while Uwen laid the staff beside him.

"Old Master," Cefwyn said. "Master Grayfrock. Come back. Come back to us. Can you hear?"

The old man's eyes slitted, ever so little, and the pupils rolled just slightly toward him.

"Tristen has gone?" Emuin asked.

"He went after them."

Emuin shook his head. "I tried."

"That you did," Cefwyn said, holding Emuin fast, while the fire blazed and crackled, impotent against the chill in the old man. "Come now. Wake, wake, do you hear me? None of this slipping back again. Stay out of that place you go. Tristen is on their track and needs no help. There's mulled wine. Uwen Lewen's-son is here. So is Crissand. Wake and make sense to me. Tristen is out looking for them, I say."

The eyes drifted shut. Slitted open a second time. The brow knit, much as if the old man was trying to think of a long-forgotten fact. "He shouldn't be out there, the fool."

"Who? Tristen?"

"He's in danger. He's particularly in danger. The boy has that book."

"What sort of book? What sort of book is it, Master Emuin?"

"His unmaking." Coughing racked the frail body, and Cefwyn propped him up until it stopped—propped him up and took the offered cup of wine, touching the merest edge of it to the old man's lips.

"Wine, if you can manage it, old master."

"Ale," the old man said, never opening his eyes. "I'd rather ale. I'm dry as dust."

"It's here, Your Majesty." The servants had brought up every likely need, when they had been sitting in this room. Liquid splashed into a deep tankard, and a yeasty smell spread through the air before the cup even reached Cefwyn's hand.

"Here," he said, and this time the old wizard's hand reached up and steadied the tankard, and he drank three deep gulps before he breathed.

"Where are my boys?" Cefwyn asked, running short on compassion. The old man seemed less dying than frozen, and warmth was getting back to him. "Where did you leave them?"

"If I knew that, they wouldn't be lost!" Master Emuin said. "But they're together. They fell away together."

CHAPTER TEN

i

THE GRAY SPACE ROARED WITH TROUBLED WINDS. THERE WAS EVERY DANGER of being cast back to the icy waste, and Tristen kept Cefwyn and Uwen very much in mind, his link to the world. He was alone here, but confused and treacherous as things could become, he had deliberately left ties to draw him back, and as quickly as the bitter cold bit to the bone he drew in a deep breath and set his feet, making his own warmth, that of living flesh.

He had his sword. Unlike most weapons, this sword had value here, even with ghosts. He had his protections, not least in those ties he maintained to the world of Men. He was glad not to sense Emuin in this place. Emuin had not tried to follow him, having no strength to do so, none, either, to tell him what way he had come—but the track Emuin had left in his passage was still clear, a bright trail shredding on the winds.

He followed it, carefully extending his presence from his staying-place in Henas'amef along that roiled, chill breeze through the void that defined that recent passage.

He saw shapes, hazed in the gray. Going farther, he found two horses where no creatures of Men ought to be, and one he knew: they ran in panic, but he drew his sword and parted the gray space to give them their escape into the world they wanted . . . natural creatures, nothing of the sort this place could harbor long. Their fear had roiled everything around them, and destroyed the track Emuin had made, lines of passage confused and broken.

A shard of ice thrust itself up. *That* place tried to form again around him, and he knew its warning signs, and hurled himself back.

Everything shifted. Every track he had followed was gone, confounded and confused.

"Elfwyn!" he called down the winds. "Elfwyn Aswydd! Answer if you hear!"

A wisp of something wafted back at his call. He reached for it.

ii

AEWYN NEVER YET STIRRED FROM UNCONSCIOUSNESS, OR WIZARD-CAST SLEEP, or whatever held him in its grip, despite the fall into a snowbank. Sweating despite the cold, Elfwyn hauled him up into his arms, the wind skirling about them and moaning through old trees. He rocked, as Gran had used to do with him when the night was full of noises; but there was no old man any longer, there was no roof over their head. Master Emuin had left them and there was not the least clue where they were, except in the midst of a woods that could be some lord's copse or the dark heart of Marna itself. There had been no woods, he said to himself, no woods at all near the cottage. And they had no shelter, no way to ride out of here.

"It's all right," he said, over and over again, in time with his moving, in time with the worst shrieks of the wind. "It's just the wind. It's the trees making that sound. It's all right. It's all right, Aewyn. I'm still here; I won't leave you, I promise."

Aewyn moved, lifted a hand as if to fend something off.

"Aewyn?"

A hand caught him in the chin, bringing blood to his lip. Aewyn flailed out, kicking and gasping, and he wrapped his arms about his brother, hard as he could.

"We're not falling, we shan't fall," he said, and felt Aewyn's breath go out of him and come back. "I'm here. I'm here."

"Otter?"

"We fell, Aewyn. Something hit the door, the old man left, and we fell."

"Where are we?" Aewyn asked in a hoarse thread of a voice. "Gods! Where are we?"

"I don't know. Somewhere in a forest. He was going to take us to your father, and then I couldn't hold on to you, and I did, and we're here, is all."

"Freezing in the snow," Aewyn said, trying to sit up, and wincing. It wasn't deep snow here: the trees kept it off, but they were in the edge of a drift, in the dark, in the wind, in a clear spot in the woods. "Have we lost the horses, too?"

"I don't know where we are." Elfwyn tried to get to his feet, managed as far as one knee, stiff with cold. "I don't think he meant to drop us. He might come back. I did ward us here. I did what I could." He had trampled a line all around them, and done it three times, on his knees, with the wind knocked out of him. The old man had told him, the old man had chided him about his carelessness with protections. He was not to be caught being a fool again.

But Aewyn lurched to his feet and walked a staggering step or two, which took him immediately outside the sorry little circle he had made, and Elfwyn scrambled up and seized Aewyn's arm to bring him back.

"Where are we?" Aewyn asked desperately, and turned. Now, above their ragged breathing, there began to be noises in the woods around them. Brush cracked, first on this side, then that.

They were still outside his small circle. Elfwyn pulled him back in, and looking between the trees he saw slashes appear in the snow.

"Go away!" he yelled at whatever it was. "Get back! Get away from us!"

The fog swept in about them both. Shadows moved in it, tall shadows, soldiers with pikes, and swords. He heard shouts, and the clangor of weapons, and the ground seemed to go out from under their feet and come back again with a thump that staggered them where they stood.

The fog broke in a rush of snowy wind, and left them, not in a woods, but on flat, open ground, beside a snowy heap of stones, a tall pillar of stones, in a sea of snowdrifts.

It was a cairn, and a flat stone was set against it: writing on it was obscured by snow, and when Elfwyn brushed the face of it clear . . .

Andas, it said. Just that.

"Andas Andas-son," Aewyn said. "The standard-bearer. This is where the standard-bearer fell. Oh, gods, Otter, this isn't a good place! We're at Lewen Field!"

All around them in the dim, snow-sifted light, as Elfwyn turned to look, the snowdrifts blew off other cairns piercing the white, hundreds of low hummocks of stone that had gathered snow, looking for all the world like drifts, and unnaturally blowing clear all at once. He seized Aewyn's arm, and all of a sudden the fog began to close in again about them, in a rush of shouting and tumult, the clash of armed men and the howl of a dark edge so, so close to them . . .

iii

GONE. TRISTEN REACHED OUT, BUT WHEN HE REACHED FOR THE BOYS, THE GRAY space shifted again, and things that had been on the left were above him, and things that had been above him were below. The diminishing trail of a living and double presence retreated on winds he himself had generated, just by moving, like leaves in autumn—while around him, everywhere around him, shadows moved.

"My lord!" some cried, and others howled in rage or screamed in fear. Lewen Field, it was, the old battlefield seething with sorcery, and magic. Here, his enemy had evaded him, had attacked those who followed him, bitter, bitter lesson. Now the battlefield teemed with shadows, some beseeching him, some cursing him, some attempting to go home, some to find their lords, their comrades, their brothers: the whole place had gone down in chaos, and chaos bred and broke out like plague, sweeping into the winds.

Darkness lurked here, too, a dark wind, an ominous track. It had come at him in that day. But where it went now, he turned to see.

It eluded him, and swept away on the course the boys had taken—a stalking presence risen between him and them.

But when he risked leaving his hold on Uwen Lewen's-son and attempted to follow that trail through the gray space, chill winds flung him or it elsewhere. It was as if the harder he reached to take hold of anything, the farther what he sought retreated.

Once more, he made the attempt. Once the faint whisper of presence that was the boy Elfwyn wafted right past him, but when he reached for it, the boy was immediately far distant, like flotsam on another current, trailing blue fire—magic let loose, and part of it within his grasp, a mystery to him.

Elfwyn he might snatch, *might*. But Aewyn was lost if he did that. Aewyn resisted. Aewyn clung to the world, and the result slung the brothers no knowing where, a leaf's mad course through a windstorm.

The gale narrowed, however. A gap appeared in a wall of shards that baffled him: such a wall had never existed, within his ken. Winds wailed through that keyhole of a gap, and if the boys went that way, they might be swept through and lost.

Those were wards, he thought. Wards of unprecedented strength, veiling a power that might suck the boys right through: to him it appeared as an impenetrable wall, when most were gossamer, and shredded when he casually reached through them.

He was dismayed—helpless to prevent the boys' sweeping course toward that narrow gap, and not knowing, if he passed through that one necessary breach, whether he could rescue the boys, or even save himself.

Two swordlike spires of ice thrust up, blocking his path. One cut his reaching hand. Blood fell, and streamed away like smoke. More shards rose.

"Aewyn Marhanen!" he called out, attempting to enlist that recalcitrant mote. But he had not seen the Guelen brother in years, and had nothing to hold to, no inkling how to compel the one resisting element of that retreating image. "Elfwyn Aswydd!"

Suddenly the track of both boys curled away and vanished, more smoke than substance, streaming among shards of ice, bristling precursors of that wall.

The gray space curled up and stretched out again, and all the shards revised themselves. They became part of the barrier.

He might risk it. For two such lives, even so, he might risk that barrier.

"M'lord," Uwen said, or he thought Uwen said.

Solid as the mortal earth, Uwen was, and long ago, he had given Uwen the command of him. He began to retreat without deciding.

Overheated air met him, like fire, burning his wounded hand. Blood dripped, Uwen seized him, face-to-face as he caught his balance on solid stone. Cefwyn and Crissand, with Master Emuin, turned in alarm.

"I lost them, too," he said in despair, and Uwen caught his wounded hand and held on to him, warmth, like the room, and Crissand seized a heavy chair and shoved it under him.

Rest and warmth came welcome. His body was exhausted. And from where he sat, he could look across to Master Emuin, whose face was still unnaturally pale. "Wherever I went, whenever I reached for them, it drove them farther. Well that I came back, before I made matters worse than they are—they stopped, they stopped, somewhere just short of where another power meant to take them. They are fighting. How long they can fight—"

"A book, lad," Emuin said hoarsely. "We thought it burned . . . and 'twas hidden in the library wall. It's come loose in the world now."

"There was something . . . " A chill came through his flesh, a memory of that place, and of that blue trail through the winds. He recalled of the Zeide library, a pile of ash, and a basket of burned fragments that resisted every effort to put them back together—fallen to dust, now.

But the boys had fought their fate. Some sort of magic was with them. Magic drew them along the winds, but in their determination—or the determination of one of them—they fought being drawn. That, and at least the one thing of power in the possession of one of them, was how they still held on to the world.

"One book survived," Emuin said faintly. "One book someone most wanted, time meaning very little to him. Mauryl's notebook, if I'm a wizard, and Elfwyn has it. He carries it with him."

Cold settled about his heart, deep suspicion what power would have had the deftness to hide such a thing from Emuin and from him all this time, despite their searching, the deftness to hide it and the patience to wait for years to lay hands on it. Men were born and died, but that ancient soul had maintained a key in the world to get at it. It was not an immortal creature: nor was he, brought into the world for one purpose—to oppose it.

So a book of Mauryl Gestaurien's had survived, as they had thought—Mauryl, who had taught Hasufin Heltain, but *not* taught him all he wanted.

Mauryl, in his battle with Hasufin Heltain, had called *him* into being at the last. Tristen's own making might be in such a book. He had looked for that in the ashes they had found in the library, a burning that had not been complete, and in books they had gotten back at the riverside . . . to no avail. Now there was a book, which no one could find before.

Now, now the key emerged—the boy with the hollow at his heart, the book that was not burned, the burst tomb, and the sister vanished from her tower . . .

Hasufin had no pity, nor any desire but one: life and power to hold on to it. He knew his enemy, having reached to the depth of him. And Hasufin knew him: if there was one thing Hasufin wanted most in all the world it was to see him out of it . . . because Hasufin would not have life until he took and destroyed Mauryl's own key in the world—his greatest spell, his Shaping clothed in flesh, that walked and breathed and held lordship over Ynefel, where, until Tristen was gone, Hasufin could not be.

The blood dripped down from his hand and puddled on the stones. Uwen was attempting to staunch it with a piece of cloth, but it was cut to the bone. Once he thought of it, he healed himself, only because it distressed Uwen. He was trying to think what else in recent days might be the enemy's working, the gathering of pieces, the arrangement of items that suited his working.

His and Uwen's confusion in coming here—oh, that was beyond doubt part and parcel of it: they were not meant to have come here too early. Once things moved, then they could move like lightning. Emuin could reach this place. Tristan had arrived, alas, just a little later than Emuin, having come farther, he suspected.

"Are they lost?" Cefwyn asked him . . . the dread in his eyes was hard to bear.

"No," he said quickly and, for Cefwyn, he took a risk: he cast out into the world of Men, sure of a location, at least, now that he knew *what* the boy was carrying, and hoping only not to dislodge them again in the mere attempt to locate them. North, he thought. North of Henas'amef, at the bridge. "I know where they are," he said. "They're well enough for the moment."

"What can we do?"

"I've lost Owl somewhere," he said, not at all extraneously. It was part and parcel of the difficulty they were all in, part of his being lost, part of his immediate helplessness to reach the boys, and that Owl had strayed from him in Marna and not come back was all of a piece with the rest of it, this sudden abstraction of resources that belonged to Ynefel and Mauryl, and to him. Their enemy was pouring a great deal of effort into this working, a very great deal, and moving quickly. "They are north of us, not all the way into Elwynor. If I should reach for them, I fear they would move out of reach."

"Tristen," Cefwyn said, laying a hand on his arm. "Tristen, *Ninévrisë* is in Elwynor. With the baby. Could they be going toward her?"

It was not good news. He shook his head. "The two boys are *in* this world. I believe they are. I cannot reach them, but I shall try to hold them on this side of the river, as much as I can. No, I do not think it would be a good thing."

"Is it that damned woman? Is it Tarien Aswydd?"

"She hasn't done this alone," Emuin said.

"Hasufin," Tristen said quietly. And: "Get horses. We must go in this world, as quickly as we can. If I am nearer to them than he is, I believe I can hold them."

"The book," Emuin said. "The book evaded her when he took it; in his hands it is not compliant, and the boy's will is not inconsiderable. He defied me—and I dared not take it in my own hands—I doubt I could have held on to it, or survived the attempt. He's done quite well at holding on to it, thus far. But I fear that book is still dragging him bit by bit where he ought not to go, and dragging your other son along with him."

"If it alone is the cause," Tristen said. Pieces unfolded to him, bits of knowledge, the rest eluding him; but at his heart was the cold thought that his time in the world, already longer than he had expected, might be running out, and that with scattered pieces that had been Hasufin Heltain coming unstuck from their separate places in the world, it was not good for two unskilled boys to try to hold onto one of them. "It's going where it's bespelled to go," he said, thinking of the fate of the rest of that trove of books. "Where it was always bespelled to go. When we recovered the other manuscripts, they were at the river, were they not, and failed to cross. Best we hurry. The river is some sort of barrier to it, at least for a time."

"Horses," Cefwyn said. "Horses, Crissand! Now!"

iii

THE WIND HAD LET THEM GO AGAIN, AND THEIR FEET HAD FOUND THE GROUND, the two of them clinging together by both hands, refusing to be parted—separately, Elfwyn thought, they would be carried who knew where, but they were down again, standing next to other stonework, next to a wall that broke the wind.

A cliff dropped away at their feet, and the river lay below them, all frozen, in the strange storm light, and a great bridge spanned it.

"Everything is mad," Elfwyn said. "I don't know what to do. We aren't at Lewen Field any longer, I think."

"That is certainly the Lenúalim," Aewyn said, his voice ragged with cold. "That's the bridge. We've come to the border, is where we are." The wind began to blow again, and the fog came with it, a chill that reached the soul. "Don't let us move, Otter! Stop us!"

Elfwyn had had enough of being swept here and there. He attempted to set his feet on the earth and defy what came down on them, but Aewyn seized hold of the rock face itself and dragged Elfwyn to him with one strong arm, refusing to budge. "Hold to the rock," Aewyn shouted into his ear. "Don't let it blow us away again!"

He tried to hold on. But the fog came around them—around him, bone-deep and cold.

"Lord Tristen!" he cried.

All around them, shadows moved, some soldiers, some not, some mere wisps without faces. He knew only one thing for real, which was his brother's warm grip on his hand, as if Aewyn alone held them.

"Lord Tristen!" he whispered, and had a sense of direction for the moment, as if the man he sought lay somewhere behind them, far distant. "We're here," he tried to say, but made only a raven's creak.

"Don't leave," Aewyn implored him, jerking at his arm. "Otter, stay here, stay with me. Hold on!"

"I'm in a place," he said in a thread of a voice. "I'm in a place without ground under me. I see shadows. And there's something beside us. There is."

"Don't go," his brother said. "I'm not going again, Otter! I shan't go, so you have to stop."

Someone was in the mist, something quick, and stealthy and powerful, and he reached out for it, thinking it was Tristen, and in the next beat of his heart knowing it was different . . . like Mouse with the crumb, he shied off and would not take it. He became Mouse, and slipped back again, became Otter, and dived deep, and slipped away in the currents of that place . . .

Something was hunting, something with a presence as quick as lightning: it followed him, and he dived and spun and dived deep, quicker still, and slippery as his namesake, playing the game; but this, he knew, heart thumping hard, was no game.

He treated it as one. He was Otter. He could lead the hunter indefinitely—he slid, and rose, and dived down again, hunter and prey at once. He evaded traps. He spun his own. He laughed, a wicked laugh—don't get too wise, Paisi would chide him, but he knew what he did. He led the hunter farther and farther. He might be lost, but so was the one chasing him. Aewyn couldn't find him—his brother, his anchor in the world, was utterly confused, because he relied on a world in which one place connected logically to another, in which moments followed moments and roads led where they had always led . . .

Not when Otter played. He baffled the hunter. He was smug with his triumph when he surfaced—shook off the fog that he had learned to use and found himself just where he had been, with Aewyn holding on to him.

The places were connected, he thought. *One place led to another—the house to Marna, then to the old battlefield, to the river . . . but why did this place lead to that? How were they associated? The battlefield was from before he was born. Why could they not lead where he wanted, when he wanted?*

The hunter hated to be confused, or laughed at. And he laughed. He was all these places, in his own order, and back again. He could be anywhere but where he most wanted to be, which was safe at home, which was cold ashes, and that was the trap, that the snare . . .

He evaded it, and blinked, and was back with Aewyn again.

The sun was rising above the bridge, yellow and wan, on what he took for the east.

"Otter!" Aewyn exclaimed, and snatched at him hard, while the winds died and the fog cleared. He was too numb in his lower limbs to feel pain any longer. He kept one hand clenched on his brother's and one arm locked about the rock, the bones of the earth itself, refusing to be swept up again. He grew tired. And the game grew dangerous.

Aewyn could not go where he did. He tried to move him, but Aewyn caught his arm and clung fast to the rock.

"What are you doing?" Aewyn said. "You were gone, Otter—you've been gone for hours. One moment your hand just went away, and then you were there again, holding on, and then gone again! Don't leave me. . . . Don't leave like that!"

He had never meant to. He had never meant to leave Aewyn. He just hung on, thinking—he must believe—he had done wizardry, on his own. It was something he could do.

But he was by no means sure that he governed what happened when he did. That was the frightening thing.

In time things grew calmer, and he realized all sensation had left his fingers in that hand, so tightly Aewyn held to him. The winds faded, in favor of a thick snowfall. Below, beyond their perch atop the cliff, the river ran, mostly frozen, and the ice snowed over, so that the great Lenúalim, which he had heard about all his life, seemed no wider here than it ran beside Ynefel. His mind conjured a deep chasm, here as there. He grew dizzy, thinking about that river deep. He began to hear the water. He fancied if he thought about it very, very hard, he might reach out through the fogs that came and just be there, safe, at Ynefel. Even if Lord Tristen had left, there was a place no enemy of his would dare to come.

He might try it, if he could only find a way to drag his brother through with him.

He did try, shutting his eyes and wishing very hard for the fog to come close, close, so that he could test where it might send him this time. He *could* bring his brother with him. Aewyn had been with him when they moved through Marna, and through the battlefield, had he not? So he *could* do it.

The fog came, deep and pearly-gray, lustrous as a jewel, and wrapped softly around him. He had only to think very hard of Ynefel. He had their escape.

But the hunter slipped onto his track, and now, with Aewyn failing and falling, he tried to hasten him along but failed. The shadow trailed him, tracked him, and Aewyn drifted, as if he were drowning in water.

"Brother!" Elfwyn called, shaking at him till his fair hair flew, and everything proceeded slowly as in a dream. He tried to carry Aewyn, dragging him along, away from what hunted them, his heart pounding and his breath coming so hard he knew the hunter could hear it.

A shadow loomed up before him in the fog, the shadow of a robed figure, clearer and clearer in the gray, while the hunter came behind him, dreamlike and inexorable.

"Well," the cloaked figure said.

And he knew that voice. It belonged in a tower in Henas'amef. It belonged in a prison Lord Tristen himself had sealed. It was his mother. And his heart plummeted, feeling pursuit closer and closer behind them, and her in front. "Well. Well . . ."

He tried to dart aside. She was still before him, once, twice, three times, and the hunter came nearer and nearer, a cold presence, and terrible, behind them.

"Come along," his mother said.

"No!" As the shadow spread out behind him, all-encompassing, now. "Stand away! Let me go!"

"Fool, boy. Great fool."

He was not standing where he had. The shadow behind him was at a greater distance, his mother had gained them that, but it advanced, inexorable in its pace.

"I can save you," his mother said. "Death follows you. Do you recognize it? I do."

He clung to Aewyn, who said nothing, knew nothing, drifting half-conscious beside him. He held Aewyn's arm close and dragged him with him in a sudden bid to escape.

His mother was before him, lifting her shadowy arms.

"Fool, I say, my dear boy. Let me save you. Let me bring you to warmth, and safety."

She was a shadow here, but she was imprisoned in Lord Crissand's fortress. If she brought him there, if she brought both of them with her, they would be within hail of her guards, and safe, safe in her tower, exactly where he wanted to be.

Wanting was enough. He felt Aewyn begin to slip from his arms.

"No!" he cried. "My brother, too! If we go where you like, my brother goes with me!"

"Of course," his mother said in her silkiest voice. "Of course he will. Let go, let go, dear fool. Trust me to guide us."

He did *not* trust her. He did not believe, in the next instant, that he heard anything like the truth. The hunter came close behind and, in the very moment he felt that darkness reach up for them, Aewyn slipped from his arms and plummeted away into the dark.

"Aewyn!" he called out, a last desperate bid to save him. "Aewyn! Wake up!" If his brother waked, he might escape the fog. It might be a condition of the mist that carried them, that Aewyn seemed to dream, and Aewyn's waking might drive the hunter away. It was all he could hope. His hands were empty.

And in the very moment of his concern for Aewyn, he felt the ground come up under his feet, and warmth come around him. He was with his mother in what seemed, for a heartbeat, her room.

But it differed from her tower. There were couches, and cushions, and drapes—but the colors were green and gold, not the motley brocades his mother's room had owned. There was a fireplace with an iron screen that had the aspect of a grinning monster. A harp stood in one corner, and the floor was gray, ancient stone, not wood.

"Where are we?" he demanded. It was not the Zeide. It was not Lord Crissand's fortress at all. Nothing smelled or felt the same, and his question met the empty air. "Mother?"

He was alone. There was a door. It was solid oak, and locked, and he beat his fist on it in rage.

"Mother!" he shouted, betrayed—she had deceived him, but never lied. She still had not lied. He had assumed everything and lost everything, even his brother. He raged, and beat at the door, and yelled until his voice cracked.

No answer came.

iv

SNOW COULD BE HARD, HARD ENOUGH TO KNOCK THE BREATH OUT OF A BODY— Aewyn had found that out before this. It was a long time before he wanted to move, and it was a while more before he could gather his elbows and his knees under him and get up.

"Elfwyn?" he asked the surrounding air, in which snow fell thick. He was unsteady on his feet and staggered backward when he tried to turn.

His back met something solid, and when he put out a hand and turned about, he found himself next to a man-high stone wall.

Lucky, he thought, not to have come down on that. Or perhaps he had. The only parts of him that did not hurt were only numb with cold, and his head ached—there was a lump on his brow, he thought, but his fingers were too cold to tell.

"Elfwyn?" he shouted, thinking his brother might well have fallen onto some roof, or onto the other side of the wall. He waded through the snow, following the wall, hoping it would lead to a window, a door, a gate, or some living person—Guelen he was, and Guelen he looked, in Amefel, which did not love Guelenfolk; but he thought he could count on hospitality, Lord Crissand being his father's friend. He would call Lord Crissand the aetheling when he referred to him, the way Amefin liked to think of him—he would be very respectful of any farmer he met, and ask a message be sent to Lord Crissand—not to his father. That would be the politic way to do things in this countryside.

His father would be beyond anger by now. His father would be worried sick, was what, and he was heartily ashamed, the worse since he had fainted half a dozen times and been a weight on his brother, who now had flown off somewhere by wizardry and lost himself in what he was well sure was no ordinary trick of the weather, even in Amefel. There had been ghosts—his shaken wits remembered that. There had been voices, and shadows, and they had been beside the river, but he was nowhere near it now: the river had a voice, and all he heard was the crunch of snow under his own boots and his own panting after breath.

Fool, he said to himself. He should be thinking where he was. Even if they had flown randomly about the map, there was a wall, and a wall was a structure, and structures were on his map. It might be the defensive wall, the one they had built in the war, and if that was so, he might come to the hold of Earl Drusenan of Bryn; or if it was farther south, it could even be part of old Althalen, which had been the capital of the High Kings, when the Sihhë had ruled the realm . . . So he told himself, walking along a wall that seemed to go on forever and trying to gain a sense of what direction he was going in this murk. The fog seemed to have persisted about him. He had never yet come out of it. And the wall went on and on, and seemed in worse and worse repair.

A small group of Elwynim had settled at Althalen. The map had had to be changed because of that. Old Althalen had been cursed ground—cursed by the Quinalt *and* the Bryaltines, which was uncommon; but people who had fled the wars in Elwynor had wanted to live there and farm there again. They wanted to make orchards, which they said had once flourished there. They had tried to take the curse away, so he had heard.

But part of the ground they would not build on. He had read that in notes appended to his map. In the lack of anything substantial to see in the world around him, he built his own room, his work strewn across his desk, the great parchment map fastened up above it. He had committed it all to memory. He could recall the shape of the ruins, some inner details of which were left vague because no one would venture into such a haunted place just to draw a map, even with a lord's commission. The palace ruin had a long wall on its northern side. In his own safe room he had liked to picture what the Sihhë palace had looked like, building its lost upper tiers in his imagination . . . all, all of this had filled his lonely hours when Otter had gone away south.

His own room was real enough in his vision that he wondered if he could be there as easily as he could be in the woods or at the old battlefield, if he took the chance and just wished hard enough; but if he succeeded, it would take him leagues away from his father, who would be searching the hills for him, and leagues separate from his brother, who had to be hereabouts, if he just kept looking, and damned if he would give up. They must have arrived close to each other. Perhaps, he thought, he had just started out looking in the wrong direction. Perhaps he should go the other way, and try that, since this direction had led to nothing, not even a corner to the never-ending wall. He was growing desperate in this nightmarish continuance of one solid wall, and being without Elfwyn, he grew afraid, more afraid than he had ever been in his life. Nothing he had ever met had dared threaten him. No one in Guelessar had dared stand up to him, certainly none of the boys brought in to be his associates. But this thwarted him. The unnatural fog and the blowing snow confused him.

He still knew where he was. He knew where he was, the way he knew he was standing on solid ground. It was Elfwyn who was lost.

He was surprised, even indignant, to find his legs growing weak in the struggle to walk, and his hands without feeling. He went all the way to his knees, which was no place for a prince, and he got up, astonished and ashamed, and continued walking—he had lost contact with the wall as he fell, but he found it, hoping it was the same wall, and doggedly followed it back the way he had come. He had had enough of rest, had he not? He had *slept* through the business with the old man, he had *slept* his way through the fog, when they had gotten swept away to the woods, and he was entirely put out with himself. His father would not be sleeping his way through a calamity, would he? His mother, whose blood he had in his veins, would take action and See her way through it, with that Gift she never admitted to the priests.

So Elfwyn was not the only one with wizardry in his blood. If his brother had it, he was sure his mother's son was not less gifted, only that such ability had never been encouraged in him.

And now he needed it. He so desperately needed it now.

V

IT WAS THE BOOK THAT WAS THE TROUBLE: MASTER EMUIN SAID IT. TRISTEN HAD located it briefly, and felt it move through the remainder of the dark and through the murky day, a day gray and pale as the space between, that space where Tristen emphatically dared not, at the moment, go.

It had shifted again, and the book and the enemy were very close one to the other—closer than the last time he had felt it, and as every venture he had made toward the boys had driven them farther away, now he feared anything that might upset the balance. Time itself had started to diverge: day and dark, this day and the next grew confused around him, and now, he suspected, had diverged again.

They were a small party that had ridden out from Henas'amef: himself, and Uwen, and Cefwyn, unescorted and on borrowed horses. Lord Crissand had stayed behind, much against his inclination, to bolster Emuin, with Paisi to help. Emuin was wizard enough, he hoped, to hold the Zeide itself against intrusion or attack, where it might well come. A score of the Dragon Guard would have taken to the road behind them, traveling fast, one could be sure, but not fast enough to overtake a desperate father.

Cefwyn had not waited for them. He had delayed only to put on his armor, had taken a warm cloak and headed for the stable to borrow the best horses available, while Uwen had ordered supply out of the kitchens, and they were gone, only the three of them, by the world's roads.

The shadows that had haunted their riding out by dark persisted by daylight, streaking the snow from time to time, and Tristen did not trust their company in the least—they were part of the disturbance in the gray place and attached themselves to any part of it. The boys' innocence was no longer a protection to them, not once the spell on that book was involved: he had extended his senses as quietly as he could, risking the gray space with the delicacy of a breath, when the intrusion he tracked had come down like a thunderbolt.

And moved all of them.

One bit of the road was much like another, but he had the dire feeling they had lost time as well as distance, and now their own tracks were, half-snow-covered, ahead of them.

"Someone has been by here," Cefwyn said, not yet seeing the truth.

"We have," Tristen said, and beside him, he knew Uwen understood; in the look Cefwyn gave him, he knew Cefwyn did then, too.

"That book?" Cefwyn asked. "Can a damned book do it?"

Tristen knew at least part of the answer—knew he had acted recklessly, that the boys had moved again, and he dreaded to tell Cefwyn the whole truth, but he must do something about the situation he felt; and he reined aside, due south, and away from their own tracks.

"What are we doing?" Cefwyn asked him.

"They have separated. For good or for ill, I could not stop one of them—"

"Which one?"

"Aewyn has arrived south of us. He has fallen away. He draws at the earth. He *wanted* to stop. But Elfwyn went too fast this time, too fast and too far."

"Too far," Cefwyn echoed him, shouting through the wind. Their horses drifted apart and together again, knee against knee. Uwen was a shadow on Cefwyn's other side. "Where is he?"

"We are going toward Aewyn," Tristen shouted back. "I cannot reach the other without leaving Aewyn in danger. One or the other—we have now to choose."

"What choice is that?" Cefwyn cried. "How can I?"

"I choose!" Tristen said. "On me, be it—I choose the one we can reach. Where he is, is no good place for him."

"Althalen," Cefwyn said. Cefwyn knew as well as he what lay in this direction, down a forgotten road. "There's the new village there."

"If he were there," Tristen said, "I would trust he was safe. He is not."

A new village had grown up at Althalen, and that safety might be within the boy's reach, but that was not the way he was tending. The whole place had become troubled and uncertain, a pond where a small stone had dropped and sunk, and reached depths where it was not good for one of his blood to be. Disturbance rippled through the gray space in that direction. It was a Sihhë place, a place of blood and angry ghosts . . . the home of Elfwyn's distant ancestor.

But it was home to one of the boy's own, too.

They tended south and west, and now every stride of the horses carried them aside from the book and from Elfwyn, and his own guilt rode with him. He had reached instinctively, attempting to divert both boys from plunging through that looming ward, and created disaster as he did it. The boys had been headed right for a suddenly appearing gap in the wards and Elfwyn had shot through as quickly as if he himself willed it. Perhaps he had gone so quickly because Aewyn's resistance had pulled away—Aewyn, even half-fainting, had clung to where he was with a fierceness that held them to earth; and when he had come loose, perhaps at his jostling the boys, Aewyn had plummeted somewhere in between the two places—not straight down, but aside, to a place with its own will and its own magic, old magic, and a special claim on him. The old ruin, extending constantly into the gray space, might have found a mote flying free, recognized it, and simply snatched it down into itself . . . while Elfwyn, set free of that bond, had flown like an arrow, and now was entirely out of sight, sealed behind those wards.

Folly, he said to himself: *Mauryl would have said it, most certainly.* He had tried because they were both about to vanish through that gap—but he had lost one of them in the process, and where the other had come down was not well-intentioned or safe: not by accident, such events, not even his own failure.

And while there was now every chance that, if he took them all into the gray space to save time, he might reach Aewyn safely, without flinging him into Elfwyn's predicament, there was equally well the chance that Elfwyn himself maintained some hold on his brother, and that the book's intent would snatch the second boy through if he pressed hard. The book's intent reached far, far across Amefel. It *wanted* to be found, and it *wanted* to be loose in the world, and it *wanted* at least one of the boys if not both . . . which was, Cefwyn would say, a damned great lot for a book to want.

It was that. Say rather, either Mauryl Gestaurien had laid an intent on his work to keep it out of his hands, or that the wizard who had tried to lay hands on it more than a decade ago had laid a geas on whoever found it.

Or say, equally possible, that Elfwyn, with enough magic in him to shake things loose from hiding, had had such a command laid directly on him long, long ago, in those visits to his mother. He had felt attachments he had not trusted when the boy had asked him to be his teacher.

He had said no.

And which of the two of them had done right?

Might he have told the whole uncomfortable truth to a chancy, immature boy?

He had not told all he feared to Cefwyn. He dared not, at this moment, consult Emuin about his choice to go after Aewyn—not with the gray space as chancy as it still was—and he was not sure to this hour that he had made the right choice.

He hesitated to burden Cefwyn with the likelihood that the bond between the brothers was not ordinary—least of all did he want to say what else he sensed, that it might never be broken.

Cefwyn said not a word, in the meantime. Nor had Cefwyn said anything more about Ninévrisë and his daughter being across the river, in the place defended by those icy wards.

Nothing about it boded well for his household.

But there was one more reason for turning aside after Aewyn: Elfwyn Aswydd had more than a compulsion on him: there was also his father's blood in him, there was a Syrillas brother's love, Emuin's concern, and a Sihhë blessing on him. If there was one young lad it might be difficult for any enemy to hold, it might be this one.

He made up his mind. As much as he dared nudge a set of affairs so very precariously balanced, he sent the most delicate thought curling toward what was now an iron wall—a thought that quested after the least, most insignificant gap in the barrier, the sort a brotherly bond might make. And he intended to lay hands on that brother.

CHAPTER ELEVEN

i

COUCHES, AND CUSHIONS, AND DRAPES—THEY WERE EVERYWHERE FOR COM-
fort. It was that precise green and that precise gold that had been the Aswydd
heraldry, forbidden now, but everywhere about, and the monstrous fireplace,
with what might have been a dragon, or a grinning devil. The harp. Defy-
ing his prison, having heard in Gran's tales that harps could be enchanted,
Elfwyn ran his bruised, cold-burned fingers over the strings and evoked a
rippling of notes.

No answer came.

"Ordinary," he said in his most stinging way. "Besides," he said to his
absent mother, in case she could hear him, "you never played this harp, did
you? I would never expect you to like music."

That drew an answer. The door never opened. But a figure appeared by
the fireside—not his mother, but a young man who for all the world looked
like Lord Tristen: that kind of youth that was neither young nor old; that
kind of beauty that set its owner apart from blemished mankind.

That figure faded, and in its place stood a woman, a woman with long
red hair. Her back was to him, her face to the fire, her hands lifted to it.

"Mother?" Elfwyn asked harshly. "Mother!"

The woman turned, and it was his mother's face, and his mother's cant of
the head, and it held that same kind of beauty, chilling, severe, and foreign.

"Not your mother," she said. "Your aunt. Your aunt, dear boy. I pass by
any thanks for rescue. I would never expect gratitude, not from your father's
bloodline."

"Mother!" he shouted, but the figure, like the man before it, faded before
his eyes, leaving only the fire.

ii

AEWYN'S FEET HAD LONG SINCE LOST ALL FEELING. HIS LEGS BUCKLED. IT WAS not weakness, he insisted. He was weary, but he had only stumbled this time on a bit of ice. He levered himself up, holding to the wall as he could with fingers that likewise had gone numb within his gloves . . . it was only the roughened leather that gripped the stones. His fingers would no longer bend.

He was in a predicament. He realized that, in a distant, determined sort of way. He might have made certain wrong choices, but if he turned back a second time, that would be three times down the same stretch of wall.

"Otter?" he called, and was utterly confused to find night settled about him, as if daylight, so newly born, had just given up in exhaustion. "Elf-wyn!" He shouted that out whenever he found breath. If only there were an answer, if only they were together, they could share warmth and find a nook to shelter them from the damnable wind. Or if someone heard him, it might be one of the villagers, and he could raise a general search for his brother. He would promise the village—he would promise them whatever a prince of Ylesuin could promise: cattle, sheep, horses, a grant of land, whatever they wanted, if only they could find his brother alive.

As it was, he could only put one foot in front of another, and did that because, if he stopped, he would die, and his father would never know where he was.

"Boy," someone said behind him. "Boy, what d' ye want wi' my Otter?"

He turned, blinking, as snow hit his eyes. A woman stood there, a little old woman in a shawl, then a robed woman in gray skirts, who was almost too dim to see.

"Why, 'tis Prince Aewyn, ain't it?" the first woman said, and took off her shawl and wrapped it around him, which he protested—the old woman would freeze straightway, in her light clothing. But it warmed him where it touched, warmed his hands just as he tried to give it back to her.

"I've lost Otter," he tried to say, but he stammered too much. He began to make out the other woman, like an Amefin lady, but in a faded, cobwebby gown. And he knew he should not be standing still. He had to keep moving, but he had gotten distracted and forgotten to do that.

But he was so much warmer, just where the old woman had touched his hand, and he thought he knew her. He thought it was Paisi's gran. Otter had told him she was dead, but here she was, and he had to tell Otter that his gran was safe, when he found him. He had no idea who the other lady was, but he felt safer, and warmer, though the fog closed about him for a moment.

"Grandson," an old man said from behind him, and he turned about and saw a tall, dignified man with a gold band about his brows, and a fine rich cloak. The old man looked right into his eyes. "Grandson. A fine lad. You have your mother's look about you."

"My mother is Ninévrisë, the Lady Regent of Elwynor, Queen of Ylesuin . . ."

"All these things," the old man said, "*and* my daughter. A good daughter, she is. Are you a good and honest son? I think you are."

"My mother's father is dead," he said, and that was two conversations with the dead in a matter of moments, which might be too many for safety. He looked about to see where Paisi's gran was, and if she had advice for him; but she was gone, and the old man laid a hand on his shoulder, sending warmth through him.

"Tell me about yourself," the old man said. "Tell me why you've come."

"To find my brother!" he said.

"There is no one here," the old man said.

"Then help me find him," he said—not that he failed to know he was in dire trouble, but if he was seeing his dead grandfather, and he was dying or dead, he stuck by his mission, and by his brother. "He fell away. He must have come down somewhere. Help me!"

"Then tell me about him," the old man said, and flung the great warmth of his cloak about him, and when it enfolded him, the warmth all but stole his breath. He fought to keep aware, and to keep awake—he knew better than to sleep in the snow, but the weight of the cloak bore him down, and down, and he rested against the old man's knees. He felt the touch of the old man's fingers in his hair, a caress, then something like a kiss on his temple.

"Rest," the old man said, somewhere in his hearing, and near him a blue Line sprang into being. Blue fire ran along a wall, then branched, all in squares and rectangles, until all the space about seemed alight. They were wards, and they stretched on and on and on, burning blue and covering the very hillsides.

Safety, they informed him. Safe to sleep, safe to rest.

No, he insisted to himself. *Not safe to sleep. Not while Otter's lost.*

iii

AUNT, THE WOMAN HAD CALLED HERSELF.

Orien, Emuin had named his mother's twin. Orien Aswydd. The name sent chills through Elfwyn's bones. What have you done with my mother? he wanted to ask.

But he had no one to ask. He paced, too weary to walk, but unwilling to sink down and wait patiently in soft cushions. He thought of wreaking destruction on the place, ripping down the tapestries and shredding the cushions and making himself as ungrateful a tenant as possible—but that did nothing to win his freedom, and might put him in a worse place.

He did think to search the walls and behind the hangings for any hint of a second door or a cupboard, or something he might use as a weapon. The fireplace had no poker. There were no windows. And last of all he tried the latch of the door, in the foolish notion that, who knew? Perhaps his strong wish for a way out might make one: the world had not followed ordinary rules since Master Emuin had walked into their little cottage—or maybe not for hours before that.

He pushed the latch. It gave downward, and the door opened on a night-bound waste, a howling gust of snow, and shards of ice that rose up with the sound of swords, completely to bar his escape.

He slammed the door on that ungodly sight, slammed it and leaned against it, chilled to the bone.

It was not just ice. It was a cold so intense it had burned his throat and numbed his hands. It was magical, or sorcerous, part of the deep, unnatural winter that, as often as the snow melted, had blasted out more and more and more, and never quite ceased.

It was his mother's winter. It was the winter when Gran died. It was the winter when his dream of welcome with his father had come to grief.

He wanted this winter to end. He shut his eyes and wanted it to end, with all the strength he had.

Your wards are pitiful. The voice came to him clear and strong, as if Lord Tristen himself had stood right at his shoulder. It occurred to him that he had made no wards at all, already assuming it was not his premises, and that he was the one held, not the holder. He blinked and lifted his head, stung by his own folly.

Or perhaps you forgot, the mocking voice said again, not in the air, but in his mind, and he knew it was *not* Lord Tristen. Lord Tristen, whatever else, might have cast him out of Ynefel, but mockery was not his manner—

furthest from it. Lord Tristen had been, whatever else, kind, and told him no simply by saying nothing at all.

Liar, he said to that voice, or thought it, then, gathering his courage, said it aloud: "Liar!" Not even his mother had lied to him. It seemed a low, mean sort of behavior, to pretend to be what one was not.

He moved, moreover, and walked the perimeter, and laid the wards once, twice, three times all about, in fury and defiance.

Wind blasted at him, as if every ward at once had blown inward. The force blew cushions off the couches and lifted his hair and blew his cloak back. His hand tingled, half-numb. His wards were flattened, useless.

And the same young man confronted him, standing near the fire . . . but the fire showed right through him.

"Well, well," the young man said. "Temper rarely works where skill fails."

Rage grew cold. The taunting minded him of the court of Guelemara, and the manners there, where detractors attacked with soft, sweet words. He bowed ever so slightly, drawing up the armor he had learned to use there— pride of birth, of all things, and a study of the rules of courtesy the other violated. "My name," he said with that soft sweetness, "is Elfwyn Aswydd. I own it with no shame. Do you have a name, sir wisp?"

A hit. The young man's chin lifted, and there was an angry glint in his eyes, before a smile covered it, showing teeth. "Elfwyn Aswydd." He bowed in turn. "A name, indeed. Was it from your *father*?"

"You know who I am, or you would find something else to do. Your name, sir."

"My name. My name. I think you know it. Where *is* your brother?"

That hit, too, in the heart. He kept his gaze steady. "Clearly your interest is in me, and my mother is in this. Or my aunt. Are you a kinsman of mine, too, perchance?"

"No." Again, he had nettled the young man. "Such lofty manners from a goatherd."

"A goatherd who has a name, a noble one, and old. Why should I trouble myself with a wisp?"

"Oh, waspish lad. Unbecoming in a boy." The young man left the fire, and light ceased to show through him. "Is that better?"

"I hardly know," he said, jaw set, "since you have not the courage to go by a name, or possibly are ashamed of it. *Are* you ashamed?"

"Otter, Otter, and Spider. One you call yourself and the other people call you behind your back. There are your names, boy."

"Improve my opinion of you, I beg you. It's reached very low."

"Oh, pert beyond all good sense. Shall I call your mother?"

"Is she alive?" It should, if he were virtuous, feel some pang, no matter what she was, but she had taken too much from him, and he mustered no will to care whether she lived, at the moment, except the grief of what he wished he had had from her.

The young man snapped his fingers. His mother was there. Or his aunt.

"Son," his mother said, in that intonation she had. "Are you being foolish?"

"Prideful," the young man said. "Prideful and difficult. His brother's name, I think, rouses a little passion in him."

"That Guelen whelp," his mother said. "That Guelen boy. He will be your enemy, Elfwyn. He is what he is, and he is Guelen."

He turned his shoulder and looked at a tapestry in the corner, for some better view.

But he saw instead a room in candlelight, like a vision, a blond young man with a lean, strong jaw. That jaw was clenched, and those eyes, those blue Guelen eyes, looked at him with such anger . . .

"Your enemy, in time to come," his mother said.

"Then he is alive," he said, taking that for comfort.

"He will hate you," his mother said. "He and you contend for the same power, and you cannot both have it."

"Well enough," he said lightly. "He was born to it."

A blow to his shoulder spun him half-about, and he looked up into the face of the man. It was like facing Tristen in anger. Those gray eyes bore into him, and carried such force of magic it lanced right to the heart, painful as the grip on his arm.

"Do not cast away your birthright," the young man said. "Do not resign what you do not yet possess . . . what you do not yet imagine, Elfwyn Aswydd. Will you see? Will you open your eyes and know the world to come?"

A woman appeared in his vision, a beautiful woman with violet eyes and midnight hair, a woman who looked right at him, and into him, and that expression was so determined and so open that it lanced right through him.

"This is your wife, your queen. This is Aemaryen." The view wheeled away to a giddy sight of far-flung woods and farmland, villages and a towered city. "This is Ilefinian." Another, even wider, with towers rising in scaffolding. "Guelemara." A third, low-lying, against wooded hills, and beautiful beyond any of the others. "Althalen, where you will rule."

"I shall rule, shall I?" He put mockery into his voice. "You dream."

"Is that your answer? Aewyn may kill you, while you mewl on about friendship and gratitude. Do you think he'll forget you left him, for safety? He will remember. His father will rescue him, and you and he will go down different paths. You asked Tristen Sihhë for wizardry, and he refused you—fearing you, *fearing* you, boy, as he ought. You will surpass him. You will have a magic so much greater the ground will shake, and he saw that. He knew. *He* sent you out, well knowing your gran would die if you went back just then—"

"Murdered by my mother," he said, regaining his anger.

"Fate," the young man said. "Fate had him send you out, in fear of you, fate drew you home again, fate had to destroy your gran to get you to Henas'amef, and fate drew you to the library, where your heritage mandated you be . . ."

"Sorcery killed my gran," he said bitterly, flinging the young man's hand away from him. "Sorcery killed her, sorcery wanted that thing found! I wish I'd never found it! I wish it had been you that died in that fire!" he shouted, looking straight at his mother. "That would have been justice! Now get away from me!"

"Your kingdom," the young man said, behind him, "your kingdom will not be denied. You see how cruel your own sorcery can be, if someone stands in the way—like your gran. You assured she would die, when there was no other way to get you to the library. You assured you would lose your brother, when you enticed him out into the woods—he will grow up a bitter, angry man, all your doing. If you had only taken that book to your mother, none of this pain would have happened. Who else will you kill, until you take the place you were meant to have? I assure you, there will be more pain if you go on denying your own nature. There will be more deaths. Who next? Lord Crissand? That will throw the south into confusion. There's no other lord who can rule as aetheling—except, of course, you, my prince."

"I'm no prince, nor wish to be!"

"That is the very trouble, dear," his mother said. "You blame me for the old grandmother. I assure you, I did nothing. It was you. I quite fear to be in your thoughts at all, until you know what you are, and understand what a power you do wield in the world. Everyone has to fear you, especially when you most afflict whoever loves you—innocents, like Gran, like your brother."

"You've never lied to me," he said in disgust. "At least I thought not. But you did. Everything you did was a lie."

"My dear, you know you were born by sorcery. Can you think you might be ordinary? You were born to overcome my sister's enemy, and do you know who that is?"

"I don't care to know."

"*Tristen*. Tristen Sihhë. Now do you understand how very foolish you were, to be drawn to him? He looked you over. He saw a magic too potent to confront."

He outright laughed. "A ridiculous boy who couldn't light a candle, let alone a proper fire, to save himself from freezing. He saw someone too *stupid* to teach, with too many entanglements with sorcery. Forgive me, Mother, but I had all the ride home to think about that."

"Then you quite missed the point. He entombed my sister alive, he warded *me* into the tower above so I couldn't break free, and accepting that imprisonment was the only way I could stay alive and stay near you—"

"Oh, spare me!"

"The old woman had power he lent. Oh, he is powerful, he is powerful beyond easy understanding. I fear him, but *he* fears you."

"Ridiculous, I say."

"You are not yet grown, son of mine! You are not yet grown, and even so the world bends around you—a piece of your power has come to you, not that you know how to read it, yet. Tristen would if he laid hands on it, I've no doubt; but there will come a day it comes clear to you and shows you the way to bring him down."

He didn't want to talk about the book, which clearly they knew he had, as they knew other things. Lies, he said to himself, all lies.

Aloud, he said: "All I wish is to be out of here. And, see? It failed. My wishes have no success at all. Fortunately, I put little hope in them."

"So young, so bitter," the young man said. "So impertinent toward your lady mother. She has endured years of prison for your sake, endured them teaching you to hate her, mistrust her, all these years. Endured blame, when your own rebellion killed those around you . . ."

"A lie. I will not forgive you *that* lie, sir wisp."

"I hope you will, when you rule."

"Then you'll wait a long, long time, sir wisp!"

"You will rule," his mother said. "You fear our taking the book from you, do you not? You could hardly be more wrong. The book is yours. It was always yours. It was the text old Mauryl used, and a wickeder wizard there never was than Mauryl: you saw him, at Ynefel—did Tristen point him out? The face above the door. He brought a dead soul back, in Tristen, one of the Sihhë-lords, by blackest work, and to counter *him,* Mauryl's enemy brought *you*. So none of this nonsense about subservience to Tristen Sihhë: Aewyn will never forgive what you are—the very check on his power. Your dear brother, sweet child that he is, will learn what you are, and after a certain time, he will understand quite well that he faces a choice—between Tristen, who sustains his father on the throne—or you, whose destiny is to bring down his dynasty and put it under Sihhë rule, and one cannot readily think that he will continue to be your friend. He will remember his sojourn in the snow. He will take his path, as you take yours through the world, and, oh, my son, if you continue in friendship with him, it will be a *very* painful conclusion, with only one outcome. I advise you, shed him now, and be only a remote enemy, not an intimate one. His sister will be your queen—"

"My own sister, too!" He was truly, deeply offended. And yet the eyes, the wonderful violet eyes, stayed with him, heart-wrenchingly intent on his. "Mother, that's an abomination!"

"And *you* have listened too obediently to the Quinalt and the Bryalt. Your queen, and your subject, your one love, or there will be no love at all for you in this world. And you will, like Tristen, live long, very long. Will petty rules matter so much to you, I wonder, when you rule?"

"Well, it's no matter," he said with a shrug, "since the sun will come up in the west before I rule anything. Even Gran's goats. We gave them all away, so I suppose I have no subjects."

"The pride of a king, certainly," his mother said.

"The face of one," the young man said. "The bearing and the manner, when he wills to use it. The Quinalt would have liked him better had he been humble. His speech, do you note, has the courtly lilt, but Amefin, not Guelen. Where did he learn that, I wonder?"

"Perhaps it was a spell," his mother said. "It could walk out of my cell, with him. He could carry it wherever he wished, right past the wards. I gave him many such gifts."

That chilled him to the bone. He refused to think he had carried his mother's curse home with him. If that were so, he *was* to blame for the fire.

"Well, well," the young man said. "You have reasoned with him as best you can. Let your sister set him at his lessons."

"My sister," his mother said, and spun full about, her skirts swirling. They came to rest, and she looked at him again, but with a she-wolf's look, a terrible, burning stare, and a smile he had never seen on his mother's face.

"Nephew," those same lips said. "Listen to your mother."

"Leave me alone." Horror overwhelmed him. "You're dead. You've been dead since I was born."

"Tristen is ever so much older than that," his aunt said, "and you had no fear of him. I assure you, you should have had. He did recognize you."

"My dead aunt and a wisp," he said, drawing himself up. "Small choice I have."

"He only wishes to provoke us," the man said with a tolerant smile. "Be patient. We have time. We have as much time as we wish to take." Both winked out, with a little gust of wind that disturbed the fire, and left him with a curse in his mouth and nowhere to spit it.

He stood for a moment, in case they might come back and catch him collapsed onto a bench. He stood glaring at the fire, then settled himself with as much dignity as he could muster, given aching legs and frost-stung feet and hands and face. He felt the pain of his injuries now, a pain that grew and grew, and stung his eyes with indignation.

Anger was very, very close to the surface, anger enough to wreck the room, anger enough to fling himself at the shards of ice that barred the door, and die that way, if that was all that would spite them. He had no other hope.

Anger will be your particular struggle. He recalled Emuin saying that. And of Aewyn: *He is your chance for redemption and your inclination toward utter fall. Do you understand me?*

If I betray him, he had said. And Emuin had said:

If you betray him, it will be fatal to us all.

He had not, had he, betrayed his brother? He had stayed steadfast. He meant to do so.

Emuin had said, too, regarding his mother: *As near as she can come to love, she loves you.*

Love, was it? Wrong in one, perhaps wrong in both. Perhaps Emuin had not seen as much of his nature as he ought . . .

Vision. Was that not the word Tristen had given him?

Seeing. Seeing things for what they were. Seeing the truth, without coloring it, or making it other than it was. Was that the beginning of wizardry, to know what a thing really was before one started to wish it to be something else?

Be Mouse, Tristen had said, Mouse, not Owl. Mouse looked out from the base of the walls, was low and quiet, and looked carefully before he committed himself. He more than looked, he listened, and measured his distances—was never caught too far from his hole.

He certainly had been.

And he had forgotten his other word. So much of a wizard he was.

Spider, Emuin had called him. Spider Prince. And he had said pridefully that he didn't live in a nasty hole.

He was certainly in one now. He'd spun his little web, his wards, and Sir Wisp had smashed right through them without even noticing.

All he could do was do them again, and again, and again, and maybe, as long as he might be a prisoner here, he might do them well enough to be a nuisance, then a hindrance, then, maybe, a barrier . . . spinning his web, a bit at a time.

Patience.

Patience was his other word. Now he remembered it. Patience, and waiting to talk to Paisi, and waiting to get advice, and approaching things slowly—would have saved him so much grief.

Patience instead of anger. Patience instead of rushing into things head-long. Patience, and Vision . . . would have mended so much that had gone wrong.

Lord Tristen had advised him of the truth. Would someone do that, for his enemy?

Lord Tristen might. He would have, because that was his nature to deal in truth, not lies.

And what did that say, for the advice he had just been given?

Maybe it was time not to be Otter, diving headlong from this to that, nor Mouse, watching from the peripheries of a situation, but patient Spider, simply building, over and over, and over again.

He sat, hands on his knees, and rebuilt his path, from the cottage, to the woods, to the battlefield, to the bridge, to here, in the unnatural ice that argued for somewhere not quite of the ordinary sort. The fogs that closed in had delivered them here, and here, and here, and at the last, Aewyn, Syrillas, had outright been unable to go with him, or had resisted going, and what pulled him here had been too strong . . .

Too strong for Aewyn.

Or too foreign to Aewyn, being sorcerous in nature.

Sorcery was a path that might be open to him. He might learn it and use it.

But it did not mend its nature simply because he used it; and he did not think it would improve his own.

So there was wizardry, which Tristen had refused to teach him.

Make me a wizard, he had asked. Or, had it been: Teach me wizardry?

And Lord Tristen had said: *You are not yet what you will be,* and added, *and I have been waiting for this question for longer than you know.*

How did he hear that answer now, in light of what his captors had said he was?

Teach you wizardry? He remembered Emuin saying that. *Useless. Teach you magic? I cannot. No more can I teach any Sihhë what resides in his blood and bone.*

He had scorned the answer. He had disbelieved it.

And he named you, Master Emuin had said of Lord Tristen. *Then I suspect he did see what I see.*

And he had asked, disturbed: *What did he see? What do you?*

A conjuring, Emuin had answered him. *A Summoning that opens a door.*

What door? he had asked, straight back at Emuin. *Make sense, please, sir!*

And Emuin:

You govern what door, if you have the will. Do *you have the will, Spider Prince?*

A chill ran through him, deep as bone, a chill that had him shaking in every limb. He looked down at his hand, where, forgotten, Lord Crissand's ring shone in the firelight, dull silver, and festooned with cheap silverwork.

It had not tingled since all this last mad course began. It had not warned him against Emuin. It had lain inert during their precipitate rush from Marna to Lewen Field to the river. It had not warned him of Sir Wisp or his mother. Perhaps his captors had killed the virtue in it. He wished he had given the ring to his brother when they were at the beginning of all this. Perhaps then Lord Crissand would have been able to find Aewyn, at least, and saved his father pain.

He wished . . . like the spider. He chained one wish to the other, starting not with what was impossible, but what was possible. He sat down before the fire, and wished one spark to fly out, and to land on his hand.

It flew. It landed. Without hesitation he seized it, and patiently wished the next thing. He wished the chill away, wished himself warm. One thing after another, one thing after another.

He wished Aewyn safe.

The fog appeared again—not around him—but where the door had been. He saw just the least glimmer of light.

iv

SNOW STILL FELL IN THE DARK, AND THEY RODE THROUGH THE REMNANT OF walls . . . walls lit by ghostly blue lines, which Cefwyn himself could see to-night. He rode by Tristen's side, Uwen just behind, and all around them, like a ghostly city, old Althalen rose, not just its foundations, but the outlines of its long-fallen towers, and the soaring height of domes greater than any in the realm. It was a glimpse of the Sihhë capital, as it had been, and a Marhanen king knew what his grandfather had brought low.

But things changed. There were bonds made. And the heart of that maze of blue light led to a simple place, a corner of what had been the palace, and a wall, where a tomb was set—they had not been near it a moment ago, but then they were, and Cefwyn had the heart-deep conviction Tristen had magicked them a bit, just a little, over a hill and down it.

He saw then a gathering of haunts, in a little low place, at that corner, ghosts that, at their coming, turned and stared at them with gray and troubled eyes, before they shredded away on the winds. Layer after layer of haunts fled their passage, wisps that left an uneasiness in the air.

But a young lad sat against that wall—no, he rested against the knees of a bearded old man, whose ghostly hand stroked his blond, curly head, and by that man stood, gowned in cobweb, Auld Syes, the gray lady—her, he knew for long dead; and on the other side, behind the old man he now recognized for the old Regent, his father-in-law, stood a woman in a shawl, who was his other son's gran, likewise perished. These three had his son in their keeping, and his heart froze in him. He swung down before his horse stopped moving, and ran to his son, heedless of haunts or spirits or whatever magic might be here. He was an ordinary man. He brushed it all aside, and seized his son up in his arms, and hugged him as hard as he could.

"Ow," Aewyn cried. "Papa!"

"He's alive," he called to Tristen and Uwen, who, likewise dismounted, were right behind him, and he looked around to thank the dead, at least— old friends, old allies.

But there was nothing there but a crumbling stone wall, and the stone they had set there for Uleman Syrillas.

"It was Grandfather," Aewyn murmured against his collar. "And Paisi's gran. And a lady I don't know."

The boy was half-frozen. He might lose fingers or toes. Cefwyn brought his fur-lined cloak about them both, and looked desperately at Tristen, who simply said, "Give him to me."

He did that. He had not a qualm, having Tristen take the boy from his arms and pass his hands over him. Aewyn's eyes shut, as Tristen let him down to the snow, then opened again, with a curious tranquillity, a wonder in them.

"You must be Lord Tristen," Aewyn said faintly, catching Tristen's hand. "My brother is lost. Find him. You can find him."

"I have never given him up," Tristen said, pulling him up by that hand, so that a father who had been very sure he had lost both sons, could touch one of them and be sure that he was real.

"We were by the river. And then here," Aewyn said to him, "and I tried to hold us down, and he slipped away. I don't know where he is."

Tristen, however, had looked away into the dark.

"I know," Tristen said. "I know. He has a trinket of mine."

V

AEWYN WAS THE FIRST THING ELFWYN IMAGINED WHEN HE BUILT HIS WEB, Aewyn in the snow, as he had left him, and he imagined where he had left him, but he could not make that image stay—it broke apart, in fat flakes of snow, and drifted on the wind, threads taken apart.

The wind, however, was a constant presence out there. He constructed that, stirring the trees, raising the snow in little plumes.

Fire was another presence. He constructed Aewyn's voice, telling him about maps, and a laughing fish, one evening by the coals.

He constructed Paisi, sitting by the fireside, and Gran, busy over her bread-baking. He recalled Uwen's wife, and her fireside with the lump in the stones.

And then, very carefully, he began to spin the strands that tied him to Lord Tristen.

He remembered the table by the fireside in Ynefel, while the whole fortress creaked and groaned with the wind, where the stairs sneaked furtively into new places, and faces in the stone seemed to watch someone walking by. Curiously enough, he could not recall Lord Tristen's face, nor his voice, but he could clearly recall Mouse, taking his single crumb—taking his little success, and immediately running for cover.

He recalled Mouse's enemy, Owl, on the newel post, and could see the mad glint of his huge eyes. He felt a sting, and looked down at his hand, where a mostly healed nick reminded him never to trifle with Owl.

Be Mouse, Tristen had told him.

He immediately recalled another fireside, and an old man who had asked him if he could be a spider.

Spider he was, tonight. He wove his web. He had made his mistake right after that warning. He hadn't trusted the old man: he'd held fast to Aewyn, but he hadn't trusted the old man enough when he tried to take them with him.

He would, if he met him again.

He thought about his charm of old Sihhë coins, and saw a bowl of oil on water. If he had been a real wizard, he could have made it show him something. He would have seen the truth in it, and told the truth to his father, and nothing of what had happened would have happened . . .

He kept staring at it, patient, patient as he could be, waiting to see what he would see now that he had it back. He stared and stared at the water, and saw a fog come over the surface.

It was the best he could hope for, that fog. It had carried him here. He wished it larger, and larger, and larger.

Elfwyn fell into it, and kept falling, but he was patient. He knew there would be a bottom sooner or later and that he would find it.

When he did, it was white, a long stretch of white, but when his feet hit it and skidded, and when he started walking, it was just another snowy patch of ground. It looked like a road. In the dim snowlight he could see walls on either side, and a little wish, a very little wish, made the ring tingle on his finger. He knew what way he ought to go. It was strongest in one particular direction.

So he kept walking. He pressed the book that rode inside his shirt, to be sure it was safe. He had made one mistake with a message, and was not prepared to make another. It was still there. It felt warm against his skin, and he kept his hand pressed there for a long time—growing colder as he walked, over snow that made a sound convincingly like snow.

He could endure the cold. He had endured worse, and would have endured worse, where he had been. He was determined, if another fog showed itself and tried to take him back, that he would sit down, hold to the rocks around him, and simply refuse to budge until bright daylight.

But none did.

He might have walked in that way for the better part of an hour, before he heard a strange sound behind him that was neither the wind nor the occasional cracking of ice crust under his feet. It was that sort of regular sound, but many feet—like horses.

He stopped, turned, straining his senses against the night, and saw three riders slowly overtaking him. There was nowhere for him to hide. It hardly seemed likely his mother would be riding here—but then it was not terribly likely that he would be here, either. He wondered, with a little shiver of fear, should he try wizardry again, and attempt the fog that had betrayed him.

He tried to bring it. He meant to bring it. But:

"Elfwyn!" someone called, a ragged, youngish voice.

"Aewyn?" he called back, all efforts stopped for a heartbeat. "Is it you?" His mother was full of lies, and he suspected it and was ready to run, but he stood his ground when he heard:

"Son?" That was his father. He never mistook that voice. He planted both feet in the snow and stood fast, waiting, as the three, no, four riders reached him.

One was Lord Tristen himself. Another was Uwen, who reached down a hand to lift him up. But before he could take it, Aewyn slid down from behind his father and seized him in his arms, pounding him about the back.

"Elfwyn!" Aewyn cried. "I thought we'd lost you."

"I came home," was all he could think to say. He hugged his brother, and now his father had dismounted, and put arms about him, and pressed the breath out of him.

The ring all but stung him. He looked up sharply, at Lord Tristen's shadowy form, at a Sihhë-lord in armor, with the white Star blazoned on him, the sight that belonged in Paisi's stories and not in the world as it was now.

"My lord," he said, though his own father, the king of Ylesuin, had a hand on his shoulder at the time.

"Get up behind Uwen," Tristen told him, and Uwen rode near, offering his hand a second time. He took it, hand to wrist, hauled up aboard a powerful, broad-rumped horse to settle behind Uwen Lewen's-son, while his father and his brother climbed back to the saddle of his father's horse, and Lord Tristen waited in silence. Owl showed up, and flew a curve half about him, then sped ahead.

There were a thousand questions. Aewyn answered a few of them when he said, in a voice hoarse with cold, "I never gave you up."

"Nor I, you," he answered, from behind Uwen's saddle.

He hoped that was the truth. With all his heart, he meant it to be.

My lord, he had called Tristen Sihhë. And he wished he had known how to say that to his father instead, when his father had put his arms about him; but what he had said, he had said, and meant it, as best he could.

He should have offered up the book. He should have surrendered the ring immediately. But he had given himself, instead. He supposed that counted for honesty.

EPILOGUE

SNOW FELL, AS IT HAD FALLEN FOR DAYS. SNOW LAY THICK ON ROOFTOPS OF THE town, with only this noon a promise of blue sky, a lazy slit above, as if the heavens watched, only pretending to sleep.

It was the courtyard of the Zeide, and the window from which King Cefwyn had looked out on the world as Prince Cefwyn. From this diamond-paned window he had watched, oh, so many grim things in his tenure here.

Two boys were at arms practice in the yard below, next to the armory, boys only weeks ago, but now—

Now a father saw changes. Elfwyn, the one had called himself, now and forever, but—Spider, Emuin called him, while Tristen called him Mouse. No longer Otter, to Cefwyn's sorrow. Nevermore Otter. The boy had gone places even Emuin did not guess and Tristen only hinted at. Even Elfwyn's eyes had changed, gray and seeming at times lately to look into distances, or to spark fire. The face had grown somber, the stare more direct, at times so very direct that the servants looked away.

His father would not look away from him. Cefwyn would not give him up to the enemy that had tried to take him. He had fought for his kingdom. He would fight for his sons and his daughter.

Take both boys back to Guelemara? No. Elfwyn was home, now, at least as at home as Elfwyn was ever apt to be. His was still a wild heart, but he had ceased to run. He was furtive, but that furtiveness had turned full about: it had become a hunter's stealth—the look of pursuit, not flight—that displayed itself in his sword-play.

Elfwyn got past his brother's guard. Aewyn had to jump back. Twice.

And when had *that* manner taken hold? Was it something gained at Ynefel? Or—elsewhere?

Bump and thump from great distance, from beyond the diamond panes and a floor below. Aewyn recovered, and pressed back, both boys with padded swords. Now Elfwyn retreated, and circled.

No one here in Amefel questioned a bastard's right to bear arms, no one questioned the boy's royal paternity—a few, perhaps, shuddered at the taint of sorcery on the Aswydd side, and oh, yes, the good Quinalt father—the lone Quinalt authority in this Bryalt town—had come puffing into the audience hall to express his opinion, and gone out from his king's presence much more meekly than he had arrived . . .

A hit. Aewyn, pursuing too rashly, landed on his backside in the snow, and scrambled up again, shield and sword flailing. Then swords hit the snow, shields did, and brothers tumbled, locked in each other's arms.

They rolled, they wrestled. Cefwyn afforded himself a smile, a hope of a moment's duration, that the brothers might find their innocence again—that they might somehow get back what they had left behind in this dire winter. He hoped they laughed, but the window cut him off from sound: from his vantage, he simply saw boys struggling for advantage, pounding snow down each other's necks. Surely there would by now be laughter. He hoped there was. He looked for signs of it.

Oh, there went Elfwyn free of the clinch, quick and wily, leaping onto his feet, crouched low. Elfwyn gathered up a double handful of snow and flung it, a spray of white.

Aewyn charged right through, but Elfwyn was suddenly back a good half his length, and retreating first.

My sons, my sons, Cefwyn said to himself. Both my sons. A man could do much worse. The clergy called Elfwyn a calamity. And Cefwyn had feared. He still feared, if he let worry have sway over him. But he shut out the dark thoughts, as hard, as persistently as he could. He insisted to believe in this boy, in both of them. Belief, so Emuin had taught him, was its own magic—so long as it was carefully placed, often examined, like a bridge kept in careful repair.

Brave boys. Aewyn's charge carried through Elfwyn's mists of snow, and Aewyn almost laid hands on him, but Elfwyn skipped back and back, full circle, now.

No matter to Aewyn. He kept coming, suddenly swinging fists.

Oh, be careful of temper, son of mine. That damnable Marhanen temper . . .

Aewyn struck. And Elfwyn spun half-about and stopped still, not hurt, but amazed. Indignant.

Aewyn stopped dead. The two stood looking at each other. It was Aewyn who held out his hand, held it out, pressed a step farther.

Then Elfwyn took the offering, and Aewyn clapped him on the shoulder, hugged him in comradely fashion, hugged him close, the two walking side by side away, heads down.

Cefwyn breathed. He had not known he had held his breath, but he had. He watched the two walk aside to the armorer's shed, and sit down on the bottom step together, and remain so, shoulder to shoulder, finding something mutually interesting in the snow at their feet, weapons forgotten in the snow. It was a breach of discipline, that abandonment of weapons, a fault, but Cefwyn ignored it, wishing, hoping, that he would see the two get up together, friends, brothers—children, again.

They might be talking—or might still hold a sullen peace. He saw Elfwyn take off his glove in the cold. What Elfwyn did then, bending lower, reaching into the snow, he could not tell. But he watched Aewyn staring at that hand, and saw—saw a cold gleam, bright as a mote of moonlight.

Elfwyn closed that bare hand, and opened it, and it was gone. Just gone.

Magic? The chance spark of a jewel in the winter light? Cefwyn prayed for it to be the latter, but the gray sky and the sifting snow afforded no sun at all to strike a spark off metal. The day was leaden, the snow standing on the boys' arms and backs and heads the moment they sat still. There was no natural source of light now from the heavens. Elfwyn had done it . . . whatever it was.

And what had that spark meant? What thought proceeded in that dark head, when, after his brother attacked him, he let a cold fire sit in his hand?

There was sorcery, and there was wizardry, and there was magic. Which one had his bastard son learned to practice, and *where* had he learned it?

The boys still sat together on the step. What words passed between them, there was no hint at all, except the bodies were quiet, the heads bowed.

Two things had sparked out there—the cold fire and the hot, the fire in the hand, and the fire in Aewyn's heart, the ungovernable temper that had damned the Marhanen house through three generations . . . that had done murder, and earned damnation. . .

Gods, let one quench the other. Let them be brothers.

A step intruded. A servant, he thought at first: very few dared come and go without at least a cough.

It came just that degree closer than a servant at work and he turned his head, his hand already moving; but it was Tristen who had come in—doubtless an open door, the servants coming and going about their business—but not necessarily, Tristen being what he was. Cefwyn's hand went back to the window sill, his attention back to the view below. He welcomed the presence by him, the other overseer of the witch's son—and the queen's. His friend. Always his friend, whatever the world said.

"Elfwyn has wizardry," Cefwyn murmured, knowing he was not wrong. "I ever so hope it was your teaching."

A moment of silence. "The boy was offered many things on his journey. He found something within himself, where it always was."

Cefwyn turned his back to the window, his face to Tristen, as if a glance could answer what had no answer, nor might have for years. "His mother's heritage, do you say?"

"His mother had a choice," Tristen said. "Both the sisters had, at the start. Neither was strong enough. Tarien came closest to escape."

He thought he understood what Tristen was telling him. He could hardly imagine that Tarien Aswydd could have been like Emuin, that the choice of wizardry rather than sorcery had been within her reach. Some Aswydd far back in the line had made a certain fatal choice, was what he had believed, a choice that had damned all the line.

And he had, in his folly, joined that bloodline to his own, linked these two boys, these brothers.

He looked back at his sons, saw they had risen from the step. Aewyn put his arm about Elfwyn's shoulders.

Elfwyn's arm went about Aewyn's. Two boys, pushing and shoving at each other, meandered back to their fallen weaponry. They gathered swords and shields up out of the snow and, falling in together with a second round of elbows and now evident laughter, passed out of view.

Tracks remained, a serpentine in winter white, one set of tracks, weaving this way and that, but going side by side.